WRESTLING WITH HOPE

D.H. STARR

Cover art by L.C. Chase

Second Edition published by Rocky Ridge Books

Print ISBN-13 978-1-62622-061-4

Join the Rocky Ridge newsletter for the latest on D.H. Starr, the Wrestling series, and more.

ONE

Christmas Eve

Scott Thayer stared at the flickering light of the candles Derek Thompson had lit as it danced off the ceiling and walls. With Derek's parents downstairs, he should've been nervous. Instead, he scooched over on the bed, making room for his greatest love, the person who kept him anchored to earth, to slide behind him and spoon him in strong arms. He couldn't imagine a happier place to be.

Derek's breath washed across Scott's neck and cheek. Heat from Derek's bare chest soaked into Scott's back, his own personal blanket. No, life didn't get better than this.

"Can you believe it's Christmas Eve?" Derek squeezed Scott from behind, kissing the nape of his neck.

"Mmm-hmm." A hum was all Scott could manage. If he let himself, he'd fall asleep within a few minutes.

Another kiss to his neck, then Derek slid closer, folding Scott into him in a tangle of arms and legs.

"I was thinking about the school dance and the song you mixed for me." Scott tempted fate, and the ire of parents who might choose to check in on them at any moment, wriggling his ass against Derek's groin. Maybe he'd inspire Derek into some private Christmas Eve fun.

"Hey, you know the rules." Derek blocked the seduction with a firm hand on Scott's hip. "I was thinking about the dance too. Can you believe we're already halfway done with sophomore year?"

Scott sighed. *Guess fooling around will have to wait.* "That song, *Happy* by Pharrell Williams, was amazing." The memory of Derek's tribute to their relationship, the way he'd represented their love in booming, technological form, had Scott's heart racing…not to mention his cock filling out.

Scott swallowed against the rising emotion swelling in his chest. The song had lit up the room. Students exploded with energy. Smiles and laughter and dancing. Happiness. The message embedded within Derek's gift, reinforced by every kiss, each touch, the silent times they shared where no words were needed to know they belonged to one another.

"You think we have time to fool around?" Derek shifted his hips, pressing his hard shaft against Scott's ass.

Scott laughed. "You're the one who just put the brakes on." He held his breath, reminding himself he had the power to say *no* even when every cell in his body screamed *yes*. "I mean, your mom's cool, but I don't know if she'd appreciate walking in on the two of us—ooohhh!"

Derek pressed his bare cock against Scott's ass, the thin fabric of Scott's boxer briefs serving as a tenuous barrier. *Wasn't he just in his underwear?* "She'd knock first. Besides, we could be really quiet." He slipped his hand under the waistband of Scott's briefs, wrapping his slender fingers around Scott's cock and stroking with practiced confidence, up and down.

Damn him. Derek never played fair when he wanted something badly enough. No sense in fighting the inevitable.

Scott swiveled in Derek's arms, staring directly into eyes. Even in the dimly lit room, he could see the flames of desire raging in their amber depths. Or was that the flame from the candles? Drawn magnetically, Scott pressed his lips against Derek's.

Derek opened to him, sliding his tongue along Scott's teeth and gums before probing the depths of his mouth. A hint of lemon danced along Scott's taste buds, probably from their after-dinner tea.

Scott slipped his boxers over his ass and wriggled them down his legs without breaking his kiss. Seconds later, Derek's legs wrapped around him, drawing Scott closer. "It's your turn."

Raising his head an inch, Scott placed a quick kiss on the tip of Derek's nose. "We don't have to keep score, you know."

A squeeze of thighs. The slow drag of nails along Scott's back. Hot stiffness pressing against Scott's stomach. Launch sequence initiated. No stopping the flood of need now.

Sealing their mouths together again, Scott devoured Derek. A war of tongues, Scott's favorite kind of wrestling.

"Fuck me." Derek demanded on a whisper before recapturing Scott's mouth.

Scott rolled Derek to his back, settling on top. Derek wrapped his legs around Scott's waist. Bless the man for his flexibility. A slight hip adjustment and Scott edged his cock into the crack of Derek's ass, precum serving as a natural lubricant. Thank God, since he didn't want to waste any time rummaging through the nightstand and finding whatever brand of lube they'd bought. Double thanks, since they'd long ago committed to one another, gotten tested, and no longer needed to use condoms.

Each pass of his shaft generated more friction and heat. Derek's hole pulsed, grabbing at Scott's cock head. Easing the tip against Derek's opening, he only had to push forward and he'd sink into the man he loved.

But he needed one thing first.

Tearing out of the kiss, he supported himself on his arms and observed his lover. Derek's closed eyes and contented smile told a story of pure satisfaction. They'd never specifically discussed looking into each other's eyes at the instant of penetration, but Scott needed the link each and every time. The pause must have been enough to cue Derek, who opened his eyes, twin pools of fiery amber burning a flame of desire straight to Scott's heart.

"Love you." Scott lowered himself as he said the words, pressing his full weight onto Derek while breaching his lover's pre-cum lubricated ass in a smooth motion.

Derek arched his hips, helping Scott to bury his cock all the way inside. "Yessssss."

"Shh. Your mom." Scott dipped his head, trailing his nose along Derek's cheek, past his ear, to his neck, securing his mouth along the tendon under the skin. He bit down, Derek's familiar squirming letting Scott know he'd hit the right spot.

Derek tightened his grip around Scott with quivering legs.

Slow and steady, Scott rocked against Derek, the tight ring of Derek's ass pure bliss against Scott's cock. Satiny warmth glided along his shaft as he sank in further until buried to the hilt. When he drew his hips back, the hairs surrounding Derek's hole created extra friction along his skin, better than any hand ever could. Scott's muscles coiled. Another plunge back into his lover's body.

Derek tilted his head back. "Ahhh. Yeah."

This was where Scott loved to be. Not in Derek's room, or even their dorm room, but connected body to body, inside and out. A hiking trip. New York City. The shower. They were all places, but Derek was home.

Ragged breaths drew Scott's attention and he found himself immediately captured in Derek's gaze. Need, raw and primal, slammed into Scott. Lost in the wide-eyed picture of bliss and happiness below him, he let the floodgates open.

Steady rhythm increased to frenzied pumping. Derek bucked up with as much force as Scott slammed down. The flickering candle cast an orange glow against Derek's chest and face, reflecting off damp skin.

In a hoarse whisper, Derek uttered the words that drove Scott crazy with need: "I'm gonna come."

Scott's arms burned as he supported his entire upper body and watched Derek. So beautiful. Writhing. Lower lip caught between teeth. Whispered groans serenading their love. "Me too. Go ahead."

Derek gripped his cock and beat himself in time with Scott's thrusts. Each plunge forced Derek's cock through the slick circle of fingers and palm. His cock shone with liquid, his glans bulging.

Derek drew in a sharp gasp. A prickling current of electricity sparked along Scott's skin. He sank all the way into Derek, as deep as he could get. Derek's ass clenched and released in a steady rhythm. A thick rope of cum shot from Derek's cock, splashing against his chest and neck. The sweet, acrid scent of semen surrounded Scott, filtering into him.

With one last surge of energy, Scott withdrew and drove back into Derek. For a suspended second, time froze. Heat danced along his skin. His balls tingled and his ass clenched as he fought to savor the few seconds he had left before his world exploded in the best possibly way.

Derek still writhed beneath him, muffled growls fighting to escape through clenched lips. Each movement highlighted the sharp relief of his lover's muscles.

Fucking beautiful. So fucking perfect. His vision blurred. His heart raced. Scott sucked in a deep breath. "I'm…" His whole body tightened, currents of sensation racing to his core, building, burning with passion, "…coming!"

Scott gritted his teeth and braced himself as the first wave of his orgasm hit, Derek's insides, silky and hot, multiplying the sensation. His balls pulled up close to his body, cum racing up his shaft and exploding into Derek.

Wet heat surrounded his cock as his release filled Derek's ass. Another pulse and cum trickled out of Derek's hole and dripped down Scott's sack.

A few more pulses and Scott could breathe again. He held himself, buried deep inside Derek, arms supporting his weight, and gazing at his lover. "Holy shit."

"No. I think Holy *Night*." Derek wiped his glistening forehead, then placed his palm against Scott's cheek.

His wet fingers smelled distinctly of Derek. Scott turned his head to the side and took one of Derek's fingers into his mouth. Salty, both sweat and cum mixing together. "Baby, I don't care what day it is. What we just did was *not* holy."

Derek laughed. "Anyways, I told you we wouldn't get caught."

Scott collapsed on top of Derek, his body throbbing as his heart struggled to calm its staccato beat. Fucking Derek made a better workout than any visit to the gym or wrestling practice, and was a hell of a lot more fun. "Congratulations. You were right."

"Brat!" Derek slipped his hand against the back of Scott's neck and pulled him into a kiss. Their lips formed a perfect seal. Derek swiped his tongue deep into Scott's mouth, swirling in gentle circles.

Scott released a contented, "Mmmmm." Derek didn't play fair when it came to their bedroom activities. He knew every trick to turn Scott into putty. At the top of the list? Deep kisses. When Derek kissed him, everything else faded and they were the only two people in the world.

Seconds, minutes, hours might've passed for all Scott knew. He'd spend an eternity in this bed with Derek if he could.

Derek gently nudged Scott to the side until they faced each other, nose to nose. "I love you."

If words could make a person defy gravity, those were the ones for Scott, at least when they came from Derek. Three words meaning more than Derek could possibly know. After all, Scott hadn't grown up with a belief in unconditional love. Nope, his father had always laced his affection with a million demands and his mom hadn't stood up to the man until two years ago.

Scott forced thoughts of his childhood aside and snuggled into the crook of Derek's neck. Derek wrapped his arm around Scott, keeping his free hand on his belly. A glint on his finger caught Scott's attention. The ring, one of a matching pair he'd bought for the two of them and given to Derek when they hiked Mount Washington the previous summer. "I love you too."

He closed his eyes. Derek's breathing lulled Scott into a heavy restfulness. Yes. His life finally headed in the right direction with the perfect man by his side. Nothing from his past could pull him down when Derek's love created his future.

Later, in his own bed, Scott stared at his ceiling. In the morning, he and his mother would go back to Derek's house to spend Christmas with his family. Funny how two years earlier, before he'd ever met Derek, each holiday carried a degree of mystery. *Where will we be living? Who will we celebrate with?*

Now there didn't seem to be any question what they'd do. This year, next, and for all the years to come. How he'd lucked into the Megamillions jackpot by meeting Derek he'd never know. If he were prone to believing in destiny being anything but what a person made of their lives, he'd have to admit perhaps the two of them were designed to be together.

Maybe they'd been lovers in other lifetimes. Did souls exist, moving through eras like wind blowing from one tree to the next? Had they always been men?

Idiot. Scott swung his legs over the side of the bed and stood. At least the idea of either one of them being a woman snapped him out of his "deep thoughts" moment. *Christ. We only get one go around and better make the most of every minute because who knows what comes next?*

Scott stretched his arms over his head. The strain to his muscles gave relief to the overused brain cells. After all, he rarely devoted more than a few seconds at a time to philosophical thinking. He'd met Derek. Their families merged into one. Simple truths.

Except they weren't. Their families couldn't be more different. Somewhere out there his father lived a life Scott knew nothing about. Had he moved from Massachusetts? Had he met anyone new? Did he think about them? Was he sorry for all the years of icy distance and uprooting their family time and again?

Seriously? Since when had Scott become such a dramatic head case? He slipped out of his pajama bottoms, secured a towel around his waist, and strode down the hallway to the bathroom and into the shower.

Hot water washing through his longer winter hair formed a curtain over his head and around his ears, protecting him from the world outside himself. The pelt of droplets massaged his back, millions of tiny fingers working tautness out of him.

Focusing on the physical. Yes. The sting of heat as water touched a new spot on his body, replaced almost instantly by soothing warmth.

Derek, a few blocks away, probably slept peacefully. He wasn't sitting up in the middle of the night thinking about their past and future lives or wondering where *his* father might be.

Jesus. Even a shower couldn't distract Scott for more than a few minutes.

Okay, time for serious diversionary tactics. Scott lowered his head so his chin rested against the top of his chest. *Think of Derek.* Amber eyes, blazing with love. Creamy thighs locked around Scott's waist, their strength gripping onto him, drawing him closer. The stretch of Derek's ass, sliding along Scott's shaft.

"Mmmm." He gripped his cock and started stroking.

A physical touch wasn't needed for Scott to feel the softness of Derek's lips. Nor did he need to stand next to the man to fill himself with Derek's scent. Scott knew every inch of Derek's body. Could anticipate each reaction to any given situation.

Of course, some of those situations drove Scott mad with fear… like when Derek took on a new "project".

Nope, not going there. Mistakes nearly drove them apart until Scott learned not to underestimate Derek's ability to take care of himself.

He worked his hand down his shaft and beneath his balls, running the pad of his forefinger in circles around his opening. "Uhh." He poked his finger inside. Hot, smooth, tight. Surprising, since Derek drilled Scott through the mattress on a regular basis. It'd been Scott on top almost of the time at the beginning. Now? Fifty-Fifty. Which suited him just fine.

He used his free hand to stroke his cock while running a small path along his inner wall, with the pad of the finger lodged in his ass. Yes. His abdominal muscles trembled. A shock of pleasure shot through his body from his ass to his belly button. A brief jolt, no more than a second, but leaving a trail of electricity in its aftershock. Had he nudged his prostate by accident?

He rested against the shower wall to keep from crumpling to the floor. Chilly tile touched heated skin. Another stroke. A deeper probe of finger. Scott drew a shallow breath as the wave of release grew inside, bigger and bigger. He beat feverishly at his cock.

A flash of amber. Derek's eyes. The hint of a whisper. *I love you.*

Scott drew in a sharp breath right as his nerve endings fired off. His body convulsed, each fiber contracting and releasing in a powerful dance. The first jet of cum flew across the shower stall, hitting the glass sliding door, leaving a thick, white trail in its wake. The second and third pulses of his cock eased the frenetic energy ripping through him.

Panting, like after a mild run, he slid down the wall so he sat on the shower floor, draping his arms over his knees and dipping his head forward. He could focus on the water again. For several minutes he examined the floor, savoring the wash of liquid raining down.

Finally, he leaned his head back against the wall. "Well, that did the trick." No more energy for thoughts about the nature of human existence or the theory of reincarnation.

Content, Scott dried off and slipped quietly back to his room and into his bed, the cool soft sheets cocooning him in warmth and safety. A few more hours and he'd be showering again and getting dressed for Christmas.

Sleep drifted toward him like clouds passing across the sky. He needed to get through the darkness of the evening so he could wake to the brightness of a new morning. Everything seemed so much clearer with Derek, the person who'd become his family, by his side.

Images flashed through Scott's head. Derek. Mom. Hank and Claire, the parents who'd all but adopted him when he and Derek announced their relationship. And finally, Dad.

A tight knot twisted his stomach. What was the big deal about Christmas anyways? He wasn't nostalgic or overly sentimental at other times of the year, but the holiday brought thoughts of his father. Of loss. Of rejection.

And there it was. As much a part of his ritual as opening presents.

No matter how much love surrounded him, a small piece of his father lived inside, taunting, reminding Scott something within him was unlovable.

TWO

The scent of coffee wafted up the stairs to Scott's room. Ah. Christmas morning. He rubbed the sleep from his eyes, slipped out of bed, and meandered toward the kitchen, stopping at the bathroom along the way.

His mother sat at the table reading a newspaper, gripping the sides so they crinkled. "Morning." She put the paper aside, crossed the room, and placed an awkward kiss on his cheek. "Want some coffee?"

What's got her twisted in knots? "Merry Christmas, Mom. I can get it myself." Scott trudged to the cupboard, procured a mug, poured himself some coffee, and heaped two large spoonsful of sugar into the steaming black liquid. *Heaven.* The heat going down his throat. The bitter scent filtering into his nose. The caffeine which seemed to instantly filter into his system. They all melded together into one perfect waking up experience. He propped himself against the counter and closed his eyes. Coffee drinking, a bad habit he didn't intend to quit. Plus, he needed to mentally prepare for whatever his mother stressed about.

After a few sips, he opened his eyes to find his mother ogling him, her hands folded tightly. The newspaper lay forgotten on the table. "Scott, there's something I think you should see." She motioned toward the kitchen table where a white envelope took the place where his breakfast should be.

No "Merry Christmas" or "how'd you sleep?" Scott gripped the edge of the counter, preparing himself for the worst.

His mother continued without any buildup or preliminary warnings. She picked up the card. "This came for you the other day. I wasn't sure when to give it to you, and it's Christmas so I'm probably an idiot to give it to you today, but it's not right for me to hold onto it".

She's rambling. His mother handed the card to Scott, then scurried to the sink and rinsed out her mug for much longer than probably necessary.

Scott's heart skipped a beat, then pounded. He recognized the handwriting. *Dad.*

"What's this?" A stupid question, but at least asking gave him a minute to process what he held in his hand. Why would his father, after two decades of never giving him a card or any other kindness, reach out to him now?

"I think you should open it and find out for yourself." His mother kept her back to him and, upon closer inspection, her shoulders appeared pulled up close to her ears, her posture as rigid as a board.

What could be so earth-changing his negligent father would take the time to write him? For the past two years the man had dropped off the face of the planet. No phone calls. No nothing.

Scott peeled back the corner of the seal and slid his finger along the top of the envelope. Each act seemed independent from the other. Opening the envelope, retrieving the card, reading the front. Steps to prolong actually seeing what dear old Dad had to say.

No sense in delaying things any further. Scott flipped the card open.

Son,

Odd way to begin since his father never called him *son*

before. Sometimes Scott wondered if his dad remembered his name. Their interaction usually consisted of barked orders.

I know it's been a while and I'm sorry. Mom says you're doing well. I'd like to see you.

Dad.

Scott read the words three more times before placing the card on the table facedown. His heart, which had thrashed feverishly moments earlier, slowed to a steady, even beat, eerily slow and calm. *Dad asked about me? Apologized? Wants to meet?*

The room began to spin. Scott sat where his mom had been sitting. Just when his life seemed to be leveling out, *this* had to happen? "What's going on, Mom?"

His mother turned from the sink and scrutinized Scott without saying anything. By the soulful expression on her face and the shimmering in her eyes, no words were needed to let Scott know something big was up. "You'll have to make a decision about whether you want to call your father. When I spoke to him, I told him I'd let you choose what to do without getting involved."

"Mom!" Now wasn't the time for bullshit.

"All right. Okay." She wrung her hands together, the whites of her knuckles showing. "He doesn't simply want to reach out. He needs to talk to you about something."

His heart sped up again. "What!"

Nervous chuckles filled the space between them. "Was that a question or a statement?" Her tightly clenched hands revealed nervousness, but she made eye contact. "It's not for me to share, but I think you should meet with him."

Panic clasped Scott's throat with a vice grip. "Where is he? I haven't heard from him in two years. Has he been living in Massachusetts all this time?" Scott wasn't sure what he wanted the answer to be. Part of him hoped he'd moved across the country. At least that might explain why he'd simply disappeared from their lives so completely.

"He's been living out of state. He came back because..."

She closed her eyes, her lips thinning into narrow lines. "It's for him to share with you, honey. He's staying at the Marriot in Boston."

Dad, in Boston, a ten-minute subway ride away. Why reveal all of this on Christmas morning? "When does he want to see me?"

"You'll have to call him and set something up." She crossed the room and caressed Scott's cheek. Despite the fact she'd squished all the blood out of her hands, her palms were warm. "You don't have to do anything you don't want to, but at least give him a call."

Apparently, Hell finally froze over. He'd have believed icicles formed on brimstone far easier than believing his father had a sudden change of heart and wanted to get to know the son he'd ignored and used as a personal slave for the entire duration of their relationship. "He didn't leave a number."

"I've got the number right here." Mom reached into her jeans pocket and withdrew a tightly folded sheet of paper. "I told him I'd give it to you but made it clear you would be the one to decide to use it."

"Does he want me to call him today?" Scott looked at his mother's hand but made no move to retrieve the slip of paper.

As if she could read his mind, her expression softened to one of silent understanding. "I'll leave it here on the fridge." She secured the number facedown to the steel surface with a *I Heart My Gay Son* magnet.

Scott stared at the tiny slip of paper, silence growing like a storm cloud between them. No words. No thoughts. Just the thrumming of his heart and a lead weight hanging from his shoulders. He left the kitchen, tramped to the bathroom, stripped, and turned on the shower. As he waited for steam to fill the room, he inspected at himself in the mirror. Other than his mussed-up hair and a slight flush to his cheeks, this morning seemed like any other. Better. A second holiday in a row surrounded by love and warmth.

Funny how a few words written on a card and ten measly digits sticking to the refrigerator could change everything.

Scott thought knew his stance on his dad. The guy was an asshole. A cruel, unloving, abandoning butt-muncher who Scott learned to push almost entirely from his mind.

His reflection slowly disappeared from view, erased by a thin layer of fog on the glass. He stepped into the shower. Whatever decisions he needed to make, they could wait until later.

He tried thinking of Derek. Not even his cheerful smile and adoring eyes filled with love could delete the last ten minutes or the image of the slip of paper on the fridge. What in the hell did his father want? Why would he reach out now… just when Scott had finally put his past behind him and begun to view the future as bright with possibility?

"Damn him to hell." He hadn't meant to speak out loud, and he certainly hadn't meant to curse his father to eternal fire and brimstone. Forgiveness was the best cure… so said all the self-help books espousing the bullshit line. But were the strangers who wrote those thinking of his dad when they sold their psycho-crap?

Clean, shaven, and just as confused as he'd been before he entered the bathroom, Scott made quick work of dressing. Whatever he decided about calling his father, Christmas at Derek's and a day sure to be filled with holly-jolly-joy awaited him.

Derek dragged Scott upstairs to his attic bedroom within ten seconds of Scott's arrival. Scott hustled behind his sexy-as-fuck boyfriend. Maybe he'd get a repeat performance from the previous evening.

Arousal disappeared as soon as Derek closed the door and spoke. "What the fuck's wrong with you?" His voice carried no malice, but the words served as an effective slap to the face.

"What do you mean?" Like Derek couldn't read straight through him. "Everything's fine."

"I thought we had an agreement. No secrets or the secret-keeper gets punished."

Leave it to Derek to use Scott's own threat against him. Scott gave himself a mental kick. Earlier in the year, he'd withheld feelings from Derek about the support he provided to others, not wanting to impose personal fears on the man he loved as he had in the past. Epic backfire. Derek's words from the track, where they'd had a serious heart-to-heart last year, still stung whenever Scott replayed them. *You've broken me.*

While the *punishment*, submitting to the sexual whims of the offended partner, seemed more like a reward, the point been made: communicate, no matter what.

Derek folded his arms over his chest.

Scott tried to maintain a serious expression, but his lips trembled. Maybe Derek would think tears were on their way. No such luck. The way Derek planted his hands on his hips let Scott know his face had formed something more of a smirk. "Don't think for one second your sly-guy shit will get you off the hook."

Scott crossed the room and plunked down on the bed. "Believe me, I know better than to assume I can get anything by you."

Derek lowered his arms and two strides later sat next to Scott. He placed an arm around Scott's shoulders and pulled him close. "What's wrong?"

Delaying things any longer seemed pointless. "I got a card from my dad this morning. He wants me to call him."

Derek froze. "What!"

The exclamation seemed to convey an appropriate amount of shock, perhaps missing a '*the fuck*' on the end, but gratifying nonetheless. "I know."

"Are you gonna call him?" Derek brushed his lips against Scott's temple, a soft, wordless act of support. With Derek by his side, he could handle whatever came next.

"I don't know. I thought I might enjoy today and we can talk about it tomorrow." A pebble of hope flickered inside Scott. Maybe he could avoid a big discussion. The grim expression on Derek's face gave him his answer. "Or…we could talk about it now."

"Better." Derek lay on his bed and extended his arms, inviting Scott to lie next to him. Scott slid into the one place he knew he'd always be safe, welcomed by a tight squeeze. "You okay?"

"I don't know. I'm still processing." Scott huffed, a fraction of the tension loosening its hold in his chest. Letting Derek in always made obstacles seem less overwhelming.

"Totally understandable." Derek said the right words, but they came out forced.

Scott shifted so he lay entirely on top of Derek. "Are you upset with me?"

Derek's eyes widened. "No. Never. I'm trying to control my anger at your dad before I say something I'll regret."

Scott kissed him on the lips. Derek remained stiff for a second, then loosened up, opening his mouth and granting Scott access. The distinct flavor of coffee, with a hint of mocha flavoring, danced along Scott's tongue. What started sweet turned sloppy and wet.

After several minutes of kissing and grinding against one another, Scott lifted his head and fell to his side so he could look at Derek.

Slightly out of breath, Derek wiped his mouth before locking eyes with Scott. "Damn. Merry Christmas. Was that my present?"

A gentle shove. Light laughter. Warmth radiated through Scott. This, lying in bed, touching, being together was all he needed. Not even a major life event, like his fuck-up, deadbeat father reaching out to him, could break the sense of security he found with Derek. "You already got your Christmas present at school. The mix I made you, remember? And kissing hardly counts as a present…unless you count every day as a holiday."

Derek sat up. "Maybe I do." He sort of gazed at nothing.

Scott gave him a few seconds, knowing the expression all too well. "You went somewhere."

Derek's cheeks flushed. "Daydreaming, thinking about how every day really *does* feel like a holiday with you." He placed a chaste kiss on Scott's lips. "Seriously though, what do you think you'll do?"

Scott flung his arm over his eyes. Maybe if he blocked everything out, he wouldn't have to decide, but nothing could erase Derek's presence. Besides, Scott wouldn't make it out of Derek's room until he answered every question thrown his way. "I really don't know. I haven't had time to think things through. I mean, part of me says he can go straight to Hell. I don't owe him anything, and after all he's done to me, he can eat shit and die for all I care."

Derek said nothing.

"All right. You don't have to lay it on so thick."

"What? I didn't say anything."

Scott pursed his lips but couldn't maintain the expression for more than five seconds. He gave Derek a sidelong glance before rubbing his hands over his face. "You're right, of course He's my dad, and if he wants me to call him I probably should. Who knows what he wants? Maybe he wants to apologize for being such a bastard my whole life. Maybe he wants to help Mom pay for my college tuition. Maybe…" What? What could his father possibly want from him after all this time?

Derek remained silent.

He'll make an amazing therapist someday. "You know, I figured out what you should be when you grow up."

Derek rolled on top of him, his weight keeping Scott safe. "I *am* grown up and don't think I'm gonna let you switch topics on me." He cocked his head to the side, one eyebrow raised. "But out of curiosity, what do you think I should be when I *grow up*?"

He ground his hips against Scott, his hard cock pressing against Scott's through their pants.

"You should be a therapist or psychiatrist or some other kind of shrink-type doctor. It's in your blood."

Derek remained still, then nodded. "Well, duh!" For a second, Scott held his breath. Had he actually succeeded in diverting attention away from himself and onto Derek? "But we can talk about that later. Right now, I want to hear what's going on inside your head."

No such luck. Scott rolled the two of them over and straddled Derek's waist. "I can't tell you one way or the other because I honestly don't know, but I should probably call him. If I don't, I'll always wonder what he wanted."

Derek nodded. "That's all I needed to hear. Now we can go back downstairs." He bucked his hips. "But you have to let me up first."

Scott rubbed his groin, readjusting his junk into a more comfortable position. "You bring me to your room, kiss me, rub all against me, and expect me to just go downstairs?"

A smirk slithered into place, Derek's expression filled with pure evil. For the first time, Scott had an idea of what Derek meant when he complained about Scott's smirking. The expression wiped his brain clean of logical thoughts.

Grudgingly, he slid off Derek and stood. He took Derek's hand and helped him off the bed.

Each step down the stairs brought Scott closer and closer to the thought he'd been avoiding since he'd arrived: what to do with the sheet of paper with his dad's number on the fridge.

His mother and Claire, Derek's mom, were in the kitchen, placing hors d'oeuvres on platters. They glanced up at the same time. Their smiles, bright and shiny, slipped into flat lines, followed by matching pink hues to their cheeks. *Do they think we just fucked?*

Claire broke the silence first. Wiping her hands on a dish

towel, she crossed the kitchen and gave Scott a hug. "Your mom and I were talking. Are you okay?"

Ah. She's worried about Dad contacting me.

"I'm fine. Why don't we enjoy Christmas? I'm sure we'll have plenty of time over the next couple days to talk about this."

Claire squeezed Scott a bit tighter than usual before releasing him. "Of course. You boys go into the living room. We'll be out in a minute."

Derek led them to the couch and sat down. Henry, Derek's dad, gazed at the television while gripping the armrests of his chair. The sound of football announcers let Scott know the Patriots game had begun.

Scott took a seat next to Derek. "Who're they playing?"

"Giants." Henry tore his attention away from the screen long enough to greet Scott, extending his hand.

Scott gripped Henry's hand, friendship pouring through the contact from a person who'd always accepted him. Settling onto the couch, placing his arm around Derek's shoulder. Derek scooted in a little closer.

Henry picked up a bowl of chips and handed them to Derek.

The Giants held a seven to ten with only a few minutes remaining until half time. Henry wrung his hands and shouted at the screen.

In all his years growing up, Scott had never once sat in the living room with his dad, passing snacks back and forth, watching a game.

A knot formed in his throat which he swallowed hard to dislodge. The room suddenly seemed too small. He kissed the side of Derek's head. "I'm thirsty. You want a drink?"

Derek grunted something incomprehensible and shot upright as Tom Brady threw the ball fifty yards, only to have his heroic effort intercepted. "What the hell!"

Scott wandered towards the kitchen, taking his time as he

went. The distinct sound of his mother and Claire's conversation stopped him dead in his tracks. They'd said his name.

"I don't know, Claire. It seems like an awful lot for him. Especially now. He's finally settled into a good life here." His mother's voice sounded strained. Scott heard the pat-pat-pat of her feet. Likely, she paced the kitchen back and forth as she spoke.

"You should encourage him to call. This is too important." Claire sounded more like a counselor than a friend, her voice even, free from any judgment. *Now I know where Derek gets his tendency to help others from.*

His mother's voice drew his attention back to the secret conversation taking place. "You don't understand. This is..." Scott crept a bit closer to the kitchen door, slinking along the wall like he stood on the ledge of a cliff and might fall. "...I don't know how he'll take the news."

News? So, his father hadn't reached out simply to reconnect. He wanted something. Maybe he planned to remarry. Sure. That made sense and explained his mother's secrecy. *Bastard!*

"Shannon. You *have* to let Scott be a part of this. If you don't—"

Scott felt a tickle in his nose. *No, please, I'm about to find out what dad wants.* Unable to stop it, he let out a loud sneeze. If he'd been on an actual ledge, he'd be hurtling to his death.

Mom and Claire appeared in the hallway seconds later, twin expressions of shock on their faces. His mother spoke first. "Scott, were you eavesdropping on us?"

He frantically searched his scrambled brain for a response. *Yes.* "Derek. Thirsty. Me too."

Claire squeezed Shannon's shoulder. "Of course, honey. Want some eggnog?"

"Yeah." He studied his mother, a million questions racing through his head. "Thanks."

Claire hustled out of sight, leaving Scott alone with his

mother. He dug his hands into his pockets. *Should I confront her?* He certainly wanted to, but at Derek's and on Christmas Day?

"Listen." Apparently, his mother would make the decision for him. "I'm sorry you heard us talking." She glanced at her feet for a second, but regained composure. "What exactly did you hear?"

"Never mind." Anger. An emotion he'd not experienced for nearly two years, since his dad left, welled to the surface. "Why are you keeping secrets from me?"

His mother held his gaze, opened her mouth a few times, but said nothing. Finally, she took a step closer to Scott. "This is something you need to find out for yourself."

Cryptic much? It took all his willpower not to grab her by the shoulders and shake some answers out of her. "What do I need to find out?"

Tears welled in her eyes and Scott's anger evaporated, replaced immediately by guilt. The lump in his throat grew, although he choked out a weak, "Sorry."

"No, no. You're right to be upset." She wiped at her eyes. "This is something you need to speak to your dad about."

"Why?" What in the hell could be so important his dad would show up after two years without giving the slightest heads up about what to expect?

A new round of tears filled his mother's eyes. "I wish I could answer your question, Scott, but Dad made me promise to let him tell you."

Anger bloomed to life again. Still, making his mother cry, twice, on Christmas, seemed cruel. Claire showed up with two cups of eggnog and a napkin. "Here you go, honey." She handed over the cups to Scott and the napkin to Shannon.

Scott held his breath for a beat, then released a sigh along with all the fight building up inside. This wasn't the time for arguments or the revealing of secrets. For the second year of his life, Christmas would be a time for happiness and joy. "Thanks, Claire."

He gave his mother a quick peck on the cheek, took the glasses into the living room, and handed one to Derek, who nestled back into Scott's embrace.

The eggnog contained a hint of nutmeg. Upon closer inspection, tiny specks of the spice permeated the liquid. Or maybe vanilla bean. Who knew or cared? The drink comforted him and helped to keep the lump in his throat down.

Henry shouted at the television, drawing Scott's attention to the game. The score remained seven to ten, the Giants in the lead, but the Patriots stood ten yards from the endzone and two downs to go.

He focused on the game. Whatever his father needed to talk to him about could wait.

THREE

Scott should have enjoyed the space of time between Christmas and New Year's Eve, content with a stable home and Derek in his life. Instead, he sat at a table facing the entrance of the Starbucks in Harvard Square, scanning each person who came through the doors, waiting for his father to show up.

He swirled his coffee, now cold. The thought of taking a sip only added to his nausea. He chided himself for ordering the double espresso, which had seemed a good choice to keep him alert. Green tea would've been a better idea.

A buzz from his cell diverted his attention. A text from Derek.

You okay?

Scott typed in a quick, *He's not here yet*, turned off his phone, and shoved it in his pocket. No matter how good Derek's intentions might be, Scott needed to focus. Thinking about his concerned boyfriend only served to agitate his already frayed nerves.

Just as he finished his cup, the familiar, yet somehow strange, vision of Ronald Thayer filled the entrance of the coffee shop. Scott's breath caught in his chest. Odd how the man who'd had nothing to do with him for the past two years still seemed large and intimidating. Like his presence alone could fill the whole store.

Holding his breath, Scott stood. What should he do? Hug? Shake hands? The urge to punch the man certainly fought for dominance in his list of choices.

As his dad approached, he seemed to shrink exponentially. The set of his shoulders slouched. His face had aged, wrinkles etched deeper than Scott remembered. The hairline had receded into a sparse horseshoe. Even the luster of his eyes, which normally shone with life, appeared dull.

"Scott." Even his voice seemed weaker. Older. "You've grown. You look like a man now."

Scott let out his breath on a measured count. "It's been two years." The ice in his voice matched the chill running up his spine.

His father nodded. "Yes. It's been a long time. Can I get you something?"

No thanks jumped to the tip of his tongue, but Scott bit back the refusal. "A decaf herbal tea would be nice. Thanks."

As his father trod toward the counter, Scott noted the slow gate of his pace, no sign of the commanding strides of an impatient man.

His heart slowed, no longer thrashing about like a caged bird. Whatever this man had to say, Scott's instinctual fear and cowering lay dormant. He slumped down and rubbed his cell through his pocket. Even though he'd turned his phone off, Derek being a simple text away offered comfort.

"Here you go." Dad placed a tall cup in front of Scott. "I didn't know if you wanted honey or sugar, so I left it plain for you."

"Thanks." Scott raised the cup to his lips and inhaled. Nothing like the clean, fresh aroma to ease stress. "I take it plain."

His father pulled out the chair opposite Scott and settled

onto the seat with a huff. He surveyed Scott, his gaze moving from head to body and back, before speaking. "You've really grown into a young man. In my mind, you were always a boy."

Heat crawled along Scott's back, his fingers clenching the coffee cup. If he weren't careful it might crush. "Did you want to meet so you could comment on my aging process?" Far saltier than necessary, but somewhat gratifying nonetheless.

"I suppose I deserve that." His father took a sip of his coffee, his eyes becoming slightly unfocused, before honing back in on Scott. "First and foremost, I wanted to apologize to you. "

Too little, too late. The words didn't ring true even though Scott desperately wanted them to. Despite himself, he leaned forward resting his arms on the table. "Okay." He could only trust one-word responses for fear of cracking under the powerful storm clouds thundering in his head.

Scott grit his teeth. *Easy. Find out what he wants.* He drew a long breath through his nose and let it out through pursed lips. "Saying *first and foremost* implies there's more."

His father surveyed him, this time, his brows furrowed. The air ran thick as Scott waited for a response.

Scott was about to excuse himself and leave when his father finally broke the silence. "Can't we talk for a bit?" His voice sounded airy, each word taking effort to speak. Whether from discomfort at confronting his abandoned son or from something else, Scott had no idea.

Dad doesn't deserve your sympathy or concern. Scott wished the inner voice sounded like Derek, the voice of reason, rather than the remnant of an unhappy, younger version of himself. "Honestly, I'm not sure what we have to talk about. Things are good for me. You didn't care when you were around. Why do you care now?"

Dad held the cup of coffee with bony fingers, eyes unwavering from Scott's. "Maybe I want to know who my son is. You're right, I didn't pay attention to you when I had the chance."

Whoa! Did he admit to faulty parenting? "And that's supposed to make everything all right? It's not so easy, Dad." The word *Dad* slipped out far too easily.

"No. I suppose it's not, but I *would* like to get to know you."

Scott searched for the punchline. On the wrestling mat he constantly watched for an opponent to make a move. "Suppose you don't like what you learn?"

Dad chuckled, leaning back in his chair and seeming relaxed for the first time since he'd arrived. "I'm hardly in a position to judge you, Scott."

The words were spoken with an even tone. Scott waited for anger or disapproval. Familiar responses. Ones Scott knew a reaction to.

He waited, but the expected scorn never came. Despite his gut instinct to remain on guard, his shoulders lowered and he settled back into his chair. "Fine. You want to know who I am?" His near shout drew the attention of people sitting near them.

"I do." Again, he spoke evenly, words free from any underlying malice.

"Okay. You asked for it. I'm gay." Scott studied at his father. The anticipated hardening of his dad's piercing green eyes, the only part which reminded him of the man he'd known, never came. "And I've been in a relationship with Derek for the past two years."

"I could tell during your senior year of high school how happy he made you." For the first time his father cast his eyes down.

Ha. There he is. "Yeah. He does. He cares about me. He does whatever he can to make me feel like I belong somewhere. So do his parents." Scott heard the childish tone in his voice, acting like his younger self, using his words as weapons instead of communicating like the grownup his father seemed to finally recognize.

"Great." No thinning of the lips or stiffening of the shoulders.

"We both know how you tried to keep me from being friends with him in high school. Tried to keep me from going out with my other friends. Well none of it worked." His father nodded, no reddening of cheeks or gritting of teeth. "I have more friends than ever. Derek stuck by me despite all your efforts to keep us apart. The last two years have been the happiest of my life. Mom's too."

Scott maintained eye contact long enough to witness the color drain from his father's face and the light dim in his eyes. "I'm not surprised you found your own happiness. I can't blame you for resenting me."

Too much. Nothing Scott said evoked the desired effect. He wasn't sure what he tried to draw out of his father, but compassionate understanding wasn't his goal. "What do you want? 'Cause honestly, I don't feel like filling you in on my life. You should've been around to learn the details for yourself."

His dad placed his cup down, gazing blankly at the table. Finally, he lifted his head. His skin had gone a bit greenish and his lips were pressed together tightly. "Would you excuse me?" Without waiting for Scott to answer, he stood and rushed towards the restrooms.

Scott followed his father's progress with his eyes, a mixture of frustration and concern dueling in his head. A few minutes later his father returned, his eyes slightly reddened. "Sorry."

"You all right?" Along with pallid skin, a sheen of perspiration covered his father's face.

"I'm fine." He rearranged himself in his seat a few times before resting his arms heavily on the table. "You were telling me about Derek and the happiness you've found in your life."

The man sitting across the table bore no resemblance to the person Scott had grown up with. No. *That* man was strong and hard as stone. Where had the sternness disappeared to? Since when had Scott's happiness ever mattered?

"Why did you want to see me, Dad?" There was that word again, coming out far too easily. Anger Scott could handle, but the constriction in his lungs and the fuzziness clouding the edges of the picture he'd cemented of his father were too much. Scott closed his eyes and drew in a deep breath. Hadn't Derek told him cleansing breaths helped stave off a rising panic attack?

When his father said nothing, Scott slid from his seat and stood, equal measures relief and disappointment coursing through him. Cutting a fire trail out of the coffee shop seemed appealing. "Listen, I came here because you said you wanted to see me, but if all you want to do is chat, I've got better things to do with my time." His attempted bravado failed to give him the push he needed to make his legs start moving.

Again, his father remained silent, although his direct eye contact bore directly into Scott, freezing him to the spot. Scott maintained his stance. Maybe he'd actually hoped for something earthshattering, something to make him *want* to stay. Stupid. He'd actually hoped…

Scott shook off thoughts which would only lead to sadness and disappointment. "I'm gonna go." He started for the entrance.

"Wait." The request came out a bit too loud, drawing the attention of other patrons. "I *do* have something we need to talk about. Please. Sit."

With leaden feet, Scott took the two steps to return to his seat. In slow motion, he lowered himself so he sat opposite his father, this stranger who barely resembled the giant of Scott's youth. "Okay. You've got my attention." And perhaps the attention of a half the coffee shop.

His father glanced about the room and leaned forward, resting his arms on the table.

He hadn't been aware of doing so until their faces were mere inches apart, but Scott found himself angling forward as well. Nothing about the situation matched what Scott had anticipated. Hiding behind indifference or a mask of anger had been his plan, but all the questions he'd spent the last two years burying deep inside raced to the front of his mind.

"Man. Every time I have to say this it's just as difficult." His father clenched and unclenched his hands a few times, gazing anywhere but at Scott. When he lifted his head, his eyes drew Scott in like a magnet.

Every cell in Scott's body charged to full alert. His muscles tensed, ready for the inevitable fight or flight instinct to kick in. Whatever his father had to say would cement itself as a permanent memory. No question about it.

"I have cancer."

Scott gripped the edge of the table so tightly it cut into his hands. Oxygen seemed to evaporate. No air. "Cancer?" His voice came out a mere whisper, sounding like the innocent, bad-things-don't-happen boy of his youth.

"I'm sorry, son. There's no easy way to drop that kind of news." Dad reached toward one of Scott's hands.

The barrier separating him from his body shattered and Scott recoiled, pushing his chair a few inches from the table. To touch, to speak, meant to acknowledge the reality of the words his father'd just spoken. The guy'd always been there… until he wasn't anymore. Even then, he was somewhere. Now? One little word could take the man out of the world altogether.

Sadness washed over his father's face, his cheeks sagging a bit.

Scott could vaguely make out muffled sound of conversation, and the airy whoosh of the steam wand behind the counter barely registered in his spinning brain. One word rang with absolute clarity, repeating itself over and over in his head. *Cancer. Cancer. Cancer.* Why should his father's sickness matter so much to him, other than not wanting anyone to suffer from the vile disease? He'd gotten used to the idea of an absentee dad, but losing his father with the chance of seeing him again was very different than losing him altogether. Instead, of the expected ambivalence at the idea of a world without his father, hollow emptiness clutched his heart.

The room started spinning and tea mixed with bile rose up his throat, burning an angry path.

"You okay?" To his credit, his father made no move to touch Scott again.

A breath in. Good start. Rubbing his sweaty palms on his jeans. Small actions gave Scott the precious seconds he needed to compose himself.

With precision, he focused on his legs, then his stomach, scanning his body from foot to head for any signs of weakness. No major warning signs except for the inferno in his chest. *Right. Breathe.*

He drew in a deep breath and exhaled slowly. "I'm so sorry, Dad." He didn't know which felt weirder, calling the man "Dad" or the fact he'd apologized for something when no blame existed.

"I'd really appreciate it if you could look at me." No harsh directive his in the tone of his father's request. No hurt or judgment, although both must have been present.

Lifting his head took more effort than it should have. Scott's cheeks raged with heat. The thump of his heart pounded at a rapid pace. His vision blurred and a lump, which might as well have been a sugar cube based on the discomfort, lodged in his throat. Still, he said nothing.

"Thank you." His father smiled weakly. "I thought you should know."

A tear streaked down Scott's cheek. *Keep it together.* "Are you going to die?" *What! The! Fuck!*

"I hope not. I've got leukemia and I'm in the middle of chemotherapy. I won't know how the treatment is going until I finish the course."

The even tone and clinical explanation helped to settle the pressure building up inside Scott's chest. "When'd you find out?"

"A few months ago. I was tired. No. Worn down and exhausted. Getting out of bed. Reading a book. Hell, taking a shower. All of it became too much. So I went to the doctor." A wry chuckle sliced through the air. "I sure didn't expect to find out I've got the big C."

What should he say? *Thanks for telling me?* Scott would've gone the rest of his life without hearing those words if he had the choice. He'd already said he was sorry. Who came up with *I'm sorry* as the right thing to say when people were sick anyways? Besides, Scott still had no idea why his father chose to tell him or what he wanted.

"Isn't Sloan Kettering the place to go when you've got cancer? They're the best, right?" Where he'd picked up the tidbit of information and why he chose to ask the idiotic question escaped him.

His father chuckled again, this time with a hint of amusement. "Yes. They're very good, but Boston has excellent hospitals as well. Plus, you're not in New York. You're here and I wanted to..." His father closed his mouth and froze. After a short pause he heaved a breathy sigh. "I want to spend time with you."

Scott swallowed hard. On what evil planet had he been dropped? Hours earlier the thought of spending time with Dad incited rage. Now, he had to make a choice between spending time with his father or rejecting a man with a deadly disease. "Dad, it's been a long time." *Okay, non-committal.* He wasn't rejecting his father but wasn't agreeing to anything either.

"It has and I don't expect you to make any decisions right now, but think about it." Was that pleading Scott heard in Dad's voice? "Please consider whether we could spend some time together so I can get to know you. Make up for..." His father's voice trailed off and he cleared his throat a few times. Scott's people-reading skills weren't as sharp as Derek's, but the sudden flush from pale white to beet red on his father's face was impossible to miss.

Scott swallowed hard before speaking. "I can do that." No internal arguments. Apparently, he meant what he said.

"Thank you." His father's face returned to a slightly less angry red. "I'm growing quite tired. This was difficult for me. Difficult for you. I think I'll head back to my hotel. Maybe you can give me a call in the next couple days to let me know your decision."

Scott remained silent, not knowing what to say or do. Luckily his father stood, making the decision for both of them. "I'm going to leave you to sort through your thoughts. Call me when you're ready."

Dad trod toward the entrance. Scott watched his retreat until the door closed behind him with a quiet click.

Then the world caught up with him. The humming conversation of patrons whose lives hadn't just been upended surrounded him. He registered the sweat plastering his t-shirt to his chest under his fleece.

Tears poured from his eyes without warning as he dug his phone from his pocket and hit the power button. His cell buzzed immediately. Scott glanced at the screen. *Shit!* Five missed texts and two missed calls. He opened his messenger app and started reading.

Are you okay? (11:15)

What did your dad want? (11:21)

I'm freaking out. Please let me know how you are. (11:28)

Seriously. I've called you twice and go right to voicemail. (11:31)

Call me as soon as you have a chance. I'm worried about you. (11:38)

Well hell! He hit speed dial. Derek picked up on the first ring.

Evenly spaced lights flashed by the subway window as Scott took the Red Line from Harvard Square several stops west to his home. He trudged up the station steps and emerged above ground, the freezing air biting at his skin.

At least the sensation gave him something to focus on. He couldn't grip onto one emotion long enough to find direction. His plan of aloof indifference in meeting his dad. Failure. Squashed by the wall of terror risen by one six-letter word.

At home, he took the steps slowly. Facing his mother would make the explosion to his world far more real.

Funny how minutes seemed to stretch into nothingness on the ride and walk home, yet these last few seconds seemed to fly by in hyperdrive.

A shock of hot air blasted Scott when he opened the door. Rather than serving as a blanket of warmth, the heat burned against his chilled skin.

He tore off his jacket and threw it aside. His muscles trembled, nervous energy coursing through him. He glanced around the foyer, not focusing on anything, at a loss for what to do. Pressure bubbled and rose within him, spilling over the second his mother stepped into view at the top of the stairs.

It only took one look and she flew down the stairs and tugged Scott into a tight hug. Normally Scott merely tolerated these knock-the-breath-out-of-you embraces. This time, held safely in his mother's arms, he could finally let go. Squeezing his mother, Scott buried his face on her shoulder, sobs wracking his body.

"Shh. I know." Mom soothed, reminding him of the same comfort offered when he'd been younger. Content to accept his mother's protective embrace, Scott let his mind shut down. No need to think for the time being.

Eventually, Mom loosened her hold and ran circles along Scott's back with her hand. "Come on. I'll make you some tea and we can talk."

Scott followed his mother as she ushered him to the table. He limply slumped into the chair she pulled out for him. Funny how he'd longed for independence his whole life, yet his mom's presence couldn't have been more perfect.

Independence. He'd spent his whole life fighting against all the moving, the uprooting, the trying to live up to standards he'd never reach in his father's eyes. Yet the man had swooped into his life and wreaked havoc all over again. "I hate him. Why'd he have to come back and dump this on me?"

His mother's sharp tone snapped him out of his mindlessness. "Scott. I know you're in shock, but he's your father. The only one you've got. Don't talk about him like that. Especially not now."

Scott pushed his chair away from the table and stood, squaring off against his mother, who was pouring the tea. To her credit, she didn't even flinch. "You're taking *his* side? After everything he's done to us, to you, I'd think you'd be glad he's finally suffering."

He realized the grave error of his comment the instant the words escaped his mouth. What kind of evil, twisted fuck derived even the smallest amount of satisfaction at someone else's misfortune, especially when the problem came in the form of a life-threatening disease? Regardless of any wrongs the man had inflicted on either of them, he was still his father. "I'm sorry. It's just—"

"A lot to take in. You have all of these mixed emotions banging against each other inside you…which is why Dad wanted to give you some time to process what he shared with you." His mother stood by the seat Scott had vacated. "Sit down, honey. Your tea's ready."

Scott wiped a stray tear from his cheek, hardly able to make eye contact with his mom. At twenty, he should be able to contain childish outbursts. If Derek had been there Scott would be able to spill his guts and say whatever he wanted without the aggravation of guilt nagging at him.

Hell, who am I kidding? Mom let me off easy compared to the lashing Derek would've given me. Still, hadn't he been through enough?

After eighteen years of uncertainty, he'd spent the last two putting the scattered pieces of his world back together. For the first time he stood on stable ground.

After Dad left, Scott and his mom started to live honestly. He'd learned to trust the things which mattered in his life. Like Derek and unconditional love.

And there it was, the thing Scott struggled against, staring him straight in the face. Unconditional love. His father might not know the meaning of the words, but Derek had shown Scott how to believe. How to hope for the best and shape his own future. The simple act of standing by his side, loving him, sharing the good and the bad…these were the things Derek brought to Scott's life.

How could he deny his father anything when two pillars of strength supported him? Maybe his father had squandered a lifetime of developing a relationship with him, but Scott didn't have to make the same mistake.

Taking a sip of his tea, Scott determined to open his heart. He'd see whether his father really wanted to get to know him or if the man would once against serve as a bitter disappointment.

FOUR

SCOTT'S FIRST WRESTLING PRACTICE AFTER BREAK COULDN'T come soon enough. He circled his partner, best friend, and captain all rolled up in one, searching for the perfect opening to take Marcus down. *Brain tells body what to do. Execute.* So much easier than dealing with everyone's deliberate avoidance of talking about his dad, silently waiting for Scott to make a call. He'd call when he was damn good and ready.

Marcus hopped back and forth from one foot to the other. Scott moved to his right, forcing Marcus to circle with him, and within seconds found his opening. Marcus stepped back a bit too far, exposing one leg. Scott dove, swept the leg into his arms, and then brought his opponent to the mat.

"You may have fifteen pounds on me, but you're sloppy." Scott released Marcus and hopped to his feet.

"Fuck, man. You're faster than lightening." Marcus wiped his brow with his arm. "You're gonna kill it this season."

Scott extended his hand and helped Marcus to his feet. "Yeah. Yeah. Let's go again."

Although he'd never s confess aloud, he'd set his sights on the championship for his friend's weight class. During his freshman year he'd done well, making varsity, but he'd not placed in the division tournament. This year he planned on landing back on top…like he'd done all through high school. Better to maintain his strength by wrestling at a weight easily maintained. Maybe Marcus would bump up a weight class.

The coach blew the whistle and called the group to the center of the mat. "Nice practice, guys. Our first meet is three days away. I'm working you to the bone tomorrow, then we'll have a light day, mostly stamina, so you can recover. As you know, we're playing against Columbia and it's a home match. Let's publicize the shit out of this and fill the stands."

The team cheered, settled down, and listened intently. "The first match sets the tone. It lets everyone else know who means business. And we mean business."

Another cheer rose from the team.

"Go hit the showers and get plenty of rest tonight. You'll need your energy tomorrow."

The team stood huddled in the middle of the mat and screamed a communal *Go Team!* before exiting the wrestling room.

Scott had one foot out the door when his coach called for him. "Thayer. Hang back a minute, I want to talk to you."

Marcus gave Scott a quick side glance, shrugged, and dashed from the room. Scott crossed to the edge of the mat where coach shoved his clipboard and a few sheets of paper into his bag. "Yeah, coach?"

"Everything all right with you?" He remained crouched by his bag, rearranging the contents and not looking at Scott as he asked the question.

"Sure, Coach. Why would you ask?" Was he wearing his troubles on his sleeve?

"You seemed intense during practice today. You have a good holiday break?" Coach stood and placed a hand on Scott's shoulder, the closest he came to showing any kind of warmth to anyone. "Your mom's doing well? Things are good between you and Derek?"

Jesus! Personal much? "Mom's good. Everything's great between me and Derek. I guess I'm hyper-focused on the season and this first match." *Yeah, and the fact my dad told me he has cancer and everyone close to me is silently freaking out because I haven't called him back.* No need to share everything.

Coach regarded Scott, the end of his pen in his mouth. "Good man. You were the first freshman to make varsity here in a decade, and with your new bulk and focus I think you might be able to place in this year's tournament."

"You think so? My weight class is usually one of the toughest ones. Most of the guys are juniors and seniors." The one hundred fifty-seven bracket was notoriously the most difficult. Still, Scott couldn't deny his excitement at the prospect of becoming a champion again.

"You're right, which makes my vote of confidence in you all the more complimentary." Coach picked up his bag and headed toward the door. Scott scurried behind him. "Something's changed in you, kid. You've got a drive I didn't see in you last year."

"I appreciate the pep talk. I won't let you down." He'd seen Coach's *pep talks* before, thankfully directed at others, and they rarely left the receiver feeling encouraged.

"I'm sure you won't. Go hit the showers and get some sleep. I'm gonna work your ass off tomorrow." Coach didn't wait for a reply, he simply slung his bag higher on his shoulder and trotted down the stairs toward the locker room.

Scott returned to the wrestling room and ambled to the center circle. Come Saturday, the mat would sit on the basketball court where stands lining both walls would be filled, mostly with BU students and families of home team members.

His heart beat a little faster. This was *his* year. He had a loving mother, two additional parents in Claire and Henry, and most importantly, he had Derek. For once he could count on the future to map out according to his own plans. He had the support of people who believed in him, not the harsh judgment of an uncaring and unloving father.

Thinking about his father in the negative was a natural instinct, like breathing, but the man he'd met in the coffee house a week earlier wasn't uncaring. In fact, *Dad* seemed more like a stranger. Someone Scott could enjoy. Someone who needed, or at least wanted, Scott to give him a chance.

He grasped for the anger that helped him maintain distance, but for the first time since meeting with his father, he couldn't find any. In fact, he couldn't feel anything except for the hollowness in his chest. No one had pushed, yet putting off the decision he'd already made became harder with each passing day. He needed to make the call.

Snuggled in Derek's embrace, Scott closed his eyes. The comfort of loving arms wrapped around him couldn't push thoughts and worries away. Even in sleep, he couldn't escape dreams of his father, making for restless nights…not to mention severe exhaustion each morning.

Scott rested his head on Derek's chest and listened to the strong thrum of his love's heart. Derek silently worked his fingers through Scott's hair, gently massaging his scalp.

"All right. I'll call him tomorrow." Scott froze, waiting for Derek's response.

Finger stroking stopped, as did Derek's breathing for a second, but the pounding of Derek's heart knocked up a few beats per minute. Still, he said nothing.

"I know you've been stressing out about me, so you can quit your worrying and relax."

"I didn't say anything." Derek tightened his grip around Scott.

Scott slid a leg over Derek's, meshing them together in a

tangle of skin and heat. Yes. He'd call Dad. Tomorrow. For now, Derek and his warm presence was all that mattered. "What should I say to him?"

"What do you want to say?" Damn his answering questions with questions. He'd make a fantastic psycho-social-worker-therapist-whatever someday.

"I don't know." *Derek won't accept that.*

Derek ran his hand along Scott's arm, scratching gently with his nails.

Hmmm. A gentle hum. Scott's eyelids becoming harder to keep open. "Maybe I'll invite him to come to my meet on Saturday. He never came to one before. Plus, I'll have the buffer of you, Mom, your parents, the team, and all our friends in case things go south with my dad."

Derek responded with a squeeze.

"Maybe I'll grab a bite to eat with him after. You could come too. I want him to get to know you.

"Whatever you need."

"We could go to Java's and get a sandwich and coffee. We haven't been there since we came back from break."

Silence and the steady massage of Derek's rubbing seemed to be all the answer he'd get.

"He said he's glad I'd found someone who makes me happy." Had his father actually said those words? No, he'd said he wasn't surprised Scott had found happiness. Not the same thing.

Heat sliced through Scott's gut and speared outward. *Like the cancer spreading through Dad. Whoa! Where'd that come from?*

Derek stopped caressing Scott. "You okay?"

"How am I supposed to do this? Let go of all my anger."

"I don't think you have to. Your anger is real." Derek shuffled around, resting on his arm, facing Scott. "He wants to know you. Only way to do that is to be real."

So simple. So true. "Have I told you how much I love you?"

Derek scrunched up his face in a playful tease, like he probably did when he was five. "Yeah, but I never get tired of hearing it."

Scott's eyes burned, filling with unshed tears. "I love you so much."

Impossibly plump lips drew closer until they pressed against Scott's. The subtle trace of mint permeated the air around him as Derek let out a sigh. When Derek withdrew, his features had shifted, playfulness replaced by pure adoration, shining through wide amber eyes. "You're my world, Scott."

Scott cradled his lover, wrapping his arms around a strong torso. Sleep drifted closer and closer until blackness settled in.

Friday. The day before his first meet. The day he'd agreed to have lunch with his dad between classes. The waves of nausea grew stronger the closer he got to Bean Town Beef. Why he thought a burger and fries would be a good choice for him or his father was beyond him.

Mechanical steps, paced, anything to distract him from seeing his dad. Soon enough he'd have to release control and submit to whatever happened over lunch, but at least he could maintain as cool a head as possible until then.

Even before he opened the door, he spotted his father sitting at a window table, eyes trained on the hands folded in front of him. After a second, he looked up and immediately straightened his posture. He raised one hand tentatively. *Was that a wave?* Seemed more like an involuntary spasm.

Scott gripped the door handle and pulled. *Rip off the Band-Aid.* He approached the host. "I'm meeting someone." The host nodded and focused on something on the computer screen in front of him.

Despite the conversations and clink of silverware on plates filling the room, Scott could still hear the *phoom-phoom-phoom* of blood rushing behind his ears, his heart racing; totally opposite from the slow motion of his steps.

His father looked smaller than he had a week earlier. Weaker. How could Scott confront a sick man, demanding explanations for a lifetime of inflicted pain?

"The seat won't bite." His father's voice cut through the haze of rushing thoughts.

Scott slid onto a chair. "Hi."

"Hi," Dad said on a slight chuckle. "You look pretty wound up. Something on your mind?"

Be real. Be honest. Derek's voice chimed in Scott's head, coaching him, letting Scott know he wasn't alone. "How are you? You look—" Ice formed in Scott's lungs. What should he say? *You look like shit?*

Dad spared him having to finish his sentence. "Like a man with cancer." The smile lifting his father's lips conflicted with the words he'd spoken.

"Well, yeah." With the topic on the table, Scott found breathing slightly less difficult.

"I had a chemo treatment two days ago. Be glad you didn't see me yesterday." He grimaced, but only for a second. "Anyways. What's going on with you?"

No. You don't get to drop a grenade and then switch topics on me. "What's it like? The chemo, I mean."

A slight crinkle formed between his father's eyes. He studied his hands before lifting his head and facing Scott. "It's like the worst flu sickness you can imagine. Or food poisoning. Remember when you were a kid, maybe ten or eleven, and you ate the turkey sandwich I'd left out?"

"Yeah." How could he forget? He hadn't known about salmonella back then and spent three days hurling his guts, but he remembered the worried expression on his father's face. The glasses of ginger ale Dad brought him in the middle of the night and the way his father remained by his bedside until Scott fell asleep.

"I'd take that times ten compared to chemo."

Wow. He'd come to lunch even when he probably longed for the comfort of bed. "Maybe you should rest instead of having lunch with me."

"No. I *want* to spend time with you. Don't be surprised when all I order is toast and tea." He glanced around the area. "This seems like a hot spot for you college students. Do you come here often?"

"Not often enough." Scott slung his arm over the back of his chair and crossed one leg over the other. "Derek loves it, but we usually head to Cambridge for home-cooked meals."

"Sounds nice."

Scott examined his father's face. Lips in a flat line. Eyes focused, but not lively. Hands resting on the table. *Be real.* Yeah, easier said than done. "Um, can I ask you some questions about…um—"

"The cancer?" His dad made the conversation easier than Scott had anticipated. "Ask anything you like."

"Are you scared?"

Dad's eyes softened as he reclined back in his chair, the first sign of relaxing since Scott's arrival. "What a compassionate question and a hard one to answer. On one level, of course I'm scared. I'm young. I've left so many things unfinished. So many mistakes to corr—" He cut himself off and broke eye contact, peering at the table.

He cleared his throat and lifted his head, returning his attention to Scott. "On the other hand, it's been liberating. Knowing I have this thing that could cut my plans short has helped me reprioritize."

Those words coming from someone else would inspire admiration and respect, but his father wasn't just anyone. He'd caused Scott to suffer over and over again. The dominant emotion Scott could recall was one of disapproval. Disapproval of his grades, of his performance on the mat, of everything.

"I don't know what to say." *Good, Scott. Keep it real.* He

squirmed, the hard wood of the chair unyielding against his gluts.

"I don't expect you to say anything. Do you have any other questions?"

Millions. None. "Is chemo as bad as they show on TV?" *What a fucking stupid question.* He wished he could pull the words back into his mouth.

"Again, good question. Chemo's different for everyone. I've been pretty lucky." He rubbed his head. "I still have what little hair I've got left and other than a day of feeling sick, the main side effect is exhaustion."

Too weird. Having spent his first eighteen years fearing the man and the last two years hating him, yet there sat his dad, weak, open, and vulnerable. The two men, the father from Scott's youth and the one with him now weren't the same people. Why couldn't his dad have figured out he wanted to make amends without facing death?

Anger swelled in his chest, familiar and safe. Every instinct cried for him to tell his father to piss off. What came out was, "Do you want to come to my meet tomorrow?"

A light chuckle filled the space between them. Or maybe it was a full-hearted laugh, although it became a bout of coughing. Dad grabbed for his water, taking several large gulps before replacing the glass on the table. "That's not what I expected you to say."

"Me neither." Scott snickered despite the clash of confusion and yearning swirling inside him. "It's a home meet. I'm wrestling at the one hundred fifty-seven-pound weight class, and Coach thinks I have a shot of going all the way to finals this season."

"You sure you want me there? I mean, I'd love to go, but wouldn't I distract you?"

Probably. "I don't think so. I get pretty focused on the mat." *Not that you'd know.* Scott diverted his eyes. Even though he hadn't spoken the last words aloud, he'd meant them.

"Well, I'd love to come. Shannon will be there, right?"

"Of course." Again, a mix of annoyance and confusion churned inside Scott. "She comes to *all* of my matches." Sarcasm? A passively aggressive slight toward the man who'd caused him so much pain?

"Then I'll call her. I'm sure she and I can go together." His father raised his glass to his lips again.

The whole walk back to campus, Scott replayed every minute of lunch. As much as he wanted to find an excuse to shut his dad out, to find a reason to break all ties, he couldn't deny he'd enjoyed himself. Despite the darkness Scott associated with his childhood, all at the hands of one man, he still found the sparse light struggling to shine through. He wanted to believe this time things would be different.

He'd accelerated to a jog by the time he reached campus, anxious to get to practice, determined to make his father proud the next day.

FIVE

After a fitful sleep filled with dreams of his father--the one he'd grown up with, not the one from lunch the previous day--Scott should've been exhausted, but excitement charged him from head to toe. His first meet, at home. How he performed would set the tone for the season. Icing on the cake? His father would be there. Surprising how the idea brought warmth instead of ice.

Scott slid his legs out of bed and hopped onto the floor. He didn't even mind the sting to his feet. Nope. Nothing could get him down. Derek slept peacefully, his smooth torso and chest on display, a sizable tent lifting the sheet at his groin.

The temptation to squeeze in a morning blowjob seemed cruel when his love appeared so peaceful. There'd be plenty of time to use his mouth, and more, later on...*after* he'd kicked the Columbia wrestler's ass.

Already naked, Scott wrapped a towel around his waist and jetted for the showers. At six-thirty, he had the bathroom to himself. He took his time lathering, enjoying the sudsy waterfall sliding along body. A quick scrub of shampoo in his hair sent more silken bubbles trailing down his wet skin.

Heat sank into him, comforting him through and through. Yet his cock remained at full mast. *No bueno.*

Scott rested against the cool tile wall of the stall and slid his hand along his abdomen. He traced his fingertips along the crevices of his ribbed stomach and brushed at the edges of the neatly cropped pubic hair. Finally, he wrapped long fingers around his shaft and started a slow journey, stroking from base to head and back again.

Nerves along his cock fired all at once, ripping a groan out of Scott. He froze, but only for a second, remembering he was alone. Still, he made a note to muffle his noises.

Back and forth, up and down, Scott stroked, squeezing and releasing his grip intermittently. Quaking thighs and rubbery knees forced him to use the cold tile as support. Cold bit at his back, completely opposite from the heat in his belly and the tingling in his balls.

Breathing became shallow. His chest rose and fell in time with the pumping of his fist along his cock. His balls drew tighter, every fiber in his body revving faster towards what promised to be an exquisite release.

Wet heat along his skin and encircling his shaft became Derek's mouth. The firm grip of his hand, Derek's plump, beautiful lips. In. Out. Faster.

And then he exploded, capturing his lower lip between his teeth in an effort to stifle the cry itching to burst out of him. His whole body pulsed. Come travelled the length of his dick and blasted out the tip, forcing a blissful shudder to wash through Scott. Wave after wave rocked him, each one subsiding marginally, until at last, Scott could support his own weight without relying on the wall to keep him from falling.

Able to take in his surroundings, a string of his semen leaked down the far wall of the stall. Creamy ropes swirled the drain before disappearing. Scott squirted some mango-scented body wash onto his hands and thoroughly washed his cock, balls and ass. No sense in smelling like sex. It would only make him think about Derek. Not a recipe for paying attention in class.

Scott squirted a bit of body wash onto the floor and used his foot to clean the stall. He toweled off and stepped into the crisp air of the bathroom. Although he'd taken care of *business*, when he glanced at himself in the mirror, he could still make out a sizable lump in the front.

He ran into two freshman girls in the hallway, books in their arms and ambling toward the stairwell. They stopped dead in their tracks when they faced Scott, their mouths hanging open wide enough to catch flies.

Scott didn't skip a beat. Sauntering past them, he uttered a friendly, "Morning" and winked before entering his room. He made out one girl's comment before shutting the door. "Oh! My! Gawd! He's so fucking hot I'm getting wet."

No way. He closed the door most of the way, leaving a crack so he could eavesdrop.

"You know he's gay, right?" The other girl sounded like she was telling her friend off, but Scott could detect a hint of longing in her voice as well. "All the good ones are gay."

"I don't care what he is. If I could spend five minutes in a room with him standing there naked and not touching me, I'd probably still have the best sex of my life."

Scott let out a loud, "Ha!" Silence filled the hallway followed by urgent whispers and the tapping of running feet. Once he heard the stairwell door close, he pushed his own door shut and dropped the towel to the floor.

"Morning, sexy."

Scott whipped around, clutching his chest. "Derek! You're up."

Derek lay in bed, resting on one elbow, the slight torque of his body casting his muscles into slight definition. "Whatchya listening to?" he asked with a sing-songy tone.

"Uh…" Damn. He'd been caught. "Two freshmen were

talking about me after they saw me come out of the bathroom like this."

Derek's eyes widened, one eyebrow rising close to his hairline. "Like that?"

Scott peeked down at himself, realizing he was entirely nude. "Not *exactly* like this, but you get the idea."

"And these freshmen, were they guys or girls?"

"Aw, I think it's cute you can get jealous after all this time."

"And what did these lovely ladies have to say?" Derek sat up, a smirk tugging at one corner of his mouth. And fuck if it wasn't sexy as hell. Scott's cock started to fill out again.

"They said all the good guys are gay." More heat, some flowing toward his groin and some towards his cheeks.

"Nothing else?" Derek hugged his knees to his chest.

"Well, one of them did mention something about wanting me to pose nude for her so she could have the best sex of her life." If possible, Scott thought his cheeks might burst into flames.

Derek shook his head. "The last thing you need is more people inflating your already large head."

Scott picked up the damp towel from the floor and chucked it at Derek. "Brat."

Derek pursed his lips. "Yeah, but I'm *your* brat."

"Yes. You will always be my sexy, foxy, take-my-breath-away brat and I'll love you no matter how annoying you get."

Scott ducked as Derek flung the towel across the room.

Weigh-in, a pre-game ritual which allowed opponents to get a sneak peek at their competition. Columbia's team lined up on one side of the locker room scale in ascending order from lowest weight class to heavyweight, Boston University on the other. Each opponent took their turn on the scale to make sure they were at or below their weight limit. A technicality really, since Scott had never witnessed a disqualification because of an extra pound of two, but for him, the competition always began as he faced his opponent at the scale.

His Columbia opponent was taller than Scott, but leaner. Lanky arms and legs made for easy takedowns, although longer limbs provided more wiggle room to escape any hold Scott might try. Perhaps he'd have to focus on take-down and back exposure points. A technical win was still a win, but not nearly as satisfying as a pin; not as many team points.

Safely back in the wrestling room, the team sat in a circle around Coach. Through the window looking down on the basketball court, Scott watched the stands filling up with people. BU's red flooded the room with an assortment of flags, banners, sweatshirts, and ball caps. A small patch of blue congregated in one portion of the stands, to be expected since anyone following Columbia would've had to make the four-hour trip to watch the match.

Coach scanned the circle of wrestlers surrounding him, making eye contact with each member of the team. "Today's your day, boys, and this year is our year. When we enter that room, I want you to own the very air people breathe. Make noise. Crowd the mat to support your teammates. Let's show Columbia who's the best in the division, and let our message spread to all the other schools."

Energy coiled inside Scott, charging him to the point of exploding. He hopped in place as Coach rallied the team. "I've known some of you for four years, others I've only begun to know, but I can tell you this. You are winners. In the last two decades, we've never had such a strong lineup. So fight. Push. Let's show Columbia they're no match for the BU Terriers."

The team cheered, then Marcus stood next to Coach. "All right, let's line up by weight class. We're gonna bust through those doors and run straight onto the mat. A quick warm up and then Columbia will have their turn for a few minutes. You ready to kill it?"

"Go team!" The team's voices bounced off the walls.

"I said, you ready to *kill* it?" Marcus's balled his fists, raising them above his head.

"Go team!" Everyone jumped to their feet and rushed to the door, lining up.

"All right, boys." Coach's voice rose above the cheering and chanting of the team. "Let's go."

Feet stomped on stairs. The doors to the basketball court burst open to a wall of shouts and hollers flooding the room. Marcus led the team in a quick round of spins to get the blood flowing, followed by thirty seconds of drops, and the BU team hustled off to their side of the mat so Columbia could warm up.

Scott took his place along the edge of the mat with the rest of the team. Scanning the bleachers, he immediately found Derek, who'd painted half his face red and the other half white. Claire and Henry sat with him, along with Mom. His father wasn't there.

Scott's gut twisted. Anger? Sadness? Frustration? Maybe a combination of all three. He swallowed back his disappointment and focused on his opponent, who spun with a partner in the middle of the mat.

Movement from the entrance to the gym caught his attention. Dad. The man wore a heavy winter jacket, despite the stuffiness of the crowded room. His skin looked more pallid than it had the day before, and his sunken eyes seemed dark enough to appear bruised.

Worry should've dominated Scott's thoughts, along with a silent rebuke toward Mom for not driving his father, but nothing surpassed the jolt of excitement at seeing his dad.

He came.

After a second, they made eye contact and his father brightened, making him appear a bit less fragile. Dad trod slowly to where Mom sat and plunked down heavily next to her. To her credit, she placed an arm around his shoulder and kissed his cheek.

Scott watched them, recalling times from long ago, and forced himself to look away. He couldn't afford distractions.

There were nine weight classes, ranging from one hundred twenty-five to two hundred eighty-five, and Scott's one hundred fifty-seven was smack in the middle. Scott loved the combination of individual and team effort involved in wrestling. On the mat, he had only himself to rely upon. His skill. His determination. No one to assist if he made a wrong move. Yet his performance made a difference for the team.

The first two guys from the BU lineup lost their matches, although only by a narrow margin. The next two won, also by narrow margins, leaving the team scores at six to six by the time the ref called Scott's weight class.

Scott snuck a quick peek over his shoulder at the stands. Derek cupped his hands over his mouth and shouted something. The cheering crowd made him impossible to hear. Better to imagine what he might've said. All four parents clapped, his father raising his arm and giving Scott a thumbs up.

Turning back to the mat, Scott strode to the center. As he shook his opponent's hand, Scott could sense the energy coursing through his own body, electric, buzzing, ready to obey his every command. *He gave me a thumbs up!*

When the ref blew the whistle, Scott dove for the guy's leg, sweeping it into his arms with ease. He brought his opponent down to all fours and secured a firm hold.

One yank on an ankle while driving his weight forward forced the guy flat on his belly. He slid a half nelson into place and torqued his opponent to his back. As he suspected, the grip was difficult to hold.

Lanky bastard! Oh, Lanky, perfect nickname. Scott exposed Lanky's back a few more times, earning him several points, but couldn't finish off the first period with a pin.

Entering the second period, Scott took bottom position. The

second the ref blew the whistle he shot to his feet, spun out of Lanky's grip, and took the guy back down to the mat again. Since normal pinning moves wouldn't work, Scott had to focus on strength.

He wrenched Lanky to his back, locking his arms in a vice grip, and arched as far as his back allowed, driving his feet into the soft mat and ploughing his entire body against Lanky's chest. His muscles burned and sweat formed on his forehead and temples, dripping down his cheeks. A technical win by points would have been fine, and certainly much easier to achieve, but Scott wanted the pin. His dad had come to see the match, the first match he'd ever attended, driving Scott to wrestle to perfection.

Lanky tried to twist out of Scott's grip, but each movement allowed Scott to tighten his hold. Finally, the ref started counting, and after a quick one-two-three, slammed the mat.

Scott released Lanky and jumped to his feet in one fluid motion. The crowd roared, but the noise seemed more like a dull buzzing. Scott placed his hands on his knees and hunched over, sucking in gulps of air, the thrill of the win coursing through him.

Once his heart slowed from its fevered staccato pace to a heavy thumping, he scanned the bleachers, immediately catching sight of a jumping Derek, wildly clapping his hands. Claire and Henry were also clapping, although they weren't hopping around like his drunken monkey boyfriend. His mother stared directly at him, a broad grin on her face, but even from twenty feet away, Scott could tell the happiness was only surface. She glanced at his father, who remained seated, her lips thin, like she had to work to seem happy.

Scott strode to center mat, shook hands with Lanky, and the ref lifted his hand into the air. He watched the scoreboard, giving himself a silent cheer as his team score increased by six points. The moment he stepped off the mat, the thrill of winning subsided.

Scott peered to the part of the bleachers where his family sat, noticing the sag in Dad's shoulders and the way he sort of collapsed against Mom. Tearing his eyes away, he willed himself to focus on the next match.

The rest of the meet went much as the first half had gone, two wins for BU and two wins for Columbia. In the end, the team won eighteen to fifteen. Scott's pin had secured a team win. No doubt news of his performance would spread to other teams once the results published on the Division One website. Faster, probably, since players and fans posted pictures and comments on Facebook.

Coach gave a short pep talk, congratulating the team, then released them to join their friends and families.

Derek rushed to Scott's side, pulling him into a tight hug and kissing him gently on the lips. "You were awesome. I was worried when I saw your opponent. Those tall thin guys are your weak spot."

Scott peered over Derek's shoulder toward his parents, cringing when he noticed his father observing the two of them. The slight smile, only barely curling his lips, seemed so foreign. At least he was standing and didn't seem as tired.

Scott faced Derek, kissing him once more. "I don't know. I think my weakness is athletic guys a couple inches shorter than me with brown hair and amber eyes."

Derek hugged him and took Scott's hand. "C'mon. Your dad was so excited for you." He led Scott toward their parents.

Scott tugged on Derek's hand to stop their progress. "Is Dad okay?"

Derek frowned, though only for a second. "I think he's fine. Tired and weak, but he's here and he cheered for you."

"Really?" Scott peered directly in Derek's eyes, needing to see the truth.

Derek stepped closer. "Definitely." He held Scott's gaze for a few heartbeats, then the corner of his lip curled up. "They're waiting for you."

Scott's mom engulfed him in a bear hug as soon as he reached the bleachers. "You were wonderful, honey. Congratulations."

Claire and Henry sidled next to him, Henry clapping him on the shoulder. "Well done. We've missed going to meets." He tilted his head in Derek's direction. "This one keeps saying he's too busy to join the team."

"I've been hounding him to join since the beginning of last year, so if you have any tricks I don't know, please share them." Scott chuckled, gazing at the loving faces around him, finally settling on his father. A bit of the spirited energy surrounding him faded.

Before Scott had a chance to say anything, his father chimed in, "I really enjoyed watching you wrestle, son. Your focus was impressive."

Scott froze. All he'd ever wanted from his dad was an attaboy.

"I mean, the way you persisted. When you couldn't make your first move work, you plotted a new course." Dad stepped forward and gripped Scott's shoulder. "I'm proud of you."

Too much. His lungs constricted. His vision blurred. How long had he yearned for his father's acceptance?

Derek slipped his arm around Scott's waist. Instinctively, Scott wrapped his arm over Derek's shoulders and pulled him close.

Breathing became easier as Scott inhaled, taking in Derek's scent. A million comments swirled in his head. Better to keep them stored there for the time being. "Thanks, Dad."

Awkward silence hung around them. Claire, ever the peacemaker, spoke first. "We're all going to the restaurant you guys talk about. Boston Town Burgers, is it?"

Derek shook his head. "Bean Town Beef. How many times do I have to tell you?"

"Oh, hush." She swatted Derek's arm. "Shall we head out?"

Everyone turned to face Scott's father. "Thanks for the offer, but I should head to my hotel room. I can't do much these days without exhausting myself."

Disappointment hedged in on Scott's happiness. If his dad sincerely wanted to know him, why wouldn't he go to lunch? One look at his father gave him his answer. His father made it to the match. Based on his sagging shoulders and the deep lines in his face, the effort cost him quite a bit of energy. "It's all right, Dad. Thanks for coming."

"I'll call you this week if it's all right." Pressure seemed to evaporate after Scott spoke.

"That'd be great." Scott fought the sudden urge to step forward and hug the frail man who seemed so alone.

"Okay, then. I think I'll be off." His father kissed Mom on the cheek, hugged Claire, and shook Henry's hand. He stopped in front of Derek. "I'm glad Scott has you." He patted Derek's shoulder and turned to Scott. "Let's get together later this week?"

"Okay." No need to consider the truth of the words. He knew he meant them to his core.

Dad held eye contact with Scott for a brief pause, then nodded and hobbled in the direction of the entrance.

Again, Scott tamped down the need to rush to his father's side. Each step seemed an effort for the man who'd loomed so large in all Scott's memories.

His dad glanced back at Scott when he reached the doors and disappeared with the crowd. The second he fell out of sight, Scott's world came back into focus. Derek's embrace. The chatter of Mom and Derek's parents. The shouts and cheers bouncing off the walls. All the noise and celebration surrounded him, jarring the haze of memories of an unloving man. *I didn't even shake his hand.* Scott forced his lips to curve upward. "It will only take me a few minutes to get ready. I'll meet you in the main lobby of the athletic building.

One look at Derek let Scott know his internal battle hadn't gone unnoticed. He might've seemed content to most people, but Scott knew for sure a serious discussion loomed in his very near future.

SIX

DEREK SHOWED ENOUGH GRACE TO ALLOW SCOTT TO CHOOSE the venue of their little *talk*, as he put it: The Student Center. They found a booth located amidst an assortment of pool playing, computer wielding, or idly chatting fellow classmates. The way Derek folded his arms and fixed his gaze on Scott let him know a highly public setting wouldn't deter Derek from his goal.

"What? You heard him. He's tired. The invitation included him." Scott winced at how pathetic his excuse sounded.

Derek leaned back in his chair and said nothing.

"I mean, I'll admit I could've pushed. Maybe suggested someplace a bit quieter where he would've felt more comfortable." Scott gnawed on his bottom lip. Truth be told, he'd been relieved when his father begged out. The meal had been far more pleasant surrounded by the people he trusted without question.

"I mean, you can't expect me to just forgive and forget a lifetime of rejection, can you? He made my life a living hell." Scott took a sip of his ginger ale, the carbonation burning a trail down his throat.

Amber eyes, unblinking, focused directly on him. Scott

squirmed, unable to get comfortable. "I mean, c'mon. He shows up out of nowhere, comes to my meet, and says shit like he's proud of me. It's like he's been taken over by an alien."

Derek cupped his coffee in his hands, raising the flimsy cardstock to his lips. Scott shook his head. "I won't deny, hearing him say those words felt great. He's reminding me of the person I knew when I was really young. The dad who paid attention. A lifetime ago. Back when we lived in Phoenix and before we started moving around all over the place."

A clear picture formed in Scott's head.

Saturday morning. A regular weekend. No holiday or birthday or special occasion. He'd crawled into his parent's bed, as he always did when he woke up, about to fall back to sleep when his father nudged him.

"Morning, champ."

"Morning, Daddy."

"I heard something outside last night in the driveway. Did you hear it too?"

"No, Daddy. I didn't hear anything."

"Huh. Let's go check it out."

"Okay."

They'd crept out of bed, careful not to wake Scott's mother, and tiptoed down the stairs to the basement door leading to the garage.

"Shh. We don't want to wake Mommy." His father crept between the two cars parked in the dark space and stood by one of the garage doors. "Close the basement door so Mom doesn't hear the noise."

Scott closed the door, reveling in his secret mission with Dad and without Mom. "Okay, Daddy."

Inch by inch his dad lifted the door, light filtering into the darkened area. Once the door was all the way opened, Scott stepped outside. Sitting in the middle of their driveway, in bright blue, red, and yellow, with a huge red bow on top, was a Big Wheel.

He rode his Big Wheel all day and into the night until his mother came outside and threatened to take it from him if he didn't come in for dinner.

. . .

Scott could recall the way he'd clapped his hands and jumped up and down. Could remember the pit-pat of his feet rushing to the precious gift. The sound of the wheels grinding against asphalt and then skidding to a stop when he braked.

But more than anything, the light reaching all the way to his father's eyes as he stood outside the garage entrance, remained the strongest memory.

Scott shook his head, forcing the image to dissolve into nothing. Those happy times rarely occurred. For every Big Wheel, there were a hundred bitter disappointments.

"Seriously, Derek, what do you expect from me? I can't forget all those years of pain and suffering." Scott slumped back in his seat, a huff escaping him. "He was a mean bastard and now I'm supposed to forgive him because he's got cancer? I mean, I feel bad, but it doesn't change how he treated me."

Derek edged forward, placing his hands on the table, palms up. Scott clasped Derek's hands, his heart pounding as he searched Derek's eyes for empathy. "You agree with me, right? I'm not being an ass for doubting he's changed?"

Derek maintained the same even expression, no challenge or judgment. Scott squirmed in his seat, the power of Derek's gaze forcing him to face the truth he so desperately wanted to avoid. "All right, so maybe I'm being a little harsh, but who could blame me? After everything he's done, I have a right to question his intentions."

Who am I kidding? How could a sick man, a dying man, have sinister intentions? Scott blew a tuft of hair out of his eyes. "Fine. You've made your point. I'll call him and set up another get together, and this time I'll try to keep an open mind. Are you satisfied now?"

Derek squeezed Scott's hands, then raised one to his lips, kissing Scott's knuckles.

Scott let out a sigh. "Good. Then stop hounding me, would you?"

Weight training. The steady strain on his muscles by pushing heavy plates up and down. After the *talking to* Derek had given him, Scott needed to burn off energy. Amazing how Derek could communicate so much without uttering a single word.

He pressed the bar away from his body, enjoying the way his muscles tensed, mechanically driving the one hundred seventy-five pounds at a steady pace. Lowering the weights with the same care created a welcome burn, his pecs and biceps straining to maintain precise control.

A year earlier, he'd weighted fifteen pounds less and could barely bench one sixty. Now, his body bulged, and not just in areas Derek influenced. He couldn't even fit into his Tasmanian Devil shirt, the one he wore on his first day at Brampton High. The day he met Derek their senior year. Of course, the shirt could hardly be considered his own anymore since Derek wore it so much.

Up, down, repeat. The burn in his arms caused his muscles to tremble. Only three more reps and done. Then a hot shower.

An hour later, Scott exited the athletic complex, muscles sore, but not uncomfortable. The bitter winter wind whipped over his collar and through his still-damp hair. Derek would probably yell at him for not wearing a hat. *You'll get sick. People lose ninety percent of their body heat through their head.*

Scott laughed out loud. *Where does he find his information?*

His chest swelled as he thought of all the ways Derek had been his buoy. He'd been patient and understanding when Dad restricted Scott's activities their senior year of high school and pulled him from the wrestling team for a few weeks, effectively blocking him from seeing Derek and nearly breaking them up. Derek remained by Scott's side after his father abandoned him and his mother. He provided unconditional love, even when Scott withdrew into himself earlier in the year, afraid of repeating the mistake of making demands on Derek out of fear for Derek's safety. Though a small part of him, the less sympathetic part, had breathed a relieved breath when Tyrell had chosen to leave BU. A shudder ripped through Scott at the crystal-clear image of the psycho wielding a pen and charging Derek. So much had happened in two years, good and bad, and their love had grown stronger.

No way in hell would he let Derek down by being a stubborn jerk.

He dug his phone from his pocket and dialed the ten digits he'd committed to memory—numbers he never imagined he'd have any reason to know.

His father picked up on the first ring. "Scott. I'm so glad you called."

"I told you I would." He couldn't help the bitterness in his voice, like an instinctual reaction.

"I've been replaying your match over and over. You must be thrilled."

He would've been if he hadn't wasted so much energy trying to rebut Derek's unspoken message. *You promised him you'd try.* "I'm happy I won. It sends the right message. When word gets out, people will know I'm a contender."

"You were always a fierce competitor, Scott. Although I travelled for work, your mom kept me updated on your wrestling. Even if she hadn't, it would've been impossible to miss the trophies lining your dresser." Unmistakable admiration.

Scott shivered as a chilled wind attacked his neck. "You said you wanted to get together again. Want to make plans?"

"Do you remember how your mom and I used to take you to museums when you were little?"

Some of his best memories. Even when his relationship consisted of nothing more than "Hello" and "yes, sir", Scott had always enjoyed his visits to the local museums wherever they lived at the time. "Yeah."

"There's an exhibit at the Museum of Fine Arts exploring the results of the 2011 earthquake in East Japan. Would you be interested?" His father delivered the question casually, like asking Scott what flavor ice cream he wanted. Icy threads of suspicion raced through his veins, a natural reaction. Perhaps his father sensed Scott's hesitation because he added, "Doesn't matter which day. Let me know an evening when you're free and I'll make it happen."

He's trying to reconnect. Whose voice did he hear, his own or Derek's? Sooner or later Scott had to let the message sink through his thick, stubborn skull or he'd drive himself and everyone else crazy with frustration.

Wrestling practices kept his schedule full. Daily practices usually ran until six-thirty, leaving Scott useless afterward. Fridays were light days to preserve the team's energy for the Saturday meets. They had another home game coming up, so Scott wouldn't have to get up too early. "Friday works. It would have to be after six though."

"Sure. The museum's open until ten on Friday. We could meet there. Then maybe grab something to eat afterward." Again, so open and flexible, completely opposite from the man Scott had known for the better part of his life.

Scott could practically hear Derek's commentary. *Say yes. He's trying.* "Sounds good. I'll meet you there at around six-thirty."

"Great. See you there." His voice was laced with something between weariness and humility. "Thanks for trying. I know this must be hard on you."

Too much to process. This man who'd reentered Scott's life couldn't possibly be the same one he'd grown up fearing. "I'll see you Friday." He pressed the *End* button before his father could say anything else.

The rest of the week progressed uneventfully. Practice. Sex. Eating. Still, as Friday drew closer, Scott couldn't deny the growing pressure in his chest. Excitement or nervousness? Hard to tell, the sensations often similar. One thing he knew for sure: Voluntarily getting together with Dad felt strange.

He took a quick shower after practice and hustled out of the athletic complex, not stopping to chat with his teammates. A short text from Derek wished him good luck. Hell, Luck didn't come into play. Meeting his dad was a choice…one he struggled to reconcile against his natural instinct of avoidance. Always had.

This man who'd resurfaced seemed different. Why wouldn't he be? After all, movies and books depicted people who tried to make amends as they came to terms with fatal diseases. Why should his dad be any different?

Which brought on a new round of resentment. Cancer shouldn't have been the catalyst pushing his father to give Scott acceptance and love him.

Scott shook his head. No sense in getting himself riled up. Worst case scenario, he'd feel uncomfortable for a few hours while enjoying a highly acclaimed exhibit.

The museum wasn't too far from campus, although practice had run a bit late and he didn't have the time to walk. Pity, since the exertion would've given him something to focus on other than his nervous stomach.

He hailed a cab and five minutes later arrived at the museum. His father stood slouched over a cane next to the front doors. Scott hesitated, the door to the cab still open. A simple hop back into the taxi and he could return to his dorm…to Derek. Of course, facing Derek after blowing off his dad would be worse than anything the next few hours could present.

Scott climbed the steps and joined his father. "You been waiting long?"

"No. I got here a few minutes ago." Although he propped heavily on his cane, the whites of his knuckles pronounced, energy radiated off the man. "I've heard amazing things about the exhibit. The photographs depict the devastation to Tohoku, Japan. First an earthquake, followed by tidal flooding and the destruction of the Fukushima nuclear power plant. The event sparked one of the greatest surges in photo journalism the country had seen in decades."

"Wow. I had no idea you were so into history." *And why would I? Not like you ever shared anything with me.* Scott mentally berated himself. He'd promised Derek he'd try, and harboring negative thoughts wasn't helping.

Dad purchased the tickets and led them to the section with the Tohoku exhibit. On the far wall, a detailed photograph took up about a ten-by-ten-foot space. The artist had played with color, giving the ground a dark metallic blue and the sky a fiery red. Bare skeletons of buildings dotted an otherwise cracked earth, the ground appearing like skin cells under a microscope.

Wordlessly, Scott drew closer, taking in finer details. The metal within the structures jutted out at odd angles, their edges ridged like angry knives. So reminiscent of the wreckage after the terrorist attacks in 2001. Thin plumes of smoke rose from the ground, curling into the air.

As he drew closer, he spotted a shape which didn't quite seem to fit. Step by step he approached, the room eerily quiet despite the several dozen people present. About fifteen feet away he made out the shape: a man, his arms hanging limply by his sides, peering out of the picture, as if regarding Scott directly. The choice to place a man in the middle of the desolate scene accentuated the breadth of the devastation. He was no more than a tiny ant amidst a sea of destruction.

"Takes your breath away, doesn't it?" His father's voice came from right behind him.

"Sure does." Scott took a few more steps toward the image. How long must it have taken the guy to walk to the middle of the scene? What was he thinking about? The resignation in his body language helped Scott to make an educated guess, but he'd never personally experienced anything so dead and empty on such a grand scale.

"I get how the guy must feel." His father merely whispered.

Scott forced himself to turn from the picture. "What do you mean?"

"I don't know if I can explain it." His father studied the picture and said nothing. When he did speak again, he didn't face Scott. "The day of your birth was the happiest day of my life. You probably think I'm exaggerating to emphasize the importance of a moment in time, but for me, it's literally the truth."

Scott had no idea what to say so he remained silent.

"You were perfect. Your mom and I were so in love. I was beginning to move up the ladder at work. We'd created the family I'd always dreamed of." He took another few steps toward the painting without looking at Scott.

"I had such hopes and dreams for us back then. A house, neighborhood barbeques, coaching your soccer and baseball teams." Finally, he leveled his gaze on Scott. Soulful green eyes bore into him. Scott had never noticed them before, but looking at them now he knew who he'd inherited his own green eyes from. His father's lacked the passion Scott remembered, making him seem tired and older.

"But life has a way of beating dreams into the ground. One day everything is bright flowers and beautiful sunshine. The next, it can all blow up in your face." He lifted his arm, extending his fingers and reaching towards Scott's shoulder, but stopped midway and let his arm drop to his side…like the man in the painting.

"Your mom wanted to stay home to take care of you and I felt a sense of duty to earn money to support my family. I worked longer hours, applied for promotion after promotion. From a business standpoint I was successful." Dad shook his head, his lips pressed together. "In one sense I achieved what I'd set out to accomplish, but I didn't know at what cost until too late."

"What do you mean?" Scott asked, despite his unease about the conversation's direction.

"Life's a funny thing. You plan and plan. You work hard trying to make dreams come true. Each milestone is like a badge of honor, a visible sign to the outside world saying, 'Hey, look at me, I've accomplished something, but time has a way of slipping by unnoticed. A surprise dinner for your wife gets pushed to next week because of an important meeting and then a month passes and you've had two arguments. A baseball game on a Saturday gets ignored because you're traveling and you tell yourself, 'I'll be there for the next one'.

"Each excuse and justification to put things off pushes your real dreams farther and farther away. Before you know it, you've wasted a year neglecting your family. You tell yourself, 'I'm gonna change. This isn't who I am', but habits are hard to break and it takes effort to change. Courage isn't an easy trait to exercise." His father opened and closed his mouth a few times, never breaking eye contact with Scott. When he finally spoke, his voice seemed distant, like he was talking to himself and not to Scott. "You're twenty and already proved you're a far braver man than me."

So not the words Scott ever expected to hear. "How?"

"Son, you're living honestly as a gay man. Can't be easy, no matter how progressive the world's become. You've agreed to see me even though I effectively neglected you over and over again."

His father gestured toward the painting on the wall. "I created a wasteland for myself. Devastation all around. In the end, I'm standing in the middle of nothing." He returned his attention to Scott. "But you. You're seizing each moment. You're making them count while you live them. That takes far more courage than I ever showed."

Did his father feel like the man in the middle of the picture? If his father knew how many times Scott'd succumbed to insecurity, using his upbringing as an excuse, he might have a different idea about Scott's bravery. "I—I had no idea."

"Funny thing is, I wouldn't have been able to put it into words like this before. It took cancer and facing my own mortality to speak the feelings I've been living with."

Made sense. "I don't know what to say."

"Why don't we walk around and look at the artwork." His father strolled to the right side of the room, stopping before each photograph. Most images depicted landscapes, either gaping holes from the quake or decimated buildings and homes. Very few had people in them, although the ones that did caught Scott's attention the most. Without fail, the expressions on those faces were the same...vacant. The storm hadn't merely destroyed the land, but the people as well.

He caught up to his father standing in front of another photograph. Three children, two boys and a girl, formed a circle, none of them facing the photographer. They held hands and appeared to be playing some sort of game. Or perhaps they were dancing based on the way the girl's hair hung mid-air. Behind them in the distance a cityscape, or what used to be a city, loomed like a row of shattered teeth.

Scott sucked in a breath, surprised at the tightening of his chest and the sudden burn in his eyes. Even amidst devastation, the human will to find joy and happiness survived.

A tear welled in Scott's eye, then dripped down his cheek. His father stepped beside him.

The urge to touch his father, to slip an arm around his shoulder, swept through Scott, but he forced himself to remain still. He kept his eyes glued to the picture, a snapshot of Scott's life in image form.

Had this been Dad's intention all along? Could he possibly know enough about Scott to understand what this particular image would represent? He'd thought his father simply wanted to spend time with him, and likely he did, but Scott needed to see the underlying message here.

He contemplated the picture, unaware of how much time passed, how many people surrounded him. He simply gazed at the three children, playing or dancing. Happiness.

Derek's song from the winter dance came to mind. Happiness had been the message in the mix, the gift he'd created for Scott. Yes. Despite the wreckage of years lost to anger and loneliness, Scott had allowed the good to shine through.

Dad's voice cut through the haze of his thoughts. "You've been standing here for ten minutes. Everything okay?"

"Yeah. Everything's fine." Scott studied the picture more closely. One of the boys, smaller than the other two children, seemed to be laughing the hardest. There'd been lots of laughter for Scott when he'd been so young. He could remember wrestling in the back yard with his father, flying kites, taking trips to the pond down the road from the first home Scott ever lived in. "Good things find a way to shine, even when a whole lot of bad stuff happens."

The answer resonated deep in his heart, although he wished he hadn't made the statement out loud. His intention wasn't to hurt Dad. Based on his reaction to the first picture, his dad was doing a lot of thinking about his own life and reflecting on the same memories as Scott.

"I see it, but the picture says something different to me." Dad stepped forward, his back to Scott. "It's never too late to try to move forward."

Is that why you reached out to me? The hairs on the back of his neck prickled. Scott hugged himself. Spending time with his father was a chore, not pleasure. Despite the words and appearance, Ron Thayer made Scott's life miserable. No good intentions could erase any of those memories, nor could they ease his resentment.

Dad sighed, his whole body sagging. "I've had time to process all choices I've made and what steps I want to take to make things better. I don't expect you to let your guard down all at once." He grasped Scott's shoulder. Despite the frailty of his body, he managed a firm grip. "Thank you for joining me tonight. I hope each time we get together your comfort increases, even if only bit by bit." He looked at Scott, then nodded. "I think I'll head back to the hotel. I'd love to get together again soon though."

Scott bit his lip, not wanting to reveal the excitement bubbling inside. He wasn't ready to let his dad in yet. Not until his dad proved he planned on sticking around.

Silence hung in the air between them. Should he say something? Dad made the decision for the both of them. "Well, give me a call in the next few days so we can plan something." He hobbled toward the door.

A coil wound tighter inside Scott's stomach as he watched his father retreat. Then the coil snapped, freeing a part of Scott he'd kept locked up. The part, if he let it free, which would break down the protective barrier he'd built around his heart to block out his father. "Dad. Wait!"

His father closed the distance between them, his eyes a bit brighter. "Yes?"

"I have another match tomorrow. It's home again so if you'd like to come that would be cool." With the invitation extended, bands loosened from Scott's chest, breathing suddenly easier.

"I'd like to. Thanks for the invitation." He turned away again and traversed the room slowly.

Scott waited until his father left the room. *Okay. It's okay.* He faced the picture of the happy children one more time. *This time everything will be okay.*

Safely ensconced in Derek's embrace, Scott could process the evening. Hell, the past few weeks had been a whirlwind of emotions.

Derek kissed Scott's neck and hugged him tight as they lay together in bed. "Wanna talk about it?" He did, but so many thoughts raced through his mind that he had no idea where to start. Lucky for Scott, Derek could read even the most subtle behavior. "Which is worse, the anger or the confusion?"

"The confusion. No doubt." Hmmm. The answer came easily. "I'm used to anger, but Dad's being so…awesome. I don't know how to react. My gut tells me to look for the criticisms in his words. My body's primed for flight over fight. It's work to keep an open mind."

"Too much work?" Derek whispered the question into his ear.

"No." Again, the answer came without the need to think. "Just work. Like everything I say and do has to be filtered."

"How do you feel after you're with him?"

"Good. Everything leading up to seeing him is the worst. I'm anticipating bad and experiencing good. Know what I mean?"

Derek cuddled Scott in answer.

"Like tonight. The whole cab ride to the museum I dreaded having to be around him, but he's being so open and honest. It's like he's apologizing for all the years of letting me down." Scott chuckled, although without humor. "Am I even making sense?"

"Perfect sense. Words mean far less than actions. You already know that."

"Yeah." Scott'd lost count of the number of times he'd simply held Derek's hand. The moments when Derek placed a kiss to Scott's cheek. Comfortable silence meant far more than confessions of love.

"I'm really proud of you, Scott. What you're doing is hard. Lots of people wouldn't try like you are. Blindly holding onto anger and negativity is far easier as far as I can tell. To actually open yourself up to change, especially changing your opinion about someone who's hurt you, takes a fuck load of courage."

Scott pulled Derek close. "Huh."

"What?" Derek propped himself on his elbow.

"My dad said the same thing. I have courage." Scott slid his hand behind Derek's neck and pulled down, kissing his forehead. "Let's get some sleep. I've got a big day tomorrow."

Derek rested his head on Scott's chest, and within a few minutes a hint of a snore broke through the silence in the room.

Scott closed his eyes, the painting of the three children playing amidst wreckage coming to animated life in his thoughts. Had those kids found their own joy? Were they aware of the ruin surrounding them? Or had their parents encouraged them to play, protecting them from the worries of rebuilding something from nothing?

Whether from exhaustion or strain from the past two weeks of spending time with his father, heaviness settled over Scott, dragging him closer and closer to sleep. Whatever his future held, time would yield the answers. In the meantime, Scott had a match the next day and needed to get some sleep.

He'd see Dad again at his match--if he kept his word and showed up.

SEVEN

SCOTT WOKE TO FIND THE BEDCOVERS BUNCHED AROUND HIS and Derek's feet. Apparently one or both of them tossed and turned during the night, and they hadn't even had sex. Derek shifted as Scott reached for the down comforter, and settled back into the crook of Scott's arm once Scott blanketed them in warmth again.

A quick glance at the clock showed only six-thirty. Not surprising he'd wake up so early. Adrenaline and anticipation always made for energized competition days, but no reason to rush, especially when he had such a hot man lying next to him.

His meet was against Harvard, a solid team. Being a home game, the stands would probably be filled like the first match. He had no information on his opponent other than knowing he'd won against the Rutgers player. And there lay the excitement of season matches. Each person he wrestled gave him more information about wrestlers he hadn't yet faced.

Derek chuckled in his ear. "I know that look. You're plotting the next few weeks of wins, aren't you?"

"You know me too well."

"Not possible!" Derek widened his eyes in mock horror.

"Weirdo." Scott rolled on top of Derek and closed his mouth over his lover's. Derek always complained about wake-up kisses, worrying his mouth tasted like ass. Stupid man. Scott always loved the taste of Derek's ass.

Derek struggled to keep his mouth closed, caving after the third pass of Scott's tongue along his lips. Gentle, wet caresses of carefree morning kissing, easy and relaxed, a perfect way to wake up.

Derek turned his head, breaking the kiss. "At least let me brush my teeth."

Scott sealed their lips together again, exploring Derek's mouth with greater intensity. After a few seconds he pushed himself off of Derek, supporting his weight on his arms. "Mmm. There's a whole other part of my body interested in playing if you want to move away from our mouths."

Derek wrapped his fingers around Scott's shaft. "Oh yeah?" Derek flashed his sly smile. Damn if it wasn't sexy. "But you set the rules at the beginning of this season. No sex on match days until after the meet."

Scott vaguely recalled the rule, along with his foolish reasoning. The buildup of energy served him well on the mat.

Derek slid from under Scott and hopped off the bed. "I'm gonna take care of this disgusting morning mouth and take a shower." Already naked, his form dazzled Scott, causing his cock to throb with greater enthusiasm. Muscles bulged in his lover from broader shoulders to a tight, round ass. *When did that happen?* Derek glanced over his shoulder. "Care to join me?"

No way in hell could Scott join Derek in the bathroom without fucking him senseless in the shower. "I better wait here until you're done."

"Suit yourself." Derek sauntered toward their door. Each step caused his muscles to ripple and Scott nearly decided to break his own rule. Luckily, Derek slid the towel around his waist, removing the source of temptation from immediate view, and exited their room.

"Fuck me!" Scott worked hard to keep his hands off his cock as he spoke to the empty room.

The freezing chill served as a welcome distraction, cutting through the buildup of desire for Derek's body. He had to squint against the glare of a million crystalline sparkles as the sun bounced off the snow-covered quad.

What a day! Admittedly, winter had drawbacks for Scott since he wasn't terribly fond of cold. Nor did he prefer to wear layers of bulky clothes, but nothing beat the clean views and smells. Not to mention the warmth of holding Derek's hand, something he wouldn't have done publicly one year earlier.

As they exited the gates leading from the enclosed dorms into Boston, the grey slush on the sidewalk burst Scott's ideal bubble of winter wonderfulness. Cars sped by, the whoosh of tires skimming through water adding to the dreck of arctic nastiness.

His stomach grumbled, drawing Scott's thoughts to more practical matters. "Breakfast, and then maybe some studying until I have to get ready?"

Derek gave him a playful shoulder nudge. "All right. You can watch me eat while you nosh on fruit and toast. I don't know why you even bother eating at all on meet days. May as well drink an energy shake and save your appetite for a celebratory dinner."

Warmth spread through Scott's body, originating in his heart and spearing outward. Derek's unwavering confidence had seen Scott through a million obstacles over the past two years.

With several hours to kill before the team would gather in the locker room, Scott had time to allow his mind to wander. "I could think of something far tastier than a shake to curb my appetite."

Derek used his free hand to adjust his groin. "Keep talking

and I might let you break your own rule."

"I have no idea what you're talking about." Unfortunately, Scott hadn't mastered the art of mock innocence, earning him a sidelong glance from Derek. "What? I'm one hundred percent centered on the upcoming meet."

Derek stopped in the middle of the sidewalk and glared at Scott. "All right. Would you like your *meal* right here or did you have another place in mind?"

Damn him for calling Scott's bluff. "No, the cafeteria will do." He'd have to make good on his threats one day. Maybe not in downtown Boston, but plenty of dark alleyways with dumpsters offered the privacy he needed to thrust Derek against a wall, unzip his pants, and suck the come right out of him. Hmm, another scenario.

Seated and with food in front of him, Scott's libido settled. Coffee and a grapefruit along with a scone with raisins and heaped with butter made an adequate second choice to his preferred breakfast option.

"You worried about today?" Derek shoveled a forkful of eggs into his mouth.

"I don't know much about the guy I'm wrestling, but I'm ready."

Derek popped some bacon into his mouth. "That's not what I meant. Your dad's coming to the meet, right?"

Oh, that's what he meant. "Yeah. And no. I'm kinda looking forward to it."

Derek shook his head, the corner of his mouth creeping up and a dimple making an appearance. "I'm impressed. I would've expected this whole reunion thing to take a far greater toll on you. I anticipated some foul moods, but you seem to genuinely enjoy your time with Ronald."

"*Enjoy* might be a strong word."

Derek finished off his bacon then rubbed his belly. "I've got to stop eating like this. I'm gonna turn into a blimp."

Hardly possible. If anything, Derek seemed to be growing

into a stronger and sturdier man. Still, Scott couldn't resist teasing. "Bring it on. More to love."

"Shut up." Derek scowled, although the twinkle in his eyes let Scott know the comment had been taken as intended.

"I meant to ask this morning, but I noticed you're getting bigger…I mean in the good way, not the blimp way."

Derek laughed. "I wondered how long it would take for you to notice."

"Oh, I noticed long before now." Scott made a show of scanning every visible inch of Derek's body. "Me likey!"

Derek tossed a balled-up napkin at Scott's head. "I have to admit, I'm getting itchy for wrestling. Maybe next year I'll join the team."

Scott shot upright in his seat. "Don't wait. You'd kick the shit out of Sean, the guy at the one hundred twenty-five-pound weight class."

Derek shook his head. "Next year."

"You sound like a broken record." Scott fell back into his seat and bit into his scone, crumbs falling onto his shirt.

"Hope you're not so clumsy on the mat." Derek chuckled.

"Brat."

Snapping his singlet straps against his shoulders and shifting his hips so he settled into the skin-forming uniform, Scott thanked what little self-control he had for not fucking Derek in bed or in the middle of Boston. His muscles coiled, pent-up energy rippling through his body. The Harvard guy was toast, and then Derek's ass.

Scott's cock stirred and he focused on moldy goat cheese wrapped in cabbage to deflate himself before anyone noticed. As it was, his cock already formed a sizable pouch in the skimpy fabric.

A quick round of spins and drops got Scott's blood coursing

and his heart pounding. The Harvard team took the mat and Scott scouted the one hundred fifty-seven-pound wrestler. Solid, like Scott, and about the same height and size. All the better, because fairly equally built rivals meant Scott had to rely entirely on skill. No one could outmaneuver Scott on the mat. Well, except Derek, who remained the most technically skilled wrestler Scott had encountered.

Both teams warmed up and lined on either side of the mat. Scott scanned for his family. Or, more precisely, the one family member he questioned would be there. He spotted his mother pretty easily. His father sat next to her, beaming.

A surge of electricity shot through Scott from head to toe, charging him with extra excitement. Now Dad would be able to see more than brute force and strength like Scott used during the Columbia match.

The players performed as they had in the first meet, the lightest two weight classes winning and the next two losing. *Coach is gonna have a field day with that.* Scott had a much more important task to focus on than the futures of his teammates.

Stepping onto the mat, he squared his shoulders. A deep intake of breath puffed up his chest. All show, but posturing went a long way in taking the upper hand.

His solid handshake met an equally strong grip. Seemed like Scott would have to work for the win. Game on!

The ref blew the whistle and Scott circled his opponent. The guy matched him move for move, although he seemed a bit defensive, waiting rather than going for a take down.

Not a bad strategy, but not good enough to stop Scott.

Careful to keep his legs protected, Scott reached forward and gripped his opponent's forearm. Man, those muscles were made of hard metal. *Ah, a nickname.*

A slight tug and Metal Man gave Scott his opening. He stepped forward to brace against the forced momentum and Scott swooped down, securing a hold on the guy's leg and driving forward. They both fell to the mat.

Metal Man arched his back, nearly throwing Scott off of him, but Scott wrapped his legs around his opponent's in half a second. Still, even with two points under his belt for a takedown, maneuvering this wall of muscle was no easy feat.

Scott squeezed tighter, lifting his opponent's legs from the mat. If Metal Man couldn't find foot purchase on the spongy mat, he couldn't fight back with another swift move, Scott swept one arm beneath the guy's neck and tugged up, forcing the mountain of muscle to rock helplessly beneath him. The ref started counting, but after two swipes of his arm, Metal Man bucked beneath Scott, throwing him off. Both wrestlers rolled away from each other and shot to their feet.

Scott led by three, having earned two more points for exposing the guy's back, but the Harvard wrestler earned one point for escaping. Fire blazed in his eyes.

Scott fought back the satisfaction of seeing his opponent so riled up. Arrogance had no place on the mat and Scott made a habit of remaining humble until the match ended.

He wasn't going to be able to use the same tug and sweep move as before. Metal Man was too smart to fall for the same trick twice. Instead, Scott lowered his center of gravity, dancing in a circle, nimble on his feet. His opponent's muscles flexed, legs thick and sturdy.

On a steady count of three, Scott prepared for his move. He circled his opponent, swaying a bit to keep him off balance, then dove for the guy's leg. Metal Man sprawled on top of Scott, an iron plate of sheer hardness crushing him down to the mat. Scott linked his fingers together, holding on as tightly as he could to his opponent's leg. If he let go, the guy would earn two points for the takedown.

Seconds ticked by, slower and slower it seemed. Scott's arms burned from the effort of holding Metal Man's leg. He only needed to hold on until the end of the period. How could thirty seconds last so long?

When the buzzer finally sounded, Scott pushed himself onto

his hands and knees before standing up. Luckily, his opponent appeared to be in no better shape. He might be made of steel, but he didn't have better stamina. God bless Derek for forcing all those summer morning runs.

Scott took bottom position to start the second period, his opponent sliding behind him. The ref blew the whistle and Scott swung his legs in front of him and spun out of Metal Man's hold, jumping to his feet and facing off. The guy froze for a fraction of a second, maybe from shock at Scott's quick escape. Whatever. A fraction of a second was all Scott needed to whip forward, taking Metal Man to the mat.

He'd earned himself three more points, one for the escape and two for the take down, but no amount of muscle seemed to work to maneuver this guy to his back. Scott threw a half nelson hold in place, cranking with all his might to roll the Harvard wrestler, but he may as well have pushed against a brick wall.

By the time they approached the center of the mat to begin the third period, sweat poured down Scott's back and dampened his arms and legs. At least the slick would make securing a hold more difficult for Metal Man. Unfortunately, it would make them hard for Scott as well.

He took top position and gripped the Harvard guy's ankle the second the period began. Yanking with all his might, Scott threw Metal Man off balance and flattened him to the mat.

As in the second period, try as his might, Scott couldn't achieve back exposure. He didn't dare look at the clock. Any distraction could cost him the match.

His muscles trembled, sharp aches radiating through each fiber.

I have to keep control. He led in points, but more importantly, Metal Man made a worthy adversary. Scott rarely had to work to pin his opponents. The Harvard wrestler could easily turn things around if Scott weren't careful.

The cheer of the crowd cut through Scott's senses. A gentle chant, rhythmic. Slowly, he made out words. *Scott! Scott! Scott!* He gripped his opponent harder, driving his own feet into the mat, hoping to use the full benefit of his body mass to roll the guy over.

"Keep pushing, Scott. You can do it!" The world froze for a split second, then rushed forward, a tidal wave of energy flooding through Scott. The one sound he'd always wanted to hear at a match, but never had: his dad cheering him on.

Spent muscles became a mere blip. The heaving of his chest and the slickness of his skin inconsequential. Not with his dad a few feet away believing in him. Scott pressed forward with untapped reserves of power. Slowly, inch by inch, he rolled Metal Man to his side, then to his back.

The buzzer sounded before Scott secured the Harvard wrestler's shoulders to the mat, but not before Scott earned three additional points.

Scott rolled off the Harvard wrestler, chest heaving and heart sledgehammering against his ribs. He sucked in a deep breath and forced himself to roll to his stomach, push himself onto his hands and knees, and finally to stand. Metal Man remained on his knees, so Scott extended his hand.

His rival accepted the offering and, to Scott's surprise, pulled him into a loose hug. "Great match, man."

Never before had Scott experienced such an intimate connection with another wrestler on the mat. The sportsmanship of the action added a whole new level of awesomeness to wrestling. The cherry on the cake? His father cheered him on.

Scott made a mental note to talk to the guy later so he could attach a proper name as opposed to the ridiculous one he'd made up.

The ref lifted Scott's hand in the air. The crowd roared. People stomped, making an absurd amount of noise. But his father, pride radiating off him like rays from the sun, captured his full attention.

The parents made quick arrangements to meet for dinner with Derek and Scott. Derek practically dragged Scott from the athletic building. Scott couldn't have cared less. His dad agreed to join them.

Back to their dorm, Derek issued a sharp, uncharacteristic command. "You! Naked! Now!"

No time to question. Scott stripped naked and found himself falling backwards onto the bed. A gasp later found Derek's mouth clamped to Scott's neck.

Scott slipped a hand behind Derek's neck and pulled him into a tender kiss, Scott's favorite kind of wrestling. All other thoughts evaporated as he spread his legs, hooking his feet against Derek's lower back.

Derek hooked his arms behind Scott's knees. At the same time, he slid his cock into Scott's crack, using precome as natural lubricant. Skin against skin, Derek glided his hard member back and forth, his head nudging Scott's opening but not breaching him.

Digging his fingers into Derek's solid back, Scott arched his hips, trying to capture Derek's cock, eager to feel the stretch and burn.

His lover thwarted each effort with slight adjustments to his hips. When Derek lifted his head to gaze down at Scott, his eyes shone with an urgent need. "I'm in charge tonight."

Sparks shot through Scott straight to his cock. Fuck, but he loved when Derek got aggressive. "Whatever you say, babe." He arched his hips again, trying unsuccessfully to seat himself on his lover's cock. "For the love of everything we hold sacred, fuck me already."

Derek let out a strained, *"Ha!"* Then drove home, sliding the entire length of his cock into Scott without warning.

"Fuck!" Scott hissed through clenched teeth as the burn radiated through his ass.

Derek hesitated, raising one eyebrow in a practiced

unspoken question about whether he could continue or should wait.

Scott thrust back in answer.

Rocking, Derek's cock stretching Scott's hole, filling him with solid heat. Then a slow withdrawal, the hollowness inside needing to be filled again.

Derek lowered his head and nipped at Scott's neck on his next inward thrust.

Scott shuddered, tingles dancing along his skin. Man, Derek knew each of Scott's weak spots. With just the crown of his cock lodged inside, Derek froze. Scott faced his lover, captured in a fiery gaze, followed by a sharp intake of breath as Derek slammed back in. Scott managed a somewhat coherent, "Fuck yeah!".

Derek pressed his lips sloppily against Scott's, rolling them so Scott straddled Derek's waist. "Ride me."

Scott fought the smirk ready to emerge. Normally he gave orders, but he'd learned more than once to obey when Derek took charge.

"Not gonna last long." Derek's comment came out more a grunt, mirroring the strain on his face.

Scott spread his legs wider, giving Derek better access. On the next thrust, stars burst behind his eyes. Derek nailed his sweet spot dead center. "Fuck!"

Derek froze. Whatever expression Scott wore must have screamed *keep doing what you just did*, because Derek picked up the tempo.

Nothing matched the sensation of Derek pounding into him. Sure, on the mat Scott dominated, but to let control slip away, giving himself completely to Derek's onslaught, brought on a whole new kind of pleasure. His balls tightened and his muscles quaked.

Derek let out a muffled grunt, snapping his hips up and burying himself to the hilt. He gasped and unleashed inside Scott, liquid heat coating Scott's insides. Too much, each pulse forcing Derek's cockhead to rub against Scott's most sensitive gland.

He tried to hold off the final second before climax, but lasted for a count of one before his own orgasm ripped through him. Strings of cum shot from his cock, coating his stomach and sealing his skin to Derek's. His entire body shook with the force of his muscle's contractions until several waves left him limp.

Gasping for breath, Scott closed his eyes and squeezed Derek close. Words were impossible. After several seconds passed, Derek rolled off Scott, dislodging in the process. Come drooled from Scott's hole and onto the sheets, the scent of sweat and sex perfuming the air.

Scott slung his arm over his head, panting rapidly. "Damn. Just…damn."

Derek chuckled, his chest heaving as he caught his breath. "It's been a while since I topped you."

Scott tilted his head to the side, marveling at the sheen causing Derek's skin to glisten, reflecting the light from the ceiling fixture. "Too long."

He reached over the side of the bed and grabbed the towel he'd left on the floor from his morning shower. He scrubbed them both, finally wiping at the pool of semen soaking the sheets. "We better do laundry today. These sheets are more cum than cotton."

Derek shut Scott up by kissing him. "Let's lay here for a while. You never minded laying in our mess before."

No words had ever been truer. Scott pulled Derek into a hug, and before long Derek's breathing evened out, rhythmic and deep.

Fully satisfied, his lover tucked against his body, Scott closed his eyes. The day couldn't get much better.

Still, he had dinner to look forward to. The familiar sense of dread and excitement whirled together, each struggling for dominance, but slowly, excitement began to win the battle.

EIGHT

SCOTT DRAGGED DEREK TO THE DOOR. BETWEEN FUCKING, kissing, and talking, they'd let time slip past them and, if they didn't hurry, would be late for dinner.

While Scott started their trip to the restaurant by tugging at Derek, the closer they got the more he fell into a slower gait. Eventually, he stopped in the middle of the sidewalk, forcing Derek to stop as well.

"What's wrong?" Derek tilted his head to the side, exposing an all-too-kissable neck

No time for distractions. "Were you sitting next to my dad during the match?" Scott hated how insecure he sounded.

"Yeah." Derek's squinty-eyed expression revealed his confusion.

"He cheered for me." Scott fiddled with his palm, studying at the lines etched into the skin.

Derek responded without hesitation. "He did. He could see how hard you were fighting for the win and he was proud."

"Really?" Again with the little boy innocence in his voice, the one Scott lost so many years earlier.

"He turned to me during the match and said, *'He's one hell of a fighter, isn't he?'"* Derek took Scott's hand, forcing Scott to meet his gaze. "What I said was, *'Yes.'*, although I wondered whether he referred to the match or to something else?"

Scott tensed. "What do you mean?"

Derek smiled, although a hint of sadness leaked into his expression. "I think you already know the answer."

Of course, Derek knew what conclusions could be drawn from such a comment. It took Scott a little longer to connect the dots. "You think he's proud of me for persevering despite the way he treated me growing up. In life, I mean."

"Don't you?" A simple question, asked with no hint of an expectation for an answer.

"It's so hard to accept he's changed. I spent my whole life with my guard up, trying to protect what few things I could count as mine. Wrestling. Mom. You and your family. Everything else he took away from me." Tendrils of anger licked along his esophagus like flames climbing along the edges of newspaper.

The twitch at the corner of Derek's mouth let Scott know he had something to say but held back.

Swallowing hard, he pushed words out. "I'm so afraid if I lower my guard and let myself believe he really wants to repair our relationship, I'll get hurt all over again."

Derek placed his hand along Scott's cheek, the warmth grounding him in love and acceptance. "The point is you're giving him a chance. No matter how this all turns out, you'll always know you opened your heart."

"You really believe that, don't you?" If he were honest, Scott believed it too. At least he hoped he and his father could mend their scarred past.

"I believe in *you*, Scott. You'll end up on the winning end of whatever happens." Derek kissed Scott on the lips and tugged his hand, urging Scott along the sidewalk to the restaurant entrance.

As soon as they entered warmth enveloped them. Several

chefs worked feverishly in an open kitchen lining the back wall, white caps bobbing to and fro. Tables, both two and four-tops, dotted the middle of the room, flanked by booths. The walls, the flooring tile, even the tablecloths and plates beamed a sterile white, contrasted by the wait staff dressed entirely in black.

Claire stood and waved them over, her typical cheerfulness lifting her face. Scott gripped Derek's hand and dragged him through the crowded room.

Rigid and trembling, he drew in a solid breath when Mom stood and squeezed him in a tight hug. "You must be so happy."

Henry shouted a "*Here! Here!*" followed by Claire replacing Mom and planting an embarrassing kiss on Scott's cheek. Derek lifted his thumb and rubbed the pad along the spot. "Lipstick."

Scott huffed, then took a seat next to his father, the only parent who'd remained silent. "Quite a match, son. I'm still running on the energy from watching you."

Bonds surrounding Scott's heart loosened. At the meet, all the BU fans cheered him on. Now, in the restaurant, sitting next to Dad, the words felt more personal, the approval he always wanted washing through him. *Could this really be the beginning of something new?*

Hope. A sneaky little bitch, weaseling its way past guards and defenses with seemingly little effort. "Thanks. Chet's one hell of a wrestler."

Derek stared at Scott. "You're on a first name basis with your competition?"

"Not usually, but the nickname I came up with sucked." Scott took a sip of water, hoping to force his heart, which had leapt to his throat, back into his chest. "So, I asked him his name when we went back to the locker room. Why? Jealous?"

Derek shook his head. "No." His cheeks flushed. "Whatever." Derek shoved Scott with his shoulder, then busied himself perusing the menu.

Scott felt the corner of his mouth curve up. Cute how Derek could still get jealous.

Thirty minutes later, a wide variety of appetizers filled the table. Everyone dug in except for his father, who nursed a small bowl of miso soup. Scott reached for the chicken pad Thai. "Want some, Dad?"

He shook his head. "No, thanks. I'm fine with the soup."

Scott heaped a healthy portion of the steaming noodles onto his own plate, before handing the platter over to Derek, who'd returned to his normal confident self.

Claire, Henry, and Mom chatted idly, although Scott couldn't help but notice their side glances at him and his father. "Our next meet is an away game. We're traveling to upstate New York to wrestle against Cornell."

"Do you know anything about your competition?" His dad's question surprised Scott.

"No. I know he's a senior and he placed third last year in our weight class. Most of the wrestlers are new to one hundred fifty-seven, so I have no one to compare him to." Which only meant once he'd completed the match, another piece of the puzzle would be in place and help him map out a plan for the final tournament in April.

"Senior, huh? Has he been varsity all four years?" Again, an intelligent question, one Scott wouldn't have expected from someone who'd basically ignored him.

"I don't know. Doesn't matter though. Once I get on the mat, I'll know who I'm up against and take it from there." Kind of like his meetings with his father, never knowing what to expect and making instinctual adjustments on the spot.

"I suppose." His father took another sip of his soup, then placed the bowl down, spilling a bit of the contents. "Would you excuse me?"

Dad pushed his seat away from the table, looking a bit gray, and rushed in the direction of the restrooms. The remaining parents shared an unspoken moment of eye contact before resuming forced conversation. Scott looked to Derek, who watched the hasty departure.

Scott took one of Derek's hands. "He'll be all right."

Derek faced, him, worry etched in his eyes. "He turned pale so quickly."

"It happens sometimes, but Dad says it's only bad for like a day or two." Scott paused, surprised he'd absorbed such an intimate detail about his father.

Derek scooched closer, taking both of Scott's hands in his own. "You've really become involved."

"I have." The realization probably surprised him as much as it did Derek. "But I think we have a tense situation to diffuse." He nodded in Claire's direction.

Claire sat with rigid posture, her lips taut and eyes trained on Henry and Scott's mom.

Scott opened his mouth, ready to ask what they weren't saying, but the air hung thick with unspoken nervousness. Nothing to be done about the parents. Derek, on the other hand, served the perfect diversion. "It's kind of cute how you can still get jealous."

Derek giggled. "Don't get used to it."

The tension snapped. For the first time in a long while, *he'd* been the one to have the positive outlook. Maybe, if Scott kept his heart open wide enough and let his dad in completely, he could truly believe good won out in the end.

When Dad did come back to the table, his skin had gone a bit green and appeared damp, snuffing out the rising hope within Scott. "I'm sorry. I'm afraid I'm going to have to excuse myself."

Scott stood, sliding his arm around his father's shoulders, immediately sensing the slight tremor to the man's body. "You okay?"

"Why don't you walk me outside? There's something I need to talk to you about."

Scott looked to Derek, who gave him a nod, then glanced at his mom, who studied a shrimp on her fork with concentrated attention. "Yeah. That's fine." He followed Dad, the uncomfortable pounding of his heart an all too frequent experience lately.

Outside, the frosty air brushed along his cheeks and neck, helping to ease the tightness in his chest. "Is everything all right?"

"No." Not even a pause. "My chemo's not working. I just found out yesterday and didn't know when to tell you."

Fear clenched at Scott's throat, cutting off his air supply. He wobbled, gripping his father's shoulder to keep from falling over. "What do you mean?"

"I mean the cancer is still there, more of it. This treatment isn't working and I've run out of options." He spoke the words without emotion, not like a man facing death.

"Can't something be done?" This couldn't be happening. Not now. Not when he was finally getting what he'd always wanted. At least now he knew why the other parents had been acting so weird at the table.

Dad remained silent longer than Scott would have expected. When he did speak, the words came out fast. "The only option is one I'm not willing to consider. We should enjoy the time we have. I've enjoyed getting to know you as a man. To see you with Derek and watch your wrestling."

"No!" Scott's voice boomed far more forcefully than he'd intended. Almost a yell. "What's the other option?"

"I'm not sure there *is* another option, but my doctor told me a bone marrow transplant could work. *If* you're a match." His father maintained eye contact. "But I'm not willing to put you through that. It's painful and there's no guarantee of success. Plus, if the transplant doesn't take, I'll lose what little time I have left."

"We're doing it." Scott surprised himself with the strength of his conviction. "End of discussion."

"No, Scott. We're not." His father narrowed his eyes. "This isn't a negotiation."

"You've got *that* right." Anger, was a far more familiar

emotion, and one Scott could handle. "You don't get to walk back into my life, get me to start to care, and then take everything away." The turn of events shouldn't have surprised him. Hadn't his father proven time and again he'd disappoint Scott? Only this time, Dad wasn't the enemy.

"Look, I'm too tired to argue." His father dropped his gaze to the ground between them. "There's no point."

"There's *every* point." Scott stepped into his father's personal space. "Why'd you even come back? Why'd you reach out to me if you're willing to give up so easily?" An apology for his outburst struggled to escape his mouth, but Scott clamped his lips tight.

"You think—" He cut himself off, remnants of childhood fury rising to the surface. Dad took a moment of silence. When he spoke, he'd regained a calm tone. "I came back because I wanted to make things right between us while I still could."

No question of the honesty behind his father's words. Arguing wouldn't get Scott what he wanted. Luckily, Scott had a boyfriend who'd know exactly how to handle a situation like this. Channeling Derek, Scott faced his father. "You're probably in shock from the news and need some time to think things through."

"Scott, I—"

"—need to go home and sleep. Take some time to think about this and we'll talk tomorrow." There. He'd bought himself a day to map out a plan to convince his dad to at least try.

Scott could see a retort forming in the way Dad opened, then closed, his mouth. He saw it in the balling of Dad's fists and the crinkle in his brow. Then all fight seemed to drain out of him. "All right. I'll go home and think about it, but my decision is made. I really don't see the point of fighting during what time we have left."

"Thank you." If Scott said anything else he'd ruin what he'd just accomplished. Anger and fear led to poor judgment. Too many dreams had come true in the last few weeks. Scott wasn't ready to throw away the possibility of a future of more dreams coming true simply because he couldn't shut the fuck up.

His father looked at him, then nodded and turned toward the curb. He hailed a cab and hopped in, carried away toward the Marriott.

Scott remained glued to the spot until the cab turned a corner, out of sight.

On heavy feet, Scott trudged back into the restaurant. Four sets of eyes trained on him and, once he sat down, silence hung in the air. For the rest of dinner, Claire filled the awkwardness with idle chatter, Mom and Henry all too willing to chime in.

Scott didn't look at anyone except for one gloomy glance at Derek, who remained uncharacteristically quiet. No doubt they'd talk after dinner.

"We're walking home." Derek's voice remained chipper, but the brief eye-contact between them let Scott know Derek wanted to talk.

"Seriously? In this weather? It's arctic."

"I don't care if your dick freezes off. You clearly need to talk. What happened back there? One minute everything was fine and the next you were like a zombie." Derek clenched his fists. "I mean, I get this is a tough time for you, but you can't leave me in the dark about things."

Scott closed the small distance between them and cupped Derek's face in his hands. Derek would take whatever Scott dished out, of that he had no doubt. He brushed his lips against Derek's. When Scott withdrew some of the ice had melted from Derek's glare. "My dad told me his chemotherapy isn't working. He's dying."

Scott found himself tugged into a tight hug. "Oh, my God. I'm so sorry. Why didn't you tell me?"

Scott hugged him back, tears threatening to spill over. "When did I have a chance?"

"True." Derek held Scott for a few minutes. Hand in hand, they strolled in the direction of the dorms. "What are you going to do?"

"Dad said a bone marrow transplant might help save him. He doesn't want me to get tested to see if I'm a match." Scott quickened his pace, a fresh burst of anger exploding from his gut and through his body.

"But if it could save him—"

"—I know. I bought some time by sending him home to think about it. If I pushed tonight, I knew he'd dig his heels in like he always did when I wanted something growing up." Scott grabbed Derek's hand tighter and sped them toward the university. "So, I've got to come up with a plan, one he can't refuse. I'm not about to lose him again, not when he's finally here for the right reasons." Strange how certain he was of his father's intentions.

Once they'd arrived at the dorms, Scott whipped the door open and clomped inside, Derek trailing behind. He only stopped when Derek said, "Uh, Scott, you're kinda breaking the bones in my hand."

"Sorry." He released Derek and stormed up the stairs.

They undressed in silence and climbed into bed.

Nestled against Derek, Scott closed his eyes, trying to fall asleep. Flying to the moon without a spaceship would've been an easier task.

"You'll convince him." Derek's voice was a mere whisper in Scott's ear.

"Yeah? How can you be so sure?"

Derek squeezed him close. "Because you're going to tell him the truth. Everything. You're going to spill your guts how you feel, and there's no way he'll be able to refuse. And if he does, he'll have a good reason."

"You sound so sure of yourself." Scott wished he possessed

even a fraction of Derek's confidence. How stupid to trust the brief moment during dinner when he finally glimpsed the silver lining in his life without Derek's help.

"I'm sure of you, and I know how convincing you can be." Derek kissed Scott's cheek. "And I didn't mean that in the way your dirty mind works."

Despite the adrenaline coursing through him, Scott relaxed for the first time since he'd watched his father drive off from the restaurant. "I hope you're right."

"It's not your decision to make." Dad raised his voice, reminiscent of the days when they'd lived together.

"Then why would you come back at all? To make me care and then die?" Venom dripped from Scott's lips, only partially tempered by the sobs.

"You can cry all you like, but you're not the one dealing with this." His dad crossed his arms over his chest, daring Scott to respond.

Scott deflated, falling back onto the chair in the posh hotel room. "You came back. You told me there's a solution. I don't care about the pain. Let me get tested."

"It's not about the pain. Don't you understand?" His father's body shook despite the fact he hadn't budged from the spot where he'd been standing for five minutes. "It's about the hope. Hope that maybe you'll be a match. Hope that maybe the transplant will work. Then maybe—"

Scott rose to his feet, slowly, taking tentative steps forward. "And maybe you and I can keep spending time together. Maybe we can still have the relationship we both dreamed of?"

His father sagged, barely holding himself up. "Yes. Exactly. I can't bring myself to face another disappointment."

"No. Better to be *the disappointment again."*

Scott shot up in bed. He grasped at his chest, his heart pounding. Sweat dampened his skin, causing the sheets to stick to him.

"What's wrong?" Derek rubbed soothing circles along Scott's back with his strong hands. "You're soaked."

The thick darkness of the room eased, light from under the door helping Scott to acclimate to the room. *Dreaming. I was just dreaming.* He leaned into Derek, seeking the warmth of his lover. "Nothing's wrong. I know what I have to do."

NINE

SCOTT COULDN'T GET OUT OF BED FAST ENOUGH THE NEXT morning. Despite the early hour, he snatched his phone and scrolled for his father's number. He hit the green phone icon, surprised when his dad picked up on the first ring. "Scott? Is everything all right?"

He spit the words out before he could change his mind. "We need to meet. I've been thinking about what you told me last night and I want to see you."

"Scott, I—"

"—will meet me for coffee at Java's in half an hour." Scott waited for the rebuttal, which never came. "I take it from your silence you'll be there."

"I'll see you in half an hour." Even over the phone, Scott could hear the wariness in his father's voice.

Scott slipped out of bed as quietly as possibly, relieved when Derek rolled over, a snore escaping him in the process.

Angry grey clouds blanketed the sky when he stepped outside, the air thick, like it might snow any minute. Scott hugged his coat closer around himself and trekked along the walkway toward Commonwealth Avenue.

Five minutes later, he arrived at Java's and entered, blowing hot air into his hands and glancing around the room. His father sat at a small table for two off to the side of the room. Scott gave him a brief nod, then approached the barista. "Tall mocha, skim and two Equal."

The skinny kid, probably eighteen, with a mop of hair on his head that basically covered half his face, took a snap inventory of Scott's body based on the quick dip and lift of his head, then turned to the coffee machine, wagging his ass like a display item.

Scott bit back his annoyance.

The kid slid the coffee to him. "On the house."

Flipping open his wallet, he dug out the five bucks he owed, palmed it on the counter a bit harder than necessary, plus an extra dollar, and strode away from the counter.

His father maintained eye contact as Scott crossed the coffee shop. Scott slid into the seat opposite his dad, placing the cup between them with a satisfying tap. "I'm getting tested."

His dad opened his mouth, presumably to protest, but Scott cut him off. "I'm not asking for permission. You came back into my life and said you wanted to reconnect…to make things better between us. You can't just show up and expect me to do nothing when there's a possibility I could help."

"I didn't come back to ask for your bone marrow." His voice sounded strong despite the frailty of his wasting body. "I still have time. *We* still have time."

A flame burst somewhere deep in Scott's chest, licking along his insides, feeding his determination. "Dad. I never expected you to come back into my life. I certainly didn't expect to enjoy having you show up again. You proved me wrong on both counts. We're doing this."

His dad rested is elbows on the table, cradling his head in his hands. "I told you last night. I appreciate your wanting to help, but I can't take another crushing letdown."

"Neither can I." Scott wasn't prepared for the sting in his

eyes, nor for the following tears. "I just got you back, Dad. You can't go away again. Not now, after..."

Silence hung in the air between them. Scott knew exactly what he'd almost said. Why he'd held back he had no idea. His father lifted his head and studied him. "After what, Scott?"

"After..." Could he bare himself before the man who, up until a few weeks ago, he'd easily dismissed as a bitter disappointment? His throat tightened, words trying to escape and some other part of him holding them back. To Dad's credit, he remained still, patiently waiting. "You're giving me things I always wanted from you."

Dad nodded, his lips tightening. Scott bit his lip, waiting as his father had a minute earlier. This decision carried too much importance and, Scott suspected, he'd inherited his stubborn streak from his dad, not his mom. To push could prove fatal. Literally.

After what felt like an hour, when a simple peek at the clock indicated only a minute had ticked by, his dad sighed. "You don't know what you're agreeing to."

Scott used every ounce of self-control not to leap out of his chair in victory. "I don't care. If it could help, I want to do it."

"It could kill me just as easily as save me." So matter-of-fact, like telling Scott the frozen ground would thaw again when spring came around. *Maybe Dad will be better by spring.*

Scott picked up his coffee, refusing to allow his father's doubts to diminish his own excitement. "Why don't you explain it to me? Maybe we can make this decision together."

His father shook his head. "Nothing much to tell. You get tested. If you're a match, I get a transplant, in which case one of two things happen. One, the match doesn't take and, since they must obliterate my immune system, it won't have a good chance of recovering and I'll die. Or, the transplant takes and I go into remission. Either way, I run the risk of infections and have a long road to recovery...one with no true end."

"There's one other option you left out." Scott waited until

his father met his gaze head-on. "You do nothing and you die for sure."

"True." If a man could sound any more exhausted or defeated, Scott sure didn't know how. "Let's go down this road a bit. You get tested and are a match. Then they blast the cancer with chemo and radiation, obliterating what little immune system I have left. They collect your bone marrow. I go in for surgery and the transplant takes place. I wake up, weak as hell, spend most of my days in the hospital in recovery and rehabilitation. Months go by. Maybe even a year, before I'm anything close to living a semi-normal life."

"And I get to spend more time with you." Scott held his breath. His father's next words would make or break his future. If Derek, or his mom, or anyone would've told him he'd crave time with his father he'd have laughed them out of the room. Now, Scott feared the loss would be worse than any he'd ever experienced.

Dad sighed. "You know, I never dreamed you would be so open to me. I mean, when I lived with you and your mom, I wasn't a very good person."

"You'd be surprised by the memories I've had over the past few weeks. It's amazing how a few fond memories from my past can help to blur years of…" What? Neglect? Disdain? Maybe even abuse? "…times that weren't so great."

His father smiled, a slight rise of the lip. "You have so much of your mother in you. Always looking for the positive."

If only he knew how wrong he was. If it hadn't of been for Derek's love, Scott never would've opened his heart in the first place. "No. I want to see where this thing goes between you and me." Scott swallowed, surprising even himself with how open he'd been. To lighten the mood, he added, "Besides, you didn't make it easy for Mom to find…" Scott punctuated the next words with air quotes, "…*positives*."

This time, when his dad laughed, life and energy reached his eyes. "You've got spirit in you. Always did. No matter how hard I rode you, nothing could keep you down."

If only he knew how *down* Scott had been all those years before Derek. No secret stash of inner strength or unwavering trust provided by the kind of security he'd always longed for. Derek anchored Scott. Maybe, in time, with his father in his life, he could learn to be his own anchor.

"You still with me?"

The question snapped Scott out of his head. "Yeah. Sorry. Let my mind wander for a second."

"Mind sharing?" Something in his father's tone and the way his eyes widened a bit, urged Scott to open up.

"I was thinking of Derek and how I probably wouldn't be sitting here right now if it weren't for him." Scott mentally debated whether to share the admission with Derek when he saw him later.

"You really love him, don't you?" Again, genuine interest, illustrated through a relaxed posture and direct eye contact.

"I do. More than I've loved anyone or anything in my life." Scott held his breath, realizing what he'd said and waiting for the hurt to register on his father's face.

"That's the one true sign of love, son." His father's eyes glossed over and he seemed to gaze at nothing in particular. "No matter how my life unfolded, all the let downs and obstacles, I always loved your mom that way."

He shouldn't have believed the words. After all, actions always spoke so much louder. Something in the gravity of the tone, or perhaps the longing beneath the surface of his father's disciplined outer appearance, let Scott know he spoke the truth.

The guy can't be all bad if he truly loved Mom.

Like magic, Dad plucked the thought right out of Scott's mind. "And no matter how hard I treated *you*, Scott, I've always loved you like that too. I had a shitty way of showing it." A grimace settled into place. "Or maybe I needed to face *this*," he motioned toward himself, "to finally *wake up*."

What a sad statement, to need to face death before prioritizing life. Of course, Scott knew enough to recognize his father wasn't the first, and wouldn't be the last, person to make such a mistake, but other people weren't *his* father. Other people weren't finally giving Scott what he'd craved for a lifetime. "If we do this, you might have more time to enjoy being *awake*." A lame attempt to use his father's words, but he made his point well enough.

Dad shook his head. "You certainly are persistent."

"Yeah." He hadn't even begun to fight yet.

"Fine. I'll arrange for you to get tested by my doctor. It's going to be painful and you'll need some time to recover." His father's eyes widened a bit. "Maybe we should wait until your season is over."

Oh, hell no. Scott could recognize an excuse from a mile away. "If I get tested on a Monday, I'll have plenty of time to recover. If I have to miss one match, I'll survive." *There, ball's in your court.*

To his credit, his dad didn't argue. "All right. I'll set it up for a week from tomorrow."

Scott let out a breath, sinking heavily into his chair. Muscles he hadn't realized he'd clenched unlocked, and a wave of calm spread through him like a wash of lukewarm water. "Okay."

Derek joined the wrestling team on the bus for the Saturday morning trip to Cornell. At six in the morning, most players still wore sweats and immediately fell back to sleep the second they took their seats.

All the research about bone marrow testing painted the same picture. Painful. Although he'd be in and out the same day. If they matched, the heavy processes would take place. No need to think about doctors until Monday. He had a meet to think about.

Scott carved a small little cozy bed of sorts for himself and

Derek, throwing a blanket on the seat, crawling on and wrapping Derek in his arms, then pulling the blanket around them both. The pure, musky scent of his unshowered lover lulled him into a deep and peaceful sleep.

He awoke to a sharp blast of cold water drenching his face. Marcus hovered over them, a shit-eating grin adorning his face. "Hey, lovebirds, we're about thirty minutes away. Time to wakey-wakey!"

Never before had Scott considered hitting a friend, but if Marcus didn't back the fuck off, and soon, his face and Scott's fist were gonna become real intimate.

"Douchebag, you better get back to your fuckin' seat before I help you and your water bottle become best friends." Derek's voice rang throughout the bus, evoking a rumble of laughter from other wrestlers.

Marcus's eyes bulged, and then he grinned. "Man, you gotta join the team. We need guys with your spunk."

Scott muffled the instinctual comment rushing to his lips. *His spunk is all mine.*

Frank, the guy who wrestled at the one hundred twenty-five weight class shouted, "Hey!" presumably insulted at his spot being so freely offered to someone else. Meanwhile, someone chucked a soda can from another part of the bus. The can plinked off Marcus's temple.

"What? All I'm sayin' is Derek would be great on the team."

Derek shook his head, sitting for the remainder of the ride. Marcus slunk back to his seat and put his headphones on. "He's a cool guy, but no tact whatsoever."

Scott chuckled and crossed his arms behind his head, resting comfortably against the cushioned seat. "I'm so glad you came on the bus. It keeps me grounded." He tilted his head to the side, only to find Derek gazing at him with those hypnotizing amber eyes. "And you really *should* join the team."

Derek inched forward and brushed a kiss to Scott's cheek. "I probably will."

Such simple interaction, the kind of familiarity and stability Scott had come to expect over the past two years. In two short days he'd find out if his world would remain solid or crack beneath his feet. At least he could enjoy the weekend with Derek by his side.

Derek pulled a book out of his backpack and flipped it open. For the rest of the ride, Scott concentrated on the upcoming match. All he knew about his opponent, except for the fact he was a senior, was that wrestled at the same weight class the previous year and had placed third in the weight class the previous year. Pulling this match off would make Scott a serious contender for the end of season tournament…just like his coach predicted.

Upon arriving at Cornell, the team hustled to the locker room, changed, and within thirty minutes of arriving, they hit the mat for warmups. The Cornell team lined the circle, watching.

Scott fought the urge to laugh. Intimidation played a natural part of any team sport, but these guys took their posturing to new levels. With their arms folded and stiff bodies, they looked more like military than college students. Except for the soft boyish faces, some of them with bleached hair sticking out in an obvious attempt at a messy-chic look.

Spinning on Marcus's back, then doing push-ups and drops, helped to prepare Scott's body for the match. He felt ready to prove to himself and everyone else just how much of a threat he was.

Until the Cornell team took the mat. Scott couldn't miss Jason Pelham, his competitor and the captain of the team, as the walking mass of muscles strode to the center of the mat. Scott's bravado flowed out of him. The guy stood at least three inches taller than Scott, and the muscles of his arms and legs rippled beneath the surface.

"How in the hell is this guy in my weight class? He's a freaking hulk." Scott wasn't talking to anyone in particular, but

Marcus clapped him on the shoulder. "You got this, my man. This is your year!"

The faith, while appreciated, did nothing to slow Scott's rising heart rate. He responded with a weak, "Yeah."

His first four teammates lost, some of them pinned and others losing only by points. By the time Scott's turn came, his confidence had shrunk to the size of a small marble.

The Hulk, the nickname he'd come up within seconds, seemed to grow exponentially as Scott approached the center of the mat. He reached out for the handshake required of all wrestlers before they competed, only to have his knuckles crushed together in a vice grip. Muscle and size would not work to his advantage. Hopefully his massive opponent didn't have the same skill level as Scott, otherwise the match might be over real quick.

The ref blew the whistle and The Hulk began to circle slowly. Scott matched his movements, searching for an opening to take the guy down. When The Hulk lurched forward, closing the distance between them, Scott shot to scoop up his leg only to find himself cemented in place. He tried to stand and take the leg with him, but his efforts barely caused a wobble.

Before Scott could think of a new move, he found himself plastered to the mat, the crushing weight of his opponent pressing his chest down and leaving him with very limited room for movement. The Hulk spun and secured a half nelson and mechanically cranked Scott to his side and then to his back.

Scott tried to arch, giving himself a few inches of space to flip back to his stomach, but every movement seemed to help his opponent secure an even tighter hold. For the remainder of the period, Scott found himself seconds away from being pinned, only to lift a shoulder or torque himself enough to force the ref to restart the three count, which would end the match.

By the time the buzzer sounded, indicating the end of the first two-minute period, Scott felt as if he'd run a marathon.

He struggled to his feet and waited, panting, as The Hulk

took bottom position. Lowering himself on rubbery legs, he took his place on top. He wrapped one hand around a thick torso and placed his other hand on triceps which could have been small tree trunks.

The second the ref blew the whistle, the monster of a competitor shot his legs out in front of him and twisted out of Scott's grip.

Scott jumped up, shocked by the speed of such a mammoth person.

The score was already eleven to zero. Four more points and the guy would earn a technical pin. In *all* of his years as a wrestler, he'd never been pinned. Flames surged through his gut as he searched for his opening. Gripping The Hulk's arms, he started circling, tugging every so often to pull the guy off balance.

After a few more tugs Scott slipped his arms so they locked around The Hulk's forearms. He then took a giant step forward and wedged his leg between his competitor's, driving forward with as much force as he could. With both of their arms locked, either wrestler could seize control once they hit the mat.

Scott measured his movements, trying to direct their fall so he could spin in a half circle, torqueing The Hulk's massive arms and forcing the giant's back into the mat. He succeeded in gaining securing a hold, earning him two points for the take down, but each time the guy arched his back Scott found himself lifted off the ground, his feet losing their purchase.

Driving forward with all his might, Scott wrapped his arm so it held both of his opponent's while slipping his free arm under his opponent's head. If he locked hands the ref would blow the whistle and set them back to neutral position. Full nelsons were not allowed, nor were strangle holds, unfortunately.

With The Hulk's arms out of commission and his head lifted slightly due to Scott's hold, the ref waved his arm for the three count which would earn Scott his pin. On the second wave of his hand, the mass of muscle beneath him bucked his hips and arched all the way onto his head, throwing Scott off and scrambling to the side.

Both wrestlers hopped to their feet and circled each other again. They ended the second period with a score of twelve to four. Scott earned two points for the take down and two more for back exposure, but The Hulk earned one point for his escape.

Sweat poured down Scott's arms, chest, and back. His legs glimmered in reflected light. At least The Hulk seemed to have strained during the previous period and, based on his ragged breath, wasn't in as good a shape as Scott. The guy probably pinned most of his opponents in the first period. *Okay, I have stamina over him.*

As Scott took the bottom position to begin the third period, he thought of his team and of Derek. He'd never let them down on the mat before.

An image of his father appeared. Not the man of his youth, but the ragged version he'd spent the past few weeks getting to know. The new dad, the one who earnestly wanted to know him, needed someone to count on. He needed someone who could cut through all the failed treatments and hits to his morale so he'd fight to survive. Scott clung to the image of his dad as The Hulk settled on top of him.

He kept his eyes glued on the ref, waiting for the man to blow his whistle. In two short days, Scott would find out whether what lived inside him could potentially save the life of a man who'd finally begun to give him the attention and respect he'd craved for the better part of his life.

Believing he could save his father started with believing in himself. Flawed logic? Sure, but if he could dig down deep enough to win against incredible odds, maybe the strength he carried inside might turn the tide for his dad. The match changed from a personal battle to a fight for his father's life.

The instant the third period began, Scott swung his legs in front of him. Normally he'd scramble out of his competitor's grip and escape. He could take neutral position on his feet and work for a take down. Not today. Scott wanted to prove things worked out in the end to himself and everyone else.

Torqueing his body so he stayed on his knees and still holding The Hulk's arms, Scott pushed forward, driving into the massive form like a bull ramming into the side of a car. He plowed the guy to his side, secured a half nelson hold, wrenched The Hulk to his back, and arched his back with all of his might so his competitor wouldn't be able to lift his shoulders off the mat.

The Hulk pressed into the mat with his feet, raising his hips and trying to buck Scott off, but each movement allowed Scott to tighten his grip. *Squeeze. Squeeze. Keep going.* He repeated the words, his muscles screaming as lactic acid robbed him of oxygen.

He vaguely made out the sound of the cheering crowd. The black and white uniform of the ref registered peripherally. More than anything, Scott pictured his dad, urging him to dig deeper, to push harder. If Scott could pull this off, then everything would turn out just the way he wanted.

In the middle of his thoughts Scott heard a sharp blow of the whistle and then the slam of the ref's hand against the mat. Still, the sound and movement didn't register and the ref had to pry Scott off his competitor before Scott finally realized the match was over and he'd pinned The Hulk.

Scott fell to his back, gasping for air. When he rolled over and tried to get up, his arms wouldn't hold his weight. The Hulk lay on his back and covered his face with his hands while his chest heaved up and down. Eventually, Marcus and one of the Cornell wrestlers assisted Scott and The Hulk to their feet.

Somehow Scott stood, legs wobbling so the ref could raise his hand in victory. He limped out of the wrestling circle in the opposite direction of his team. Air. He needed to get outside. Foregoing even a sweatshirt, Scott strode toward the exit.

He slammed the doors open, their springs unable to resist

his force as they banged against the wall. By the time he burst through the front entrance of the athletic complex into the wintery air, he was practically running.

The sun hid behind a thick blanket of clouds and the wind had picked up from earlier. The bite of freezing wind wrapped around Scott, whose skin remained damp with sweat.

He didn't care. Throwing his arms out, he inhaled deeply, closing his eyes so he could focus on the revitalizing feel of clean, fresh oxygen. He'd done it. He'd won.

Sure, The Hulk had strength, but he lacked the one trait Scott counted on. When times got tough, when he needed to dig deep, at least for the last two years, he had a weapon no competitor could match.

"Scott?" A familiar voice. Derek.

Warmth radiated pleasant tendrils of comfort along Scott's skin. He turned and faced the source of his inner strength. "It's gonna work."

Derek held out Scott's jacket. "What is?"

Seeing his jacket, the frosty air morphed from revitalizing to knifelike. Scott wrapped his coat around his shoulders. "The transplant. I know I'm going to be able to save my dad."

Derek smiled, although not enough for his dimple to make an appearance. "I'm sure you're right." He took Scott's hand and together they reentered the building.

Scott joined his team, cheering and coaching from the sidelines. They lost the meet, but at least Scott won. Word of his victory would spread like wildfire, but his victory on the mat didn't matter.

What mattered most would happen in two days.

TEN

A BITTER, STRONG WIND, GREETED SCOTT MONDAY MORNING, cutting straight through his coat and scarf. "Fuck." Rubbing his arms provided the illusion of warming up, but to no real effect. He hustled across the quad and onto the streets of Boston, toward his first class.

Like he'd be able to concentrate.

A few hours later he found himself standing outside Brigham and Women's Hospital. He could see his father sitting at one of the couches in the front lobby area. For a few short seconds, before Dad faced him, Scott paused. *God, please let me be a match.*

With his silent prayer sent out into the universe, Scott entered the warmth of the building's interior. His father greeted him. "Hey there." The energy of his voice didn't match the tightness of his grip on his cane.

Scott rushed to his father's side. "You look horrible." He bit his lower lip and shook his head. "I mean, how are you feeling?" *Derek would kick me right now.*

His father laughed. "Apparently, better than I look." He

straightened, recovering a good deal of the height Scott typically associated with him. "Shall we head up?"

"Yeah." Scott accompanied his father to the elevators, their progress slow and labored.

Seated in front of the doctor, Scott breathed a bit easier.

The doctor first studied Scott and then Dad. Scott read his name badge: Doctor Eddie Trunkle. *Dr. T?* Scott attempted to restrain a giggle.

Dr. T clasped his hands and rested them on the desk, a pronounced crinkle on his brow. "Scott, has your father explained to you his history and the process we're about to undertake?"

Humor leached out of him in an instant. Did the guy think Scott a moron? Of course, he knew why they were sitting in a hospital office. "Perhaps you could run through the procedure one more time for me." *More bees with honey.*

Dr. T nodded, resting against the chair back and crossing his legs. "Your father has acute lymphoblastic leukemia. Treatments have included radiation, chemotherapy, and autologous transplantation."

"I'm sorry, auto-whatous?" Scott wondered whether the guy threw big words around to seem smart, or if he didn't realize his language made no sense. Either way, Scott gripped his thighs a bit tighter, hoping to restrain the *Out with it already* itching to fly from his lips.

"Autologous transplantation. It means your father tried transplanting his own stem cells to himself." The doctor nodded.

Scott bunched the fabric of his jeans between clenched fists. *Oh, right, I completely understand now!* "I don't get it. Why would you use a patient's own stem cells if they already have cancer?" There, the question showed he had a brain in his head.

Dr. T picked up a pencil and twirled it in his fingers. "Good question. The fact is, stem cells still hold many mysteries. In autologous transplantation, the stem cells from the patient function the same way an external donor's would.

They either spark the system to produce normal blood cells again, or the transplant fails. The benefit is it's much easier on the patient to donate to themselves. Basically, we're dealing with blank cells and the idea is to spark marrow cell growth like those before the cancer mutation occurred. Not to mention the bonus of not putting another person through a procedure."

Scott fought to keep his eyes from crossing. "So, Dad's stem cells didn't work."

"They did for a while, but unfortunately the cells have again mutated." Dr. T finally showed what Scott considered an appropriate reaction, his lips pressing together and a slight shake of his head. "Luckily, his system didn't completely shut down, which gave us some time to explore the possibility of a match. While there are several registered donors who match, we find people who share DNA often carry a higher success rate."

Nothing like piling on the pressure. "So, if I'm not a match, there are other donors who can help my dad." Scott faced his father, who returned his gaze with an encouraging smile. Or was is sympathy? Hard to tell the difference.

"It's a possibility." Dr. T redirected his focus to Dad. "Better thing to ask is what happens if the transplant works. If your immune system resets, you'll have to get inoculated against everything all over again."

Scott squared his shoulders, feeling a bit less pressure and a lot more hopeful. "What happens today?"

The question brought on a strange excitement from Dr. T. "Today we take your blood to see if you're a match. If you are, your dad will need to go through a short round of chemo and radiation to deplete his immune system. Then we harvest stem cells from your blood and transplant them into your father. We have to wait for approval from the insurance company, but the sooner the better."

Seemed straightforward enough. Still, the most important question remained unasked.

Dad chimed in. "Doctor Trunkle, once the transplant occurs, what happens?"

A crinkle formed between Dr. T's eyes. Scott couldn't face his father, although he wanted to hug the man for asking the question. The doctor spoke to Dad when he responded. "One of two things. Either the transplant takes, in which case your body begins to produce healthy blood cells again. You'll be in remission and we'll monitor you at regular intervals."

Silence filled the small office, pressing down on Scott like a hundred-pound weight. When Dr. T spoke again, he seemed to have grown about three feet. "Or the transplant doesn't take, in which case we've decimated your immune system and your body will no longer be able to fight off infection."

Scott finally glanced at his father, shocked at the calm expression on his face. No tightly-pressed lips. No squinted eyes. He wasn't even gripping the arms of his chair. "What then?"

"Then, we explore a limited set of options."

"Such as?" Scott wanted to punch something, preferably the doctor's face.

"Why don't we take this one step at a time?" This time, the doctor directed his answer to Scott.

Dad cut in before Scott could say anything. "You're the doctor."

"Yes, well. If you don't have any more questions for me, I'll print out the work orders and you can take them to the blood lab."

"Thank you, doctor. I think we're fine for now." Dad struggled to rise into a standing position, falling back into the seat.

Scott reached under his father's elbow, giving him assistance. Surprisingly, Dad accepted the help without argument.

Twenty minutes and a puncture hole in his arm later, Scott and his father left the hospital. They trudged slowly toward the parking lot. Although freezing, the sun provided a bit of brightness in what had so far been a dreary day.

"Can I give you a ride back to your dorm?"

Scott dragged himself out of his own head. Having his blood drawn weighed heavily on him. Unlike the certainty of the outcome when he and Derek got tested for HIV, he didn't know what the results would be in this scenario. The gravity carried a strange intensity since the results were for someone else.

"Yeah. A ride would be nice. Didn't realize you rented a car."

"I didn't. I'll pay for the cab ride."

In the taxi, Scott sank into the seat and closed his eyes. "Are you scared, Dad?"

What a hell of a question for a grown man to ask someone with a terminal disease. Scott never expected a chuckle in answer.

"Of course I'm scared, but probably not for the reasons you think."

When his father said nothing more, Scott opened his eyes and turned his head. "What are the reasons?"

The same dark circles under his eyes and sagging cheeks. Odd how Scott'd begun to get used to seeing his dad this way. "I told you before…hope. If you're a match and the transplant works…"

Then you'll live. Warmth formed in Scott's chest, washing his insides with a sense of peacefulness. "And I'll have saved you." Funny how two years earlier he hated the man next to him. Now? He couldn't imagine not having his dad around.

Minutes later, they sat outside Scott's dorm, the car idling. "Well, I guess it's a sit and wait game now." Dad spoke with the casualness Scott had become used to.

The results were no game. Scott needed to be a match. After a lifetime of yearning, he finally had the father he'd wished for. No, pretty darn far away from being a game. "I hope it's a match."

"I do too, son. I do too." This time, Dad's voice carried unwavering seriousness.

Scott found Derek seated on their couch, a dreadfully thick textbook on his lap. The book found purchase on the floor and Derek stood next to Scott less than a second later. "How'd it go?"

Scott chuckled. "I see you were doing some light reading."

Derek swatted Scott's ass. "I assume everything went smoothly if you're able to be a jackass."

"Not much to report. It'll take the lab a couple days to get the results. Ask me how it went then." He added more snark to the comment than necessary, but Derek had always been tough enough to handle Scott's moods.

At least Derek had the good grace to show the disappointment Scott had experienced when learning he'd have to wait. "I guess that's true."

Whatever strings Scott used to hold himself together could finally unwind now with Derek. "The truth is, I'm terrified."

Derek's expression relaxed. "Worried about what you'll do if your test comes back negative?"

"Yeah!"

Derek didn't miss a beat, dragging Scott to the couch. "Wanna talk about it?"

Scott blinked a few times, trying to clear the sudden blurry vision while swallowing back the lump in his throat. He squeezed Derek tight, dipping his nose into his lover's hair. Freshly shampooed. "The thing is, I've been so focused on giving him a chance. You know, like forcing myself to meet him places. Pushing past all my fears about getting disappointed all over again. I guess I never saw it happen."

Derek snuggled deeper into Scott's embrace, heat seeping into Scott's chest. "It?"

"I mean, I was so busy keeping my guard up, I never noticed how he kind of snuck past it."

"Okay, maybe I'm dense, but what is this *it* you're referring to?"

"The bond Dad and I have formed." There, he'd admitted he cared. "I was surprised by my reaction when the doctor mentioned the possibility of me not being a match."

Derek tried to turn in Scott's arms, but Scott tightened his grip. Somehow, having him there but not talking face to face made his words more a reflection rather than a confession.

"All of a sudden, this wave of need swept through me. I *have* to help him. As much for me as for Dad." The words resonated truer than any thought he'd had all day. "I want to be the reason he gets to live."

Derek said nothing, but Scott couldn't miss the stiffness in his lover's body. "Don't get mad, but why?"

Fair question. If the old Dad came back into the picture, the answer would've been easy. He'd want to save his father to prove to himself the better man.

"I'm not entirely sure. I want more time with Dad. That's the biggest part right now. Which kind of has me fucked up because I never expected to *want* to spend time with him. I thought I'd moved on."

Derek tried to turn to face Scott again and this time Scott let him. "Scott, what are you saying?"

Again, a sensible question. "God, you're so beautiful." He pressed a kiss to Derek's lips. "I'm saying I want a relationship with my father. I never thought I'd hear myself say those words, but I want Dad around so he can be a part of all this good stuff I've built around me. Having him there will make my life a little more perfect. I know that sounds selfish, but…"

"It sounds incredible." A soft smile curled Derek's lips, although tears also slid from his eyes. "Do you know how amazed I am by you?"

Scott swallowed against the lump in his throat, which resurfaced. "Yes."

"Not many people would be able to look past the things Ronald did to you." Derek averted his gaze. "He went beyond being distant. He actively disapproved of you and didn't care how difficult he made your life."

A spark of defensiveness crawled along Scott's skin, but he remained quiet. Derek would never intentionally say anything to upset him.

"When your father came back into the picture," Derek spoke in a soothing tone, "I worried you might hold on to your anger. No offense, but you can get awfully stubborn when you dig your heels in."

Scott opened his mouth to protest, but what could he say? Derek was right.

A smirk. Derek's claim to victory. "The few times I've been around the two of you, I can see where some of your less appealing qualities come from. In a way, it makes me happy."

"Okay, I was gonna let you speak without interrupting, but the last comment is kinda weird." Scott draped his arm over the back of the couch so he could more comfortably face Derek.

"What I mean is, I never thought I'd have the chance to get to know where half of your personality comes from. In a way, your dad coming back into your life has brought you and me closer together." Derek's cheeks flushed. "Talk about selfish. This is supposed to be about you and I'm making it about me."

Scott kissed Derek, then ruffled his hair. "I think I know what you mean and I'm glad. In a way, it evens things out."

"Okay, now *I'm* not sure I understand what *you* mean." Derek ran his fingers through his hair, unsuccessfully neatening the mess. "We're not in competition."

"No, but you have this full family. Whenever I saw you and Henry doing stuff, it kinda rubbed salt on an old wound. Now…"

"…you have a full family too. Both parents. People who shaped who you are. I totally get it."

"Yeah." Scott reached down and placed his hand over Derek's, raising it to his lips and kissing the knuckles. "But I'm really scared. I finally have him back. What if I lose him again?"

Tears welled in Scott's eyes and he blinked hard, trying to stave them off.

Derek tugged Scott into a hug. "We'll figure it out together. You'll still be you and we'll still be us. That won't change no matter what."

One hot tear slipped from Scott's eye and ran down his cheek. He clung to Derek, breathing in his scent.

Derek massaged Scott's back, digging his fingers in with just the right amount of pressure. Eventually, he loosened his grip enough to hold Scott at arm's length. "You okay?"

Scott nodded. "I am. Thanks for being here."

Derek pulled his lips back into a smirk, which meant, Scott knew, he'd planned something secret. "I know you have practice, but I made plans for later tonight. You're not hanging with the guys afterwards, are you?"

He hadn't thought about it, but Derek's surprises were far more appealing than pizza and soda with the guys. "No. What's the plan?"

"It's a secret."

"You're *kidding*!" Scott couldn't have infused more sarcasm into his comment if he tried.

"Quiet, you. I'll text the information right about the time your practice ends." Derek hopped to his feet and sauntered toward the door. Before he exited the room, he glanced over his shoulder, a wicked smirk reducing Scott to putty. "Don't wear yourself out too much."

Scott chuckled. Leave it to Derek to lift Scott up when he needed it most. "Whatever."

Scott received Derek's text right before practice.

I'll pick you up at the Athletic Complex…in my car.

Scott focused half the time during practice, but the other half found himself wondering what Derek planned for them.

When he exited the building, both the sun and the temperature had dropped. Hugging his coat tighter around his body, Scott glanced around. Plenty of parked cars, but no Derek. *Damnit. I'm freezing my nuts off.*

He'd just turned around, deciding to wait for Derek inside, when a familiar, old-school Lincoln Towncar entered the lot. Scott couldn't suppress his laughter. *Derek borrowed his dad's pimp-mobile?*

Derek drove past Scott and attempted a three-point turn in the narrow lot. After seven points, he'd drove up alongside Scott.

Scott hopped in, laughing, his frozen nuts completely forgotten. He gripped Derek by the neck and yanked him into kiss. He bit Derek's lip, tugging at it with his teeth, then slid his hand up Derek's thigh. Slow and steady, he nearly reached his prize, the one muscle he most wanted to explore.

"Scott!" He nearly jumped out of his skin when a solid hand grasped his shoulder from behind.

Whipping around, he first registered a flash of hot pink, then red-as-an-apple lips, and finally the person sitting in the back came into focus. "Beck!" He should have known. "You scared the shit out of me."

She released an entirely Beck-like cackle. "Mission accomplished, lo-verrrr."

Scott still couldn't decide whether Derek and Beck would be friends if they hadn't grown up together. Her crass, bigger-than-life, whirlwind of energy grated at Scott as much as it amused him, but she and Derek were awesome together and Scott could always count on a few laughs around her.

Beck softened her grip on Scott's shoulder. "So, you find out in a few days about your test results?"

Derek shot her a quick glance before facing forward again. Scott hadn't missed the tightening of lips, or the narrowing of eyes. "I thought I told you tonight is for having fun. Drop the serious topics."

Beck waved her hand absently in Derek's direction. "Lighten

up, Mary. It's just a question."

"Yeah, Mary, take a pill," Scott added with an adequate amount of Beck-flair.

Derek fixed his scowling gaze on Scott for a count of three before his façade cracked and he shook his head. "I can't take you guys anywhere."

Scott slung an arm over the seat back so he could face Beck. "The doctor said we'd probably know by the end of the week. If not, we'll have to wait till Monday."

"A week!" Bless her to have the perfect reaction. "I'd be shitting soup from all the stress of waiting." Yup. Good old Beck, always there with a delicate and charming turn of phrase.

"I think I can manage." He sounded cavalier, although thinking of days ticking by, checking every time his cell phone chirped or vibrated, he could see Beck's point.

Derek drove toward I-93, nowhere near the direction of the college or either of their homes. When he pulled onto the highway he still hadn't mentioned where they were going. Asking would be pointless. When Derek set his heart on a surprise, nothing deterred him.

"Babe, are you getting bigger?" Beck gave Scott's biceps a squeeze. "Man alive, I can barely get my fingers around the bulge."

Scott choked back the comeback which flew to his lips, earning him a pout from Beck.

"You got that right, Beck," Derek chimed in. "His bulge has given me many nights of fucking bliss."

"Derek!" Scott snapped his head sideways, rebuke on the tip of his tongue. Then he remembered who they were in the car with and shook his head. No sense in fighting the inevitable. "Well, maybe Beck should try grabbing *your* bulge. You've been getting bigger, too."

"Ew! That would be like screwing my brother." Beck made a hacking sound in the back of the car.

"Hey, easy there." Derek chimed. "I'm not disgusting and

you don't even *have* a brother."

"So not the point. Scott came into the picture after puberty. You, I've known since you still wet the bed."

"Beck!" Derek caught his lower lip in his teeth, the muscle along his jaw quivering.

"Oh, please! It's not like Scott cares whether you pissed yourself every night for all of second grade."

"Wha-ha-at?" Scott covered his mouth immediately, but Beck's revelation was far too awesome to ignore. "Every night."

Derek gripped the steering wheel tightly, the jaw muscle. Started working overtime Finally, he uttered a weak, "Maybe."

"Aw. That's so cute." Scott brushed his hand against Derek's cheek but Derek jerked his head away. If it weren't for the hint of a smile tugging at his lips, Scott might've thought he'd actually upset Derek.

"You know, it's totally normal for boys in second grade to piss themselves at night." Derek maintained a straight face for exactly three seconds before he broke out laughing. "Besides, I never wet myself in school. What did they call you for the rest of first grade?"

Beck responded, her voice uncharacteristically demure. "Pee-Pee Schultzie."

"No-fuckin'-way!" Scott started laughing, which morphed to a bout of coughing. "They called you Pee-Pee Schultzie?"

"Whatever. Are we almost at Dave and Buster's yet? I've taken enough abuse in this car ride." Beck pursed her lips and glared out the window.

"Damnit, Beck! That was a surprise." Derek gripped the steering wheel tightly, clearly working hard to manage his temper.

Beck covered her mouth and, with what seemed to be genuine contrition, hunched into herself. "Oops. Sorry."

Dave and Buster's? Seemed more of a younger kid spot, or a fun date night. *Wait!* "Laser Tag!"

Derek punched the steering wheel. "Damnit, Beck!"

"What? I didn't say anything."

"Yeah, but your big mouth gave it away."

Scott gave Derek's thigh a squeeze. "Hey, take it easy. Just 'cause I figured it out now instead of in about fifteen minutes doesn't make the surprise any less awesome."

Derek immediately relaxed, his whole body settling into the seat. Scott kissed Derek's neck. A slight hint of Acqua di Gio filled his nose, mixed with undertones of Derek's natural musk. He brushed his lips against the smooth skin again, inhaling deeply. Just a smell had Scott's cock sparking to life.

He tried to readjust himself. Stealthily, but the flicker of Derek's gaze let Scott know his *problem* hadn't gone unnoticed.

Luckily, or maybe unluckily--Scott wasn't too sure since he still had some settling down to do--Derek pulled into the Braintree Mall parking lot and navigated them to the entrance nearest Dave and Buster's.

The second they entered, Scott knew the the night would be epic. A huge banner proclaiming Laser Tag Mondays covered the better half of the back wall. Sliding his hand around Derek's shoulders, Scott pulled him in close and whispered into his ear, "This is perfect. Thanks."

Derek propped himself against Scott's body. "I knew today was probably hard on you. I thought this could be a fun way to let out some energy and frustration."

"All right, guys, you two can play touch tackle after you drop me off. Right now I want to shoot up some bitches." Beck sauntered past Derek and Scott, her fuck-with-me-if-you-dare, hot-pink, body-hugging top the perfect uniform to clear a path through the crowds. Man, Scott loved her brazen confidence. Hopefully some guy would smarten up and get themselves one hell of a woman.

"C'mon. I want to make sure we're on the same team." Derek tugged Scott's toward the entrance like a kid rushing to climb onto Santa's lap.

"I didn't know there were teams in laser tag." Scott followed close behind as Derek maneuvered them closer to the darkened room.

Derek stopped dead in his tracks and faced Scott. "Wait. Have you never played laser tag before?"

If Scott didn't know better, he'd think Derek judged him. "Nope."

"Oh, my God," Derek said, in the most adorably loving tone Scott could imagine. "I'm popping your cherry."

Scott slapped Derek's ass. "Uh, I think you already did that." Was Derek purposefully trying to turn him on?

"There are teams, and we're going to be on the same one. More importantly, we're going to make sure Beck is on a different team and then we'll shoot the shit out of her. She ruined my surprise." Without another word, he hauled Scott along, managing to weasel the two of them to the front of the line, and slapped down forty dollars. He grabbed the last two green vests and guns, then dragged Scott inside the arena.

Scott spotted Beck immediately, her shirt glowing under the black lights. As she ran past them, Derek laughed so hard he snorted. The last of Scott's tension drained from him. Who could remain stressed when their boyfriend made pig sounds?

After a brief orientation video, the game began. Red, blue and green beams flew through the air. Scott ran toward a pillar, Derek close on his heels. He'd set his goal, and needed extra manpower to take the tower. He gripped Derek's arm. "C'mon. Let's head this way and approach from the rear.".

"No way." Derek followed Beck's progression throughout the room with his eyes, clearly scouting his target.

Beck was a menace to be reckoned with, dodging beams, landing shots on other players mid-center in front and back—a one-woman army. Scott couldn't suppress his laughter when she sprinted across the room, screaming at the top of her lungs like Animal from The Muppets.

Still, eliminating entire color groups, not individual players, remained the prime objective, despite Derek's clear mission to take out Beck. "Let's attack the red headquarters." Scott gripped Derek's arm. "If we cover each other we might be able to do some damage before we get stunned."

"But I want to shoot Beck." Words Scott never imagined he'd ever hear from Derek.

"If we take out their headquarters, they lose, which is even better than killing her." Scott's logic seemed flawless, at least to him.

"No, it isn't. I want to shoot Beck." Derek stomped his foot.

Scott glanced around them. There were a few other green players nearby. "We're charging the red fort. You guys in?" Several cheers and a crowd of green players rushed through the open portion of the arena.

Lasers flew everywhere, flashing by Scott's head, nailing people in their guns and shoulders. Somehow, he got within ten feet of the red fortress before being stunned by a blow to his left shoulder. Three seconds of downtime could mean death, at least for anyone who didn't have Scott's determination. He dropped to the ground, shielding himself along a ledge.

"You shot Scott. You bitch." Derek's voice cut through the chaos with unmistakable clarity.

Scott peered in his direction, only to witness Derek in a standoff with Beck. Both aimed their guns at each other. Without flinching, Derek shot, nailing Beck in her front sensor.

"Asshole." What? Beck at a loss for words? Her typical cursing came in the form of strings and not single-word utterances.

Derek fired three more times, nailing her once more in the front plate and then in her gun and shoulders, taking Beck out for at least twenty seconds if she wasn't already dead. Scott hopped to his feet and took aim for the glowing red fortress light. Derek sidled up next to him along with a few other green and blue players, and within thirty seconds the light went out, as did all the red player's vest and gun lights.

The red team members moved to the side of the room,

waiting for the next game to begin as cheers erupted from the remaining two teams. Then blue and green teams turned on each other in a web of phosphorescent laser shots.

Derek took a shot to his gun so Scott stepped in front of him, his focus sharp, like he'd become Skywalker and the force flowed through him.

Derek joined him three seconds later once his stun period ended and, back to back, they took out four blue team players and got a few good shots at the blue fortress before each taking a shot in their front panels.

Scurrying out of the line of fire, Scott ducked behind a pillar, Derek squished next to him, panting as he clung to Scott. "I killed her."

Scott marveled at Derek, a kaleidoscope of green and blue flashes illuminating his beaming face. Without thinking, not caring whether he got shot a hundred times, he slid his hands behind Derek's neck and pulled him into a kiss, pressing him into the pillar.

Derek melted into him, driving his tongue into Scott's mouth.

Scott wrapped his arms around Derek and squeezed as tight as he could. His alarm sounded just before Derek's, but Scott didn't care. They could die a hundred times. He was already in heaven.

After several seconds, Derek pulled out of the kiss, still breathing heavily, although probably not from the running and shooting. He stared into Scott's eyes, his pupils dilated and his lips puffy and red. No words were needed to convey what he wanted, because Scott's raging hard-on matched the one pressing into his thigh.

They enjoyed a quiet drive back to campus, especially since a disgruntled Beck refused to speak to either one of them. Scott contented himself with holding Derek's hand, only one thought or care on his mind:

Dorm room, as quickly as possible.

ELEVEN

BACK AT THEIR ROOM, SCOTT NEARLY TORE THE LINING FROM his pocket as he fumbled for his keys.

"Hurry up." Derek pressed against Scott from behind, his husky whisper brushing air along Scott's neck, causing the fine hairs to tickle.

The command shot through him, his pants becoming tighter. "I'm trying," he panted, attempting without much luck to steady his shaking hands.

Finally, he gripped the correct key and open their door. No sooner had the two of them crossed the threshold when Scott found himself pressed against the wall. Derek clawed at Scott's chest, tugging his shirt up, dragging Scott's arms along in the process. Some fabric tore. No matter, because Derek bit Scott's nipple and the whole world disappeared in a flash of white.

"Jesus!" Scott cradled the back of Derek's head.

One last scrape of teeth and Derek worked his way up Scott's body, scorching hot kisses along Scott's pecs, neck and cheek. With a slight tilt of his head, Derek covered Scott's lips with his own.

Through gasped breaths, they stumbled toward the bed and

collapsed, Scott crushing Derek into the mattress. "What's gotten into y—"

His words were muffled by a hungry mouth. Derek seemed to have sprouted several new hands as he grasped at Scott's chest, lightly scraped up and down his back, and pulled at his hair.

Scott succumbed to the onslaught, squirming until Derek opened his legs. He ground his already throbbing cock against Derek's, heat radiating between them.

Yanking his head out of the kiss, Scott clamped his teeth on Derek's neck, grazing the skin and evoking the desired gasp. "Clothes off. Now!

Derek scrambled for his belt, unbuckling in record speed despite having to worm his hands between their sealed bodies. He fumbled to free Scott from the confines of his jeans and only got Scott's pants around his ass before Scott pushed himself up on his hands and knees. "Roll over."

Derek's eyes widened, then a broad grin lit up his face. Wordlessly, he flipped over, his ass on prominent display.

Saliva wet Scott's mouth as he surveyed the mounded ass cheeks so freely given. With steady fingers, he slipped Derek's pants off, then started licking his way back up Derek's body. When he reached ass level again, he gripped his lover's cheeks and spread them, revealing the taut pucker hidden within.

Scott reached down with one hand and gripped his shaft, running the pad of his thumb along his cockhead and smearing precum along hot, sensitive flesh. "I'm gonna fuck you so hard."

He fumbled with the various objects on the night table, knocking several to the floor until he procured the bottle of lube. A practiced flick with his thumb opened the lid and he squeezed a generous amount onto his cock. Scott twisted his hand as he stroked himself, slow strokes, building his already ramped up need to enter Derek.

Tingles started in his belly. No way would he finish before he even started. Releasing himself, he lowered his slick hand to

Derek's ass, running the pads of his fingers up and down the crack.

Derek arched his back, causing his hips to rise slightly, an unspoken yet clear invitation.

Scott slipped his index finger inside Derek. The contented sigh let Scott know Derek was probably ready. He added his middle finger, probing deep, rotating his hand so the pads massaged Derek's inner walls.

Derek turned his head to the side and breathed out a husky, "Fuck me now!"

Scott placed one hand above Derek's shoulder and used the other to guide his cockhead to Derek's entrance, ready to breech the tight, inviting hole, but didn't have a chance to plunge into the hot depths of his lover since Derek bucked his hips back, firmly seating Scott inside.

"Fuck!" Scott clenched his teeth and closed his eyes, attempting to settle the sudden rush of silky heat sliding against his shaft. "I'm gonna come."

Derek reached back, gripped Scott's ass and pulled him down so he rested heavily on top of him. "Not yet, you aren't."

Scott froze, and once he'd reclaimed a small amount of control over his body, slowly rocked forward and back. Heated, soft skin caressed his cock, Derek's insides wet with precome and lube, far better than Scott could ever achieve with his hand.

Small grunts escaped Derek. He bucked his ass and ground into Scott's thrusts., but Scott stroked Derek's lower back, a silent reminder that too much movement could cause an explosion.

Apparently, Derek didn't care. He matched Scott's motions, increasing the pace and force of their fucking. Scott fell into the new rhythm, his breath heaving from his chest.

Derek's channel spasmed in a series of rapid quivers, sending "I'm close" signals to Scott. Knowing he'd brought Derek to the brink of release threw Scott over the edge. He pounded into Derek once, twice, and on the third thrust buried himself to the hilt and erupted.

Derek sucked in a sharp breath, then cried out with a short, "Uh!" before his whole body clenched.

The smell of come and sex surrounded Scott. Derek moaned, bucking helplessly with Scott seated deep inside. When his muscles finally relaxed and he sank into the mattress, Scott rested heavily on Derek's back.

They remained there, sweat-covered, cum-stained, and panting for a few minutes. Finally, Scott rolled them so Derek lay atop him.

Derek thrust his tongue into Scott's mouth, swirling in circles, and gradually easing into a languid caress. Eventually, he came up for air, snuggling perfectly against Scott's chest.

Scott ran his hands over Derek's back and ass, enjoying the new hardness of muscle beneath the surface, new bulges rippling in places where lean muscle had once been.

With an evening of fun, topped off by mind-boggling sex, Scott gave Derek one last squeeze and let his head sink into the pillow.

Blood tests, wrestling meets, any kind of responsibility could wait.

He had Derek and peace. With those two things, he could face anything.

Sunlight cut across Scott's closed lids, the soft red glow soothing and the warmth against his skin a pleasant way to wake up. Such a contrast to the day ahead. Cold trek to classes, another to practice, then back to the dorms.

Derek hummed next to him, reminding him not everything about Boston winters sucked.

He forced his eyes open and observed his lover, debated slipping out of bed and giving Sleeping Beauty a few more minutes of rest, but then caught sight of the way light and shadow accentuated the extra bulk filling out Derek's form.

Damn he's getting even hotter. Scott's cock pulsed a few times in full agreement. *Down, boy. You got a good ride last night.* One thought of the sexcapades of a few hours earlier and Scott caved, sliding behind Derek and lining his hard cock against his lover's ass.

"Mmm. Someone's up." Derek voice carried playfulness. He rolled over and faced Scott. "Morning."

Scott chuckled, although disappointment pierced through. *Guess there's not gonna be sex.* "Morning yourself." Scott nudged himself against Derek once more, gripping Derek's hips and pressing his hard-on against Derek's equally stiff member. *Two can play the teasing game.* He sat on the edge of the bed. Glancing over his shoulder, he caught Derek worrying his lower lip with his teeth before letting out a huff and sitting up.

Scott ran his finger along Derek's pecs. "Couldn't help but notice the new muscles you're sporting. Just kinda popped overnight."

Derek side bumped Scott with enough force to show off his increased strength. "Trying to keep up with my muscle man."

Scott slid one hand along Derek's tanned, muscled arm and cupped Derek's cheek. "You never have to catch up to me. I'm right here beside you." Perhaps he'd uttered about the cheesiest words ever, but couldn't have cared less.

Derek bypassed making the snarky comment probably at the tip of his tongue, and placed a kiss against Scott's lips. "How are you today?"

It took Scott a minute to shift gears. "I'm good." He ran a short mental check to be sure. "Really. I'm great. Thanks for taking me out last night. You always know the perfect thing to take my mind off…everything."

"I'm glad." Derek chuckled. "Although I don't think Beck will speak to either one of us for at least a month."

"Whatever." Scott stood and crossed the room to the dresser. "One day she'll realize she doesn't need so much drama in her life. I wish she'd give the guys she dates a chance. I mean, if she let down her guard for half a second she'd—" *What?*

"Find what we have?"

"Yes!" Scott grabbed a pair of boxers from the drawer and spun around. "Exactly. I want her to find what we have. She'd be so much happier."

Derek joined Scott by the dresser, still naked and sporting a half-on. "You, my amazing boyfriend, are my hero." He kissed Scott's cheek, swatted him on the ass, then grabbed a towel and sauntered out of the room, only securing the fabric around his waist seconds before a freshman girl passed by the door.

Scott shook his head. Not only was Derek blossoming into a truly magnificent man, but he'd called Scott a hero. An unlikely word to describe him, but still enough to send him flying.

He made quick work of dressing and grabbed what he needed for classes and practice. As an afterthought, he flipped open to a new page in his notebook and scrawled a short note. *You're my hero too.* He left the torn-out page on Derek's desk.

Outside, a sharp gust of wind snapped at Scott, forcing him to hunker into himself and quicken his pace. *Me a hero? I don't think so.* His dad was the one with balls of steel. It took some serious guts to look a thing like cancer in the face and say, "Fuck you".

With extra energy in his step, Scott strode down the sidewalk. He could wait a few days to find out the results of his blood test. Then maybe he'd be a hero.

TWELVE

THE REST OF THE WEEK MOVED AT BOTH A RAPID AND agonizingly slow pace. Practices, classes, and Derek filled Scott's days, but waiting for his blood results to come in remained present in everything he did. At least he'd spotted his newest competitor's results from the weekend Division One season matches. The Lehigh guy at his weight class had beaten the Rutgers wrestler. Scott had as well. No one else he'd wrestled competed against Lehigh, so comparative stats wouldn't help. At least calculating his odds of taking division helped to distract him.

When Friday rolled around and Scott made his way to the athletic complex for his evening practice, he gave up on finding out anything from the lab before the weekend.

He spotted Marcus the second he stepped into the wrestling room and busied himself with arranging and rearranging his bag. Maybe, if he could stall long enough, his best friend on the team wouldn't notice Scott's fried nerves.

No such luck. Within seconds Marcus stood by his side. "Dude. What's the matter?"

Scott counted to three before addressing his teammate. He

plastered an expression he hoped passed for a casual onto his face. "Nothing, man. Making sure I have everything I need."

Marcus folded his arms across his chest, a *I don't buy your bullshit* expression written all over his face.

Might as well tell the truth. "I hoped I'd have heard from the doctor's office by now. Looks like I'm gonna have to sweat it out all weekend."

Marcus bobbed his head a few times. "That sucks."

Scott couldn't help but chuckle. His buddy could simplify any situation. "Big time."

Marcus slung an arm around Scott's shoulder. "Well, look at it this way. You can use your pent-up frustration to wipe the mat with your opponent in tomorrow's meet."

Scott snapped his headgear into place and strode onto the mat, Marcus on his heels. After a brief warm up, the coach organized a series of short sparring rounds, enough to get the team breathing hard and sweating.

Simple take downs, escapes, and rolling Marcus to the mat helped to ease the stiffness out of Scott's muscles. At least for an hour, he could avoid focusing on his father, cancer, and doctors.

After practice, he declined the invitation to join the team at the student center for pizza and pool. Instead, he decided to jog back to his dorm. Derek would be waiting for him and most likely planned some diversionary tactics to tire Scott out so he could fall asleep peacefully.

He took off from the athletic complex at a quick pace, his bag bouncing on his back. After a few minutes Scott stopped, his heart pounding and sweat pouring down his cheeks and neck. Somehow his jog wound up a sprint.

He grabbed his waist, pressing at a fast-forming cramp. He panted rhythmically, the icy air entering his lungs and revitalizing him. *Damn, why couldn't the results've come in?*

When the pain in his side subsided enough for him to stand, he trudged in the direction of his dorm, his nerves seeming to have the upper hand. After another few minutes, he found himself speed-walking, his hands balled into fists and his teeth grinding.

What the fuck? How long did a blood sample test take? He'd been told he'd have to wait a day or two and five days had passed.

By the time he reached his dorm, he'd worked himself into a ball to tightly wound knots. Gripping the front door handle, he yanked with far more force than necessary, the resulting slam of metal against brick startling both himself and the several students standing in the front lobby. Scott closed his eyes, trying to will the stress out of his muscles. "Sorry," he said, closing the door gingerly behind him.

He wove his way toward the stairs and took them three at a time, sprinting to his room. The door stood ajar, Howie Day music blasting from Derek's computer. Scott entered the room and threw his wrestling bag on the floor. "Would you turn that down!"

Derek snapped his head up in Scott's direction, then hit the volume button on his keypad, lowering the music to barely audible. "What's wrong?" He shot to his feet and bolted to Scott's side.

Scott scooped up a piece of crumpled paper on the floor and tossed it, watching the smooth arc through the air and uninspiring landing in the middle of their bed. Wordlessly he toed his shoes from his feet, crossed the room, and picked up the projectile. Smoothing the paper out in his hand he glanced at the flyer. *Valentine's Day Bash! Student Center Event from 7 – 11.* "Um, what's this doing on the floor?"

Derek took the paper from him and tossed it into the trash next to his desk. "I was practicing my aim toward your trash can and missed."

Scott couldn't help the smile tugging at his lips. "The target is in the corner. This landed in the middle of the floor."

"Which is why I don't play basketball." Derek plunked down

onto the couch. "Care to fill me in on why you're in such a foul mood?"

Scott's fight drained from him in a rush. He crossed the room and sat next to Derek. "My blood results didn't come in."

"Oh." Derek wrapped an arm around Scott's shoulder and pulled him until he lay with his head on Derek's lap. "I'm sorry."

Derek wove his fingers through Scott's hair, which had grown about an inch over the past month. "You should let your hair grow long again. I like it when it's all wavy."

Scott laughed. "You're so stupid."

"Yup. Doesn't change the fact I like your hair better when it's longer." Derek tugged playfully at Scott's head and ran his fingers along Scott's scalp. "Sorry you didn't hear about the results."

The heaviness Scott'd carried around for the whole week sapped him of his energy. "Thanks." He adjusted his head so he could look at Derek, noting the bulk in thigh muscle which hadn't been there a few months earlier. "Dude, are you on steroids?"

"Yeah, right. Like I'd put dick-shriveling poison in my body. I've been working out more."

"Why?" Had Scott's stress taken such a toll Derek needed the gym to cope?

Derek heaved q sigh, setting Scott on full alert. "Man, you're pushy. I'm bulking up so I'll be in prime shape for next year when I *finally* cave in and join the damn team."

Scott bolted up, abandoning the comfortable pillow of Derek's lap. "You could join the wrestling team now. The guy at the one hundred thirty-five weight class isn't nearly as good as you."

Derek shook his head. "I've got too much on my plate with courses, The Alliance, and Peer Counseling."

"You could manage, and then we could have after-practice wrestling sessions." Scott lean in and skimmed his nose along the smooth skin of Derek's neck until he nuzzled behind Derek's ear. "Remember how we almost got caught screwing around on our high school mat?"

"I remember." Derek squirmed a little, reaching for his groin and readjusting the noticeable lump beneath the fabric.

Scott replaced Derek's hand with his own, rubbing back and forth and savoring the heat radiating into his palm. He kissed a trail along Derek's jaw, working his way to the plump lips he so adored. Derek opened to him and sank into a languid play of tongue on tongue.

Within seconds, Scott's cock raged to full mast. Crawling onto his hands and knees without breaking the kiss, Scott guided them until Derek lay flat on his back. He sank between Derek's legs, grinding his hardness into his squirming lover.

With a twist of his head, Derek broke the kiss, the sound of his panting filling the space between them.

"What's wrong?"

"Nothing. It's just—" Derek bit his bottom lip the way he always did when he couldn't find the words to express himself. "Maybe we should go to bed."

"What! I thought—"

"Baby, it's not like that. You *know* I love when you get all aggressive and sexified, but maybe tonight isn't the right time for sex. Maybe we can put on the television, pop in a movie or watch some stupid Lifetime show, and—" Again, he chewed on his lower lip.

"And…?"

"And maybe we can talk about your feelings about the blood results and your dad?" Derek seemed to shrink in size after he got the words out.

Scott couldn't deny the surge of frustration forcing his heart to beat harder and his blood to flow faster, but one look at Derek and his anger melted away. "We haven't had a snuggle night in a while. Sounds like a good idea to me."

Luckily, Derek left the whole *talking about things* part alone.

Derek clicked on the TV, stripped off his shirt, and pulled back the covers, sliding into bed and leaving a space for Scott.

"If I didn't know any better, I'd think you had this whole evening planned out." Scott flipped the light switch so the walls reflected the wavering gray light from the television.

He stripped out of his clothes and burrowed next to Derek, too tired to find pajama bottoms. Warmth surrounded him even before Derek lowered the comforter. A kiss to his temple drew Scott's attention to the man next to him. In a soothing, whisper, Derek said, "I get it."

THIRTEEN

Scott woke to Derek's even breathing. He loved the rare moments when he could simply watch Derek sleep. Most mornings he rose to an empty bed, no recollection of Derek having gotten up.

Perfectly relaxed eyelids, slightly parted lips, no hint of worry lines on his forehead. Derek, the definition of peaceful when awake, seemed like a pure angel in sleep.

Scott placed a kiss on Derek's lips and slipped out of bed. Since he'd gone to sleep nude, he only needed to grab his towel and head into the bathroom to take a shower.

He felt particularly well rested. Surprising given the amount of stress he'd carried for the whole week. He didn't linger under the hot spray, like most mornings, instead, brushing his teeth, shaving, and returning to his room in record time.

Derek remained asleep. Scott quietly dressed in sweats and exited the room as quietly as possible.

The team wrestling Lehigh included a four to five-hour bus ride each way. His father wouldn't be able to make the trip, although Derek had traded his counseling shift with a friend so he could be with Scott.

The sun shone in a cloudless sky, helping to cut some of the chill from the air. He only had to walk a few blocks from the dorm to reach a Dunkin Donuts, where he ordered two ham, egg and cheese croissants and double espresso coffees, extra sugar, extra cream.

He rushed back to their room, not wanting the food to get cold. Derek stirred in the bed the second Scott opened the door, and moments later opened his eyes. "Mmmm. Coffee!"

Scott crossed the room and sat on the edge of the bed. "Yup." He hoped the coffee would help wake Derek, although freezing skin would probably shock Derek awake faster than the coffee, but freezing his boyfriend seemed cruel given he'd agreed to spend most of the day on a bus. "Your favorite breakfast sandwich too."

Derek's eyes snapped open and he sat up. "Give it!" He reached toward Scott like a kid grabbing for a present on Christmas.

Unable to contain his laughter, Scott handed over the bag and watched Derek tear into his meal. "Eat up and get dressed, we have a long day ahead of us."

Derek stuck out his tongue, but did exactly as Scott instructed, devouring the sandwich within a minute and grabbing the coffee to wash down the last bites. "Oh, double espresso. Nice call."

Scott plopped onto the bed and rested his back against the wall. "I know. Go take a shower."

A quick flip of covers towards the foot of the bed and Derek leapt to his feet, stripped, and grabbed the towel Scott had left on the floor. "I'll only be a minute."

Scott took in the rippling muscles running up and down Derek's body. "Seriously, babe, you look amazing."

"Flattery will get you everything." Derek disappeared into the hallway, leaving the door open.

Shaking his head, Scott got up, closed the door, and started picking up clothes strewn about the room and soda can's decorating their coffee table. By the time Derek returned to the room, a mop of brown, shaggy hair covering his eyes, both desks were completely organized and the throw pillows on their couch rearranged.

Glistening droplets of water dripped from Derek's hair and onto his smooth chest. A few rivulets of liquid ran down his pectoral muscles and along the ridges of his taut abdomen. By the time Scott's view reached Derek's groin, he'd sprouted a hard-on, which tented the front of his own sweats.

Derek dipped his eyes to Scott's midsection, then slowly rose to meet Scott's eyes. He dropped his towel. "You're lookin' pretty amazing yourself."

It took all of Scott's self-control to keep from ripping his sweats off and throwing Derek onto the bed. "Yeah, yeah. Let's get dressed. The bus leaves in an hour."

"Then we have plenty of time to take care of your little, um, problem." Derek licked his lips and took a step closer.

"Save it for when we get back." Scott bit the inside of his cheek hard enough to cause pain. Otherwise he'd cave and never leave their room.

"Seriously?" Derek produced and irresistibly adorable pout.

"Payback for last night." Scott busied himself with stuffing his travel bag.

Derek sputtered a few incomprehensible words, and, apparently unable to come up with a retort, started to dry his hair by violently rubbing the towel against his head.

With the immediate danger of Derek's magnetic charm dismantled, Scott could look at him again without an insurmountable urge to fuck him senseless. "Hey, why don't you wear my Taz shirt today? I know you love it and, quite frankly, I love you in it."

With a nod, Derek indicated a pile of clothes on the dresser, the one spot Scott hadn't thought to clean. The famed shirt sat on the top of the pile. "Already taken care of."

Scott picked up and unfolded the shirt, and studied at the

cracked image of his favorite cartoon character clinging to the threadbare material. "Let me help you put it on."

Derek swiveled so he faced Scott. "Look at you being all sweet and stuff." He strode across the room, bare assed, and wrapped his arms around Scott's neck. "You're in a good mood."

No denying the truth. No matter how stressed out he became, the past two years with Derek allowed Scott to finally count on at least one solid thing to keep him grounded. He placed a kiss on Derek's lips, then stepped back and held the shirt for Derek to put on.

Scott couldn't help noticing how muscles pressed at the seams, more proof of Derek's increased bulk. "You sure you don't want to join the team this year?"

"Don't push your luck. I told you. Next year." Derek slipped his boxer briefs on. "Let's focus on you winning today's match instead of me"

Scott couldn't quit babbling the entire ride to Lehigh. "The Rutgers guy, who Lance already beat, is strong as hell. All muscle and kind of stocky."

"Lance?" Derek asked.

"The Lehigh wrestler at my weight class. Keep up." Scott elbowed Derek and resumed piecing together the puzzle of his competition. "That means Lance is either the same or he's tall, thin, flexible, and really, really skilled." Strength Scott could fight. Wrestlers relying on strength usually didn't think strategically.

Skilled wrestlers were a whole different animal. They knew how to take advantage of every opportunity. They knew how to assess their opponent within the first few seconds of a match and pick from a deep arsenal of moves.

"No sense in playing guessing games. Unless…" Derek

grabbed his phone and started typing feverishly. After a minute he handed his phone to Scott. "Here, he's the one on the far left." Derek shoved his phone into Scott's hands.

Scott looked at the picture. Tall and lanky, so probably skilled. "See, this is why I take you places. You help me prepare for meets."

"Yeah, *that's* why you take me places." Derek gave Scott a playful shove, shifted so his back rested against the window, and stretched his legs across Scott's lap. "So, what's your strategy going to be?"

"I'll beat the guy with technical maneuvers. If I'm lucky, maybe I can pin him, but you know me and the tall, thin guys. I can never get a secure hold and they always weasel their way out of my grip."

"Technical pins are almost as good as an actual pin. Only a difference of one team point." Derek yawned, tucking his sweatshirt in a wad behind his head and closing his eyes. Minutes later, he slept.

With nothing to distract him aside from the snores and occasional farts and burps of his teammates, thoughts of his father bombarded Scott.

What if?

What if he wasn't a good donor? Did Dad have any other options at all?

Even more frightening to think on, what if he *did* test positive and could donate his marrow? Would Dad die sooner? How bad would recovery be if he survived? Would he return to the same person he'd been before the cancer?

Like a yo-yo, Scott toggled back and forth between excitement, fear, anger, and back again.

Not to mention the upcoming competition against Lance, whom he knew virtually nothing about.

Scott's heart beat faster, the beginnings of a headache throbbing at his temples.

Vrrrbp. Vrrrbp. Vrrrbp.

His phone's vibrations jolted Scott out of his thoughts. Who might be calling him at seven in the morning on a Saturday, Scott had no idea.

Unless…

He dug into his pocket, his heart skipping a beat when he saw the name emblazoned on the screen.

Dad!

"What's wrong?" Scott spoke louder than he'd intended. Derek stirred in his lap, but nestled back into sleep.

Chuckling wasn't the response Scott expected. "Nothing's wrong, son. I wanted to call and wish you good luck on your game today."

"Actually, they're called mee…never mind. Thanks." Scott absentmindedly stroked Derek's leg, worries slowly dissipating. "You sure you're okay?"

"I'm fine. Tired, but that's normal for me. You, on the other hand, sound stressed."

No denying the truth. "Guess I've got a lot on my mind."

"I hope you're not wasting energy worrying about me when you've got something far more important to focus on right now."

"Dad, you shouldn't–"

"I'm just kidding. Sort of." His father laughed half-heartedly. "To be honest, I wanted to make sure *you* were okay. I know the results didn't come in and I'm concerned not knowing may distract you from your goals today."

Wow. In a million years he never would've expected those words from his father. "I'm good. Derek's with me making sure I don't jump off a ledge."

"Well, tell him thanks for me." His dad coughed, the wheeze and ragged breath sounding clearly through the phone. "Son, don't let a silly thing you can't control deter you from what you've set out to accomplish. We'll get the results when we do and deal with them when the time comes. For now, go beat your opponent."

"I will, dad." Scott peered down at Derek, just as peaceful as he'd been earlier in bed. "Thanks for calling."

"Of course. Be sure to let me know how you do."

The rest of the ride to Lehigh sped by in a blur, thoughts of his father's call bolstering Scott.

I'll win the match for you, Dad. Then I'll win the battle against cancer with you.

Scott spotted Lance immediately upon entering the wrestling room. The tallest guy on the team, he stood in the center of the mat with a much bigger wrestler, probably their heavyweight, the rest of the team surrounding them on the mat.

Scott studied Lance's series of spins, drops, and arches. Fast. Maybe as fast as Scott. An unpleasant lump formed in his chest

"You're overthinking right now," Derek whispered in his ear. "You got this. Wait until your match, then go do what you do best."

Scott shook his head. "How do you know what I'm thinking?"

Derek answered with a kiss on Scott's cheek. "Warm up and let your body take over."

Marcus and the other BU captain took the center of the mat and Scott hustled onto the outer ring. The team did a few sprints in place, drops, and spins, and hustled off to their side of the mat. The ref spoke to both coaches by the scoreboard. Scott looked over his shoulder to find Derek.

Scott loved wrestling in small practice rooms. Sweat seemed to permeate the closed space with a heavier scent. The moisture and heat added to the intensity of a man using his muscles and skill to overcome another man. Somehow, he could picture himself as a Roman or Greek in ancient times, preparing for a battle of strength and honor.

Grumbling jarred Scott to attention. Marcus squared off

against Lance chest-to-chest. "What'd you say? I don't think I heard you."

Lance pushed Marcus away from him. "I said I'm gonna destroy that faggot on your team."

Marcus growled, clenching his fists into balls. He took a menacing step toward Lance, his shoulders rising until his shoulders practically touched his ears.

Oh, hell no!

Scott jumped to his feet and darted between Marcus and Lance. "Faggot" told him all he needed to know. Asshat, Lance's new nickname, saw Derek kiss him and opened his big, homophobic mouth.

"You think you're tough? I'll show you tough." Marcus gripped Scott's shoulder and pushed him sideways.

Prepared, Scott made sure Marcus met a brick wall of resistance. "Hey, chill out man. Do you really think I gave a shit what this string bean has to say?"

In truth, Lance did Scott a solid favor. Anyone so insecure they made an ass of themselves in front of their own and a visiting team couldn't be much competition. His ego would be his undoing.

Marcus locked eyes with Scott, anger brimming beneath the surface, but slowly, he let out a breath and dropped his defensive stance.

Scott gripped Marcus' shoulders. "How about we let *this* faggot," he said loud enough for both teams to hear, "teach him a lesson he won't forget?" His entire team whooped while the other team struggled to pull Lance away.

The coaches hustled the teams to their respective sides. The ref strode to the Lehigh team and handed Lance a yellow slip. *Good, he got a warning.* He then crossed the mat to Scott and handed him a warning as well. "Sorry. I hate to do it, but you can't use the word 'faggot.'" He turned from Scott, but stopped and faced Scott once more. "Hope you show him he's not so great just 'cause he's straight."

Scott's entire team hooted, then huddled together, arms around each other's shoulders. Coach chimed in, "All right, let's put the bullshit behind us. We travelled a long way and this is an important meet."

"Yes, coach," the team shouted.

"First match will start in about two minutes, get yourselves ready." Coach tapped Scott's shoulder while the other teammates gathered at the edge of the mat, nodding his head to a spot a few feet away from the others. "You all right?"

Scott responded without hesitation. "I'm better than fine."

"Good." He tightened his lips and pinched the bridge of his nose between two fingers. Finally, he uttered a short phrase, sending electricity through Scott: "Kick that fucker's ass."

What the fuck? Coach huffed and marched away. *I'll be damned.*

The distraction caused by Lance-—to be referred to as Asshat for the remainder of his life—helped center Scott. His dad's phone call further bolstered him. He'd win for his dad. He had to. If he could pull this off, he knew things would work out with the blood test. Superstitious or not, Scott couldn't deny how positive events often strung together. No need to think about how the same held true for negatives.

Scott crossed the outer ring of the wrestler's circle. With each step toward the center, he sensed his muscles filling with blood and oxygen. Laser-sharp and focused, he shook Asshat's hand for the required handshake at the beginning of matches and the whistle blew.

Like lightning, Scott scooped up a gangly leg, stepped behind the foot still on the mat, and took Asshat down straight onto his back. He hooked both legs around Lance's and arched. He had to stretch further than usual to counter Asshat's long limbs, but Scott would suffer stiff muscles to pin this prick in the first period.

Lance flailed his arms, trying to twist his back away from the mat. Scott first secured one arm, hooking his own around thin biceps, then captured the other arm in the same fashion.

With his opponent immobilized, Scott struggled to hold the squirming nuisance still for three seconds for the pin. An idea hit with the force of a freight train. He made direct eye contact with Lance.

One flash of locked gazes let Scott see the subtle shift. Adrenaline dissipated for a brief second and they faced one another, wrestler to wrestler, the inevitable conclusion registering in Asshat's eyes.

A rush of energy flooded through Scott, filling him. He winked, mouthed a taunting air kiss, then squeezed with all his might. He arched his back, pulling his opponent's head and feet off the mat, completely pinning his back to the ground. The ref waved his hands three times and slapped the mat.

Scott hopped to his feet. A quick peek at the clock showed a minute and twenty-three seconds still on the clock. He'd pinned the homophobic gnat in thirty-seven seconds. News would travel fast, especially to the Rutger's wrestler who would likely pay close attention to this match.

The trip to center mat never felt so good. He made sure to squeeze when he shook hands. Asshat glared at their joined hands. Scott mouthed "Loser" and released his grip when the ref lifted his arm in triumph.

The BU wrestlers hopped up and down, cheering. Marcus gyrated in an obnoxious victory dance, pointing at the Lehigh team.

Coach stepped in the middle of the team. "Hey! Morons! Stop dancing like monkeys and sit your asses down!" The team scurried to the side of the mat as the next wrestler stepped into the center circle.

Scott remained standing, his heart pounding. He watched Coach glance at the team, shake his head, the corner of his mouth creeping upwards. With a short nod, he said, "I'm proud of you, kid." Then he returned his attention to the wrestler on the mat.

"I'd have to agree with him." Derek slipped his arm around Scott's waist. "You kicked his ass."

Scott draped his arm around Derek's shoulders, glaring in the Lehigh team's direction to make sure he caught Asshat's attention. The glare he received sent warmth throughout his body. He'd won. Not just the match, but the moral battle as well. As an added bonus, he'd made his dad proud. This was the beginning of a lucky streak.

The moon rode high in the sky by the time everyone packed onto the busses. Scott lay with his back against the window and Derek nestled in his arms.

"So, how're you doing?" Derek asked.

Scott should've guessed he wouldn't be allowed to sleep. "Do I have a choice whether or not to talk?"

"Of course you do, but I'd really like to talk to you." Derek rested his head on Scott's chest, the weight like an anchor.

"Honestly, Lance's outburst during the match didn't bother me. I guess it should have, but once the words were out, I knew what kind of a person he was."

Derek grunted. "I wanted to jump on the guy and start scratching."

Scott hugged Derek tighter, trying to suppress his amusement. "Look at Mr. Therapy getting all irrational and stuff." An elbow to his side effectively shut him up.

"I'm entitled to fits of blinding anger once in a while. I don't indulge in them very often. Besides, that's not what I meant."

No. Scott knew better. Derek wanted to him to spill his guts about his dad.

He paused to examine his feelings. The previous day he'd

been a bundle of nerves, twitching every time he sensed the slightest vibration from his cell. Yet Scott couldn't have been more relaxed.

"Surprisingly, I'm awesome. Dad called me today and we had a really good conversation. Then, when that idiot started spouting at the mouth my nervousness about the match faded away. I've got this good feeling things would work out. You know?"

Derek shook his head. "No. I have absolutely no idea."

"Okay." Scott huffed a short laugh. "Let me try to spell it out." He waited for some quip from Derek. Nothing. "I kind of set it in my mind if I beat Asshat today then everything would turn out the way I want it to with my dad too. Kinda like a karma thing. Like I'm due a streak of good luck."

Derek remained silent for a long time. When he spoke, his voice sounded solemn and quiet, never a good sign. "You do know one thing has nothing to do with the other, right?"

So not the response Scott wanted. "Of course I know the two *events* aren't related. I'm talking about a general sense of something good on the horizon. Like things are lining up the way they're supposed to. Superstitious or not, I felt in control of what would happen today. The feeling kind of spread to other things in my life…especially Dad."

"I'm sorry. I didn't mean to sound discouraging and I totally get the good vibes feeling. I want to make sure I know where you're at." Derek nuzzled into Scott's chest. "You know, like, so I can be there for you the way you need me to be."

Scott's defenses melted. "You've been amazing. I know everything I'm going through is pretty heavy and distracting. You've been a rock through it all." He kissed Derek on the lips and then on his nose.

Derek lay his head back against Scott's chest. "I'm gonna try and sleep."

"K." Scott squeezed Derek and closed his eyes. Yeah, Derek

had been awesome ever since Scott got the news about his dad. The sense of something good waiting for him, however, came from someplace within himself.

The next few weeks would start a whole new chapter in his life.

FOURTEEN

WAITING, WAITING, WAITING.

Glaring at his watch for the twentieth time, Scott tore a page out of his notebook and crumpled it into a tight ball. Each minute seemed to draw out, stretching like gum stuck to the bottom of his shoe on a hot sidewalk.

Derek said he wanted to meet for lunch at Panera at noon, giving Scott something to think about. The winter scenery seemed more like spring, with a blue sky and bright sunshine. Still, the wind carried an icy sting. Another welcome distraction.

When he entered the restaurant, a wave of heat blasted him. He shrugged off his coat while scanning the room. Derek sat at a window table overlooking Boylston Street. The hustle and bustle of midday downtown Boston fueled Scott with its ambient energy.

He sidled to the hostess, pointing to Derek. "Hi, I'm meeting that guy over there."

"The hot one with the bubble butt?" Laura, as her nametag indicated, waited for Scott to make eye contact. She winked and gave a nod in Derek's direction.

Scott shook his head. "Okay. Thanks." He strode about

halfway to the table, then stopped and glanced back over his shoulder. Laura ogled him, the eraser end of her pencil gripped between her teeth and a dreamy expression clouding her eyes.

Derek stood when Scott reached the table and gave him a quick hug and peck on the cheek. A sharp pinch to his ass startled Scott, but not enough for him to miss the gasp from Laura on the other side of the room.

"Derek!" Scott fought the laughter crawling up his throat.

"What? She practically fucked with you with her eyes. A guy's got to mark his territory." Derek took a seat and moved the number card to the edge of the table. "I ordered for both of us. I hope you don't mind."

Scott didn't even have to ask. A grilled chicken panini with lettuce, chipotle mustard, and a side of lentil soup. "Thanks. I'm starving."

"No problem." Derek examined Scott intently. After a brief pause, he threw his hands in the air. "All right, I can't read you at all. Have you heard anything, or at least talked with your dad?"

"You *know* I'd've told you if I had. And no, I haven't talked to Dad. He'd call if he had news." Scott checked his watch and grimaced. "Although half the day is gone already. What's taking them so long?"

Derek settled more comfortably into his chair. "There's the Scott I expected. I knew this weighed on you. I think you should call your dad."

Scott's gut instinct to protest flared, but for the first time he could remember in his relationship with Derek, he simply took the advice and dug his phone out of his pocket to call his father.

Derek's mouth dropped open, but he snapped it shut and nodded.

When the phone rang his brief reverie shattered and an unpleasant fluttering rampaged towards Scott's stomach. Or nausea? Luckily, he only had to wait for two rings before his father picked up.

"Scott, I was about to call you. Good news. You're a match."

Contagious energy radiated through the phone, knocking the pesky butterflies from Scott's stomach. "You're *kidding* me."

"I wouldn't joke about this." Dad's serious tone only lasted a second before returning to a jubilant lilt. "I got the call from the doctor. I have an appointment tomorrow to go over the next steps and wanted to know if you were available at four."

Scott mentally ran through his schedule. Tuesday, so morning classes. He'd be done early afternoon and didn't have practice until six. "Four's perfect."

"Great. See you tomorrow." Silence stretched between them. His father spoke again, voice far more subdued. "Scott, I can't tell you how much it means to me you've decided to…."

A sensation Scott had never experienced, at least not when communicating with his dad, overtook him. Squeezing words around the lump in his throat, he managed, "I know, Dad. You don't need to say anything. I'll see you tomorrow."

He hit end and put the phone back into his pocket. Gazing at the street, Scott noticed pigeons climbing over each other a few feet down the block. A torn piece of bread bounced from beak to beak as the frenzy escalated. Rather than his typical reaction of disgust, Scott let out a short chuckle.

Through his peripheral vision, he spotted Derek's tilted head and gaping mouth. *Yeah, I probably look like a crazy man.* "I kind of understand how those pigeons feel."

He tugged his attention from the street to Derek, the raised brow adorning his boyfriend's brow expected. "They're driven by anticipation and adrenaline, or whatever the pigeon equivalent for adrenaline is."

Derek looked at the feathery frenzy. "Um. Care to elaborate?" A hint of laughter simmered under the surface of his words.

Scott gripped Derek's hands. "I'm a match for my dad."

Derek's face lit up. "No way!"

Scott nodded. "It really is. Everything's coming together. I told you. I could feel it. Things are working out exactly how I hoped they would and if this works…when it works…".

"Then you can build a relationship with your dad." Pure understanding enfolded Scott in safety and love.

"Then I can build a relationship with my dad," Scott repeated. He shook his head, amazed at how easily he'd pieced his feelings together. Usually, he waited for Derek to spin his brilliant web of insight to help Scott figure things out.

Derek took a sip of his coffee, studying Scott with an unreadable expression. Finally, he broke the silence. "Um, Scott."

"Yeah."

"Did you really say you know how *pigeons* feel?"

Scott released Derek's hands and stuck out his tongue. "You're such a brat!" he said through laughter.

Bad enough the minutes had dragged the day before. Sitting next to his father in the doctor's reception area, each second seemed to stretch for an eternity. Dad sat calmly next to Scott, his head resting against the wall and eyes closed.

"Can I ask you something?" Scott forced the words out.

"Anything."

"Do you think…I mean, I thought…," Scott exhaled on a huff. Simple questions shouldn't be so hard to ask. "When this is over and you're healthy again, would you consider going camping with me and Derek?"

His father opened his eyes. "I'd love to."

They were the right words, but somehow, missing excitement. Maybe Dad was just nervous. Scott could certainly relate. "Derek and I love camping and I thought it might be a good way for you and me to share something together…and for you to get to know Derek."

"I'd really like that. On both accounts. The invitation means a lot." His dad rested his arms on his thighs. "Let's take things one step at a time though. We have a lot of hoops to jump through before I'm *healthy*."

Scott didn't know what to say. A nurse appeared at the door leading to the doctors' offices and called for them to enter before he had to come up with anything.

Minutes later, they sat across the desk from Dr. T. "So, this is really good news. The match is as near to perfect as I've seen. Now, for the logistics." The doctor flipped through a few pages on the chart in front of him before speaking again. "Now that we know you're a match, transplantation is the course of treatment. First we need to kill all the cancer in your body, which means your immune system will also be decimated. You're looking at both chemo and radiation treatments."

Scott's chest clenched.

Dad, on the other hand, remained cool, the smile never leaving his face. "How soon can we get started?"

Dr. T chuckled. "I admire your attitude. We can begin as soon as tomorrow. I think two or three weeks of aggressive treatment would work. Or we could stretch it out over two months to ease your discomfort. Then we schedule the transplant. After that we see how it takes and make our next decision."

Clearly mapped out. Concrete actions Scott could understand. Especially the consequences if the procedure failed. "Is there anything I can do?"

"Nope. Your dad's the one doing the work for now. Just support him. The radiation and chemo won't be easy on him, especially since he's already weakened, but positive energy has super healing powers."

Scott bit back disappointment. If things had to get worse in order to get amazing, he'd suffer through. "I can do that."

His father rested his hand on Scott's knee and gave a squeeze. "Thank you, son."

Scott nodded, blinking away the burn in his eyes.

Coach seemed to be in a particularly sadistic mood at evening practice. Marcus faked right, shot for Scott's legs, and took him down. Wow! Marcus never pulled the move successfully before.

"Thompson, you planning on letting your opponent flip you on your ass on Saturday?"

Biting back a string of curses, Scott pushed hopped up. "No, sir."

"Good. Again." Coach moved on to another wrestler and started yelling again.

"Dude, what's up with you? You're a million miles away." Marcus got ready for another sparring round.

"I'm a match for my dad and he's starting chemo tomorrow." Scott couldn't believe how easily the words came.

Marcus stood all the way up and clapped Scott's shoulder. "Oh, my God. Are you serious? That's…great?"

Scott laughed at the uncertainty on Marcus's face. "Yeah. It is."

"I thought so. It just seems weird to say chemo is great."

True. Lots of weird things had happened over the past few months. Like Scott never would've invited his father to go camping…with Derek, no less. "It's cool, man. I'm just worried about him and excited for us. I mean, my dad and me."

"Noted." Marcus squeezed Scott's shoulder.

"So, now you know where my head's at."

"Ladies, they're serving tea and biscuits down the street if you need to chat." Coach's voice shattered their brief conversation.

"Right, Coach," Scott called over his shoulder. He squared off against Marcus and continued wrestling.

Derek's breathing evened out as he lay next to Scott in bed.

Scott tossed back and forth purposefully, hoping to jar Derek awake but making it seem like an accident. Derek only stirred slightly.

Next, Scott lifted his head and flipped his pillow so the cool side of the sheets would soothe his cheek. He made sure to fluff as noisily as possible.

Derek simply let out a short snore and lay still.

Finally, Scott stretched his arms, intending to rap the headboard with his knuckles. Unfortunately, he clocked Derek on the jaw.

"Ugh! What the fuck, Scott?" Derek rubbed his jaw and pushed himself up.

"Oh, you're awake." Scott sat up as well.

Derek glared at him. "*Now* I am."

"Yeah, um, sorry." Scott allowed himself half a second's remorse. "So, got a minute?"

Derek shook his head. "For Christ's sake, Scott, you don't have to beat me up to get me to talk."

"I asked my dad to go camping with us when all of this is over," Scott blurted before he lost his nerve.

Derek paused for a second, then nodded. "I think that's a great idea."

"Really?" Scott winced at the doubt in his voice. He shouldn't have expected any other reaction. Well, perhaps a bit crankier since Scott had punched him.

"Absolutely." Derek rubbed his eyes, feeding Scott's guilt at having woken his lover. "I never would've guessed you'd open up so much and so quickly to your father."

A pleasant tingle rushed though Scott's stomach. "You didn't?"

A small chuckle filled the space between them. "I mean, if you would've asked me last year, I'd of bet against those words ever coming out of your mouth."

Being honest with himself, Scott never would've guessed either.

"I'm really proud of you." Derek gave Scott a quick peck. He lay back down, opening his arms in invitation.

Scott curled into Derek's embrace, resting his head in the crook of Derek's shoulder. "It feels like I've had this puzzle with one piece missing and had accepted the fact it would always be *mostly* complete, but never truly whole."

"Most people feel that way. I don't think anyone feels entirely whole." Derek placed another kiss to the top of Scott's head, breathing in deeply as he did. "Mmm. You washed your hair with lavender shampoo."

Scott tightened his grip around Derek's torso. "I can't believe how lucky I am. Finding you is all I need, but to have my dad come back into my life in such a positive way. I just…I feel like my life is perfect now."

Derek ran his hand along Scott's arm. "You deserve to be happy, Scott. I don't want to hear you saying you don't. The fact you see your life as perfect is another reason you're my hero."

"Yeah." Scott sighed. Um, what did Derek mean?

And damn if Derek wasn't a mind reader, because he launched into an explanation before Scott could ask a question. "What I mean is, most people wouldn't view their life as perfect if they were in your shoes. Your dad has cancer and is about to go through a really tough time."

True. Most people would probably see that as a negative. Still, he couldn't shake the idea of his life turning out exactly the way he'd always dreamed. "I guess so."

"I *know* so. Most people would wonder why their lives sucked so *bad*. They'd ask, 'Why'd this have to happen to me?' But you're focused on a renewed relationship with your father. One you'd always hoped for. I'd say you're pretty heroic. Ronald's lucky to have you in his life."

Scott allowed Derek's words to sink in before responding. He'd never considered himself a hero until Derek mentioned it the other day. He certainly hadn't taken into account the way other people might react if they were in the same situation. "I guess you're right."

Derek dipped his finger under Scott's chin, lifting gently until their eyes locked. His lips parted slightly, plump and firm.

Scott sealed his mouth to Derek's.

When they parted, Derek slid back, holding the covers for Scott to nestle into place as well. Safely ensconced in his lover's arms, Scott closed his eyes and sighed.

Perhaps the next few weeks would bring challenges, but the finish line drew closer and closer. One day, he'd walk out the hospital doors with his dad. His healthy, cancer-free dad.

FIFTEEN

Scott sat in his father's cramped hotel room, staring at anything that would catch his eye.

Nothing could drown out the sounds coming from the bathroom. Full body retches echoed throughout the small space. To make matters worse, Dad clearly stated he didn't want any help.

Scott'd known what to expect from the treatments on a clinical level.

Of course, doctors never painted a true picture of what cancer treatments did to a person. He'd expected the vomiting. Having nightmares about the way his father's skin went from clammy and pale to green seconds before his rush to the bathroom came as a surprise.

The discomfort which his father couldn't hide remained a constant companion. Sure, they gave him pills for the nausea and pain, but nothing, it seemed, could fully erase the struggle of willingly poisoning one's body.

To his credit, Dad wore a brave face. Aside from the physical outer signs, Scott couldn't possibly know what the chemo did to the man. He couldn't even guess what life was like minute to minute. Whoever discovered the treatments for cancer was brilliant, no doubt, but probably sadistic as well.

His father reappeared a few minutes later, his face covered in a sheen of sweat. "Well, I could do without *that* happening again." He stumbled to the plush chair next to the couch where Scott sat and collapsed into the soft cushion.

The chair reminded him of the one from home, tied to some of the only good memories he carried from his youth. Rarely did his father allow him into the home office, a sterile room with lots of shelves, mostly bare, a desk and lamp nestled to one side. The wooden floors and white painted walls did nothing to give a sense of warmth. The chair, sitting on a small circular rug, its leather edges worn and blistered, served as his perch.

Back when he'd been young, maybe three or four, he'd sat in that chair when his mother went shopping, the only time his father allowed him in the room. Most days he played with a hand-held game device or read a book.

But one day his father put work aside and slipped a package from his desk drawer, wrapped in bright silver and red paper. It was summer, Scott remembered, nowhere near his birthday or Christmas. A book, *Small Pig*, by Arnold Lobel, the same guy who wrote the *Frog and Toad* stories.

He'd forced his father to read the story to him over and over. They'd only spent a few weekends reading together, but seeing the chair brought each detail into clear focus in his memory.

Of course, the *Small Pig* moments were overshadowed by the countless times he'd sat alone in the office, consigned to the same chair, waiting for his father to reprimand him for some failure or another. Earning a B+ on a mid-term, losing a wrestling match…existing, as far as Scott could tell.

Familiar tendrils of resentment crawled along Scott's skin, but one look at his father and negative thoughts flitted away like leaves carried on the wind.

"How much longer for treatments?" he asked, needing to fill the crushing silence in the room.

His father's raspy chuckle seemed foreign coming from such a withered man. "The doctor will run a full course and then check my blood. If my system is where it needs to be, then we should be ready for the transplant."

Spoken so casually, Scott might've thought they were discussing how the Sox would do in the spring. "Is there anything I can do?" He'd asked the question enough times he wasn't surprised by the response.

"No, son. This part is for me to deal with. The fact you're here spending time with me is enough." He closed his eyes. "Too much, actually. Don't you have practice in about an hour?"

Scott had shown up late to several practices over the past few weeks. Coach accepted the cryptic *I need to miss a few practices* without any further explanation and hadn't given Scott shit… yet…but how long could he borrow pity and concern before it affected his game? *Selfish much?*

"You need to keep up with your wrestling. Don't let me stand in your way."

People were getting too good at reading his mind.

What, another command? His father telling him what to do evoked customary responses. "I'm old enough to make up my own mind about how to spend my time." He crossed his arms over his chest. "And I know when to go to practice."

His father held up his hands defensively. "Whoa! I'm not telling you what to do. All I'm saying is I don't want to be the reason you lose focus, especially when it comes to your wrestling."

Of course! Scott's shoulders sagged. "Sorry. Gut reaction, I guess."

"Yeah." His father's voice trailed off along with his gaze, which settled on nothing in particular three or four inches in front of his face. Finally, he sighed. "It's not surprising."

He lumbered to the couch and plunked down next to Scott. "I never treated you like a person who deserved respect and consideration. I knew what I wanted you to do and expected you to do it."

The air in the room thickened, sticking in Scott's throat. He swallowed as best he could, given his suddenly dry mouth. "Dad," came out a mere gasp.

His father smiled, although his eyes remained sad. "It's okay. I'm glad we have a chance to get some of these things out in the open. I was a shitty father. I made so many mistakes I wish I could take back." He cupped Scott's cheek. Clammy palms, too cool, forcing an involuntary shudder. His dad removed his hand. "I'm sorry, I—"

Heat climbed up his spine one vertebra at a time, flooding into his cheeks. "No, it's fine. I'm not used to us…talking so genuinely." Scott's brow dampened.

"I think, given our current situation, this is a good time for us to talk honestly. Don't you?"

Scott counted each pulse of his own thundering heartbeat, not knowing where to begin. Luckily, he only got to thirty before his father chimed in. "What's the biggest disappointment you have in me, Scott?"

The question shocked him out of his stupor. "Dad, this is hardly the time to—"

"This is *exactly* the time." His father placed a hand tentatively on Scott's knee, giving a squeeze.

Scott worked to remain still.

Several thoughts raced through Scott's mind at once, bouncing off each other with the same frenzied anarchy of the last few minutes. "You were never there," he forced out, a lone bead of moisture running from his hairline down the side of his face.

"Fair enough." His dad nodded, his voice gentle. "I know I travelled a lot and that bothered you?"

"Yes. No. I mean, yeah, but that's not what I mean. I knew you had to travel for your work. I'm kind of freaking out right now because I think this is the first real conversation we've ever had. At least where I'm not distracted by blindly hating you."

His father froze, his expression etching into Scott's brain for what he knew would be forever. Shock, mixed with pain, poured through his saucer eyes and gaping mouth. To his credit, he masked his initial reaction. "You had every reason to hate me and you're right, I didn't pay attention to you."

Scott buried his face in his hands. "No. There's never a reason to hate someone. It's a wasted emotion. There are so many memories of you standing directly between me and what I wanted. It's hard for me to trust what's happening now is real."

"What else could it be?"

"It could be you're desperate. You'll do anything in order to survive, and once you're cured, you'll go right back to the way you always used to be." Scott shot up from the couch. "I'm sorry. I don't know why I said that. I don't even believe it."

His father stood. Two quick steps closed the space between them, his father gripping Scott by the shoulders, forcing eye to eye contact. "Relax. I asked to talk. This is what I want."

"How can spitting my disappointment at you help?"

"Because it's real." He locked eyes with Scott, waiting long enough for Scott to breathe again. "Sit down and let's talk."

Scott allowed his father to guide him back to the couch.

Once seated, Dad jumped right in. "If there's one thing this damn cancer has done, it's forced me to take a hard look at my life and you know what?"

Scott shook his head.

"I don't like what I see. Every phase of my life has been a letdown. My childhood with parents who had high expectations and made all my choices for me. My marriage where I fell so easily into the role of provider, thinking if I made enough money to support you and your mom, I'd done my job. Perhaps worst of all, seeing you, my son, as a nuisance instead of a gift. I've squandered what life has put in front of me and now I'm dying." He spoke with as much emotion as reading from a grocery list.

"My God, Dad, morose much? There has to be something you're proud of. Something you think back on with fondness."

His father nodded. "You're right, of course. The picture I paint nowadays is bleak, but there are many bright times filled with happiness which boost me when I'm down. Like meeting your mom and when you were born."

The knot in Scott's chest seemed to loosen a bit. "Yeah. The small things make the biggest difference. I wish we'd had more of them."

"You've grown into a far smarter man than me. I envy you, but I'm so proud and happy too." His father lay back and closed his eyes again.

"Tell me about how you met Mom. You've never told me the story before."

His father opened his eyes and sat upright. "You want to hear about meeting your mom? I'll need a glass of water since I'm parched." He stood and crossed the room with greater energy than when he'd entered, disappearing into the kitchen.

Scott pulled his cell out of his pocket, finger poised over the Message app. A million weird things had happened within the span of ten minutes, and he needed a solid dose of Derek to bring him back down to earth. Instead of texting, he returned his phone to his pocket, smiling as his dad returned to the room with two glasses in his hands.

Scott felt well rested on the bus ride to Sacred Heart for his next match, but only because he'd skipped three practices. Each night his father told him stories of their past, some of them sad. Most of them pleasantly nostalgic and bringing with them a mood of happiness.

His teammates texted him after the first missed practice,

knocked down his door after the second, and cornered him in the cafeteria on the third day with Coach in tow.

His conversation with Coach hadn't been pleasant, especially since Scott still wouldn't provide specific details about why he missed practice. He could've trusted Marcus, but something inside wanted to keep the new relationship with his dad private for a while. At least until he felt confident they were forming something lasting.

Derek lay cradled in Scott's arms, sleeping peacefully. Scott sniffed in his scent, then reclined in the bus seat and observed the scenery. Trees sped by, mostly pines, brown and green blurring together.

Patches of light cut through the branches, revealing a bright, cloudless blue sky. The night before, his father had recalled the story of Scott's first tree climb. He'd been three and had actually climbed a really big rhododendron bush. Still, his dad had told him about how Scott giggled.

"Look, Daddy, green. Look, blue," he'd said, pointing his tiny fingers up toward the sky.

"That's right. The sky is blue."

"Daddy. Daddy. That cloud looks like a birdie!" He'd become so engrossed in looking at the bird, he'd forgotten to hold tight and fell.

"Scotty!" His dad rushed to his side, carefully lifted him off the ground, and cradled Scott on his lap. "Are you okay? Let me look at you."

Scott smiled, remembering the last words his father said to end the story. "And I'll be damned, but you were beaming, even with a scratch etched in your cheek and another along your calf. Yet you were smiling and reached toward me calling out 'Daddy' and giggling in your cute little voice."

"Mmm. Everything okay?" Derek's voice cut through Scott's thoughts in a raspy whisper. "You squeezed me awake."

Scott wasn't quite ready to reveal the stories his father

shared over the past few days, wanting to keep them just for him and Dad for now. He kissed the tip of Derek's nose. "Do I need a reason to hold you tight?"

Derek let out a contented hum. "No." He sat up, stretching his hands above his head. "We almost there?"

Scott glanced at his watch: 7:00. "We have about half an hour before we get there. Then the match at eight." How had two hours flown by? More importantly, why did they have to have a meet at eight in the morning?

"You ready? You said the Sacred Heart wrestler is undefeated. What will your standings be after this match?"

Derek's question helped Scott to concentrate on wrestling instead of wandering down Memory Lane. He'd gone over his opponent's stats a million times, yet he hadn't thought of them once on the trip to the meet. "If I win, I'm pretty much guaranteed to be seeded number one for the tournament at the end of the season. If I lose then I could still seed two or three."

How he performed in the match couldn't have been more important. If he won, his victory would send a message to all other wrestlers in his weight class. So why wasn't he focusing every inch of his concentration on strategy?

Derek seemed oblivious to Scott's internal worries. "You'll win. Start getting yourself mentally prepared."

A soft brush of lips skimmed along Scott's jawline, ending beneath his ear. Scott tugged Derek close and closed his eyes, thankful no one could hear the turmoil rumbling about in his head.

SIXTEEN

The team arrived at Sacred Heart and were ushered to the locker room. Within ten minutes they lined up for weigh-ins. His competitor looked sturdy. Roughly the same height as Scott, maybe a bit shorter, but solid. Thick arms, powerful thighs, and bulging pecs. *Fuck.*

He'd wrestled his fair share of worthy opponents, but he'd been tracking his string of good luck. Wins on the mat. Successes with his dad off the mat. This was not the time to break a streak.

When his turn came to step onto the scale, the ref stood to the side. Scott let out a few short breaths and exhaled all the air out of his body. As if the lungful would carry enough weight to put him over the limit. He'd never been eliminated for not making weigh-in and never would.

Still, the whole process of standing-off against your opponent began by the scale, and when Scott met the other kid's eyes, he knew the match would be long and drawn-out.

"Zane." The Sacred Heart wrestler extended his hand.

Scott took the offered hand and shook, examining the guy's

face. No friendliness, but he wasn't trying to intimidate either. "Scott. Good luck!"

Fuck. Fuck. Fuck. And he's nice. Scott stood by the lockers, eyeing Zane while hoping he didn't seem obvious, and mapped out a mental plan of attack.

The Sacred Heart team left the locker room to warm up first, giving Scott a minute to unclench. Marcus sidled next to him and slung an arm over his shoulder. "That guy's a brick house, man."

Scott sighed out a half-laugh. "You don't need to tell me."

Marcus responded with a clap on Scott's shoulder and moved along towards the gymnasium with the rest of the team.

Why am I working myself up? He'd always brought his A-Game and he would bring his best with him onto the mat against… Zane…Who named their kid Zane anyways?

After five minutes their team took to the mat, warming up and getting their blood flowing.

The match began.

As one after the other of the BU wrestlers lost their matches, Scott glanced toward the sea of maroon occupying a small section of the stands. He spotted Derek, standing in front of the first row of benches in an empty space that separated supporters for each school. His jeans rode low on his hips and he wore a threadbare t-shirt. Man, if his ass didn't fill out those pants nicely. And the way his arms and chest stretched the fabric of his shirt, Scott wondered how the thing hadn't shredded.

Familiar stirrings buzzed through him, forcing him to look away.

Facing the mat shocked Scott out of his trance. The fuck? Greg, wrestling in the one hundred forty-nine spot, lay on his back, arching, unsuccessfully, in an attempt to lift his shoulders. No sooner had Scott registered the situation and the ref slapped the mat.

His heart skipped a beat and his stomach sank. No time to prepare himself. No last-minute pep talks to himself. It was time.

"Scott, you're up." Coach's voice cut through the screaming in Scott's head.

"Yeah. I know." He glanced at Coach, encountering a hard glare. Normally, he'd be right by Coach's side for the whole meet, but he'd not even been watching his teammate.

Silencing his thoughts, Scott took a purposeful step toward the mat. Then another. Snapping his focus and strategy into place, he stood tall and confident facing Zane.

"Shake hands, gentlemen." The ref waited as Scott and Zane shook hands, then he blew the whistle.

Zane hit at Scott's legs faster than a blink. A second later, Scott found himself on the mat, Zane overpowering him. What the hell? Scott swung his legs out in front of him and twisted, propelling himself out of Zane's hold.

Within ten seconds Zane earned a two-point take down and Scott earned a one-point escape. Time to get his head in the game.

For the next thirty seconds, they circled each other, but whenever Scott saw an opening to scoop Zane's legs out from under him, Zane changed tactics.

And then, like lightening, Zane shot for Scott's legs. This time Scott saw the move coming and sprawled, his chest landing on Zane's back. He pivoted—thank God for spin warmups before each meet—and secured a hold.

Three to two, Scott up by one point.

The rest of the period, Scott struggled to keep his hold, then exposing Zane's back to the mat. In fact, it seemed the seconds ticked at a slow-motion pace, lactic acid building up as Scott used every muscle in his body to keep Zane beneath him.

When the ref blew the whistle ending the first period, Scott slid off Zane, panting way harder than he should've been after two minutes of wrestling.

For the second period, Scott started in the bottom position. When the ref blew the whistle, Scott shot his legs out, as before, but this time Zane was ready for him. Hooking one of Scott's arms, Zane allowed Scott's twisting motion to carry the two of them in a clumsy circle, ending up right back where they started, Zane in full control.

And then Scott realized why he'd been worried about Zane's muscles.

With a push of his feet against the mat, Zane flattened Scott belly down, then slipped an arm under Scott's, beginning the grueling process of torqueing Scott over in an attempt to expose his back to the mat for points. Two seconds of exposure earning two points, three or more earning three.

Scott clenched his arms together, trying to break the hold. He could sense each muscle contracting, sucking precious energy reserves from him. He stopped for a second to regroup and try again.

As with the first period, the entire two minutes consisted of Scott in an endless struggle to free himself from Zane's hold. He hadn't allowed Zane to expose his back, but he pushed himself up with wobbly arms to stand so Zane could take bottom position.

He shook his arms out a few times, studying the scoreboard. Three to two, Scott leading by one point.

Lowering himself on top of Zane, Scott realized his legs weren't in much better shape. Sweat poured down his neck. Combining his own dampness with the sweat on his opponent made getting a solid grip nearly impossible.

Scott took in a deep breath, prolonging the beginning of the third period. Like an extra few ticks on the clock would help to restore his depleted energy.

The ref blew the whistle.

Zane shot out of his grip in less than a second, hopping to his feet with far more nimble finesse than Scott could hope to muster. He didn't have time to curse the missed practices and workouts, which would surely have given him the stamina he needed.

On the next eye blink, Zane shot for Scott's legs, securing

them and taking Scott to the mat. He wasn't too tired to do the mental calculations in his brain. One point escape. Two points take down. The scoreboard now displayed five to three, Scott lagging behind.

He could make out general sounds coming from the edges of the wrestling circle. His teammates, most likely, telling him what to do. A more clouded din came from the stands, although Scott couldn't distinguish between those cheering him on and the home team spectators supporting Zane.

Forcing himself to buck backwards, Scott pushed to his feet and ducked out of Zane's grip. One more point for Scott, but he still trailed behind five to four.

He locked arms with Zane, gripping an elbow, but Zane was too slick and fast for Scott to try a throw. Yanking back on one of Zane's arms forced him to step forward. Scott knew he wouldn't get *that* leg and keep it. Zane would be expecting such a tactic.

Instead, he waited until Zane brought the stabilizing leg back, leaving his other one exposed and vulnerable.

Scott pounced, drawing on the very last shreds of his energy. He scooped the leg up, immediately stepping between Zane's legs and bringing him to the mat in a backwards fall. Scott crashed his full weight onto Zane's chest and used what he knew would be a moment of shock to hook both of Zane's arms in his own. He fumbled for a few seconds, trying to scoop Zane's knees with the heels of his feet. If the guy couldn't put pressure on the mat with head or feet, Scott could ride the rest of the period out.

Scott could barely keep Zane's legs immobilized for more than pieces of seconds. Still, he exposed the guy's back and earned points on top of the two for the take down.

Zane arched and spun, flopping hard onto his stomach, then pushed himself onto hands and knees despite every one of Scott's efforts to stop him. Seconds later, the two were standing, facing off again.

Two points take down and two or three back points puts me ahead eight or nine to five. One point escape for Zane, so worst case scenario, I'm ahead eight to six.

He didn't dare glance at the score, needing to ride out however much time remained on the clock trying for a takedown.

They circled, each gripping the other experimentally. Scott used the seconds to draw in ragged breaths, grateful his muscles weren't on full throttle.

Whether a quick shove to his shoulder, or perhaps a pull to the other arm, Scott couldn't tell as he fell off balance. Before he could hop away from his opponent, Zane attacked his legs and Scott tumbled down, smacking his cheek hard against the mat.

Zane pounced, somehow wrenching his arm to secure a half-nelson—a human crane, or a bulldozer, the way he steadily twisted Scott from face down to his side, and then toward his back.

Scott fought against the move, curling his arm with all of his might to break the hold. His biceps bulged, over-swelling with blood from the effort.

Every time he tried to maneuver himself back to his stomach, Zane counter moved.

Whereas the sideline noise had been hazy before, Scott clearly heard Coach's voice. "Roll through it."

To roll through a half-nelson ran the risk of allowing Zane to secure his grip and secure Scott's shoulders to the mat. As it stood, he trailed by at least one point, maybe two. The only move to win would be an escape and takedown or a reversal and back points. Either choice required Scott to take a huge risk.

No time to contemplate. Better a tie than a loss and he wasn't about to let his lucky streak end with this match.

Dad counted on him.

His team counted on him.

Time moved at a pace Scott couldn't measure. He could

have thirty seconds left or two, but he already felt like he'd been wrestling for hours.

Digging to the very center of his core, Scott prepared for another burst of effort to muscle out of the hold. He pictured his move, knowing he'd have to exert greater force on his already worn-out biceps. How much energy Zane had left, Scott couldn't tell, but he felt like he fought against a brick wall.

On a mental count of three, Scott squeezed his hand into a fist, the one attached to the arm being yanked like a rope, and flexed as hard as he could, trying to force himself back to his stomach. The effort conjured an image of trying to punch a rock with someone holding his arm back.

He budged an inch, his body tilting so his chest at least angled toward the mat. He could do this. He could get to the safety of his stomach and escape for the tie.

Zane must have had the same thoughts as Scott because he surged into Scott with rocket launching force, not only rolling Scott to his side, but all the way to his back. The seconds counted down and Zane's points ticked up.

Scott's shoulders never touched the mat, but when the final buzzer sounded, Scott knew he'd lost.

He fell to his back, chest heaving, as reality sank in. He'd lost, for the first time in his college career.

His streak was over.

He'd let everyone, especially his dad, down.

He flipped to his hands and knees in order to prop himself up and stand. Zane stood in the middle ring, looking worn and covered in a thick sheen of sweat.

Scott approached, each step like a march of supplication to his victor, and, once he reached the center of the mat, extended his hand to Zane in keeping with tradition at the end of each match.

The ref placed one hand on each of their wrists, and raised Zane's in triumph. Scott peeked at the scoreboard. He'd been right. If he could only have escaped, at least he would have tied nine to nine. The back exposure earned Zane three points and a victory score of twelve to eight.

Before Scott could skulk away, Zane gripped his shoulder, pulling him close. “Nice match, man.”

And damn it all to hell. He’s a good sport too.

The absence of typical chatter and rehashing of matches filled the bus with a loud, heavy silence. All but three of the team had lost.

Scott consigned himself to a miserable ride and closed his eyes. Maybe he could sleep away his disappointment.

No such luck.

“Thayer. Up here. Now!” Coach’s command cut through the quiet of the bus with reverberating power.

A quick exchange of glances with Derek and Marcus told Scott they had no idea what Coach wanted either. He climbed over Derek and ambled toward the front of the bus, a walk of shame as he passed each of his teammates. Coach loomed large in his seat. With a final mental reminder he could take whatever came next, Scott plunked down in the empty seat next to the lumbering and scowl-faced man.

“Something’s up with you.” Coach wasted no time diving right in. “You’ve missed practices. You’re out of shape and today you lost an important match. One I think you could’ve won if you had your priorities straight.”

Flames burned an angry path through Scott’s chest. Nerve endings shot off warning signals, his fingers and toes clenching and unclenching. Fight or flight with nowhere to run.

“I told you. I have some personal stuff going on right now.” Scott struggled to contain the string of words he’d surely regret later.

“Not good enough!”

“I’m sorry about today. I’ll try not to miss any more practices. I'm probably more disappointed about today than you are." No need to tell him the disappointment came in the form of fear. He'd broken his streak. What did that mean for Dad?

"Do you hear yourself? You'll *try* not to miss any more practices." Coach gritted his teeth together, his jaw muscles bulging. "I'm trying to understand, kid. I can't help you if you don't tell me what's going on."

Scott studied at his hands. Maybe the words he needed to get out of this conversation would magically appear. "I appreciate that coach, but I'm not ready to talk yet."

Coach slammed his hands on his lap. Scott whipped his head up at the sudden, aggressive movement. "We need everyone's head in the game. Yours isn't."

Scott bit the inside of his lip, twitchy hands and burning anger resurfacing. He wouldn't get anywhere by snapping at Coach. Better to say nothing.

"You got nothin' to say. Maybe you shouldn't be on the team while you work your *stuff* out." Coach locked eyes with Scott, daring him to respond.

"Do what you have to do, Coach." Scott stood without waiting for permission and slunk back to his seat. At least he hadn't disrespected Coach.

Derek remained relatively quiet for the rest of the ride, chatting occasionally with Marcus, who sat across the aisle from him.

Back in their room, he seemed anxious, pacing back and forth in the small space between the two beds.

"Something on your mind?" Scott hadn't meant for the question to come out sarcastic, but Derek stiffened nonetheless.

Derek relaxed for the first time since they'd left Sacred Heart. "So, wanna talk about it?"

Scott cupped Derek's cheek. "Actually, I think I'd like to go home and talk to Mom."

Derek's mouth fell open and snapped shut again. To his credit, he rebounded pretty well. "Whatever you need."

Scott scratched the back of his head. "Uh, actually, could I borrow your car? My muscles are dead, so jogging's out of the question, and I don't want to deal with public transportation right now."

Derek crossed the room to his desk, scooped up the keys, and tossed them to Scott. No words needed. He simply started fiddling with his laptop.

Scott gripped the keys, stole a sparing glance at Derek, and left the room with a quick, "I love you."

"You too." Derek looked up at Scott for a second, but his relaxed expression let Scott know Derek was okay.

Twenty minutes later, he pulled up in front of the house he'd moved to a few years earlier, the only one where he'd experienced any happiness except for his first home. He padded up the steps and let himself in. "Mom."

His mother came out of the kitchen in a rush, her hand over her chest. "Scott. You scared me half to death." She took a deep breath, crinkles forming on her brow. "Is something wrong? Is Derek all right? Did something happen with your father?"

Scott couldn't help a chuckle. "No, Mom. Nothing like that. I lost my match today against the Sacred Heart guy."

"Oh." His mother placed her hands on her hips, shaking her head a few times. "And you couldn't call before coming over?"

Bristles rose along Scott's spine. "Why should I call? Aren't I welcome here whenever I want?"

Mom's snicker did nothing to sooth Scott's irritation. "Looks like someone's in a mood." She turned from Scott and reentered the kitchen. "You hungry?"

Since she asked, Scott realized he was starving. "Whatya got?" As if he'd refuse anything. His stomach growled in agreement.

"Oh, a little of this and that. Want some coffee?" His mother's voice bounced merrily through the air, lifting a bit of the weigh Scott seemed hell bent on carrying around.

"Coffee, but only if you already have some ready." He

clomped up the stairs, shedding and slinging his jacket over his shoulder as he went.

"It's no problem, dear. Two secs."

Scott took a seat at the table and watched his mother move about the kitchen with a relaxed ease.

Finally, once she'd thrown together a turkey sandwich and set the coffee to brew, she sat next to Scott, setting her elbows on the table and resting her head in her open palms. "So, to what do I owe this pleasure?"

Again with the cheerful voice. He couldn't remember his mom ever living so carefree and easy-going. He only remembered a quiet nervousness and twitchy movements, like a bird, whenever his father was home. "Just feeling down and wanted to see you."

Mom sat upright, head tilted slightly to the side and eyes penetrating straight through him. God, Scott hated when she looked so maternal. Like he was so fragile he might break. "Aw, sweetie, it's just a match. You've lost matches before."

He knew she wasn't belittling his sport or his loss, so the comment actually sank in. Why was he so upset about this loss? Sure, he'd hoped to enter the tournament with an undefeated record in order to boost his own confidence, but a loss didn't mean he wouldn't get a good seed in the rankings, and he could still take the weight class with a lot of hard work and no more skipped practices.

The last thought caused Scott to squirm in his seat. No missed practices? He'd never wanted to before, but over the past couple weeks, wrestling had felt more like a burden than a passion.

Plucking thoughts out of his head, Mom placed one of her hands over Scott's. "Why didn't you win today?"

"Because I wasn't focused."

"And what were you focused on instead?"

"Dad."

She nodded, a knowing smile on her lips. Had she known all

along this moment would come? "Care to fill me in?" Had she started taking lessons from Derek on how to probe to the deepest part of his soul?

Still, the questions led him exactly where he wanted to go.

Unsure why he'd become so defensive, Scott reminded himself he'd come specifically to talk to his mom. "I've been spending more time with him and I missed a few practices this week and, well, I wasn't ready for today's match."

"There's nothing wrong with spending time with you father, and I certainly don't think missing a few practices is going to ruin your whole season." The perfect, understanding comment. "Why did you choose to skip practices this week?"

Coming from Mom, maybe because of their shared history together with Dad, the answer to the question he'd struggled with solidified. "Because Dad's telling me stories about when I was younger, before we moved around. I like knowing he paid attention. Maybe I was too young to recall everything, but as he tells the stories, I feel like I can remember them."

Mom extended her hand and brushed his cheek. "You've come a long way, kiddo."

Scott didn't need to ask. He knew what she meant, but it still felt good hearing her say so. "What has you in such a good mood? You're practically dancing around this place."

Did a sudden a blush color his mother's cheeks? "Well, I haven't had a good time to mention this, but now seems the perfect time. "I've sort of met someone."

He laughed with a loud "Ha!" and slapped a hand over his mouth. "Sorry. You sounded like a teenager." He observed his mother through a new set of lenses, ones other men might use. Despite all they'd been through, she still had a great figure, good looks, and most important, a resiliency. Just like Scott, she'd pieced her life together. "Sounds like you've come a long way too."

A dreamy kind of somewhere-out-there expression caused

her features to relax and glow. "Yes," she finally said, "I suppose I have."

"Tell me about him. What's he like? What's he do? When do I meet him?"

The blush deepened, but she locked eyes with Scott, merriment sweeping away, replaced by a thinning of her lips. "You didn't come here for that. I want to talk about your father and wrestling. That's what's bothering you."

Taking ownership, leading their discussion, parenting him. Everything he'd always hoped she'd do happened over the span of ten minutes. The lump in his throat surprised him when he tried to speak. "I don't know what's going on with me. My priorities are shifting, I guess. Wrestling doesn't seem like the most important thing I want to do anymore."

"And that scares you?"

"Hell yes."

To her credit, the corner of her lip only twitched and she made no comment about his language. "It's all part of growing up." She plowed on before he could roll his eyes. "What I mean is, the older you get the more perspective you have on things. Right now, your dad's come back into your life and is giving you something you've always wanted from him. Wrestling has always given you what you wanted, but for the first time, it's interfering with things you'd rather be doing."

"I know. What I don't get is why I can't make space for both. I've always been good at balancing things. I had to." The last comment might have been unnecessary as he'd blamed her as much as he'd resented Dad for his unstable upbringing, but his mother didn't react.

"Yes, in a rational way, you understand what's going on, but what about emotionally? Have you considered that?"

Scott waited for the punch line. Did he consider his emotions? He couldn't possibly exist in a relationship with Derek without examining his emotions at least once a day. "Of course."

"And what are they telling you?"

Scott's blood to pump a bit faster. "I'm feeling frustrated."

"Because…" her voice hung in the air.

"Because I can't seem to manage all the things I need to."

"Which are…"

A serious thought of storming from the table almost made Scott get out of his seat. Instead, he closed his eyes and considered the things in his life battling for attention. His dad, wrestling, Derek, classes. Although none demanded time he didn't want to give, he didn't have enough time to fit everything in.

With more than a little bit of petulance, Scott conceded his mother had carried him down the right train of thought. "I want to experience this thing with Dad all the way, not half-assed." He glanced down at the table. "Sorry."

She gave Scott's forearm a squeeze. "And wrestling takes up so much time you feel like you're being…half-assed…in your time with your father?"

Wow! His mom never swore in front of him. "No, my mind isn't focused on wrestling and I'm not mentally in the game. That's not fair to me, the team, or…"

Dad.

He'd never wanted to invest time in in his father before. "Actually, yes. I think because I'm enjoying my time with him, and he's filling in spaces inside me I always thought would remain empty, it's like I'm starving for his attention and every minute feels like it's important right now."

A short intake of breath caught Scott's attention. His mother raised her hand to her chest and remained silent before continuing. "Then you need to take a break from wrestling."

"Mom, I didn't mean–"

"I know." She wiped at her eyes even though Scott couldn't see any moisture forming. "I wish I'd been stronger for you. It's a regret I have to work through." She shook her head. "But we're not talking about me and I know how hurt you've been by your father's absence. Which is why I believe taking a break from wrestling is the right choice."

"I can't."

She smiled. "Sure you can."

Could he? Everyone counted on him. Wrestling became the one thing he counted on no matter what. Well, until Derek came into the picture, but Derek and wrestling never pulled for his time in one direction over the other.

"I know you have a strong sense of loyalty and commitment. Once you start something, you finish it." Mom stood. No! She couldn't walk away! She ambled over to the coffee machine and poured him a cup. Scott relaxed.

Placing the cup in front of him, she took her seat again. "Sometimes you have to direct fierce devotion toward yourself. It's not always about everyone and everything else. Sometimes you should be your own primary focus."

Completely the opposite thing he'd expect any parent to ever tell their child. "So, you're telling me to be selfish." It wasn't a question.

"Yes. In this, your need to be with your father is more important than wrestling. If your coach and teammates can't accept that, it's their problem. The question is, can *you* accept it?"

Baffled by his mother's words, he racked his brain to remember what *it* was. *Right. Needing time to do what's most important to me.* Why shouldn't he put his own needs first? *Because it's plain selfish.* Scott snapped his head toward his mother. "My God."

Shannon froze. "What is it?"

"I realized I see myself as selfish." He dropped his head onto his folded arms resting on the table.

"Oh, honey, you're being way too hard on yourself, and maybe a wee bit dramatic."

He suppressed the urge to flip his mother off, managing to keep his reaction to a simple grunt.

"Think about it. You've never had a say in anything that's

happened to you. At least not until we moved here." She paused, piquing Scott's interest enough for him to raise his head and look at her. "Except for wrestling. You took to wrestling like a fish takes to water."

"Adages, Mom, really?" Scott dropped his head onto his arms again, running through the many ways he'd been a selfish, little brat over and over again. Playing sports because he thought being an athlete would get his father to pay attention to him. Getting good grades to spite his father who rode him for every A- he earned. Pushing his own needs onto Derek, who'd been nothing but a rock for him.

Mom ignored his comment, seemingly unaware of the running tally of egocentricity he generated internally. "Look. All I'm saying is you deserve a chance to get to know your father. I mean, I did marry him for a reason. You never got a chance to meet the man I fell in love with."

The genuine outpouring snapped Scott out of his own head. He looked at his mom again, this time as a woman and not just the person who'd given birth to him. She was a person who saw deeply, even though she tended to remain at the fringe of everything around her.

Scott took his turn covering his mother's hands with his own. "Mom. You never said anything about this before."

"What could I have said? By the time you were old enough to even begin to understand what I'm saying now, Dad had… changed." She withdrew her hands from Scott's grasp and folded them on her lap. "I suppose I could have done more to pave the way between the two of you, but to be honest, once you were old enough to join little league teams and go on trips, he was never around.

"And you were changing schools so often you'd become quiet. It took at least six months at every new school before you even started to come out of your shell. Then, wham, we'd move again."

"Mom." She ranted and Scott couldn't see any discernible

relationship between the various things she said. "I'm kind of losing your point here."

At least she laughed instead of looking hurt. "You're right. Maybe I should be spending some time with your father too. There are several wounds I carry he could help begin to heal." Her eyes lit up and she sucked in a short breath. "And there it is."

Scott opened his mouth to speak but his mother raised her hand, cutting him off. "Sometime life offers you windows of opportunity. Moments you can seize before they pass you by. Right now, with your dad, you have a tremendous opportunity to bring closure to some of the hurt and damage. You have a chance to get to know him and, I assume, to confront him with the ways he's hurt you."

Mesmerized, Scott remained silent. He wouldn't have known what to say even if he tried.

"Do what you think is best, Scott, but know you may have a limit to this kind of time with your father."

Not something he wanted to think about. A day earlier he'd been so sure everything would work out exactly the way he wanted. He'd save his dad, take the tournament, live blissfully with Derek, and live happily ever after.

"Should I just tell Coach and the guys, it's been nice knowin' ya. Later dudes." He didn't even try to cut the sarcasm from his voice.

His mother shook her head. "So stubborn. You always have been. You sit down with the coach and explain to him your situation. You gauge his reaction, remain strong in your convictions, and maintain respect no matter how he responds."

Could smoothing things over with the team really be that easy? "He's going to be disappointed in me. The guys will too. Especially Marcus."

"Honey, they aren't the ones who have to live your life." She picked up Scott's still-full mug. "That's probably cold by now."

As his mother strolled to the sink, Scott got out of his chair. "Mom." She turned to face him. "I love you so much."

She placed the mug on the counter next to hers and opened her arms, the same way she used to do whenever Scott was upset or hurt himself growing up. "I love you too, sweetheart."

Scott sank into his mother's embrace. She slowly rocked him as they stood there, holding one another. If he could've stopped time and remained in her safe embrace he would have.

But he couldn't hide in his mother's arms. He needed to talk to Coach.

SEVENTEEN

Derek still sat at his desk when Scott returned to their room, earbuds in and staring at his computer screen. Mixing most likely. He looked up when Scott entered, his smile immediate, although it didn't light up his entire face.

Well, no big surprise there. Scott had basically clammed up and left Derek to his inevitable worrying.

Scott crossed the room and stood behind Derek. He placed his hands on Derek's shoulders, mentally cursing himself at the knots he hadn't expected to find. He kneaded slowly, squeezing with practiced force at the muscles running from Derek's neck to his shoulders.

Derek groaned, resting his head on Scott's abdomen. He popped out his earbuds and sighed. "That feels like heaven."

Scott inhaled deeply as he kissed Derek's head. The musky scent of his lover surrounded him, igniting familiar stirrings. His cock started to fill out, but this wasn't the time for ravaging his boyfriend. He needed to open up about his deepest thoughts without prompting.

"I've made a decision."

Derek stiffened, his shoulders tensing noticeably. Scott gave them one more squeeze, then took Derek's hand and led him to the couch. "I'm taking a break from wrestling."

Derek's mouth fell open. "Wha—"

Scott blurted, "See, the thing is, today's match showed me something I've been trying to hide from. The match wasn't important enough to me to make it a priority. You are."

"Scott." Derek tried unsuccessfully to twist out of Scott's grip, "I never asked you to—"

"I know. Dad's been telling me stories over the past few weeks. About when I was younger."

"You never told me." Derek tried to turn again and this time Scott let him.

"I wasn't trying to hide anything. It's…I don't know. I've never had something just for me and Dad. These stories are like our special way of connecting." Scott uttered a silent prayer, hoping Derek wouldn't take offense.

"I totally understand." Derek stepped forward, wrapping Scott in a tight hug.

Scott swallowed against the damn lump in his throat, which seemed to make frequent appearances lately. "Anyways, I feel like it's more important for me to spend time with my dad than to devote all my time to wrestling. Things are getting…" What? "Good" would seem a strange way to describe his current situation. "We're starting to know each other. He's reminding me of things I've either forgotten or blocked. Times he and I spent together before our first move, when things were more stable with his job and whatever."

Derek kept hold of Scott.

For his part, Scott said all he could think of to say and waited until Derek broke the silence.

Finally, after what might have been an awkward length of time with anyone else, Derek released Scott. His eyes shimmered with unshed tears, and his lips curved into the irresistible smirk Scott could never resist. "Wow."

Encouraged, Scott plowed ahead. "I need some help. How should I approach this with Coach?"

Derek laughed, snapping right back into his natural manner of therapist. "Tell him the truth. Exactly what you just told me. If he disapproves, who cares?"

Simple and perfect. Of course, Derek reiterated exactly what Mom said, but Derek's support cemented his decision. "Listen, about earlier."

Derek silenced him with a gaze so intense Scott lost his breath. "Do *not* apologize for holding onto your thoughts for a while. *Or* about going to your mom instead of talking to me."

Scott heaved a sigh, relieved Derek understood, although the new mind-reading abilities were a little frightening. "Okay. Still, you know it's not that I didn't want to talk to you, right?"

Something in Derek's expression softened, sadness mixing with love through a soulful gaze. "Of course I do. Everything you do lets me know how much you love me."

Relief. Regret. Happiness. Fear. A war constantly raging within him. At least he'd finally discussed what he needed with the two people who mattered most to him. "Mom said the weirdest thing earlier. She said there's nothing wrong with being selfish sometimes."

"There isn't. You're always putting other people first." Derek took Scott's hand in his own, turning it pad up and running a finger along the etched lines. He pushed on without making eye contact, his voice slightly softer. "I'll admit it kind of stung when you didn't want to talk to me earlier."

Scott moved closer and pulled Derek into his arms. "Baby, I know. I'm guess I've taken you for granted lately."

Derek sunk into Scott's embrace. "No, you haven't, but I love hearing the words." He slid an arm around Scott's waist and squeezed. "I've been worried about you."

"I think you can stop worrying so much. This feels right to me." He'd go to the athletic complex on Monday and talk to Coach before practice. *Rip the Band-Aid off, right?*

With Derek pressed against him, Scott mapped out the next few steps he'd need to take. He'd made a bunch of decisions without consulting his dad, but he couldn't foresee any resistance. In fact, his father would probably enjoy the extra time they could spend together.

Scott held Derek at arm's length, needing to see his face, waiting until their eyes locked before speaking. "Will you come and spend some time with me and Dad?"

Derek's grin spread all the way across his face. "Yes!" He flung his arms around Scott's shoulders and hugged him tightly.

Scott cringed at the unfamiliar sound of Derek's sniffling. *Shit.* "What's wrong? What did I do?"

Derek's muffled response took some effort to understand. "You asked me to come spend time with your dad."

Scott squeezed Derek tighter. "Jesus."

In bed, Scott found himself staring at the ceiling. "I'm shittin' bricks about talking to Coach."

"Go in and say what you have to say. You can't dictate how Coach reacts." Derek kissed Scott's cheek. "But from what I know about him, which isn't much, I think he'll be okay with it. Disappointed, but he's not a monster."

Derek was right, for the most part. It didn't change the guilt at abandoning a whole bunch of people. "I hate I can't do everything."

A puff of breath wisped over his nipple as Derek chuckled. "I know." Propping himself on an elbow, he gazed down at Scott. With the darkness, Scott mostly saw the silhouette of Derek's frame, although his pale skin seemed to radiate slightly with its own glow. "Twenty years from now, are you going to look back on this moment and wish you hadn't taken some time to spend with your dad?"

A resounding No! "You're right. I'm over-thinking things."

Derek settled back into Scott's arms and before long, his breathing evened out.

Scott wasn't far behind, but as he drifted off, images of him standing before Coach filled his mind.

Monday morning when Scott knocked on Coach's office door, he was greeted with a grim expression. "Come on in. Take a seat." Friendly enough, although lacking warmth, if ball-busting coaching could be considered warm.

Scott entered the room and tentatively sat down. "Yeah. Um. I need to talk to you about something."

Coach glared, his eyes boring into Scott's. Finally, he rested his arms on his desk, closing the distance between them and looming a big larger. "What can I do for you?"

No amount of planning, of which there'd been very little, would've prevented Scott's stomach from dropping to his feet. "It's about the meet this weekend, and some thinking I've done since then."

Coach raised his brow. "Go on."

"I was totally unfocused from the moment we left for Sacred Heart."

"No arguments from me. I already told you so." Coach reclined in his chair, appearing more relaxed. "So, what conclusion have you reached?"

"The thing is," he couldn't quite bring himself to meet Coach's eyes, "my dad's been going through a lot lately and I've been spending more time with him and—"

"Wait. Your dad? I didn't know you had a dad in the picture. You've never mentioned him before." Scott couldn't tell whether Coach radiated concern or irritation.

"Well, he wasn't until recently. You remember the thin guy sitting by my mom and Derek and his parents? That's my dad. He's got cancer." Scott took a deep breath before forging ahead. "He needs a bone marrow transfusion, so I got tested and I'm a match."

"That's good news, right?"

"Yes. It's really good. Great even." Scott fought against the rising nausea, thankful he hadn't eaten earlier. His morning coffee burned an angry trail up his esophagus. "And during the past few weeks, he and I have been spending a lot of time together. It's why I asked to miss some practices last week."

"I wondered why you were so vague with your excuses." Coach breathed in, puffing his chest. "Listen, Scott. A team can only succeed if they communicate and are honest. I appreciate your honesty now, but the guys look up to you. Not showing up for practice and then losing sends a bad message and hurts team morale."

Scott fought the anger crawling along his skin and closed his eyes to concentrate on easing his steel grip on his chair's armrests. "I'm not quite through telling you what you need to know." At least anger loosened his tongue.

"What more is there to say? I'm sorry about your dad and understand. I also know you're one of the most promising young wrestlers to come through this program in a long time." Coach sat taller in his chair, angling himself toward Scott. "I wouldn't be surprised if you get elected captain with Marcus next year after Max graduates. I don't think you realize how much you have riding on this season."

"Coach, I'm taking time off from the team so I can be with my dad." Scott fell back into his chair, finally able to look Coach directly in the eyes.

Coach stood with such force his chair rolled back and hit the wall with a loud crack. "You what!"

"I'm taking time off. Maybe the rest of the season. My dad needs me and, well, I guess I need him too." Scott stood, not knowing what else to say and preparing for a quick escape if necessary.

"You leave the team, you're off it completely." Coach set a hard gaze on Scott, seeming to grow a few more inches.

"I'm sorry to hear you say that." Scott's heart faltered but he wouldn't give Coach the satisfaction of knowing how badly the words stung. He marched toward the door.

Just as he grabbed the handle, Coach called out. "Hold up. Sit. I'm sorry. I didn't mean what I said." Coach gestured toward the seat Scott had vacated.

Scott sat back down, eyeing Coach warily.

"Listen. If you asked, I wouldn't know the first thing about how to give you advice about Derek, but dads I know something about." At least he wasn't yelling.

"Okay." Scott still thought the idea of hightailing it out of there seemed like his best option.

"So, your dad." Coach scratched the back of his head. "You're gonna donate bone marrow for him?"

"That's the plan." The chill of his tone would've kept ice cubes frozen.

"And you've been hanging out with him?"

Scott stood and brought his face closer to Coach's. "Listen, I'm not really in the mood to get into this right now. I wanted to let you know my situation and what I need to do about it." He started to leave but Coach grabbed Scott's wrist.

His hand balled into a fist, but one look at Coach and Scott regained control. For once, the man didn't seem angry. "Seriously, Scott. Hear me out." Once they'd both settled into seats, Coach picked up a pencil on his desk and tapped it against the glass surface of his desk a few times, and placed it back where he'd found it. "You don't see any way to fit both in?"

"Look, if you're trying to convince me to change my—"

"All right. I needed to see how serious you are before I let one of my best wrestlers go." He got up and rounded the desk, pulling up another chair and sitting next to Scott. "My dad passed from cancer. Twenty years now and it still chokes me up every once in a while."

Scott hadn't ever considered Coach having a life outside of BU. The guy wasn't married, no kids. It seemed his life revolved around the school. "I didn't know. I'm sorry."

"If you have a chance at helping your dad beat this thing, you gotta take it. I get that." He studied Scott, remaining silent long enough for Scott to start squirming. "You mind sharing why it's so important to you, aside from helping him get better, of course?"

Scott hadn't planned on telling his entire story, especially when Coach tried to strong-arm him into staying on the team. "I'm not sure what to say. There's a lot of history between me and him and I need to take advantage of the time we have right now." He hoped his explanation would suffice because he didn't plan on offering anything else.

Coach nodded. They both stood and took a few steps toward the door. "All right, then. I hope you find what you're looking for."

"Thanks." Too bad compassion had only come after bullying didn't work.

He'd stepped into the hallway when Coach's voice stopped him mid-step. "Scott."

Scott turned but said nothing.

"When you're ready to come back to us, we're here." He gave Scott a quick nod, then returned to his desk and picked up a folder.

The right words, although stated far too late and after damage had already been done. Saying nothing, he strode towards the building entrance.

He took his time going back to the dorm. He didn't have classes for another few hours and felt way more tired than he should after a weekend.

Derek exited the dorm just as Scott arrived. He gave Scott a hug and kiss, then stepped back and surveyed him.

He knew full well Derek would read him within seconds, but having made his decision and following through, a weight had been lifted. Even Derek's interrogations couldn't tire him out.

"He's an ass." Derek hadn't asked a question.

"Yeah, but he said I'm welcome back whenever I'm ready."

"What the fuck's that supposed to mean? He'll let you back on the team? Like anyone could beat you for the spot." Derek placed his bag on the ground, rolling up the sleeves of his sweat-shirt, his eyes narrowed to tight slits.

"Easy there, killer. No witch hunts today. I said what I had to say and now it's done." Scott scooped up Derek's bag and slung it over his shoulder, then hooked his other arm in Derek's, dragging him in the direction of his first class. "Let's walk together. I have a proposal."

"Ohhhh! I already like the sound of this."

"Not that kind of proposal. Wait, what kind of proposal do you think I mean?"

"Sex." Derek darted a quick glance at Scott. "Why? What kind of proposal did you think I…wait…did you mean?"

"Do you think I'd announce my proposal to you while walking you to class? When I propose, you're gonna be blown away." Thinking about the idea of marrying Derek had Scott's pants getting tighter.

The flush running up Derek's neck to his cheeks let Scott know the thought had the same effect on him. "So, what's this proposal?"

"A while back, after I started believing Dad is really trying, I asked him if he wanted to go camping with the two of us."

Derek stopped dead in his tracks, forcing Scott to face him. Despite the chill, heat radiated between the two of them, warming Scott by sheer proximity. A tear formed at the corner of Derek's eye and started a slow journey down his cheek. Scott started to wipe the tear away with his finger, but Derek grabbed his hand, holding it in place against his cheek. "I'd love that."

"Good, because I'm seeing Dad after class today and planned on asking him if he's free this weekend."

EIGHTEEN

SCOTT MADE AN UNANNOUNCED VISIT TO HIS DAD AFTER HIS eleven-thirty class. The doorman, who knew him by now, buzzed him through the doors.

He bounced on his feet impatiently as the elevator rose, desperate to tell his father about his conversation with Coach.

He knocked on the door and waited about a minute, listening to see if he could hear any movement from inside. When he couldn't he knocked again, a bit louder.

His chest clenched, a chill running up his spine, when he still couldn't hear evidence of movement. Whipping his cell from his pocket, he dialed his father's number.

One ring. Two. Finally, on the third ring, an answer. "Hel-lo." Dad's voice sounded thick and groggy.

"Dad. Are you in your room? I've been knocking on your door." He tried to keep the panic out of his voice.

"What? Oh. Yes. Dozed off. Must not've heard you. I'll be right there."

The line disconnected and Scott used the few seconds before his father opened the door to recompose himself.

Dad answered the door wearing a robe, the top portion of it

hanging loosely on his shoulders, his ribs and sternum prominent against pale skin. Scott fought back a gasp. "Everything okay?"

His father glanced at himself, then back at Scott. "Just tired. I'm sure I look much worse than I feel."

Scott certainly hoped so. "Seriously. You look worse than when I saw you on Friday. Is there anything you're not telling me?"

"No, Scott. This is how it works. I'm going to look a lot worse before we're ready for the transplant." He cracked a weak smile. "And thanks for the compliment."

If the man could joke, he couldn't be too bad. "Sorry."

"It's fine. Come on in." Dad gestured toward the couch. "What brings you here?"

Scott's cheeks flamed. "I'm sorry. I should have—"

"Relax. I'm happy to see you." He took a seat even though Scott still hadn't. "You're a bundle of nerves. Maybe I should be asking if everything's okay with *you*."

Was he completely obvious? "Actually, I've had a rough day already."

Dad glanced at his watch. "Scott, it's only two-thirty."

He couldn't help but chuckle. "Yeah. Well, I've always been an over-achiever. I can accomplish more by two-thirty than most can fit into a whole day." He clasped his hands, realizing they kind of flailed around as he spoke. "But the reason *today's* been a rough day is because I talked to my wrestling coach. I told him I'm taking some time off from the team to spend with you."

The little color left in his father's skin drained away. "You can't."

"You didn't ask me. I chose it." Scott took a seat on the couch, unable to get comfortable. "I thought you'd be happy." Familiar barricades started to swing into place. He'd learned how to protect himself against disappointment through extensive practice.

"Please, don't get me wrong. I'm thrilled at the sentiment,

but to give up wrestling," He glanced toward the window overlooking Boston Harbor. "I don't want this choice to be something you resent later."

Understandable, given their history. He waited until his dad faced him before speaking, leaving them in silence for a long, awkward minute. "I lost my match on Saturday because I'm not focused. I'm more interested in hearing the stories you've been telling me and feel like wrestling is a burden right now. This isn't so much for you as it's for me. Does that make sense?"

"Actually, it does. I find it hard to believe you've come to a place like this in such a brief period of time. I'd hoped I could repair some of the damage I'd done, but dared not hope our relationship could grow so quickly."

Scott rested his arms on his legs and looked at his father. "That's the point. The history. Sure, most of what I remember isn't so good, but you're helping me to recall things weren't always bad between us. I want more of this while—"

While what? He'd carefully avoided allowing his mind to travel too far past each day. Each new task. Blood test, compatibility, Dad's chemo-radiation. Next came transplant.

But the thoughts coursing through his brain extended beyond treatment and concrete plans. For the first time he considered the several possible branches the journey could take, one of them very, very final.

"While I'm still around to tell them?" His father asked in a soft voice.

"Yes." The brutal fact Scott didn't want to face. "I want to remember this time for the rest of my life. Whatever happens next, I want now to really count."

"I can tell you've thought this through and know what you want. Remember, you're the one who knows what you need. Promise me you'll return to wrestling when to the time is right."

Easy enough. "Of course." Scott settled back in soft cushion, pleased at the direction their conversation took. "I did come here to talk about something else. Remember I asked you to come camping with me and Derek? I thought this weekend would be great."

"I'm not sure camping is something I can handle right now. I'm weak. I don't think I could hike a mountain or sleep in a tent."

Scott kicked himself for not thinking of his father's physical condition. Just as quickly, a new idea formed. "What if it wasn't camping so much as a weekend getaway in a cabin? We could rent one somewhere in New Hampshire or Vermont. If you're not feeling energized you could stay in a bed and chill out while Derek and I explore." He'd saved up a bit of money through sparse living and Derek continued to rake in random mixing gigs for dorm parties. Why not spend it on something worthwhile?

"That, my boy, sounds like an excellent idea. Make the plans. I'm in."

Scott found a surprisingly affordable a cabin in Stratton, Vermont. A quaint town, where they could enjoy dining out and still feel like they were in the middle of the wilderness. Buttressed by mountains, forests, and lakes, all within walking or driving distance from their location, they would have plenty of different excursions to choose from.

Derek started a list of things they'd need before Scott even solidified plans. Such a simple thing, inviting Derek to camp with his dad, and he'd clearly made Derek happier than anything he'd done over the past year.

He should've known Derek would catch him in a moment of reflection. "What's going on in your handsome head?"

Scott crossed the room and, sliding his arms around Derek until his hands rested on Derek's ass, gave him a quick peck on the lips. "Nothing much."

Derek squinted and his mouth crinkled up, pulling toward

his cheek. Classic Derek expression whenever he tried to read someone. Finally, he simply kissed Scott on the cheek and returned to his list.

Scott waited outside his Friday afternoon mixing class. Right on schedule, Derek pulled up the curb and rolled down the window. "Need a ride, mister?"

Scott huffed a short laugh, tossed his bag into the trunk, and hopped into the passenger seat. "Did you thank your dad for lending us the car?"

Derek rotated his head slowly to the right, leveling Scott with an emotionless expression.

Scott held his fingers up in the peace sign. "Right. Stupid question."

The corner of Derek's mouth curved up. "If your dad's ready and traffic isn't too bad, we should make it to the cabin around seven and have time to go into town for dinner."

"Whatever the two of you want." Scott had no intention of overthinking anything this weekend. Saturday's plans would depend on the weather and they'd leave around noon on Sunday after a nice breakfast of whatever, doused in butter and maple syrup. Lots and lots of maple syrup. May as well take advantage of the fact he didn't have to watch his weight anymore. He'd simply enjoy time with the man he loved and the man he hoped to love again.

Thirty minutes later, with Dad in the back seat, they left Boston.

It didn't take long for city to give way to more open rural areas. Exit signs appeared less frequently, replaced by twists and turns and hills.

Scott switched from radio to CD once reception became spotty. Derek's mix of Happy from the Alliance party before Christmas, his present to Scott, filled the car. Whenever Scott listened to the mix, whatever stress he held dropped away as if nothing could tether him.

He closed his eyes, recalling the heat from Derek's body as

they held each other on the stage as the music played. The memory stirred familiar yearning, his cock beginning to fill out, as it had back then.

Derek cleared his throat, jarring Scott from his thoughts. He glanced to the side and caught Derek shaking his head. With a quick dip of his eyes to Scott's lap and then another toward the back seat, Scott realized what he'd done. He rolled down the window and let a blast of bitter air smack him in the face. "Sorry, about the cold." Scott twisted around so he could look at his father, "I farted."

Derek let out a choked laugh, gripping the steering wheel tighter.

Scott's dad, who'd been silent since he got in the car, scooted to the middle of the back seat so Scott could see him through his peripheral vision. "I know this song, but it's not like the version on the radio."

"I'm sorry. This is our travel music. I can put something else on if you want." Scott reached for the radio.

"No. I really like it. I've been so tired lately. This music has energy." Just then the part with the sirens kicked in. "Oh my. This is wonderful. My heart's beating faster. It makes me want to dance."

Scott didn't miss the way Derek sat a bit taller. Dad had no idea he'd praised the artist. Scott gave Derek another few seconds. After all, he never accepted admiration, always deflecting focus on others. On Scott.

"Derek actually mixed that song. Everything on this CD is Derek's work."

"Really." Eyebrows raised, his father nodded. "Impressive. How long have you done this sort of thing?"

"Mixing?" Derek kept his eyes on the road as he drove. "I've always played around with music, but the serious mixing started in high school when I noticed the tech board used by the drama club. I was fascinated by how one platform could control everything and wanted to learn more. I started hanging out with some of the tech geeks and they were all too happy to teach me what they knew."

"Were you into dramatics in high school?"

"No. I also wrestled. I miss it now."

And was that a little encouragement sent Scott's way? May as well lather on some more praise. "I've been trying to get him to join the team since the beginning of last year, but Derek's taken on a lot. He's an officer in the school LGBTQ club, The Alliance, mixes for parties, and is working to establish the school's crisis hotline and walk-in center for students who need someone their own age to talk to."

"Quite impressive. Your parents must be very proud of you." Dad squeezed Derek's shoulder.

Scott glanced at Derek, noting the slight widening of his eyes. Yeah, Derek deserved all the recognition he could get. "His parents can't shut up about him."

"Whatever." Derek's cheeks ran red.

Scott kissed Derek on the cheek. "Don't be modest. You've accomplished an amazing amount in a very short period of time."

"It's true," Dad chimed in from the back, "it's all too easy to fall into ruts, and there's safety in routine. Pay attention to these years. College is a training ground for how to live the rest of your adult lives."

Silence filled the car, thick and heavy. Scott wondered what Derek made of his father's comment. Knowing him, he probably dissected every word, exploring all the possible root causes of such a cryptic statement. To his credit, his next question didn't probe Dad's inner psyche. "So, Scott tells me you've been catching up on the earlier years of his life. Tell, me, where did he get his competitiveness from? He definitely gets sour when he doesn't win."

Scott winced, Derek's comment rubbing over the still open wound of his recent loss to Zane. Derek's hand on his thigh, the warmth of his touch and drumming of his fingers, settled Scott's nerves.

"Oh, Scott was always a very determined kid. We bought him his first bike, well tricycle, for his second birthday. Most children dread the thought of taking off the training wheels, but Scott would watch the bigger kids zoom up and down the street, their hands in the air, managing to pedal and balance themselves without holding the handle bars. He begged and begged for us to take the training wheels off."

Derek giggles. "I can totally picture it."

"Shannon and I had several fights about it. She insisted he would get hurt. I tried to explain how getting hurt was part of boys growing up. You have to fall down and get back up to learn how to persevere in life."

"Dad, you're awfully full of sage wisdom today." Scott tried to insert levity to his voice, but the two pairs of eyes that snapped in his direction suggested he hadn't been too successful.

"What happened?" Derek artfully redirected the conversation.

"Well, I ended up taking off the training wheels, telling Scott he could only ride on the grass until he got a sense of how to stay up." A chuckle emanated from inside his father's frail body. "I learned a bigger lesson than the one I wanted to teach my son."

Derek gripped the wheel tighter. "And what lesson was that?"

"If you tell your kid not to do something, it's as good as ensuring they'll do it." He shook his head. "Scott did well the first day. Trying and failing, over and over, the bike chain leaving grease stains on his body and clothes. Scratches running up and down his legs and arms."

A picture of the small bike with a black seat and silver body formed clearly in Scott's mind. He'd completely forgotten about it, along with the desire to ride like a big boy.

"The very next day, after I left for work, Scott took the bike onto the driveway. Luckily we had a large square of pavement in front of the double bin garage and another long strip of pavement leading to the road." Dad shook his head. "I'd only been at work for an hour before I got a frantic call from Shannon, screaming about how Scott had fallen off the bike and had a gash running the full length of his leg."

Scott laughed. "I remember. If blood appeared, she called it a gash. I had a nasty raspberry on my hip and a lot of tears, if I recall correctly."

"Yes, it scabbed over and wasn't really much bigger than the size of a sand dollar. Bruised up pretty nicely with purple and yellow coloring."

"Yeah, and Mom put those training wheels right back on the bike and wouldn't let me use it without direct supervision for a year." Scott could remember how panicked Mom had been. What a big deal she'd made over his injury. He remembered how much he craved his mother's attention while he was still hurt.

But he recalled the sense of pride, of feeling like a big boy, when his father came home, glanced at the cut, and rubbed his head. "Fell down and got back up?" he'd asked. Not worried at all.

"It wasn't a year. You're exaggerating." Dad's comment brought Scott back to the car. "Shannon policed the training wheels issue, so Scott moved on to new ways of exploring his body and balance. He climbed the swing set, trying to walk along the top ladder. The first time he fell his mother burned rubber on the driveway taking him to the hospital for x-rays. Literally left tire marks on our driveway, but Scott was right up there again the next day.

"It seemed he always had a new scrape or bruise every day from whatever misadventure he got himself into. Still, he'd always bound into my arms when I got home to tell me about what he'd done."

"My parents were the same way, Mom always coddling me

and dad pushing me to explore." Derek nodded at the road sign ahead of them. "We're about an hour away. Anyone need to use the bathroom or a take a stretch break?"

"I'm good." Dad gazed out the window, a far-off expression on his face.

Scott turned the volume of Derek's mix up and for the rest of the ride they listened to the music, the lack of conversation no longer stifling.

By the time they arrived at the cabin, Scott's father snored gently in the back seat. In sleep, he looked peaceful, but the hollow of his cheeks and dark circles beneath his eyes also seemed more pronounced. Scott touched his father's shoulder, shocked at the lack of muscle. A shake got his dad to open his eyes. He glanced around for a second, his gaze finally settling on Scott. "Did I fall asleep?"

"We're here. Let's unpack the car and get settled in." His dad still needed to use a cane, so Scott helped him into the cabin without grabbing any bags. He ushered the frail man to a couch over by a window overlooking a wooded area. "Derek and I will get the stuff. You relax."

Scott joined Derek at the car and helped unloading bags, hoisting several out at once. His back protested, but he muscled through, the strain distracting him from other more frightening thoughts.

He could sense Derek studying him, but Derek said nothing. He led the way back to the cabin and opened the door so Scott could maneuver himself and his load inside.

The immediate room upon entering was a large living area, and a small kitchen lay off to the right with a dining table separating the open space into two sections. Stairs led to a second floor. Scott fumbled his way, step by step, until he reached the top step, finding a small landing with a door on either side of the hallway and another in front of him.

Derek opened the door to the left, which turned out to be a

bedroom, then opened the other two, revealing a second bedroom and a bathroom.

Scott dropped the bags and heaved a breath. "Which room do you want?"

"They're identical so it doesn't really matter." Without waiting for a response, Derek grabbed his and Scott's things and brought them into one of the bedrooms, leaving Scott to set his father's stuff on the dresser in the other.

He knew he probably shouldn't snoop, but justified opening his father's suitcase as an act of generosity.

He regretted his choice as soon as he opened the case, counting at least seven bottles of pills in a plastic bag, nestled on top of clothes. Jesus. What could he need so many pills for?

He closed the suitcase and zipped it back up, deciding to pretend he'd never opened it in the first place.

Derek had already unpacked half of his clothes. Scott joined him and together they filled the dresser and placed their toiletries in the bathroom.

Before heading back downstairs, Derek grabbed Scott's arm. "What's wrong?"

He should've known Derek could read his discomfort. "I opened my dad's bag and saw a million bottles of pills."

He couldn't quite bring himself to look at Derek, embarrassed he'd been snooping in the first place. "Why does he need all those pills?"

"I don't know." Derek slipped an arm around Scott's shoulder, giving him a side hug. "And you can't ask because then he'd know you looked in his bag."

Scott tensed, urging a tighter squeeze from Derek. "It's not even about the pills. It's what they represent."

"I don't get what you mean." Derek released Scott and plopped down on the bed.

"I mean, he's so weak. He's so sick. The doctor explained this would happen, but to see it up close and personal—" Scott closed his eyes, hoping the darkness might block out images and thoughts he didn't want to face. The opposite occurred, so he opened his eyes. "What if he doesn't make it?" Tears blurred his vision.

Derek shot off the bed and tugged him into a tight embrace. "One step at a time. Let's go downstairs and figure out what Ronald wants for dinner."

They found his dad reclined on the couch and sleeping again. Scott's stomach rumbled, hunger mixing with worry and stress. "You think he'll be all right if we run out to get something to eat?"

Derek took Scott's hand, leading him toward the door. "He's sleeping, Scott. He'll be fine. There's a diner we passed a few miles down the road. I could go for something breakfasty for dinner." He brushed his lips against Scott's neck and blew against his ear.

Tightness eased from Scott's muscles, his mind able to focus on the warmth of Derek's breath, a stark contrast to the bite of the winter air. "I hope they have a lumberjack special."

Derek released Scott and, after writing a brief note, led him to the car and hopped into the passenger seat. "You drive."

Maneuvering the car around twists and turns on the dirt mountain road helped to take Scott's mind off his father. The sun had set, but a deep bluish-purple light still filtered through the black outlines of branches on leafless trees.

When they arrived at the diner, Scott's hunger ratcheted up a notch, his stomach groaning. "Man, I'm fuckin' starved."

Derek hopped out of the car without a word, walking toward the diner's entrance. Although chilly, Scott suspected his speed had nothing to do with the weather.

They sat at a table tucked off to a corner, silently perusing the menu. A minute later, their waitress arrived. They ordered two lumberjack specials, a side of fries, and vanilla milkshakes. Scott also ordered a burger, well-done, and chips to go for his father.

The waitress gave them a sweet, elderly nod. "You dolls

want some coffee or water while you wait?"

Derek flashed a toothy smile. "We're fine, thanks."

She winked at Derek and hustled toward the kitchen area, shouting, "Two Bunyans and a side of sticks and one burnt up cow."

Scott chuckled. "I guess I should've expected something like that in the northern woods of New England."

"It's charming." Derek rubbed his belly. "I hope the food comes out fast."

Right on cue, their waitress returned to their table, plunking two enormous plates down with a heavy thunk. Eggs, waffles, pancakes and bacon piled in sloppy heaps, leaving no surface uncovered. "Shakes'll be up in a minute."

They ate with quiet urgency for a few minutes, only stopping when their drinks arrived. Finally, after about five minutes, Scott leaned back, rubbing his belly on a deep sigh. "My God. Fantastic."

Derek simply nodded, shoveling another forkful of eggs into his mouth, managing a garbled, "Fuckin' right it is." He swallowed, then let out a large burp, instantly glancing around the room. Scott did too, noticing several people watching them. "Excuse me."

"I can't take you anywhere." Scott caught Derek's smirk, which lasted a fraction of a second before he stuffed some bacon into his mouth and bit half of it off with a growl.

Scott cut a wedge of pancake, three thick, fluffy mounds layered one on top of the other, forking it and lifting it in the air, but he didn't pop it into his mouth right away.

His thoughts travelled back to the cabin, to his father, alone, and suddenly his appetite seemed less intense.

"He's gonna be okay. It was a long trip. He's tired. Tomorrow we can do something easy like drive to some nice little vista and sit around a campfire and talk." Derek placed his hand on Scott's.

"How do you do that? Know exactly what's going on in

my mind?"

"Because I love you and I've learned to pay attention to the subtle things you do when you're feeling different ways." A simple statement, one Scott could easily make as well, although he certainly didn't have Derek's skill of insight. For the millionth time he imagined what an amazing therapist Derek would make one day. His future was so sure. So clear and natural. Like everything lined up perfectly for him.

As for his own future, Scott couldn't see past the next day, let alone where he'd be in five years or ten. "Do you think taking him on this trip is too much for him?"

"Why?" Derek placed the second half of bacon back onto his plate, focusing entirely on Scott.

"His treatments are taking a huge toll. What if he gets sick? Any complication could affect the transplant and it would be all my fault for planning this whole thing. And—"

"Stop." Derek's bark cut Scott off. "Do you think the doctors would let him go home at all if they thought the risk would be too great? He's fragile, but he's not broken."

"I know, but look at him. He's wasting away to nothing." Why did he have to poke holes in Derek's logic when Derek said everything he wanted to hear?

"What's this really about? I mean, I think I already know, but I want you to put it into words."

A flare of resistance ignited deep in Scott's chest, his urge to tell Derek not to psychoanalyze him poised on the tip of his tongue. Experience taught him, when Derek wanted Scott to talk, Scott talked. "I'm afraid."

"I know. I am too."

Scott snapped his gaze from their joined hands to Derek's eyes. "What?"

Heat radiated between them, warm and soothing, their bond as tethered to nature and Earth as trees rooted to the ground. "You're healing. You're letting your dad in. You may even love him a little bit now. And—" He caught his lower lip between his teeth, the war between continuing or clamming up evidenced in the crinkle of his brow. "If he dies, I'm afraid a piece of you will die too."

Scott considered Derek's words, not knowing what to make of them. The connection between him and his father had grown undeniably stronger. He certainly hoped for a future where they could one day have a relationship resembling the one he'd craved growing up, but he also knew the very real possibility of losing his father.

He tried to imagine a life where part of him was dead. How would living with and loving someone who'd lost a bit of himself affect Derek? Could Scott actually be what Derek deserved if he lost his ability to hope?

"Derek, I know what the possible outcomes are. I know my dad might not make it." Funny how he couldn't use the word "die." "I know I made this choice to be with Dad instead of wrestling because, deep down, I know this may be all the time I have left. I think, if I didn't take advantage of now, I'd be at far greater risk of losing an important piece of myself."

Speaking so frankly forced the rest of Scott's appetite out of him. "I'd rather look back on now and be able to say I did everything I could rather than play it safe and avoid a broken heart."

The intensity behind Derek's eyes eased up. He released Scott's hands and settled back against the booth cushion. "Wow. Just, wow."

"I know, right?" Scott caught a whiff of the food on his plate, his appetite coming back to life.

"Right." Derek returned to inhaling his food.

On the ride back to the cabin, Dad's burger and fries in a Styrofoam container, Scott plotted out the next day. An easy hike through the woods, a flat trail so his father wouldn't have to strain himself, followed by a relaxing evening sitting around a fire. Maybe he could prevent his father from sharing more embarrassing childhood. stories.

NINETEEN

SCOTT WOKE TO THE SMELL OF COFFEE WAFTING UP THE stairs, followed by a sharp sizzling sound. "You boys hungry?" His father shouted up the stairs.

"Dad?" A piece of Scott's heart swelled. Dad couldn't be in too bad shape if he got up before anyone else. "Yeah. Starving."

"I hope you don't mind," he called, "but I took the car to buy some groceries. Eggs, bacon, pancakes."

If Scott still wrestled, he'd surely not make his next weigh-in. Bad enough he'd eaten three days' worth of calories the night before, but to do it all over again the next morning? Not good. And so perfect. "We'll be right down."

Scott squeezed a yawning Derek close. "Dad's making breakfast for us."

Derek hugged Scott back, then peered at him. "Why are you acting like it's Christmas morning?"

"Because Dad's making us breakfast. He's up and took your car out and he's doing stuff. That's good, right?" Hope blossomed in Scott's chest, fanning through his body.

"Yes. Very good."

They made quick work of dressing and dashed down the stairs and wolfed down the food already set on the table.

"I thought we might find a nice place to do an easy hike." Scott held his breath, gauging his father's response.

"Absolutely. After the restful sleep yesterday, I'm ready to take on the world." Dad collected the dishes and brought them to the sink.

"I can get that, Dad." Scott shot out of his seat.

"Sit. Drink your coffee." His dad waved a hand absently in Scott's direction. "I can clean up."

Dished stacked up to dry, they tugged on thick winter jackets and ventured outside. Bright, evergreen pines offset a crystal blue sky, offering a sense of warmth despite the crisp air. Several trodden paths laced through the site. "Why don't we explore the woods behind the cabin?" Scott suggested.

The paths were well worn, fallen pine needles and crumpled maple leaves scattered where snow hadn't coated the ground. The wind died down as they ventured deeper into the woods, the chirps of birds serenading them. Every once in a while, a scuffling of leaves would draw Scott's attention and he'd catch sight of a chipmunk dashing from one hiding spot to another. Owls slept during the day, making this the only time they could safely find food.

As he'd hoped, the path stayed fairly level, several smaller offshoots winding into areas thickly settled with bushes.

After they'd hiked a mile or so, Scott heard a trickling sound. He inhaled fresh and clean air. "I bet there's a spring around here."

The three of them remained silent, unmoving, attempting to determine where the sound came from. It seemed to originate a bit further ahead of them on the path they were already on, so they continued until they reached a circular open area, clear of trees. To the right, rocks sloped up at hard angles, leading to a peak. To their left, a panoramic view of the mountains.

Stunned into silence, Scott took a few steps toward the spectacular view. He noticed an abrupt drop off and wondered at the absence of warning signs. The edge of the clearing consisted of large boulders, pine needles swept away by wind. In the middle, running from the mountain and over the edge in a mini waterfall, they found a thin stream, only about six inches wide. Moss grew on either side. Scott knelt down, cupped his hands, scooped up some of the icy water, and drank. He swallowed, feeling its path down his throat and settling in his stomach. "This is the best damn water I've ever tasted."

His father hobbled over and knelt down, scooping up some water for himself and tasting. "You're right. I think you found the fountain of youth. I feel energized. Scott, fetch my canteen from my bag. I want to bring some of this back to the cabin."

Scott handed over the whole bag and together, he and Derek watched as his father carefully lowered the opening into the stream. "This place is so alive."

Derek took Scott's hand. "Let's go to the edge of the overhang."

Scott glanced at his dad, who waved them on. "I'm going to explore near the rocks over there. Life thrives around natural springs. Even where life has died out in other places, nature has a way of renewing itself in spots like this."

Derek and Scott glanced at each other, then Derek shrugged and led Scott toward the outcropping of rock. At the edge, Scott noticed the substantial drop off, perhaps two hundred feet to more rocks below. "This is freaking gorgeous, but dangerous as hell." He reflexively placed an arm around Derek, pulling him close.

Derek slipped his arm around Scott's waist. "Maybe, but it's awe-inspiring."

They sat, allowing their feet to dangle over the edge. Scott glanced over his shoulder and spotted his dad stooping near the area of rock where the water originated from. Satisfied Dad didn't need immediate assistance, he returned to gaze to the scene before him. The landscape consisted of a mixture of lush pine and leafless maple trees. The evergreens colored the vista, a sharp contrast to the dark angles of bare branches spearing in different directions.

The further out he scanned in the horizon, the more blurred together the colors and shapes became. "Does it seem like Dad's being kind of philosophical?" He asked the question without looking at Derek.

"I'm sure he's been doing a lot of reflecting. After all, he's facing the biggest challenge of his life. It only makes sense he would kind of theorize about life and what everything means."

"Boys, come look what I've found!" Dad studied at something in the palm of his hand. "Come. Look."

Scott stood next to his father and glanced at the small green leafy thing. "It's a four-leaf clover." He tried to sound appropriately impressed, but wasn't exactly sure why a mere clover generated so much excitement.

"Do you know the odds of finding a four-leaf clover?" He didn't wait for Scott to answer. "Ten-thousand to one. That's means…," he crinkled his eyes, his lips moving slightly, "you have one one-hundredth percent chance of finding one." He nodded. Perhaps he thought his revelation explained the importance of the clover.

Apparently, Scott's expression must have seemed less enlightened, because his father laughed and patted him on the back. "It's a fairly common superstition that these particular clovers are seen as good luck. Probably because of the unlikely odds of finding one. If you're lucky enough to stumble upon one of these anomalies, it could mean you should expect good things in other areas of your life as well."

Funny, Scott had thought the same thing about his winning streak in wrestling.

Carefully, Scott picked the clover from his father's hand and studied the plant. He didn't feel any magical pulse from the small object, nor any tie with nature or fate. "That's awesome, Dad." He tried to infuse enthusiasm into his comment.

Derek, who'd been standing by their side, rubbed a small circle at the base of Scott's back. "Let's go back to the cabin and put it somewhere safe. Maybe we can preserve it." To Scott he whispered, "Do you not get what he's saying?"

"What a wonderful idea, Derek." Scott's father didn't wait for the boys to lead the way, grabbing his cane and shuffling with greater energy than Scott had seen in a while.

Scott followed behind him, considering his father's words. Luck. Scott certainly stumbled upon more than his fair share of luck in meeting Derek and with love in his life, everything else blossomed. It only took one catalyst to set everything else in motion.

Maybe that's what his father meant. The clover gave Dad hope.

When they entered the cabin, Scott hung back, watching his father and Derek dampen a paper towel, place the clover delicately in the middle, fold the napkin around it, and place the whole thing in one of the plastic shopping bags from his father's earlier shopping trip.

Derek tied the ends and placed the bag in the refrigerator. "I think it should keep nicely in there."

"I think it will. Thank you, Derek." Dad clapped Derek on the back and maintained contact. To Scott, he said, "He's a great catch. Hold onto him."

"I fully intend to." Scott crossed the room to where they stood and kissed Derek on the lips. "How about we drive around and see if there are any other areas we'd like to explore?"

Sitting around the fire, an orange glow flickered against Derek's face, casting shadows, highlighting his strong jawline and high cheek bones. His hair, slightly longer than usual, brushed lazily along his forehead. He gazed through the flames at Scott, his amber eyes glowing, and a wicked grin creeping into place.

Scott gasped, his cock sparking to life.

Still eye-locked with Scott, Derek asked, "So, Ronald, got any more stories of Scott as a young kid? Anything I might be able to reference in the future if he gets on my nerves?" He licked his lips slowly, his gaze unwavering.

Scott had no question about Derek's evil plan. None whatsoever. He planned on getting the information he desired. The way he stared let Scott know the events later on would satisfy a whole other set of needs and wants.

The throbbing of Scott's cock kept pace with his racing heart as he hung, suspended in a vulnerable limbo, between domination and submission.

"Well, there's the birthday party where Scott wouldn't keep his clothes on. Would you like to hear about that?" Dad couldn't have sounded more unaware of what was happening right in front of him.

Derek released his lower lip, a flash of white teeth flickering with the reflection of lively flames. "Would I ever!"

Heat raced up Scott's spine, forcing a shiver through his body. "This is not happening."

Derek hadn't broken eye contact with Scott the entire time. "Oh, it's happening." His voice dripped of sex. "It's gonna happen."

"Well, birthdays were always a big deal in our neighborhood." Dad remained blessedly oblivious to the double meaning behind Derek's words. "Families used the opportunity to get together and socialize. Needless to say, Scott's actions stuck with him right until we moved for the first time."

Derek finally severed eye contact, turning his attention to Scott's father.

For the next thirty minutes, Scott suffered through one of

the most humiliating stories of his childhood, knowing full well Derek would find some way to use it against him in some adorable and infuriating way.

Luckily, Dad let out a yawn at the end of the story. "Well, today has been fantastic, but I'm quite tired. Maybe we should call it a night."

Back in their room Derek took his time undressing. With the lights off, the moon shone through the window, creating interweaving lines of light and shadow along pale, muscled skin. "And to think, if I'd known you back then, I would have gotten a sneak preview of a naked Scott Thayer."

"I'm still mad at you." Scott could barely muster more than a whisper, his breath coming in short gasps.

"Uh huh." Derek sauntered to the bed and knelt on the floor between Scott's legs. He gripped Scott's belt, undoing the buckle with practiced ease. "Should I stop?"

"You know I was only two at the time." Scott propped himself on his elbows to get a better view of Derek's actions.

Derek lifted his gaze from Scott's groin and gawked at Scott. "Are you kidding me? I can't wait to get my hands on, what did Ronald say? Oh yeah, your teeny *weeny*."

Scott fell back, flinging his arm over his eyes. Maybe blocking Derek from view could ease some of his embarrassment. "You know full well I don't have a teeny weeny anymore."

Derek slipped his fingers beneath the waistband of Scott's underwear, pulling them down. Scott lifted his hips to assist, abandoning the pretense of anger. Warm fingers wrapped around his cock and lingering thoughts of righteous indignation flew out the window.

Derek nudged Scott's legs further apart. Hot breath skimmed along the surface of Scott's cock, forcing a slight tingle to rush along his skin. Steady strokes from the base of his cock to the tip had Scott groaning. He placed a pillow over his face, not wanting his father to overhear anything. Just in time, it would seem, since Derek close his mouth over Scott's cock and skillfully slid halfway down the mast.

He swirled his tongue around the head a few times, massaging the bundle of nerves under the glans. He withdrew, breathing slightly more heavily. "You're right. You definitely don't have a teeny weeny anymore."

Scott used the pillow covering his face as a weapon, smacking Derek on the side of his head.

Derek wobbled, but only a little, regaining his place between Scott's legs. "Big mistake." He slipped his hands behind Scott's knees and pushed them forward, diving between Scott's legs again. This time he bypassed Scott's cock, aiming straight for a far more sensitive target.

The first pass of tongue around Scott's hole turned quivering muscles to putty. Had Derek not been holding his legs, he would've collapsed in a useless heap. Instead, he used his free hands to grab his own ass and spread his cheeks further.

After an evening of Derek eye-fucking him around, Scott was more than ready to experience the real thing. Slick pressure nudged at his opening and he bit his lip to keep from crying out.

Derek worked with both index fingers, prying Scott open and thrusting his tongue inside.

Muscles deep in Scott's core contracted and released, churning his need for Derek to fill him more completely.

Derek pressed at Scott, urging him to scoot further onto the bed, crawling onto the mattress after him, and using his body weight to press Scott's legs even further apart. He probed one last time and sat back on his heels.

Scott lifted his head, unable to coordinate the rest of his body. Derek placed two fingers in his mouth and withdrew them slowly, then reached between Scott's legs and inserted them into Scott's entrance. Only a slight stretch instead of the expected burn. "Need you to fuck me."

Derek's grin morphed into a smirk. He slid one more finger inside of Scott. A slight burn sent a rush of electricity up Scott's spine, but wore off far too soon. "Please." His voice barely came out a whisper.

Something changed in Derek's expression. His eyes blazed a path up Scott's torso until he'd locked eyes with Scott. Wordlessly he bent forward, sealing their lips together.

Scott clung to Derek, afraid he'd fall into an abyss if he let go. Derek's weight settled on top of him, pinning him to the bed. He wrapped his legs around Derek's waist.

Without using his hands, Derek guided his cock until the head pressed against Scott's hole. Without warning, he plunged into Scott, sinking balls deep and stretching Scott from the inside out. "You want this?"

Scott thrust his hips against Derek's pelvis, attempting to draw even more of Derek into him. "God, yes."

Derek withdrew at a tortuously slow pace, only to slam back into Scott with enough force to cause his whole body to rock against the sheets. The bed gave a slight lurch, the legs scraping against the floor.

Neither of them spoke, but Derek stilled for a second. Scott craned his neck, listening for anything from his father's room. A snore echoed through the air.

After a brief glance at one another, Derek resumed, although with a bit less force than before.

Which was better and worse at the same time.

Derek took his time, gliding in and out of Scott, withdrawing all the way out just to the point of withdrawing completely and plundering him once more. Each thrust created a stretching burn, replaced by radiating warmth rushing through him.

Each wave increased in intensity, with Scott pushing back, trying to hold Derek deep inside.

Derek's breathing grew shallow, his gritted teeth gleaming.

Scott gripped his own cock and started pumping, his release building at an alarming rate.

After a few more pumps, Derek called out in a strangled voice, "I'm coming."

The first pulse of Derek's cock brushed directly against Scott's prostate and sent him flying over the edge, hot semen shooting across his belly.

Derek crashed on top of Scott, wriggling his hips in small rutting motions as he unloaded deep inside Scott.

After several spasms, Derek went slack, his head buried in the pillow next to Scott, panted breath blowing against Scott's neck. "Fucking amazing."

Scott still couldn't form full thoughts. Instead, he wiped the sweat from his brow. "Agreed."

Eventually, Derek rolled onto his back, a shock of air chilling Scott's sticky chest and belly, enough to relax his breathing and slow his racing heart. Scott cupped Derek's cheek, drawing their lips together in a soft brush of skin. "Let's clean up."

"Won't it wake your father?" Derek didn't show any indication of moving.

"Maybe, but he'll fall back to sleep." Scott slipped out of bed and yanked Derek so half his body hung over the edge. "Better put your feet beneath you."

"So pushy." Derek sounded indignant, although he had the shower going before Scott even stepped into the hallway.

Scott stood under the spray, partially holding Derek while also running a hand along his own body to get the dried come off his chest and stomach. Derek rested his head on Scott's shoulder, swaying a little and doing nothing to clean himself.

With the sliminess washed away, Scott pulled Derek close, the water falling over both their heads, enclosing them in a private waterfall for two. His simply wrapped his arms around Derek, resting his hands at the small of Derek's back.

Derek wrapped his arms around Scott's neck. "Thank you for inviting me to join you and your dad."

"There's nothing to thank me for. I wanted you here." *Despite the fact you've weaseled enough ammunition out of my dad to last you months.* "But if you ever tell anyone the teeny weeny story, no sex for a year."

Derek let out a full-voiced, "Yeah right!!" then covered his mouth, glancing toward the door. He whispered. "Like you could hold off for a year."

"Hey. My right hand and I were best friends for years before I met you. I've been meaning to get back in touch with him." Scott nipped at Derek's neck, loving the easy banter.

Derek stepped out of Scott's embrace, picked up their favorite mango-pomegranate body wash, and poured a healthy amount into his palm. A think, sudsy foam coated Scott's body as Derek scrubbed at his chest and stomach. Random sprays of water finding a path past Derek's body washed some of the soap away, a velvety trail of bubbles sliding along Scott's skin.

The crisp citrusy scent carried on the steam, filling the small room. He took the bottle from Derek and cleaned his lover, paying special attention to Derek's cock, buried deep inside Scott a few minutes earlier. Not surprisingly, Derek lengthened in Scott's hand.

Scott tilted his head to the side in order to catch Derek's expression. His eyes were closed and he bit his lower lip with a fair amount of pressure. "Really?"

"I can't help it," Derek let out on a huff. "Whenever you touch me I get so turned on." He dipped his head under the water, thickly-lathered shampoo washing out, then got busy scrubbing Scott's hair. "You've let this get a little long for wrestling."

Derek froze, his body going rigid for a split second. Scott placed his palm over Derek's heart. "It's okay. I know it's weird I've taken a break. It's not like me."

"Oh, it's totally like you, Scott. In the most amazing way." Derek made his hands into claws, massaging Scott's scalp. "You always give, give, give. You're putting your dad's needs first. You invited me here. You gave up the thing you love second best in the world."

"Right. Second best. You'll always be number one." Scott tried to kiss Derek, but Derek took advantage of Scott's longer hair, grabbing two fistfuls and holding Scott in place, devouring his mouth in a ravenous attack.

Scott dished back as good as Derek gave, and before he realized he'd moved, he pressed Derek against the tile wall of the shower stall. He cupped each side of Derek's face, tilting his head so he could fall deeply into the kiss.

Derek grabbed onto Scott's sides, his fingers curving around to Scott's back and kneading solid muscles like dough. What started as a devouring attack eased into a swirling dance of tongues, water and saliva mixing in their mouths.

Scott could have kissed Derek until the hot water ran out and would have still felt hot even after the spray ran ice cold, but Derek slipped his hands to Scott's chest and gave a slight push. "Are you having a good time?"

"Doesn't it seem like I'm enjoying myself?"

Derek shook his head. "That's not what I meant."

Oh. A sarcastic response would have been easier, but Derek deserved seriousness. "It's hard seeing him so weak, and I won't lie, he's been more…I don't know…cryptic than usual. It makes me kind of nervous, like maybe he knows something he's not telling me. Overall, yes. I'm having a really good time."

Derek glanced down at their feet. When he raised his head back up Scott detected sadness by the slight sag in his shoulders and the downward curve of his lips.

He gently massaged Derek's shoulders. "And now you're a part of this directly, experiencing what I am moment to moment. I don't feel so alone in this anymore."

His words had the desired effect as Derek's whole body inflated. "Thank you."

Scott hugged Derek, noting the water had run from scalding hot to lukewarm. He turned the nozzle off, still holding Derek, reached for an oversized towel, and wrapped the fluffy terrycloth around the both of them. "No matter what happens, I'll always want you by my side."

He could have said more, shared how he'd need Derek's strength should the situation take a turn towards his fears. He could have shared how Derek would need to be patient with him should his father lose his battle with cancer. Those things didn't need to be said out loud, at least not yet.

TWENTY

DEREK KEPT FISHING FOR STORIES FOR THE REST OF SUNDAY, seeming particularly interested about the famous *Supermarket Tantrum*. Derek couldn't breathe from laughing so hard. Scott remained stoic in the face of humiliation, but no doubt he'd have to put his foot down at some point if Derek abused his newfound ammo.

It had been easier to push the immediacy of their next steps aside after the weekend in Vermont, but before he knew it, two weeks had passed. Time for the dreaded doctor's appointment.

Friday found him sitting in front of Dr. T, Dad's rail-thin frame in the seat next to his own. Dr. T folded his hands over his desk, not even bothering with a cursory glance at the medical folder in front of him. "I have good news."

Dad said nothing. Dr. T continued. "I'm sure you're feeling incredibly tired and weak. Your bloodwork shows you're ready for the transplant. We should schedule the procedure for Monday or Tuesday. As soon as possible. Right now, you're susceptible to the smallest of germs people with normal immune systems don't have to worry about."

Scott nodded even though the doctor hadn't said a word to

him yet. When he did finally speak, Scott hung on every word. "The procedure isn't terribly difficult for you in terms of preparation or recovery, but I want to make sure you're aware of what happens next. After the transplant, I mean."

"You told me it works or it doesn't." He couldn't prevent the annoyance dripping from his lips and glanced to his father.

His dad's expression hadn't changed. Or perhaps Scott spied a hint of a smile. "Why don't you explain it once more?"

Dr. T settled his gaze on Scott. "We've done rounds of chemotherapy and radiation to kill any remaining cancer cells in his body. As you've seen, it's a weakening procedure and puts the patient at risk for infections normal people could fight off."

"Yes, I understand. We've gone over it a million times." Didn't the guy know Scott wanted the real news, not a recap?

"Now we're ready for the transplant. Stem cells from your bone marrow will be transplanted into your father. These stem cells are meant to jumpstart your father's healthy bone marrow function and he'll be able to produce the right amounts and types of blood cells." He paused.

Scott fidgeted. "Okay."

"I've presented the best-case scenario. With a successful transplant, your father will take months to recover as his immune system heals itself."

"Okay." Scott's defenses lowered a bit. After all, how did one comfortably talk about leukemia and bone marrow transplants?

"Then there's the worst-case scenario." Again with a pause.

Scott swallowed hard, trying to force a lump down his suddenly dry throat. "What would that be?"

"There's something called graft-versus-host-disease where the donor cells see the recipient as a virus. Then the transplanted marrow will attack the recipient and mortality follows rather quickly."

"You mean he dies! Right away?" Scott snapped.

"I'm afraid so."

Scott twisted in his seat towards his father. "I knew this was a risky procedure, but I never realized you'd be gone really fast if it doesn't work."

"What did you think would to happen?" The sharpness of Dad's tone shut Scott up. "I'm sorry." His whole body sagged. "You're getting worked up. If we don't do this procedure I die anyways. At least with the transplant there's a chance I could live."

"But you could keep doing chemo and radiation. Aren't there trials he can take part in?" Scott ping-ponged his head back and forth between his dad and Dr. T.

"Believe me, Scott." Scott finally settled his attention on the doctor. "We've tried just about everything. The trials, if there are any currently going on your father would qualify for, have some serious side effects.

"And, at some point along treatment, a person has to make a decision about how to proceed." His eyes widened a bit, drawing Scott's attention even deeper. "I say *decision* because the treatments make living hell. When all is said and done, at some point people want the suffering to stop and to enjoy whatever time they have left."

The words were logical and humane, yet seemed all kinds of wrong coming from a doctor. Scott swiveled again, gazing at his father. "Is that what we've been doing for the past few months, Dad? Have you been making the most of the time you have left?"

"Yes and no." Dad maintained a calm demeanor, off-setting and somewhat eerie. "Of course I hope this works. I'll keep making the most of what life has to offer, but I'm prepared for the alternate ending. If it doesn't work, at least I had this time with you. To get to know the man you've become and, maybe, to let you know how much I've always loved you, even if I had a lousy way of showing it."

Scott chuckled involuntarily and then tears flew down his cheeks. The words were everything he'd ever wanted to hear, heart-felt and holding the promise of a future he'd always hoped for.

A future which could be cut short before it even had a chance to blossom. He could lose his dad right when his dad had finally found him.

Though the tears eased, Scott's head grew heavy. The image of his bed, Derek's arms, darkness, sucked what little energy he had left in him. "Is this what you really want, Dad? Because I'm gonna be so fuckin' pissed at you if you die."

His father pressed his lips together in a thin line, revealing more resignation than anything else. "Son. This is what I want. I really hope I don't disappoint you…again."

What could Scott say? "One step at a time, right, Dad?

"Right. One step at a time."

Scott found himself with a lot of spare time, his father too tired to do much more than spend a few hours talking. Saturday morning had him groaning against the sunlight peeking through the window. Derek, far more productive, already had a jog, Starbucks coffee, and currently took a shower.

Still trying to push aside the remnants of a rather ugly nightmare involving his father and mortality and all sorts of other heavy stuff, Scott wanted to sleep for the rest of the day. He pictured Derek, hands on hips staring down at him, both understanding and disapproving, and forced himself up.

Rubbing the sleep from his eyes took longer than usual. Of course, the steaming cup of coffee Derek left on Scott's desk helped. He slipped out of bed and stretched, taking time to feel each muscle, then grabbed the coffee and brought it to his lips. Perfection. Black and piping hot, the acrid scent filling his nose. The first hot sip slid down his throat and he was ready to tackle the day.

Derek entered their room, a rosy tint to his otherwise pale

skin. With a towel covering enticing portions from the waist down, Scott had to limit his appreciation to the definition of strong abs and the swollen pecs which formed a slight crevice over his sternum. He'd had always been strong, but he'd been leaner, more vulnerable. This Derek had grown into a sturdy man. A really hot, muscly, God-I-need-you-now man. Scruff colored his jawline hadn't been there before. Since when did Derek skip a day shaving?

Scott abandoned his coffee and had Derek wrapped in his arms before registering he'd made a choice to do so. "You shouldn't have taken a shower."

Derek's eyes widened. "What?"

Instead of answering, Scott shoved Derek to the couch, forcing him onto his back. The damn towel hadn't shaken loose and kind of got in the way of Scott's goal. "Lose that."

Derek didn't skip a beat. The towel flew across the room and hadn't hit the floor by the time Scott knelt between Derek's knees.

Wasting no time, Scott gave Derek's cock a stroke, cupping Derek's balls in his other hand. The skin around them loose and pliable. He rolled them with tender care as he stroked Derek at a steady pace until he felt a heartbeat pulsing in his hands.

Releasing Derek's cock, he slid his hands along creamy thighs, spreading Derek to reveal his hole. The entire picture, Derek's cock head hovering over his belly, pulsing and at full hardness, had Scott salivating. One look at Derek's opening as it clenched and loosened, pink and clean, framed by strong ass muscles, and Scott's cock started drooling.

He angled his cock toward Derek's hole, using his precome as lube.

Derek sucked in a short breath, muscles dancing underneath the skin.

His hole opened, gripping at Scott's cock.

And all at once, Scott slid in until his pelvis made contact with skin.

Derek let out a deep groan, his eyes rolling, arms limp and splayed on either side of him. "Fuck yeah!"

Ignoring the signs of premature release his body screamed at him, he pulled out and pressed in again, this time harder, forcing Derek against the couch cushion. Gripping the upper edge of the couch, he rocked harder.

Derek leaked freely, a pool of semen forming in the crevices of his upper abdomen. The tang of Derek's sent filtered into Scott, fueling the fire in a way only Derek could. He maintained his onslaught of thrusts, but his legs trembled. Sensation overtook the ability to think.

He didn't know who came first, or if they'd come together, but as his own climax exploded out of him, the first jets of come splashed out of Derek's cock and hit him on the cheek.

Still rutting inside Derek, Scott lowered his head and licked the white rope of thick liquid into his mouth. The sound of two men panting filled the room. Scott only dared to move once his breathing eased. "I think you need another shower."

A smile lit up Derek's face. "You and me both, but we have to be quick. I've planned something for us and we don't have much time."

"Wh— You planned something and didn't tell me?" And this was a surprise because…?

Derek narrowed his eyes. "Listen. I didn't think you'd want me to do this and I didn't want you to say no, so—" He bit his bottom lip and pasted his staple innocent look into place, the one Scott could never resist. "Please don't be mad at me."

"What did you do?" He'd infused a sufficient amount of droll into his tone.

"We're meeting up with Marcus and going hiking." Derek spit the words out fast and returned to his don't-be-mad-at-me expression.

Every muscle in Scott's body tensed, earning a slight whimper from Derek. "Why'd you do that?"

"Because you quit wrestling, not your friends." This time

Derek spoke with assertiveness. "He's been worried about you and he misses you."

Scott shook his head. "When are we meeting him?"

Derek's smile brightened. "Eight."

"Ei—" Scott bit back his growl. "Text him and say it'll be more like nine."

"But I—"

Rolling off of Derek, Scott grabbed his cock, already filling out again. "You made *your* demand. I'm not allowed to get mad. Now I'm making *mine*." Scott gripped the base of his cock and wagged it in Derek's direction.

Derek flashed a sly grin. "In the shower. After I've cleaned you. It's just been in my butt after all."

Scott barely contained his laughter. "Charming."

~ ~ ~ ~ ~

Scott hadn't realized how much he missed his friend standing in front of his dorm. Derek pulled up to the curb and Scott hopped out before the car stopped moving. "Marcus. It's so good to see you."

Marcus grabbed Scott in a bear hug and squeezed. "I've missed you, man." He stepped out of the hug and grabbed Scott by his arms. "And I have a bone to pick with you."

The joy of seeing his friend remained, but Scott became serious in a flash. "Dude. I know. I should have told you."

Marcus opened his mouth to speak, but nothing came out. When finally spoke, he sounded defeated. "You think I'm pissed because you left the team without telling me first?"

Not the question Scott expected. "Aren't you?"

Marcus sighed, studying the ground between them. Without looking up, he said, "I'm bummed because I got to see my friend every day at practice and now I don't even talk to him anymore."

Man, if words could strike an actual blow. "I'm sorry. I

didn't, I mean I…sorry, man."

Marcus shrugged, lifting his bag and toting it toward the trunk of Derek's car. "It's cool man. We're hanging out now, right?"

Scott glanced at Derek, who only met his eyes briefly, confirming through one look Scott had a lot of making up to do. Deflated, he slugged to the car and buckled himself into the passenger's seat.

Derek did his best at making small talk as they drove west into the rural, mountainy portion of Massachusetts. City landscapes gave way to farms and wide-open fields, and eventually, to steep inclines of trees and rock.

He pulled into a small camping site about halfway up a particularly large and winding road. Scott read the sign. Mount Holyoke Range State Park.

He stepped out of the car and spun a slow circle, taking in the vista.

Marcus let out a long whistle. "You don't see this in Boston." He turned to Scott, the beginnings of a smirk curling one side of his mouth. "This is gonna be fun. Can't wait to get all sweaty with ya again." He nudged Scott with his shoulder, then hefted his hiking pack out of the trunk. At least some of the heaviness from the ride lifted.

"Look up there." Derek squeezed between Marcus and Scott, pointing toward a peak around two miles away. "We're going there." He plodded toward the entrance to the trails.

Scott and Marcus scurried behind him, and for the next half hour Derek led them into an area of the trail densely crowded with pines. There hadn't been much snow, so Scott found himself surrounded by various shades of green and brown.

Finally, Derek stopped resting against a tree. "Okay. We're following the blue markers for this hike." He nodded to a spot higher up in the tree with a blue streak of paint. "At every turn, we follow blue."

Marcus nodded, slinging his pack off his shoulders. "You're

a slave-driver, Derek. Coach doesn't even work us this hard."

Silence sliced through the air, the weight of two sets of eyes locked on Scott. He stared first at Derek, then at Marcus, not knowing what to say. Finally, he huffed, "All right, let's get this out of the way now. I'm sorry I didn't reach out to you. I thought you'd be pissed about my leaving the team." He'd been honest, even if Marcus demanded they return to the car and never wanted to speak to him again.

Instead, Marcus did what he did best: surprised Scott. "I knew it. I mean Derek said—" Another thick, airless pause ensued, before on the focus shifted to Derek. "Sorry, little dude."

"He called me and wanted to know how you were. What did you expect me to say?" The sheepish, innocent thing could only work so many times.

"Any-wayyyys," Marcus drew out the word, interrupting what could have turned into a heated argument. "We've been through a lot together. I thought you knew I'd support you in any decision."

If someone had told Scott a few months earlier he'd be standing in the middle of the woods with his best, straight friend talking about feelings, he'd have laughed them out of the room. "I guess I needed to be selfish for a little while."

"I appreciate your feelings. I respect them." Marcus closed the distance between them in more ways than one. He gripped Scott's shoulder with steadying firmness. "But pick up the phone. Check in. I care about you, Scott."

"I will. I promise." Scott had more to say but decided to let it rest. "So," he trapped Derek with an icy glare, "exactly how challenging is this hike you've planned for us?"

"Oh, it's fuckin' killer, man." Marcus clapped Scott on the back. "I told Derek where to take us. One way or the other I planned on kicking some ass today." He hoisted his pack into place and tightened the belt around his hips. He then took the lead, forging up a steep incline. "I guess kicking this mountain's ass instead of yours is a decent runner-up prize."

Scott couldn't let the challenge go unanswered. He grabbed onto a branch of one of the trees lining the path and hoisted himself onto a rock serving as a natural platform to climb the path.

Another half hour passed before they took their next break. Once they made it to level ground at the top of the slope, Scott dropped his pack on the ground, panting, supporting himself with hands on knees. Marcus wasn't in much better shape, probably because they'd been engaged in an undiscussed race.

Derek joined them about a minute later, a bit flushed, but nowhere near as wrecked as either Scott or Marcus.

"I'm gonna say it, even if the topic is taboo right now, but you are a monster, Derek. You have the stamina of a fuckin machine. When the fuck are you joining the wrestling team?" This time, at the mention of wrestling, Scott couldn't sense the awkwardness. Not in himself, and not from either of the two guys next to him.

"Probably next year." Derek lowered his pack to the ground and sat on a rock lining the path. "Babe, can I have some water?"

Scott tossed a water bottle over to Derek, who chugged half of it, then wiped his mouth with the back of his arm. He handed the water back and Scott finished it off. "When's the next steep incline?"

"No idea." Derek hauled his pack onto his back and secured the fasteners. "It's my first time hiking this mountain." He trekked down the path, following the blue markers.

"C'mon, dude. Next incline's just ahead." Marcus scurried behind Derek, leaving Scott to scramble to keep up with his hiking partners.

The trail remained relatively flat for about half a mile, then curved sharply up to the right. Clear blue sky painted the area above the looming ridge. The last push before the peak? Scott said a silent prayer and steeled himself against the work ahead.

Marcus glanced over his shoulder, shaking his head. "Dude.

You're huffing like a bitch. Maybe, if you were still on the team, you'd be able to handle a simple climb up a mountain like I can." His labored breathing, and the sweat dampening his neck, told a different story. He strode over to Scott and clapped him on the back. "Sorry. I know you need this time, but I miss the hell out of you. No one can beat my shit into the mat like you can."

"About that." Scott hadn't planned on talking about his thoughts for the next season, but Marcus acted way too smug. "I'm planning on moving up to the one hundred sixty-five spot next year, so you better make the most of the weeks you have left. Maybe you should consider putting on a few pounds."

Marcus's slack-jawed expression paired perfectly with saucer-pan eyes. "Are you shitting me?"

"I shit you not." Scott stood upright, clapped Marcus on his back with the same force Marcus had used, then started the arduous climb up the side of the mountain.

Derek settled on a large boulder about a quarter of the way up and grabbed onto a tree branch. His chest heaved, but he seemed energized, eyes sparkling.

There were plenty of natural handholds along the rocky surface. Had there been snow or ice, the climb would have taken twice as long, but Scott's goal waited, maybe thirty yards directly above him. "Don't you dare move a muscle until I reach you."

He could make out the sound of Marcus's boots on dirt behind him, accompanied by a slew of curses. Whether about the hike or Scott's revelation he had no idea, but Scott gritted his teeth and climbed toward Derek.

Fatigue set in faster than he would have expected, and he couldn't help but agree with Marcus. If he'd still been wrestling, his stamina would've been much better. At least the crisp air kept him fresh, and knowing he'd have Derek by his side kept him moving.

By the time he reached his goal, Scott's muscles had turned

to rubber. Derek had to hoist him up or else Scott would've had to wait for a good ten minutes before he could continue.

Derek hauled Scott's deadweight with ease. Once he planted his feet onto level ground, he leaned heavily into Derek, allowing his lover's sturdy frame to keep him from falling back down the portion of mountain he'd just climbed.

With gentle fingers, Derek brushed a few hairs matted to Scott's forehead out of the way and kissed his cheek. "You okay?"

"Yeah. Out of shape, I guess." He slung an arm over Derek's shoulder, attempting for the pretense of a simple act of affection. Most likely he wasn't fooling anyone, least of all Derek. He needed to hold on for a few more minutes before he trusted his legs to support him.

Marcus's hand appeared on the boulder where Derek and Scott stood. He glanced up, sweat pouring down his cheeks and neck. "If you two can take your hands off each other long enough to help me out here I'd be grateful."

Derek let go of Scott, who used a tree as support while trying to seem casual, and hoisted Marcus onto the rock.

"C'mon. We have a crest to reach." Scott cupped his eyes against the sun and spotted the gradual slope leading to the peak.

Marcus only took a minute to catch his breath, then started along the path, Derek on his heels and Scott dragging behind. Maybe he wasn't wrestling, but he could still work out.

A sudden silence drew Scott's attention to Derek and Marcus, who'd moved about a hundred yards ahead of him. They stood, side by side, unmoving. Scott had climbed enough mountains to recognize the awed reverence inspired by reaching a peak.

Digging for the remnants of his energy, he hiked the rest of the way to the top, huffing way harder than he should have been. Derek ventured toward the outer edge of the mountain-top, his form silhouetted by the sun.

Scott summoned enough reserves to cross the peak and stand next to Derek. He studied his lover, the sun reflecting off Derek's face, thin clouds of steam exiting his mouth on each exhale. "So fucking beautiful."

"I know, isn't it?" Derek faced Scott and paused. "Oh." He stepped closer to Scott and sank into his chest.

Scott wrapped his arms around Derek and finally took in the view of the scene surrounding him. Unlike with their previous hike with his father, no haze obscured the view. He could make out tall pines for miles around in every direction. "I didn't realize we'd climbed so high."

"I know. It's scary, but incredible." Derek snuggled closer to Scott. "Is all of the talk about wrestling bothering you?"

Scott considered the question. Initially, absolutely, coupled with the fact he'd been avoiding everyone on the wrestling team. It felt good to get outdoors, even in the ass-numbing months of winter, with the love of his life and his best friend by his side.

"You know, Marcus is pretty cool." Derek stepped out of Scott's embrace and nodded at the other side of the peak where Marcus chucked small rocks over the side. "He's a good friend."

"Yeah. He is." It continually amazed Scott how Derek plucked unspoken thoughts right out of his head. "Hey!"

Marcus spun around. "I feel like Superman. I bet I'm throwing these rocks about a mile. Maybe more."

Scott shook his head. "Really? You're up here with one of the most breathtaking views surrounding you on all sides, and all you can think about is how far you can throw some rocks?"

"Yup." Marcus hurled another rock in a clean arc, easily clearing the first ledge and dropping far below.

Ten minutes later all three of them were throwing stones, grunting with the effort. The sun climbed overhead and Derek found a spot to set out the snacks he'd packed. "Anyone else hungry?"

"Fuck yeah." Marcus scurried after Derek, leaving Scott to his last throw before joining them.

Lunch wasn't anything more than a big bag of trail mix to share and an orange for each of them. Still, the dried fruit and granola filled his stomach, followed by the refreshing sweetness of the orange, all washed down with more water. "We should try to find a fresh spring on the way down." Scott gathered and stuffed their trash into his pack, and started for the trail they'd climbed to reach the peak.

They descended in silence for a while, the only comments about locating the next marker or a good hand or foothold along the way. Halfway down the mountain they found a spring.

Marcus descended on the pool like he hadn't seen water his entire life. He scooped a huge handful to his mouth and slurped. "Oh, my fucking God, that's good shit!"

Scott laughed. "Leave it to you to find joy in the simplest of things."

"Oh, this isn't simple. It's nature. Life trying to thaw through the cold." Marcus scooped another handful into his mouth.

Derek followed Marcus's lead, enjoying the freezing spring water.

So much nature had forced itself into Scott's life over the past few weeks, accompanied by philosophical platitudes. First his father. Then Marcus. He ambled over, to the spring, debating whether to say anything snarky or drink, finally deciding Marcus provided way too tempting an opportunity to pass by. "Life's trying to thaw through the cold?"

Marcus met Scott's gaze directly. "Yeah. The earth tilts away from the sun and our part of the world freezes over, but the sun, animals, plants, they all work together during the day to persevere in the toughest of weather conditions. Spring water is one of a million examples of life always winning. Renewal. Cycles. You always have new beginnings. Like what's going on with you."

To hear his wrestling partner, one of the team captains, spouting truisms about the earth and renewal seemed like an invitation for some serious shit-slinging. Still, the words hit home. Maybe because of what Scott's father endured. Maybe because he and Marcus were still friends. Or maybe because he'd been thinking the same things lately. Whatever the reason, he could understand what Marcus said on a very personal level.

"You think I'm having a new beginning." Scott waited through a sudden silence. *Please, Marcus, say something!*

When Marcus finally did speak, his voice took on an unfamiliar seriousness. "Totally, man. Your dad's back in your life, you're not wrestling, pretty soon your dad will be healthy and you'll experience a whole new beginning. You're at a pivotal point, my friend. It's awesome."

One piece of Marcus's wisdom didn't make sense. "How is leaving the team a new beginning?"

"Because it's a decision you never would have made until now. Nothing would have stood between you and wrestling." Marcus paused, glancing at Derek. "Except maybe if Derek needed you for something. Now, here you are, free as a bird, clearing a path crowded with thorn bushes."

Derek stopped drinking long enough to gawk at Marcus, his mouth slightly ajar. Scott could relate. "Dude, since when did you become so philosophical about life?"

"I've always had these thoughts and assumed you'd give me shit if I shared them with you." Marcus shrugged.

"Honestly, I'm impressed. Have you ever considered joining the peer counseling group? We're getting pretty busy and plan on training a second group of students. I could recommend you." Derek, who'd remained silent for most of the hike, hopped to his feet. "We don't have any varsity athletes in our group yet, which may be why not many athletes call into the hotline or come to the walk-in sessions."

Or maybe it's because they burn off their aggression and stress. Scott sucked in a short breath, shocked at the judgment behind his thought. "How come you never asked *me* to be a part of the group?"

"First, you have no time. Second, you and I weren't exactly

communicating so well last semester. Then there's your dad." Derek slid next to Scott, hugged him around the waist, and placed a quick kiss to his lips. "Why. Are you jealous?"

Marcus snickered. "You two crack me up." He shrugged on his pack and resumed down the path. Derek gave Scott one more kiss and bounded off after Marcus, leaving Scott to his thoughts and suddenly very thirsty.

The markers were pretty clear along the trail. Finding his way wouldn't be a problem, and the others wouldn't go too far ahead without waiting. He placed his hands into the freezing stream water, the sting immediate, a welcome distraction from all the surprises he'd experienced during the hike.

He took several large gulps.

New beginnings. The words bounced in his head, suddenly making a whole lot of sense, applying to much of what he'd experienced over the past two and a half years since he'd moved to Massachusetts. Some good, some stressful, but all of them responsible for the life he now lived. Yes, he believed in a future he could shape. Because he'd allowed himself to trust, he had room to let his father back in his life.

As he hoisted his pack onto his shoulders, one thought troubled him. *What if the transplant doesn't work and Dad dies? How will that be a new beginning?* Darkness crept through his mind and he sagged, the weight of his pack seeming to increase by the second.

He splashed some of the spring water onto his face, careful to prevent any from dripping down his chest or back. He'd already sweated through his undershirt. If he got his outer layers wet too, he'd probably catch a cold.

Derek and Marcus had reached the bottom of the first steep incline, standing at the top of the path leading down to where they'd parked. Scott hustled to catch up with them.

Back at the car, he let Marcus sit up front with Derek, choosing to sit in the back. He needed some time to contemplate the deep thoughts Marcus had planted in his head.

TWENTY-ONE

SUNDAY FOUND SCOTT SORE AND EXHAUSTED. THE HIKE HAD taken more out of him than he'd expected, a reminder he'd fallen out of shape and should probably hit the gym, but he had more important things to do.

Sleeping in and taking his time in the shower, he made it out of his dorm a little past eleven. He'd texted his father, saying he'd arrive around noon. Given his new desire to work out, he considered jogging the few miles to his father's apartment, but his legs protested the instant the thought crossed his mind. Instead, he loped to the Massachusetts Avenue bus stop.

Watching the city speed by helped to lull Scott from focusing on the rapid-fire of activity the next few days would bring. Monday he'd have to rest. There were no stipulations on what he could eat or how late since he wasn't going under anesthesia, but a weird superstitious nagging told him his blood would be cleaner if he didn't eat anything after six o'clock.

Which is why he stopped off at the Chinese food store next to his father's building. Maybe his dad couldn't stomach the stuff, but if Scott had to watch what he ate the next day, he'd make up for it by splurging while watching movies in a downtown Boston hotel room.

Dad greeted Scott wearing sweats, a worn t-shirt, and a Red Sox baseball cap. "Hey, Scott." He even sounded chipper.

"Hi." Scott entered the room, trying not to seem obvious about surveying his father. The clothes definitely fit him loosely, but he didn't look as haggard as Scott had grown accustomed to. "Since when did you become a Red Sox fan?" Safe enough topic.

"I'm not. But I need something to cover this shiny dome of a head I've got." Dad's light chuckle filled the room, lifting Scott's mood. If he could laugh about how the chemo had balded him, he must be doing at least okay.

"So, what are we watching?" Scott crossed the room, sat on the couch and placed his food on the coffee table. "I should have called to see if you wanted Chinese. I assumed you wouldn't because of the nausea and everything." Funny how easily the words came. "But, you seem…good."

"I am. The queasiness has eased up. I got a decent night's sleep. You're here. And in two days a whole new chapter will begin." The string of comments had to have been the most positive and optimistic things Scott had ever heard his father say.

They watched the Star Wars trilogy, the original three, Dad sharing stories about when he'd first seen the movie, how he wanted to be Han Solo, the hero who sweeps in and saves the girl. Or how he and his friends played with light sabers late into the night until their mothers had to leave their houses and physically drag the boys back into their homes.

With each story, Scott tried to imagine his father the boy. An innocent kid with a head full of dreams. Someone who hadn't moved from place to place. Who'd been able to make friends and keep them. Yet, despite the fact Scott never had any luxuries growing up, his *dad* was the one fighting for his life. Alone, with no one to turn to except his semi-estranged son.

Guess having a stable home doesn't buy happiness. Another piece of resentment broke away with the realization.

After the final scene of *Return of the Jedi,* where the entire cast partied in Endor, his dad clicked the television off. "There's something I'd like to talk to you about."

Scott wriggled in his seat, unable to get comfortable. He settled on an awkward pose, one leg tucked under the other and an arm slung over the back of the couch. "Okay."

"It's about Tuesday." Dad studied Scott for a long time, his breathing hardly audible. Eventually he nodded so slightly Scott would have missed the gesture if he hadn't been watching so carefully. "We need to talk about what might happen if the transplant doesn't take."

Scott's lungs constricted, forcing the air out of him in a quiet huff. In a mere whisper he managed, "Do we need to talk about this today?"

"Yes." Dad got up and ambled toward the kitchen. "Come with me."

He hopped up and scurried behind his dad. His father indicated a small seat at a circular table only big enough to fit two. He opened the refrigerator and pulled out a platter of cut pineapple, apples, grapes, and melon. "I thought giving you something sweet and tasty might make the conversation go a little smoother." He sat down and popped a grape into his mouth. "Seedless."

Scott picked up a hunk of green melon and bit off a piece. Sweet fluid filled his mouth and dripped to his chin. He gulped down the food and swept a hand over his lips.

"I need you to hear me out." Dad heaved a sigh, settling into his chair. "On Tuesday, things will go one of two ways. If the transplant takes, great, but if it doesn't, we should talk about what will happen."

The bite of melon threatened to run a reverse trip. "Why do we need to think about this? Let's deal with things as they happen."

His father's expression softened. "You've grown into such a good man, but you aren't all grown up. There are experiences I've had which drive me to seize every moment I can." He became silent, peering at the grapes before locking his gaze on Scott. "I have to let you know what I want for you. After, if things are…bad…I may not be able to say any of this."

Scott closed his eyes, unable to meet the intensity in his father's. "Okay. I'm listening."

"I want you to wrestle. Go back to it. Right away. Don't go through a mourning period and put your life on hold until next year. Believe me, a year becomes two, then five, then twenty, faster than you can imagine."

Scott let the words settle, giving his initial shock a chance to simmer down. Go back to wrestling after his father died? No breaks to process? *Why would I possibly want to do something like that?* There were no answers. "Dad, I don't understand."

"You have to live, Scott. You have to be who you are all the time. If I'm gone, you can't move forward with anger." He paused long enough to urge Scott to look at him. "Anger leads to cynicism. You could view this time we've had as the universe putting me in front of you then yanking me away. My question is, how that kind of thinking helpful?"

Scott didn't respond right away, frazzled pieces of information slowly forming into the beginnings of a big idea. He didn't want to become a cynical person. Losing his father after finally getting him back would be an easy way to live with a *life sucks* attitude.

Dad nodded. "There's something else."

"Dad—"

"Give me a minute. I have papers mapping out my final wishes. I'd like to go over those with you now." He got up without waiting for the protest itching to escape Scott's lips, and disappeared into the living room.

Absence cleared with Dean? Check. Professors? Check? Free pass? Um… not so much. Assignment extensions instead.

He and Derek met his father at the hospital at nine in the morning. Having Derek by his side helped to calm the violence of Scott's heart beating in his throat as he sat next to his dad in the oncology department waiting area. When the nurse called for him, he jumped, nearly knocking his chair over.

Dad lay a steadying hand on Scott's forearm. "Relax. This is going to be painful enough for you. Worse if you're tense."

As painful as harvesting bone marrow might be, Scott's recovery didn't compare to the work his father would have to endure as he remained in the hospital for days under constant monitoring and undergoing endless tests.

Dr. T, business as usual, spared Scott another explanation of the process. Instead, he pulled out tools and instruments, letting Scott know how he'd use each.

Most of the tools seemed standard. Small injection needles, blood collection bags, gauze, tape. "This," Dr. T announced, holding up a weapon which seemed to belong in one of the Saw movies, "is what I'll use to burrow into your bone."

Scott shrunk away from the doctor. "The hell you are." He'd have a hole the size of a medium nail in him by the end of the day.

"I told you most patients are sedated for the marrow extraction. With the epidural, you're still feel a great deal of uncomfortable pressure."

Pushing thoughts of probes and holes out of his mind, Scott focused on other terrifying things as distraction. "What happens when you finish my part of the procedure?"

"We'll take your father in and transplant the marrow intravenously. His experience is far more grueling. Along with his depleted immune system putting him at risk for infection, he'll be weak and require weeks of observation and testing, not to mention the physical therapy to strengthen his muscles."

Scott couldn't help noticing the irony of the procedure being far more painful for the donor than the patient. Of course, his father had suffered through round after round of chemo and radiation, so Scott's discomfort couldn't really compare.

Dr. T took advantage of Scott's stupid, he now realized, decision to remain awake. "The hardest part for both of you," Dr. T said, "is the waiting. We really won't know anything until tomorrow after several rounds of blood tests. You should know some of the things we'll be looking for." Dr. T stared down at Scott. "First, we test to see if all the cancer is gone. The treatments prior to transplant were to remove as much cancer as possible. If any is left over, we'll have to remove it so the cancer won't come back. Also, we'll monitor the graft, looking for graft-versus-host disease. You remember what that is, right?"

"Yeah. It's where my dad's body attacks my donation." He remembered all too well, along with the quick and permanent outcome if it occurred.

"Every patient is different. Maybe the cancer returns. Maybe your father rejects the transplant, although unlikely since we tested you. The most probable complication, if there is one, is infection." A grim expression in the form of tight lips and a crinkled brow set Scott's teeth on edge.

"Okay." He didn't know what else to say.

"Your father's immune system doesn't exist. Literally anything could get him sick and could kill him. He'll need to be isolated until it's clear he's no longer at immediate risk."

What? "You mean I can't see him until after he's cleared by you for visitors?"

Dr. T chuckled. How dare he? Scott balled his hands into fists. "No. You'll have to wear a mask and, if you feel sick at all, you shouldn't see him right away."

Scott closed his eyes. No one had prepped him for not seeing his dad. The whole point of the procedure was so they could be together. "How long until you know how he's doing?"

"Like I said, it's different for every patient. Are you ready?"

What else could Scott say but yes?

A slender, blue-eyed male nurse stood by his side. "You ready, honey?"

"Like I have a choice."

"I could still sedate you, sweet cheeks."

Scott fought the urge to grab the blue-eyed, endearment-spewing, do-gooder. "Fine, knock me out." At least that way he wouldn't have to listen to the sadist any longer.

Someone called Scott's name, although the sound seemed far off and dreamlike. Next, some pressure to his shoulder caused him to shift. He opened his eyes. Hazy blurs appeared, slowly sharpening into recognizable shapes, until he found himself staring up at a man wearing hospital green scrubs. "Hey. You're up, doll. You slept like the dead." Scott peeked around the room. "Oops, probably shouldn't say stuff like that here."

The man smiled, but something shiny caught Scott's attention, drawing his focus. A name badge: Bernard. The last name began with a J but he couldn't focus his eyes long enough to figure out. "Where am I, BJ?" He chuckled, unable to help himself.

The nurse quirked his head to the side, a confused expression on his face, then tapped his badge. "Clever. Your friend warned me you might give me a nickname."

The fog started to clear. "Huh? Someone told you I'd...Derek."

"Yes. There's a young man out in the waiting area who's been checking to see how you're doing every ten minutes." BJ winked. "The receptionist is getting fairly irritated, but I found it charming." Another wink.

Scott nodded, not exactly sure why. "How long have I been out?"

"Not long. An hour, and you've been in recovery for thirty minutes."

Made sense and followed Dr. T's timeline. "My dad." He locked eyes with the nurse. "Where's my dad?"

BJ nodded slightly, understanding pouring out of him. "They're prepping him right now. The transplant is much less invasive than yours in terms of what the doctor has to do." He paused, tilting his head in the direction of the door. "Doesn't seem too busy right now. I can bring your friend in if you like."

"Thank you." Scott closed his eyes, his lids feeling too heavy to keep open.

He wasn't sure how much time passed, but like before, a soothing voice stirred Scott from his sleep. "Hey there. How're you feeling?"

"Derek." Scott tried to sit up but a sharp pain in his lower back forced him to fall back against the mattress. "Shit!"

"Baby, don't get up. You're gonna be in pretty bad shape for the next day or two." Derek's voice remained calm, but his eyes widened.

"K." Scott surveyed himself, noting the needle in his arm, and the attached tube connected to a bag of blood. Dr. T had said they'd be taking some of his blood to give back to him during recovery. "You heard anything about Dad? Did you see him?"

Color drained from Derek's face and he glanced at his hands briefly. "Only for a minute. I wouldn't leave the waiting area." A deep shade of red colored his cheeks.

Scott laughed, the movement shifting him. Laughter turned into a groan. "I think I need BJ."

Derek's eyes flew open. "Scott, what the fuck? We're in a hospital." He remained quiet, but his voice carried urgency.

What had he said? He wanted the nurse to give him something for the discomfort. BJ would certainly have something for him. Then it hit him, although he made sure not to laugh again. "The nurse's initials are B and J."

"Oh." Derek shook his head, the red deepening even more. "I'll see if I can find him."

Scott watched as Derek strutted toward the door, mumbling, "he had to come up with BJ," under his breath.

BJ released Scott after checking his vitals and handing him a prescription for pain killers. "The doctor is waiting for the bone marrow to be processed so he can begin transplantation into Mr. Thayer. Then we wait."

His mother joined them in the waiting area a few minutes later. "Oh, honey, you look so pale." Turning to BJ she asked, "Are you sure he's ready to leave?"

"Well, you need to wait for the doctor to give the official orders and instructions." BJ checked the file in his hands. "Pressure's good. Blood count's good. He's drinking fluids without feeling nausea. And he peed. Make sure he spends the next couple days in bed. It's fine if he feels up to walking around a little, but he should be supervised until he can walk up and down stairs steadily."

He addressed Scott. "This is serious. You just had a big procedure. Give yourself a little time to heal. You don't want to get any infections or to injure yourself by falling."

Scott nodded, noting how different the nurse's advice was from what his father had said two days earlier. *You have to live, Scott. Start wrestling, right away.*

Shannon and Derek both chimed in, "Oh. He'll rest."

The finality of their conviction, coupled with the sheer amount of energy it took to stand, even with support, helped Scott to accept a few days of pampering before getting down to the business of starting a new life with a healthy dad.

TWENTY-TWO

THE NEXT MORNING SCOTT WOKE UP IN HIS HOME BED, pleasantly surprised when he only experienced local discomfort in his tail bone area. The shooting bursts of pain were gone.

He chanced sliding his legs out of bed. *Holy shit! I can stand without help.* He still had intense throbbing, but could tolerate the pain. Still, BJ had told him not to push himself. Thank God Mom hadn't forbidden Derek from staying over.

"Hey. You awake?"

Derek snored peacefully.

Scott nudged Derek's shoulder. That did the trick. "I'm up. What happened?"

Scott laughed, unable to help himself. "I need to pee."

"Oh." Derek climbed out of bed, slipping Scott's arm over his shoulders.

Scott chuckled. "Would you hold my dick for me and aim it towards the toilet?"

Derek guided him as far as the bowl and stepped aside. "There are a lot of things I'll do for you, but holding your dick to pee isn't one of them."

Scott shrugged, playfully masking the lightness filling him.

Derek helped him in the shower as well, although Scott wasn't stupid enough to think he could handle anything sexual. "Can we go to the hospital right away, even if Dad isn't up?"

Derek locked eyes with Scott, biting his lower lip.

Scott grunted. "I'm not fragile. I won't break. If I'm tired, sore, or need help, I'll let you know. Promise."

Derek released his lip. "All right. Yeah. Sure. I wouldn't be able to keep you away from the hospital even if I tried. At least not without a major fight."

After a bit of heavy kissing and hastily throwing on clothes, Scott climbed into the passenger side of Derek's car, his mom wringing her hands in the doorway, watching them drive off.

Derek kept up mindless chatter about the weather, stupid Boston drivers, and courses he would need to take for his major, psychology, to no one's surprise. Reality set in when they entered the revolving doors of the hospital.

Scott took Derek's hand and they rode the elevator to the oncology floor in silence. As soon as they stepped out of the elevator, BJ walked by. He passed them without pausing, then stopped dead in his tracks and spun around. "Scott. What are you *doing* here?"

Scott bit back the snide comment crawling up his throat. "I want to see my dad. Do you know how he's doing?"

BJ's face lit up. "Of course. Makes perfect sense." His expression became serious again. "How are *you* though? Are you in a lot of pain?"

"Not as much as I would've expected."

"Good." BJ flipped back into the chipper version of himself. "Well, I'll find the doctor so he can fill you in, but your dad's awake and responding well to all the tests we've run so far. That's really good news."

Scott pulled Derek into a tight embrace, tears slipping from his eyes. "Oh, my God. This is amazing."

Derek hugged him back. From somewhere in the distance Scott thought he heard someone say something along the lines of *I'll leave you guys alone now* but only two things stood out in his mind: *Dad's doing well* and *Derek's right here.*

Dr. T approached them about five minutes later. "Your father's doing remarkably well. He's been sleeping. Numbers look good. There's some redness at the injection site we have some concerns about, but we have him on an antibiotic drip to help." He locked eyes with Scott, his expression serious. "This is the best we could have hoped for. No signs of graft versus host disease."

"Can I see him?" Scott extricated himself from Derek's embrace, realizing he'd been clutching onto his love during his conversation with Dr. T.

"I don't see why not. He's been asking for you." The doctor squinted, tapping his pen to his chin. "You'll have to wear a mask."

"It's fine." Scott took a step forward, pain shooting from the site where he'd been pierced, and up his spine. Damn, he'd chosen not to take a pain killer since he'd only felt achy when he got up. Not wanting to ruin his chances of seeing his father, he tried taking another step. If Derek hadn't been right next to him, he would have crumpled to the floor.

"You're in pain." Dr. T shook his head. "Do you need stronger pain killers?"

"No," Derek volunteered. "He thinks he's superman and didn't take one this morning."

"Didn't take…" Dr. T stopped a nurse passing by. "Please get me an apap with codeine for Mr. Thayer."

The nurse looked confused. "But doctor, why wouldn't we administer the main meds through Mr. Thayer's IV?"

Dr. T nodded toward Scott. "I meant the younger Mr. Thayer. Seems he's determined to make recovery as difficult as possible for himself."

The nurse nodded and skittered away, leaving Scott to face not one, but two men who frowned at him. "I'm going to say this again, Scott. You need to make sure you're taking time for you right now. You could hurt yourself very badly. One fall and you could break something, get a concussion, lacerate yourself, get hit by a car. I assume you get where I'm going with this." Dr. T scowled until Scott nodded, then eased his expression so there weren't quite as many crinkles on his brow. "That said, I'm impressed you had the motivation to come in at all today. You shouldn't want to move."

"He's as stubborn as a mule and acts like an *ass* half the time," Derek chimed in again, drawing a smile from the doctor and an angry glare from Scott.

"Oh, I like this one." Dr. T chuckled.

"He's okay." Scott mumbled begrudgingly, trying to stand his ground against two people who seemed hell-bent on treating him like an invalid. "So, can I see my dad now?"

"Yes. He's in room two-fourteen. Please stop by the nurse's station to pick up a mask."

Derek followed Scott as far as the station, gave Scott a quick peck on the cheek, ambled over to the lobby area, and sat in one of the uncomfortable-looking chairs.

The nurse handed him a mask and led him, or rather, supported him, Scott hated to admit, toward his father's room. "When we checked in on him about thirty minutes ago, he'd woken up from a nap. He may seem groggy to you, which is normal." She stopped outside room two-fourteen. "You sure you ready for this, sugar?"

Scott nodded, securing the mask over his face, and entered the room. He hadn't known what to expect, but his father sitting upright, reading a magazine, was not it. "Dad. You look…great."

Perhaps "great" was an exaggeration, seeing as Dad wore a paper-thin gown, remained bald and gaunt, and had several tubes running into his body at various places. Still, the life shone behind his blue eyes. "I feel great." He surveyed Scott. "You, on the other hand, look like you're in pain."

The anticipation of seeing his father had overrode the pain.

Or maybe adrenaline hid it. Whatever the reason, seeing his dad smiling at him, Scott finally had a chance to truly register the aches and pains in his body.

Throbbing emanated from his lower back, pulsing upward. Scott collapsed onto the chair next to his father's. "Maybe I kind of pushed myself a little today." Scott took a deep breath, the relief from having to support his own weight immediate.

"Well, I'm happy to see you, but you need to take care of yourself." His father winked.

Dad directed his attention to his inner arm where a needle ran into a vein. Scott noticed a red dot about a centimeter in width at the injection site, a black circle, drawn in marker, about an inch around the red dot. "Is that the infection Dr. T mentioned?"

"Yes. It's where the marrow is entering my body." He lifted his other arm. "This one is for fluids and the antibiotics." His father laughed. "I feel like a puppet."

"Why'd they draw a circle on your arm?" Scott couldn't draw his eyes away.

"To have a visual on whether the infection is getting better, or worse. If it spreads outside the black circle, we've got a problem." His father cleared his throat. "I feel fine. I'm sure the antibiotics will do their job, and in a few days, I'll feel like a new man."

"Yeah. I'm sure." Scott tried to infuse optimism into his voice, but knowing the little red splotch represented something far more dangerous lingered in his mind.

"Enough of this medical talk. We've had as much of *that* as we can stand." Dad started to reach toward the table next to his bed, then winced, glancing at his infected arm again. "Would you mind grabbing the cards? I think an old-fashioned game of gin is in order. Don't you?"

Scott retrieved the deck and shuffled the cards. His dad crushed him, although Scott barely paid attention to the game. Instead, he searched his father for signs of weakness. As minutes passed and his father remained chipper, he found it easier to accept everything would work out fine.

BJ poked his head into the room after an hour. "Um, guys, I'm sure you could spend many more hours together, but I'm afraid we'll have a problem out here if we don't cut this visit short."

Both Scott and his father stared at BJ without saying a word. "Er, well, you see, Derek and your mom are terrorizing the nurses at the front desk. I actually blocked Derek from charging here to, I quote, *drag you bodily from the room*. He's quite strong."

Scott fought back rising annoyance, but Dad simply laughed. "They're right, Scott. You should go home and rest. Put them at ease and let them take care of you for a day. I'll be here tomorrow."

Reluctantly, Scott rose from the chair, wincing as he did so. As much as he hated to admit it, he'd pushed himself too hard. BJ came to his aid, supporting him. With one final goodbye, Scott hobbled from the room and down the hallway to his waiting mother and boyfriend.

Scott dozed on the trip home and needed to be shaken awake when they arrived. Resting heavily on Derek, Scott climbed the front steps. Once inside, he took a break before tackling the steps up to the main floor. By the time he'd reached his bedroom, a sheen of moisture coated his skin. Derek helped him into bed and Scott fell asleep the second his head hit the pillow.

In his sleep, Scott dreamed of his father, the two of them returning to the mountain where they'd hiked with Derek. This time his father had a full head of hair and his muscles began to fill out. He'd been in remission for quite some time and kept fairly good pace with Scott.

Once they crested the ridge where his dad found the four-leaf clover, his father said, "Well, this couldn't have worked out any better."

"Nope. This is exactly what we wanted."

They sat together with their feet dangling over the ledge where Derek and Scott had sat before, sharing a sandwich and silently taking in the scenery before them.

A sudden jerking motion caused the images in his head to swirl and turn to blackness. "Scott. Scott!"

Scott shot up in bed. "What!" His eyes hadn't adjusted to the darkness, so he felt for Derek beside him, only to find his lover sitting bolt upright next to him.

A hand from the side of the bed gripped him gently on the shoulder. "Scott. Get up. Something's happened." Mom's voice.

Derek moved first, hopping over Scott and throwing on his sweats, a t-shirt, and rushing to the bedside to help Scott. The whole time, Mom stood by the bed, wringing her hands.

It took several minutes before Scott could make sense of anything.

"Very high fever." His mom's voice cracked. "The infection has spread."

"It's okay. I'll drive. You sit in the back with Scott. He's still weak."

Mom slipped into the back seat, tugging Scott against her. A few minutes later, Derek sped along the deserted streets to the hospital.

"What did the doctor say?" Scott winced as Derek took a turn, the pain in his back throbbing.

"The infection on his arm worsened and his temperature rose to a dangerous level. I don't know any more." Mom tightened her grip on Scott, her body shaking.

Derek dropped Scott and his mother at the front entrance of

the hospital. "I'll park and meet you inside." He drove off, but Scott was already halfway to the hospital doors.

He spotted BJ as soon as the elevator deposited them on the oncology floor. "Scott. Shannon. Follow me. He's been asking for you."

They rushed down the hallway in silence, only stopping when they'd reached Dad's room. Mom hung back. "I think you should go in by yourself, honey."

Scott didn't argue, hobbling directly to his father's bedside.

Where the man had been vibrant a few hours earlier, now lay a man wheezing through each labored breath. His head glistened with sweat and his skin appeared gray. "Dad." Scott barely got the words out through the lump in his throat.

"Scott." Dad rolled to his side, wincing and grabbing for the lines running into his arm. "I'm so glad you're here."

Scott took his father's outstretched hand in his own, careful not to jostle him. His head pounded with each powerful heartbeat, an angry hammer against his temples. "You're gonna be okay, right, Dad?" His voice broke and tears slipped from his eyes.

"I hope so, but maybe not." Dad lay his head on his pillow but didn't let go of Scott's hand. "But I want to talk to you."

"Anything you need, Dad." Scott's tears ran freely down his cheeks.

"These past few months have meant more to me than any other part of my life. Being with you has given me what I've always wanted." He choked on the last word and fell into a hacking cough.

About thirty seconds later, and with veins bulging in his neck, he resumed speaking. "There's one last thing I need from you."

"What is it?" Scott could only make out a blurred vision of his father, his eyes stinging.

"Wrestle in the tournament."

Scott froze. He couldn't possibly have heard his father right.

At a time when they should be spending every possible minute together, each one possibly their last, his dad wanted him to wrestle? "I can't. I need to be here with you."

"No. I need something to hold onto. Something to give me a reason to keep on breathing and waking up each morning. Come tell me how you did each night." Dad rolled his head to the side and gazed at Scott. "Please."

His mother squeezed his shoulder. Scott glanced in her direction, surprised he hadn't heard her enter the room. "Ronald, you can't possibly expect Scott to wrestle right now. Even if he were physically well enough by then, he'd never be able to focus. He wants…no, *needs* to be here with you."

Dad closed his eyes, his jaw tensing and unclenching. "Shannon, you have to understand. This isn't just for me." He looked at Mom and Scott followed his gaze.

The furrow of her brow smoothed out and the set of her lips loosened. His father's words had conveyed some message only the two of them understood and they weren't including him in their private conversation.

Better to cut them off before they could speak their secret agreement out loud. "No. I won't do it." Scott pounded the arms of the chair, accentuating each word. "You can't ask me to miss out on what could be…" His chest constricted, cutting off his words.

Mom pulled Scott to her, cradling his head against her chest like she had when he was young. She spoke, however, to Dad, again, how she used to do, making decisions for him despite the fact he was right there. "We'll give him two days and see how he feels by Thursday." She kissed the top of Scott's head. "Maybe you'll be better by then. Maybe your father will too."

"Yes. Maybe I will." His father fell into another coughing fit. When he regained control and spoke again, his words were a bit slurred. "I'm very tired. I think I need to sleep."

Scott wanted to grip his father by the shoulders and shake him. *Don't you dare give up! Not after everything we've been through.* He remained seated and silent, waiting for his mother to dictate his next move.

Mom urged Scott from the chair. "C'mon, honey. Why don't we get you home and rested? You'll need your strength to be able to travel back and forth from the hospital."

With no fight left in him, Scott followed his mother toward the door. He glanced back, locking eyes with his father. "You really want me to wrestle?"

"Yes. Please." Dad's eyes widened a bit, making him appear young and innocent.

With a silent nod, Scott left the room. Derek rushed to his side the moment he reached the lobby, and the three of them trod to the car.

Derek sat next to Scott in the back seat while Mom drove. "He can't possibly expect Scott to wrestle."

His mom pulled to the side of the road and put the car in park. She then turned in her seat so she could face Derek and spoke in a tone harsher than any Scott had ever heard her use. "Yes, Derek. He does. I think we should all get a good night's sleep so we can think with level heads tomorrow."

Derek's eyes shot wide open and his mouth formed an "Oh", but he remained silent, pulling Scott a little bit closer.

Back home, Derek helped Mom get Scott into bed. Scott slid to the side to make room, but his mother touched Derek's arm, directing him toward the door. "Would you mind coming into the other room to talk for a minute?" Her voice didn't carry the same bite as earlier, but she'd never behaved in such a forceful way before either.

Scott wanted to say something, but Mom was in rare form and he didn't have the strength to fight.

A few minutes later Derek entered the room, slipped out of his clothes, and crawled into bed next to Scott, letting out a sigh but saying nothing.

Scott waited for what seemed an appropriate amount of time. Three seconds seemed right. "What did she say?"

Derek rolled over and touched Scott's cheek, remaining silent for another few seconds. "She said I should keep my opinion about you wrestling to myself."

Scott glanced at the bedroom door, tempted to hop out of bed, dragging Derek with him, and demand his mother say whatever she had to say to *him*. Secrets with Dad. Secrets with Derek. Not okay.

Derek gave Scott a gentle shove, urging him to roll over so his back faced Derek.

Scott complied, surprisingly calm once Derek wrapped him in strong arms. "She's scared and doesn't know what the right thing is to do."

"She told you that?" At least Scott got some information.

"She didn't have to. You saw the way she snapped at me. She said to stay out of it and then went to her room." Derek nestled into to Scott, pulling him even closer.

Derek's weight pushed him more comfortably into the mattress, his head sinking into a cool, soft pillow. A yawn forced its way out of him, and with it, the last of Scott's energy. "She's stupid."

A swat to the side of his head woke him up from his near slumber. "Don't talk about Shannon that way."

Scott shrugged and sank back to a place of near sleep. "Sorry."

No way in hell would he allow decisions to be made for him, but at least he could let everything go for a few hours and lie safe in Derek's arms. In the morning, he'd let everyone know what *he'd* decided and they would all have to deal.

TWENTY-THREE

THE NEXT MORNING, SCOTT SAT UP AND SWIVELED HIS LEGS out of the bed, surprised by the reduced level of pain. More like someone had kicked him.

In the bathroom, as he waited for the water to warm, he studied at the injection site on his back. The skin appeared a bit purplish around the scab, surrounded by about an inch of yellowish discoloration.

He pressed at the site and barely felt any soreness at all. Pushing a little harder, he sensed the ache he'd been expecting. He stepped into the shower, pleased at how quickly his body recovered. In the next instant, his happiness turned to dread. While *his* body healed remarkably faster than he'd anticipated, his father fought a serious battle. Details from the previous night flooded Scott. He needed to get to the hospital and check on Dad. Plus, he had an announcement to make and no one, not even Derek, would sway his decision.

Scott stood in his doorway, towel around his waist and hair still dripping, enjoying the view of a yawning Derek. "Morning, sleepyhead."

Derek flipped him the bird and rubbed his eyes. "What time

is it?"

Scott glanced at the clock on his side table. "Eight." He ran through a mental list of their classes. Derek didn't have anything until eleven-thirty and Scott only had one afternoon class.

"Why'd you get up? We could've slept in." Derek began to lay back down, then snapped right back up. "Wait. How are you? Last night you could barely walk."

Scott couldn't suppress his happiness. "I know, but I feel amazing today. Amazing enough to march down to the hospital and kick my dad's ass back into shape."

Derek shook his head, an expression of understanding and concern warring for dominance on his face. "So, you've decided you…" He snapped his mouth shut.

Right. Mom told him to butt out. Well, Derek wasn't technically butting in if Scott simply told him what he'd decided. "I'm not going to do the tournament. I'm sticking with Dad and seeing him through this." *There, problem solved.*

"Are you sure? I mean, it's like a sign that your body healed so fast."

So not the response Scott wanted. "I thought you were the one who wanted me to take it easy."

Derek scooted out of the bed and to Scott's side. "I just want what's best for you. Last night I didn't think you'd be ready, but now—"

"I don't believe you." Scott tugged a shirt over his head, the fabric sticking to his slightly damp skin. He tugged a little harder, rewarded by a loud rip. "Fuck!"

He hadn't mean to shout, but the outburst released some tension. At least it did until Mom showed up at his bedroom door. "What's wrong?"

Scott couldn't see with his head tangled in white cotton, but he could hear his mother chuckle and felt Derek's stabilizing hands on his sides. "Just get this thing off me."

Derek gripped Scott tightly. "I will when you stop wriggling around." Agitation colored his tone. Whether from Scott's squirming or the imminent fight they were likely to have, he had no idea. Nor did he care.

Once Derek helped him out of the shirt, Scott regrouped. "Mom, I've decided I'm not wrestling in the tournament and, before you say anything, Derek didn't have anything to do with my decision. In fact, he now thinks I *should* wrestle."

He gave Derek a pointed glare, then his mother, daring either of them to contradict him.

Mom stared at Derek, her lips pursed, then shook her head. "You had a serious procedure. You heard what the doctor said. You could really hurt yourself, but if you're able to physically wrestle—"

"I don't need Dr. T, you, or Dad telling me what I should or shouldn't do." Scott tossed his ruined shirt into the trash can next to his desk. "What I'm going to do is march down to the hospital and give Dad the hope he needs in a way that makes sense to me…by spending time with him."

Gripping another shirt, Scott ensured he'd placed his arms through the correct openings before tugging it over his head. "And another thing." He bent over to pick up his jeans, noting again the lack of discomfort. "I don't need an escort to the hospital. I'm going on my own." He planted his hands on his hips, silently daring Derek to protest.

Derek raised his hands in surrender. "Okay. You win. Do what you want and go see your Dad by yourself."

Scott held Derek's gaze for a few seconds, then swiveled to lock eyes with his mother. Determining the resistance in the room had snapped, he finished dressing and grabbed his coat, Derek and his mother standing by silently. "I'm going to the hospital now." He kissed his mother on the cheek. "And I'm going back to the dorm tonight."

"But"

"It's decided." Scott tugged on his jacket, then strode to Derek. "I'll see you after my evening class."

Derek nodded, but said nothing.

As Scott closed the door behind him, the finality of his decision cemented itself into what felt like an impenetrable shield. No one, not his mom, not Derek, not even his dad, would convince him to do anything he didn't want to do.

A half hour later, he entered his father's hospital room. While his father still appeared weak and tired, the angry red splotch on his inner arm hadn't grown. In fact, it seemed to be exactly within the boundaries of the black circle.

"This is looking better, but you need to drink lots of fluids. I know you hate having a catheter but you need to put it to good use if you want to get better." Scott didn't recognize the new nurse, but her gray hair and commanding tone instilled a sense of authority.

Scott cleared his throat, drawing the attention of both the nurse and his father. "Sorry, bad time?"

The nurse glanced back and forth between Scott and Dad.

"Not at all." Dad pushed himself up a bit on the bed, wincing as he did so.

His actions seemed to snap the nurse back to life. "Let me help you." She tucked her hands beneath his father's shoulders and helped him sit up with what appeared to be very little effort.

Scott diverted his view to his feet, not wanting to see how frail his father had become.

The nurse ambled to a cabinet and procured a face mask. "You, young man, must wear this."

Scott's sense of self-preservation stilled his tongue. Better to do what the mean nurse asked.

When she exited the room, some of the awkwardness left with her. "Come on over and sit by the bed. Where's Derek and Shannon? I know they wouldn't let you come here by yourself."

Scott squared his shoulders in a childish act of defiance. "The hell they wouldn't. I feel a thousand times better." His words brought an immediate smile to Dad's face. "Well, maybe a hundred." He needed ammo to support his decision, but didn't need to over-exaggerate his recovery in the process.

"That's great news. Then you'll do the tournament?" Dad gaped at Scott with saucer-wide eyes.

"Listen, I know you really want me to, but I feel like I should be here with you." Scott scooted his chair a bit closer to the bed, taking his father's hand. "Don't you think it would be better for us to be together right now?"

Dad visibly deflated, falling back into his pillow. "Of course, you're right."

The silence weighed heavier than all of the arguments he'd played out in his mind. "Okay then. That went much easier than expected."

More silence. His father locked him in a steady gaze, piercing straight through to his heart. They sat without speaking for about a minute, then his dad caved. "It's just—"

"Ha. I knew it." Scott straightened in his seat, prepared for a fight.

"How perceptive of you. My point is, it's not like you to give up on something. Especially wrestling." A slight crinkle furrowed his father's brow. "I'd hate to be the reason you look back on this year with regret."

The words were more effective than any blow. "Do you really think I'd regret not going to a tournament? Every minute we've spent together has meant ten times what wrestling means to me."

"That's kind of you to say." Dad paused and looked at the red spot on his arm. "And don't get me wrong, I feel the same. We're both involved in a battle right now. It's kind of like something we can go through together. Me in here and you out there."

"I don't see how cancer and my athletic career have anything in common."

Dad chuckled. "I should have known that wouldn't work." He shifted, wincing as he did so. "I can't sit up. Could you help me?"

Scott stood and placed his arms under his father's, gripping skin and bone. Lifting him felt like moving a chair from one place to another. He bit back the questions burning to fly from him. "Better?"

"Yes. Thank you." Dad's breath came out in faint wheezes. "You have to do this. It's not for me. It's for you."

Anger. A friend he could use to put this argument to rest once and for all. "If you're asking what *I* need, then I think I've made it clear. I need to be with you. I want us to spend our time together and fight this thing side by side."

"Scott!" Some of the fight he'd known returned to his father's voice. "I am not the center of the universe and I'm still your father, even if I've been a shitty one. Let me correct past mistakes."

"I made up my mind, Dad." Petulance had always served him well.

"Okay. What about Mom? She needs you too." Dad crossed his arms over his chest and immediately unfolded them, scowling at the infection site. "She told me she's met someone. Have you even asked her about him?"

Scott averted his gaze. *No.* As much as he wanted to argue how cancer trumped new relationships, Dad had made a valid point. He'd basically ignored his mother ever since Christmas.

Dad reached out his hand and Scott took it in his own. "Don't you see it? If you sit around here and make my battle the center of your world, you're giving up. You're letting a championship slip through your fingers without a fight. You're neglecting Mom, who's stood by you like no one else. Well, no one else except for Derek. What message am I supposed to get from that?"

Heat rushed along Scott's spine and up his neck. "How about I want to be with *you*. I want to stick by you through this and see it through to the end, one way or another, and finish what you and I started. Do you think I don't know this could all end badly? And if things turn for the worse and I do what you ask, I'll never get this time back. I'd regret that far more than missing a tournament."

After several seconds of silence, Dad spoke. "You constantly impress me with how much you've grown into a man. To be honest, I *did* get the sense you were holding onto the hope of a miracle, blinding yourself to the possibility of a different result."

Scott measured his next words. "I want to be here with you. This is what I feel is most important for me."

"Okay. I'll stop trying to persuade you after you answer this last question." Dad dropped his gaze to their joined hands. "Which do you think will help me endure the hours of drugs, discomfort, and the pokes and prods from medical staff? Chats and card games here in my hospital room, or dreams of how you're performing on the mat, knowing you'll be coming to share every detail with me before I go to bed at night?"

Damn him. One simple response and Scott would get what he wanted. His dad promised no more pressure, but didn't he owe it to both of them to answer truthfully? Still, he could put in one last effort. "It's almost like you don't want me around." Petulance laced his tone. Typically an expected response, his words felt foreign on his tongue, even to him.

Dad laughed. "Really? That's the best comeback you've got?"

Scott shrugged. "I had to try."

"So, you'll do it?" Again with the wide-eyed, eager expression.

Scott fell heavily into his chair, drawing up and hugging his knees. "Fine, but you better live."

"Deal." Energy radiating from him. "One more thing."

Scott released his father's hand and crossed his own arms over his chest. "You already got what you wanted."

"Make sure to spend some time with your mother. Ask her about her life." Dad waited until Scott nodded. "Thank you. Now, fill me in on everything. Who are your biggest competitors? Who do you wrestle first?"

TWENTY-FOUR

SCOTT STOOD OUTSIDE THE ATHLETIC COMPLEX AND collected his thoughts. Dad's strength improved over the last two days, but he still had a long way to go.

Steeling himself, he opened the door and strode into the warm interior. Wrestlers from all over the country swamped the lobby area. At least Scott didn't have to travel and stay in a hotel room since BU hosted the tournament. Better yet, he could keep his promise and visit his dad each night with news of his progress.

He wove through the mass of people, finally having space to breathe when he entered the locker room.

Marcus clapped him on the shoulder as Scott opened his locker. "I can't believe you're here, man. I really didn't think you'd make it." He glanced at Scott's back. "You know, cause of the…"

"Yeah. Well, I guess I'm super-human because I feel a hundred percent." At least physically. Maybe a little bit mentally beat up after approaching Coach and asking to compete. At least he hadn't been too much of an ass.

Marcus's cheerful attitude helped erase lingering thoughts of

Coach. "Awesome, man. With you here, we have a chance at winning this thing as a team." The heavyweight wrestler passed by the locker and cracked a rat tail against Marcus's ass. Without a second's hesitation, Marcus bound after him. "Motherfucker!"

Scott chuckled, pleased for the distraction from the seriousness of the past few days. The infection on Dad's arm continued to shrink, but was still noticeably there. It could easily spread, without warning.

Scott shook the thought away. He needed to get his head ready for his first match. The fact he hadn't practiced at all didn't help either.

A few minutes later he marched into the gymnasium. Eight mats formed a four-by-two array in the middle of the room, about ten yards separating them, leaving room for people to watch individual matches. The first day of a tournament was always the busiest. Eight mats would be reduced to four the following day because of the double elimination rules.

Large posters covered the back wall of the room, each a tournament bracket for the various weight classes. Scott maneuvered through the crowd until he stood before the chart for the one hundred fifty-seven weight class.

Even having missed two meets, Scott still ranked third, placing him in the bottom bracket. Zane, the Sacred Heart wrestler who'd been annoyingly awesome as a person, appeared on the top rung. No surprise there. The guy definitely deserved his spot. Scott scanned the chart to see who held the second seed spot; the person he'd have to beat to make it to the finals.

Skipping all the names in between, Scott read the bottom name of the second bracket. *I don't believe it. Lance, the homophobic prick from Lehigh.* "Perfect."

"Is that a good perfect, or a bad one?"

Scott spun quickly to see who'd snuck up behind him? "Zane?" Up close and without adrenaline rushing through his system, he took in finer details of the only wrestler to defeat him the entire season. Zane wore an easy expression, carried through a relaxed posture and broad smile.

About to answer the question, Scott realized he couldn't remember what it was. "I'm sorry. You asked me something?"

Zane laughed, his face lighting up with warmth. "You said '*perfect*' and I couldn't tell whether you were happy or upset with something on our chart."

"Oh." Scott peeked at Lance's name again. "Yeah, not sure how to answer you. I referred to this dude." He pointed to the name. "I nicknamed him Lanky and he's a douche."

"Ah, the infamous Lance. I'm jealous he's in your bracket." He pointed to the number four seed who he'd have to wrestle in the semi-finals. "I heard you beat this guy. How'd you do it?"

"Sheer willpower."

"I hear you. The guy is like Iron Man." Zane puffed up his chest in a mock display of bravado.

Scott laughed. "You reminded me of the nickname I came up for him. I named him The Hulk because he's so big."

Zane nodded. "So, the Lehigh guy is Lanky. The Cornell dude is The Hulk. What nickname did you give me?"

"Actually, you're the one player I haven't given a name to."

For a second he looked hurt, but the expression changed to one of curiosity. "Why not?"

"Honestly, because you're such a good wrestler I needed to beat *you*, not the caricature I make of most of my opponents. Which, of course, I wasn't able to do," he added, nodding a silent acknowledgement of a match well won.

"I do too. Give names, I mean." He studied the chart on the wall. "Although Lanky isn't the one I would have chosen for Lance."

Scott remained silent and waited for Zane to finish. When it appeared their conversation had ended, Scott asked, "So, what would you name him?"

Zane's lips twitched and his cheeks flushed a deep shade of burgundy. "Stupid Fucker."

Scott hadn't meant to laugh out loud, but the words were totally unexpected. "Care to elaborate?"

"I don't know if you know this, but he's openly homophobic."

"Yeah, I seem to remember nasty words before my meet." The memory of prying Marcus away from Lance would remain cemented in his mind for years. *Why would Zane care?*

"Really? Then you know why I'd give him that name." Zane folded his arms. "Which is why I'm kind of jealous of you. You get to be the one who knocks him out of the finals."

Look at this vindictive little bitch side to Zane. I like it.

Zane suddenly stared at his feet, all bubbly cheerfulness gone. "What happened at your meet?"

Scott shrugged. "Not much of a story. My boyfriend, Derek, kissed me. Lance saw it, made some kind of comment, and my captain almost got himself kicked out of the match for beating the guy up."

"No shit. Now I'm really jealous." Zane sighed, then raised his eyes until they met Scott's. "I hope you don't think I'm weird after this, but I kind of asked around about you after the match at Sacred Heart."

Not sure of the direction of the conversation, Scott simply nodded and let Zane direct the conversation.

"See, there's not a lot of tolerance for gay life at Sacred Heart. I mean, sure, they have student groups and people aren't hostile, but it still feels like we're a side thought. You know, like, let's make sure we have a gay group so we can't be accused of discrimination." A far-off expression crossed his face. Scott knew the look, having worn the same one over the past few months. "Anyways, sounds like BU has its shit together. You and your boyfriend are open about who you are. Teammates stick up for you."

"Yeah. I'm pretty lucky." An odd thing to say given his father's circumstances.

"You are." Zane nodded slightly, as if agreeing with himself instead of Scott. "I'd like to talk to you about the school. I'm thinking of transferring here next year."

Scott's brain immediately started cranking, a string of thoughts racing through his mind. Another awesome wrestler for the team. *Would he want my weight class? Wait, will I not make varsity next year? But I already decided to bump up to one hundred sixty-five. What about Marcus? Could he handle one hundred seventy-four?*

"Sure." Scott couldn't come up with any other response while contemplating the string of unspoken questions running through his head.

"Cool. I'll catch up with you later. Good luck in your first match." Zane shook hands with Scott, then turned and disappeared into the crowd.

"What was *that* all about?" A voice, directly behind him, caused Scott to jump.

Scott spun around, relieved to find Derek standing behind him. "People need to stop sneaking up on me." The sudden start had his heart beating a little faster and his senses a bit more alert. "I think Zane just came out to me."

Derek's eyes widened. "No shit." He glanced over Scott's shoulder into the crowd, his eyes narrowing slightly. "Did he hit on you?"

Scott laughed. He hadn't meant to, but a jealous Derek was always so much fun. "I don't think so. He mentioned he might transfer to BU. I think he wants to be somewhere where he can be himself."

"Hmm." Derek returned his focus to Scott. "So long as that's *all* it is."

Scott placed a kiss to Derek's cheek. "You know it turns me on when you get like this."

Derek didn't get a chance to respond.

"Well, look who decided to show up to the tournament. I heard you were bailing out this year."

Scott didn't need to turn around to know who stood behind him. On a slow, cool rotation, Scott faced Lance. He slipped an arm around Derek's waist and pulled him close, gratified by the way Lance darted his glance to the affectionate contact and back to Scott's face. "Oh yeah, I wouldn't miss the chance to knock you around the mat again." He reached down and squeezed Derek's ass, ripping a small squeak from his otherwise silent boyfriend.

Lance grunted, but said nothing more. Turning with the flair of the most seasoned drag queen, he sauntered away.

Derek let out a breath. "You okay?"

"If I didn't know any better, I'd say that dude is gayer than you and me put together."

"Maybe. They say homophobia is one of the first signs of a person questioning their own sexuality."

"There's my cerebral, psychologist boyfriend. I wondered where you'd gotten off to. The jealous, possessive act is only fun for a few minutes." Scott nudged Derek playfully with his shoulder.

"I'm not j…I mean, I'm not posses…Shut up!" Derek's cheeks reddened in an instant. "I guess you need to have a serious conversation with Marcus."

"Yeah." Scott answered automatically, then realized he had no idea what Derek was talking about. "Huh?"

"If Zane transfers to BU, you have another reason to bump up to the next weight class. Which means Marcus will have to bump up as well if he wants to stay on the team."

Amazing how Derek could piece everything together the same way Scott just had. "That is," Scott added, "if I can beat Marcus."

Derek let out a huff, accentuated by a dismissive wave of his hand. "Please."

Scott already knew he could take Marcus. Still, it would suck to piss off his best friend on the team. A pre-emptive suggestion at a lineup including Zane might be the best course of action.

With Derek by his side, Zane and Lance adding drama to the morning, and Marcus to find, Scott easily slipped into the vibe of the room. Together they joined his team by the bleachers.

The sky was almost dark when Scott left the athletic complex. Only a streak of glowing purplish-blue spanned the horizon. He squeezed Derek's hand. "The skyline looks amazing this time of night."

Derek pressed closer to Scott, shivering slightly against him. "Yeah. Sometimes I forget you didn't grow up with this view. I guess I take it for granted."

Scott ran his hand up and down Derek's back until he felt warmth from the friction. "You're ice. You should take my jacket. I'm hopping in a cab to go to the hospital, but you're walking back to the dorms."

Surprisingly, Derek accepted the offer without debate. "Thanks. Tell Ronald I said hi. Oh, and congratulations on your victory today."

"Will do, with Dad and thanks about the match." Scott held his varsity jacket for Derek, taking extra care to make sure he snapped each button before placing a small kiss to Derek's lips.

Ten minutes later, he crawled out of a taxi in front of the hospital. He checked his phone again. No messages. Which had to be a good thing, right? Because someone would have told him if something bad happened.

Logic aside, Scott quickened his pace, speed walking to the elevators and shifting impatiently from foot to foot as he waited for the doors to open. It wasn't until he entered his father's room that his heart calmed and he could again breathe more easily.

"Scott. I've been thinking about you all day." Dad motioned to the seat next to the bed and Scott noticed how the angry red splotch on his arm shrank in size and had become a dark pink.

Sinking into the chair, a sense of peace rolled through Scott, leaving him content and relaxed for the first time since he'd gotten up. Even the pain in his back calmed to a dull throb. "I wish I had something exciting to report, but today was pretty boring. Everything went just as it should have."

"You're winning?" His dad rolled to his side, facing Scott directly.

"Winning? It's too soon to tell, but I'm on the winning track. Tomorrow is when the big matches happen. I have to get through quarter finals and then semis." An image of Lance popped into Scott's head, distracting him from his story.

"Oh, tell me about the semi-final guy. You got an angry look on your face." Dad scooched a bit closer to Scott.

Scott chuckled. If his dad wasn't careful, he'd fall out of the bed. "Easy there. Lay back before you hurt yourself." Dad complied without complaint. "The guy I have to wrestle has a problem with me. Well, not me specifically, or maybe it is me specifically, but people *like* me."

"Scott, you're making no sense. What's wrong with the person you have to wrestle?" Dad pressed his lips together and he peered a bit more intently into Scott's eyes.

"He has a problem with gay people. I had an issue with him during the season, and then he approached me today too. It was…uncomfortable." Sharing his burden felt oddly comforting. "I never thought we'd ever have a conversation like this."

Dad's eyes popped wide, but only for a split second. "I know. I don't think I would've believed it either a few months ago, but back to this schmuck who doesn't like gays."

"You know what? He doesn't even matter. Being here with you is what matters. Lance can believe whatever he wants." Scott paused, searching for internal signs of resistance to letting his father in and finding none. "And you know what else? I'm gonna encourage Zane to transfer. I can tell he wants to, and I'm sure he's not trying to get between me and Derek."

Once again, Dad's eyes popped open. "What! Scott, I think you should get the nurse. My medication must be doing strange things to me because I can't follow a word you're saying."

Scott chuckled, sinking back into the cushioned seat. "No, you're not nuts. I am. I feel so free right now, like I can say or do whatever is on my mind. Zane is this amazing wrestler from Sacred Heart, and he came out to me today, I think. He mentioned he'd noticed me and Derek and thought it would be cool to go to school where he could be more himself."

Dad nodded. "Well, if anyone can bring good things out in others, it's you. Look at what you've done with me." His gaze shifted, almost imperceptibly, but admiration suddenly took on a slightly sterner look. "Have you talked to your mom at all about her new friend?"

"Not yet." Guilt slithered through his veins. "I will though. I promise."

"Good. She's been remarkably strong for you."

Scott bit his lower lip, unhappy with the sour turn in their conversation. "You're wrong about one thing, Dad. It's Derek who brings the best out of people, not me."

"Derek is an amazing person. I'm really glad you found your match."

"He's pretty awesome." Scott tucked one leg under the other, resting more comfortably with his father allowing conversation to shift back to casual.

"Do you think he'd be willing to stop by here on his way to your tournament tomorrow?" Dad attempted to roll to his side again, but winced and lay back down. "I'd love to have a chance to get to know him a little better. You know, one-on-one."

The fact his father wanted to connect with his son's gay lover blew past Scott's wildest hopes. Given time, maybe he really could have everything he'd always wanted. "I'm sure Derek would be thrilled to swing by."

Dad sighed. "Good." He closed his eyes. "I'm tired, and you should probably rest up for tomorrow."

Scott nodded. "Okay. I'll come by again tomorrow night."

"Good."

Scott ambled toward the door, remembering he'd given Derek his jacket and would have to brave the night without one.

Dad called out. "Scott."

Scott swiveled in a smooth arc, not something he could've done without pain two days earlier.

"I'm so proud of you for making your relationship with Derek a priority. I wish I'd had your strength when I was a young man."

"Dad"

"No, it's okay. It feels good to say these kinds of things. Out with the bad, in with the good. Then we can start our lives together with a fresh slate."

"Yeah. A new beginning."

Scott ran from the street to his dorm, hugging himself tightly. While glad Derek borrowed his jacket, nothing said winter like brutal Boston cold. He entered his room, teeth chattering and body shaking.

Derek lay in their bed, only in his boxers, a book in hand. "Hey. You're back."

Scott couldn't draw his eyes away from Derek's nearly naked form, even though the sexy beast hadn't made a move to touch himself or even put the book down.

"Yeah. And freezing. I need to warm up." He stripped out of his clothes and jumped on top of Derek, nipping at his neck. A gasp and shove were not what he'd been aiming for.

"Shit. You're freezing." Derek sat up and rubbed his hands over his skin. "You shouldn't have given me your jacket. If you get sick—"

Gripping the back of Derek's neck with enough force to counter any resistance, Scott shut Derek up with a kiss.

Derek sighed, sinking into Scott.

Heat blazed from the center of Scott's core, chasing back

any remnants of cold. After what seemed hours of kissing, Scott withdrew, finally getting a good whiff of himself. "I haven't showered all day."

Derek wordlessly hopped out of bed and shucked his boxers before Scott could say another word.

Chuckling, Scott undressed, grabbed a towel, and together, he and Derek scrambled down the hallway and entered the bathroom.

Under the spray of lukewarm water, Scott took advantage of having his boyfriend against his body. So strong and sculpted, yet pliant under Scott's touch.

Exploring his power over his lover, he slid his fingers down Derek's back, giving one ass cheek a firm squeeze.

Derek rutted his cock against Scott's thigh in response. "Mmm," he hummed through their tangle of lips and tongues.

Encouraged, Scott gripped Derek's other cheek and tugged their bodies together, rewarded by an audible gasp.

Better to keep their showering tame. After all, anyone could walk in at any minute.

Returning to languid kissing, Scott gripped Derek's cock and initiated a slow journey from base to tip and back again.

Derek ground into Scott's fist, taking Scott's own swollen member into his hand as well.

The combination of his desire to please his lover and Derek's talented touches put Scott on the edge faster than he'd expected.

Derek bit down on Scott's shoulder, his body stiffening and muffled groans filling the enclosed stall.

Scott closed his eyes. The first wave of his release hit, his cock pulsing in Derek's hand.

They drew together, forehead-to-forehead, panting. When Scott could think again, he cleaned Derek, attending to every inch of skin. He knew he wouldn't have to ask Derek to return the favor.

Back in their room and nestled warmly in bed, Derek finally

broke the spell cast by their mutual releases. "Good visit with your dad?"

Scott chuckled. "Yes. Great visit, actually. I can't believe how rapidly the barriers came down between the two of us."

"I'm really happy for the you." Derek rested his head on Scott's chest. "How's he doing?"

"Seems fine. His arm is getting better." Scott squeezed Derek closer, intertwining their legs. "Oh. I almost forgot. Dad wants to know if you'd stop by for a visit before you come to the tournament tomorrow."

"Really?" Derek tried to lift his head, but Scott held him in place.

"It's no big deal. Dad and I talked about how good things are between you and me, so he wants to get to know you better."

Derek nestled back into place on Scott's chest. "Okay."

Scott closed his eyes, a yawn escaping him. An image of the bracket on the gymnasium wall flashed in his mind, Lance's name emblazoned on the bottom line coming into clear view. Only fleetingly, powerless to invade Scott's consciousness for more than a second or two.

TWENTY-FIVE

SCOTT NUDGED DEREK AWAKE EARLY THE NEXT MORNING. "Babe, you mind catch up with you at the meet later?"

Derek rolled over, half-awake. "Mmm. What?"

"I want to swing by my house." He'd honor his promise to his father. "Mom and I will go to the tournament together."

"Fine." Derek yawned, flipped onto his stomach, and fell back to sleep.

Grabbing his jacket, not willing to make the same mistake as the night before, Scott crept out of their room. A bus and subway later, he tromped up his front steps. He'd never thought about coming home unannounced as a problem before, but with his dad reminding him to ask Mom about her life, Scott hesitated, wondering what he might encounter when he entered.

Steeling himself, he unlocked the door and stepped inside to warmth and the smell of coffee. "Mom? You in the kitchen."

"Scott!" She emerged at the top of the stairs. "What are you doing here?"

"I'm not interrupting anything, am I?" Scott wasn't sure whether he'd prefer to rip the Band-Aid off if she had company or hightail it back to the dorms.

"What could you possibly interrupt? Come in. I have fresh coffee in the pot." Mom disappeared back into the kitchen.

Scott took his usual seat as she busied herself preparing a cup for him. "I'm not complaining, but don't you have a tournament to get ready for?"

"I do, but I thought we could go together." Scott took a sip of the coffee. "Strong. You always make the best wake-up tonic."

"That's sweet of you to say." She sat in the chair next to him, the cup cradled in both hands. "Is everything all right?"

How to begin? For his entire life, he'd relied on Mom, letting her direct every conversation. Well, all of them except for the one when he came out and told her about Derek. He'd initiated that one with a lot of prompting from the handsome man still asleep in their room. "I've been so caught up with Dad, I realized I haven't paid any attention to you."

Mom tilted her head to the side, her there-has-to-be-something-wrong expression crinkling her brow. "Are you sure you're ok?"

Scott frowned. Dad was right. If Mom assumed negative things every time he came home, he had some serious making up to do. "I'm fine." He scratched the back of his head. "I wondered, I mean, er, you had mentioned, um—"

"Scott, do you have a statement or question in there somewhere?"

Fuck it! "You mentioned you'd met someone. How are things going?" There, he'd asked the question.

To her credit, Mom only widened her eyes for a split second before recomposing herself. "Greg? You came here to talk about him?"

"Well, not necessarily to *talk* about him, but to hear from you about how things are going." Scott took another sip of coffee, if for no other reason than to have a reason to not talk.

Mom opened and closed her mouth a few times. Without

speaking, she ran her fingers along Scott's arm. "What brought this on?"

The truth? Perhaps it would mean more if he chose the secondary, yet clearly accurate reason for asking. "Shouldn't I show an interest in what's going on in your life? I can't always expect you to keep track of me without reciprocating." Derek would be so proud.

His mother swiped at her eyes with the back of her hand. Scott hadn't seen the teary version of Mom for quite some time. "You're growing up so fast. Greg and I are doing well. Thank you for asking."

"You don't have something a bit more detailed for me?" Scott tried to infuse humor into his voice, but the fact she held back sharing information tugged at his heart.

"You really want to know?"

"I do." And damn if he didn't mean it. Maybe growing up meant he and Mom would become friends and not just parent-child.

Mom's eyes sparkled with a girlish energy he'd never seen before. "Well, he's very romantic. Flowers. Cards. Texts and calls to check in."

"Sounds like a good guy. What's he do?"

Mom chuckled. "Oh, he's so different than your father. He's an artist. Musician actually. He plays in a jazz band."

A musician? Can he support Mom or will she end up supporting him? Scott suppressed the urge to judge out loud.

"He's also practical. He teaches music lessons and his band has a fairly successful business playing for various celebrations."

Scott nodded, glad he hadn't said anything out loud. "And you've been dating since around Christmas?"

Mom darted her gaze to the coffee cup in her hands. "Maybe a bit before then. I didn't know how to bring it up to you with everything going on at school for you. You and Derek do seem to give a mother plenty to worry about."

Scott made a note to remedy that. "We're good. Back to you. How long have you been together?"

"About six months." Mom revealed the story of meeting Greg, Scott paying close attention, only distracted by the sporadic pang of guilt he hadn't thought to ask about his Mom's life until Dad told him to.

Mom didn't stop talking the whole ride to the tournament.

The morning match flew by uneventfully, Scott pinning his opponent in the first period. Which left him several hours to wait until his semi-final match, most likely against Lance.

Barely out of breath, Scott grabbed his sweats and tugged them on, and strode for a remote hallway deep in the athletic complex.

He pulled out his cell phone and called Derek, his nerves beginning to prickle when Derek didn't pick up.

Shoving his phone back into his pocket, Scott hustled back to the gymnasium. At least he could distract himself watching his teammates. Still, he checked the screen of his phone for missed calls ten times during the two minutes it took him to reach the other BU wrestlers.

An hour later, all quarter final matches completed and the semi-final brackets filled in, Scott still hadn't heard from Derek. He searched the bleachers for his mom and couldn't find her where she'd been sitting. A quick walk around the gymnasium yielded no results.

He was about to call Derek again when a strong hand gripped his shoulder with a touch. "Dude, I think you've pulled that thing out a million times. What's going on?"

Marcus. Scott could always count on his team captain and best friend to read him like an open book. "I've been trying to reach Derek and I can't find Mom." His voice came out strained and a bit high pitched.

"I'm sure Derek is taking advantage of some extra sleep and maybe your mom went to the bathroom or something."

"Maybe." Scott wanted to believe Marcus's reasoning, although a piece of him couldn't let go of Derek not answering the phone.

"Besides, you got bigger things to worry about." Marcus gave Scott's shoulder a squeeze. "You're wrestling Lance in the semis."

Scott hadn't even thought of checking to see if Lance won. "Figures. Well, I've got all day to plan out how to kick his ass." Something he'd be able to accomplish much easier if he could reach the two people who'd apparently disappeared on him.

"Seriously, what's got you all knotted up?" Marcus guided Scott to a bleacher and urged him to sit. "Maybe if you name it, you won't feel so stressed." He scrutinized Scott with piercing eyes. "You know you can take that idiot, right?"

Scott laughed. He hadn't meant to and immediately regretted it the second Marcus's face sunk. "No, I'm not worried about Lance. I can only think of one reason Derek wouldn't answer his phone, and I can't think of any reason why Mom would leave the gym without telling me."

Marcus's brows rose. "You think something happened with your dad?"

"Yeah. Wouldn't you?" Scott surprised himself with the frankness of his own question.

"I guess." Marcus patted Scott on the back. "You need anything?"

The perfunctory question of a good friend. Unless he were to find Derek, drag his ass to the gym, and plant him directly in front of Scott, there really wasn't anything Marcus could do. "No. I'll just have to get a grip."

Marcus regarded him with squinty eyes, then nodded. "C'mon. Let's watch the guys who didn't make the semi-finals. Hopefully, they'll be able to earn third or fourth place."

Scott forced a smile. "Yeah. Good idea."

By the time the semi-finals rolled around, Scott's nerves stretched to the point of snapping. Not only had he still not heard from Derek, but Mom hadn't returned from wherever she'd disappeared to and wasn't answering her phone either. "Where the fuck *are* they?"

Marcus shook his head. How he'd put up with Scott's neurotic behavior all day was a mystery. "I don't know. You're up pretty soon, so, if possible, you should get yourself mentally prepared."

Scott's gut clenched. Lashing words sprang to his mouth, barely restrained. Marcus wasn't trying to be insensitive, he wanted to help. "Yeah. I'll go stretch."

With a silent nod, Marcus turned his attention back to the other captain, the heavyweight, who'd lost in the quarter finals and currently wrestled for third place.

Scott grimaced, envisioning the loud and curse-laden tantrum likely to occur in the locker room at the end of the day.

Finding a private corner, he sat down, extending his legs in front of him. He pushed through the pain. A tension-filled day did nothing to keep muscles limber, not to mention the remnants of achiness from his lower back from the nearly healed extraction site. Slowly, his body relaxed and he could lay his torso flat against his thighs.

Other wrestlers and families gave him a wide berth as they shuffled about the room. Wanting his phone, and glad he'd left it in his bag, Scott concentrated on the upcoming match. Lance offered a challenge, but not a big one. As long as Scott could get his head in the right place, he could make it to the finals.

The announcer's voice cut through his thoughts just as he'd finished stretching. "The quarter final match for the one hundred fifty-seven weigh class will begin in two minutes on mat four."

Scott drew in and held a deep breath for a count of three

and exhaled sharply. As ready as he would be, he strode to the center of the room.

Coach and several of his teammates lined the fringe of the mat. Marcus sidled next to him before he reached them. "You ready for this?"

"Yup." Scott glanced around the mat, not surprised when he couldn't find Derek or his mother. Pushing disappointment aside, he stepped into the circle.

Lance already stood center ring, looking tall and gangly in his singlet. *Take him down fast and secure his arms.* Scott repeated the instructions as he approached his opponent.

He could sense his team and glanced in their direction, his breath hitching in his chest when he did. Derek stood next to Marcus, neither of them looking the least bit cheerful.

With no time to work out what happened, Scott forced himself to tear his gaze away and took Lance's extended hand.

"Good luck, boys. Start on my whistle." The ref placed his hand over Scott and Lance's joined grasp, then blew the whistle.

Lance snatched Scott's leg with surprising speed.

Oh hell no. Scott reacted on instinct, diving for the mat and rolling away. No way would the son of a bitch score even one point. Jumping to his feet, he circled Lance, all of his attention focused on his task.

Like an old friend, strategies formed in his head, grounding him and, for the first time all day, tearing his thoughts completely away from his father, his mom, and Derek.

With predatory focus, Scott waited for the perfect time to secure Lance's leg. His opening came seconds later when Lance stepped forward. Perhaps he'd initiated his own move, but Scott saw the leg and seized the opportunity, stepping in front of the other leg and earning his two points for the take down.

As he'd expected, Lance's long, sinewy body was difficult to hold. With each twist and buck, Scott lost his grip and had to secure a new hold.

Lance nearly escaped, swinging his legs in front of him and twisting his body so he could slide out from under Scott.

Frustration burned inside Scott, licking at raw nerves and crawling along his skin. Lance's words, the stress of seeing Derek after not being able to reach him for hours, uncertainty about his father, all coiled together into one massive ball of fire.

In a smooth motion, Scott cupped under Lance's chin and yanked him backwards, forcing him to fall onto his back, then jumped on top so he could finish the match once and for all.

The ref blew his whistle.

Scott froze. The period couldn't possibly be over, they'd just begun and he hadn't secured Lance's shoulders to the mat for the required three seconds.

"Penalty, BU. Illegal hold. One point Lehigh." The ref turned to Scott. One more penalty disqualifies you. Both of you, back to neutral position."

Scott stood at center mat again. Only twenty seconds had passed in the first period. He glanced in the direction where Derek had been before the match and spotted him right away. In the few seconds they locked eyes, more information passed between them than if they'd had an hour-long conversation. Something bad had happened. Only, Scott didn't know how bad. Worse, he couldn't take the time to find out in the middle of a match.

Scott shook his head. No matter what else happened outside of the ring, he had to put it aside, at least for the next five minutes and forty seconds.

Scott glared at Lance, glimpsing a snide smirk on his stupid face. Instead of the surge of anger he expected, Scott calmly took the final step to center ring.

The ref gave Scott a warning glance and blew his whistle.

Lightning couldn't have moved faster.

With all the energy he could muster, Scott shot for Lance's leg, sweeping it up and off the mat easily. Again, he took the bastard to the mat, but this time, he relied on years of training and practice.

He secured a half-nelson hold and began the process of cranking Lance to his back. Two points take down, three points back exposure. Three of those and he'd earn a technical pin.

Lance arched and twisted, but Scott simply adjusted himself, countering each move.

By the end of the first period, he led ten to one. Lance opted for bottom position, which annoyed Scott only because it would take him longer to finish the match. The most he could earn from the top was three back points, unless he earned the pin, which wasn't likely.

He cranked Lance to his back, but after five seconds, he hopped off, allowing Lance to escape.

A collective gasp surrounded him. The crowd around the mat thickened.

Despite the reaming he knew he'd get from Coach, Scott had other priorities and wanted to end the match as swiftly as possible. While he'd sucked at math in high school, keeping a mental tab on the score while wrestling had been a natural talent. The three back points he'd earned put the score at thirteen to one. Scott needed a fifteen-point lead for the match to end in a technical pin. He could earn the three remaining points with a take down and back exposure.

Then he could finally get some answers.

Scott circled Lance on the mat. Lance gripped his arm, tugging, likely testing Scott's balance. "Big mistake letting me escape, faggot."

The ref blew the whistle. "Penalty, Lehigh. Inappropriate language." Scott stepped back to the center of the mat, chuckling through breathy panting. No need to respond. Lance got what he deserved. Besides, the extra point meant Scott only needed a take down to finish the match.

With precision, he secured one of Lance's legs, took him down to the mat, and, for the fourth time, maneuvered him to his back. He didn't have time to attempt back points. The ref blew the whistle.

Scott could feel the corners of his mouth lift, tugging his face into what had to be a tauntingly obnoxious grin. The luxurious gratification lasted until the ref raised his arm in the air, declaring him the winner.

And then he spotted Derek and Mom again, holding Scott's sweats and gym bag.

His spirits crashed as he trudged off the mat, wordlessly passing his coach and teammates, and following two very serious people to the exit of the gymnasium. Once they'd cleared the bulk of people-traffic, Derek handed Scott his clothes. "Here, get dressed. We have to go."

"I should shower first." A stupid thing to say, but anything to avoid hearing whatever made Derek look so serious.

"We don't have *time* for that. We have to go *now.*" Derek crossed his arms over his chest.

"Honey, Derek's right." Mom spoke calmly, although her bloodshot eyes showed she'd been crying.

Scott deflated, his chance to prolong whatever came next evaporating. "What's wrong?"

Derek's expression softened. "It's your dad. He…" Derek gaped, color draining from his face.

"Did he die?" Scott couldn't believe how easily the question slipped out of him.

"No." Mom answered., yet Scott could sense no relief in her expression. "But he's not doing well. We need to go."

Without another word, Scott tugged on his sweats. How could his father not be doing well? A day earlier he'd been full of energy. His arm was getting better. The future was unfolding as Scott hoped.

They rushed in silence to Derek's car. As Derek drove, Mom following behind in her own car, Scott stole side glances, wanting information and afraid of what he might hear. Derek's tightly sealed lips and churning jaw muscle let Scott know he'd only get bad news if he asked.

Derek drove them right up to the hospital entrance. "You go in. I'll park. Shannon and I will meet you up there."

Scott reached for the door handle, then stopped. "What am I gonna see?" Derek bit his lip. "No. Don't. Whenever you do, it means you're trying to think of what to say. Just be straight with me."

Derek's eyes widened for a fraction of a second. "Never thought I'd hear *that* request from you." The brief levity vanished as suddenly as it formed. "His infection returned, much worse than before. They're not sure…" Derek gazed at Scott, eyes wide, tears shimmering on their surface.

Nothing more needed to be said. If the roles were reversed, Scott wouldn't want to be the one to deliver those fateful words. Stretching over the console, Scott kissed Derek on the lips. "Hurry." He hopped out of the car and rushed toward the hospital entrance.

Whatever Scott imagined he'd see, nothing matched the picture of his father, gray, except for an angry purple blotch on the inside of his arm and the faint glimmer of light reflecting off his sweaty skin.

He secured a face mask into place. Forcing one foot in front of the other took concentration. As he drew closer, more details came into focus. Dad's dry, cracked lips. His cheekbones protruding with alarming clarity, offset by sunken cheeks and eyes. The gown, which barely fit his father's small frame, rested low enough on his chest to put his collar bones on prominent display.

His father lolled his head to the side and Scott knew the instant recognition set in by the way his eyes opened a bit wider.

At least there was some life there. He rushed to his father's side, a strangled, "Dad," escaping through his impossibly tight throat.

"Scott." Dad's voice came out weak, scratchy. "You're here." He started coughing, gently at first, but steadily growing into a body-shaking hack.

Scott rubbed his father's back. "You okay, Dad? Need some water?"

Dad gripped Scott's arm, drawing in several ragged breaths. He collapsed against the pillows and reached toward the side table where only a pink cup sat. "Water." Sandpaper on wood sounded smoother than his father's voice.

He gave Dad the cup and watched as the frail man took small sips. "Sorry." His tone resonated more clearly. "How did today go?"

"What?" Scott scrutinized at his father, seconds passing before he could form words. "Are you kidding me?"

Dad's whole body slumping heavily into the bed. "No. Just putting off what needs to be said."

Scott shook his head, unsure what caused him to do so. "What's going on, Dad? Please. Tell me."

His father closed his eyes and drew in a deep breath, letting it out on ragged sigh. At least he'd recovered from the coughing. "I'm afraid we have a problem." He glanced at his arm. "The infection's spread and is now in my bloodstream. I'm septic."

"Isn't that what they have antibiotics for?" Scott noticed the absence of a needle running into his father's infected arm.

"They aren't working," Dad stated matter-of-factly.

How could he be so calm? "What about a transfusion?"

"It doesn't work that way. My body has to be able to take care of infections. If my immune system doesn't want to work…" He left the rest of his sentence hanging in the air between them.

Stress from the whole day wound itself into a tight, painful ball in Scott's chest. Not being able to reach Derek or his mom, receiving a warning for the first time ever in his wrestling career.

For what? To end like this? "No. You *can't* give up. I won't let you." Tears sprang to his eyes, making his vision blurry.

Dad's eyes widened for a split second, then he relaxed again. He glanced toward the entrance of the room, prompting Scott to do the same. Mom stood in the doorway. "Is everything all right in here?"

Stupid question, from someone who kept essential information from him all day long. "No. Everything is very *far* from all right!" He hadn't meant to scream, but doing so helped dislodge the ball of fury crushing his heart. "How could you keep this from me? Why didn't you find me at the tournament?"

"Scott, I…" She darted her attention toward his father.

Dad answered the question for her. "It's okay, Shannon. Leave us so we can talk."

She wrung her hands a few times, glancing back and forth between Dad and Scott, then nodded and skittered away.

Alone, anger at the ready, Scott glared at his father, planned his next words, took aim, and fired. "So, this is it. You come into my life, make me believe we can build the relationship I've always wanted, and in the end, you leave me again."

Far harsher words than Scott intended, though his father didn't even flinch. "Do you really believe that?"

What other choice did he have but to blindly cling to the one thought with enough power to hold Scott together? "Maybe not exactly the way I said it, but the end result is the same."

"Is it?" Dad remained calm, simply watching Scott.

"Yes. In the end, I lose you all over again. It would've been better if you'd never—"

"Don't say things you'll regret later."

Scott cringed, thankful his father had stopped him before he'd been able to finish his sentence. Scott knew, without a doubt, the haunting questions he'd never have been able to answer.

The pulsing heat flowing through his veins prevented him from voicing those thoughts.

"I'm sorry, Scott. I really wish this story had a different ending, but I'm choosing to look at what we've gained instead of focusing on what we're going to lose." The words reminded him of Derek, so perfectly identical to the sort of thing his lover would say.

"I won't recover from this." Scott sank into the chair by Dad's bed, tears streaming freely down his cheeks.

"You will. Because of the time we've shared over the past few months, you'll be able to move forward as a complete and whole person. You'll know what we could have been. What we were at the end." A hint of a smile lit his face. "And so will I."

Platitudes of closure weren't what he wanted to hear, but at least the raging anger subsided. "It's not fair. This was supposed to work. We were supposed to have a second chance."

Dad took Scott's hand. "We took full advantage of the time we had."

True. "But it's not enough. I want more. I want years and decades. I want you to see who I become and to guide me along the way."

"I've already seen the man you've become and it's easy to see what your future holds. It will be filled with brilliant happiness.

Scott shook his head. "I don't see how."

"Because you have Derek," he stated.

True. Although Scott refused to admit so out loud. With Derek in his life, nothing could ever truly be bad. To speak the words would be the same as accepting this unwanted fate.

He looked at his father, barely able to make out the details of his face through the tears. "I don't want to lose you."

Dad rubbed Scott's hand. "I know, but you'll always have this, the past few months we've spent together. You'll know for the rest of your life I'm looking out for you, even if it isn't in the way either of us hoped for."

"What was the point in any of it?" Scott spit the words out with venom.

"What's the point in anything?" His father interrupted before Scott could continue his rant, "The point is, we're here for a short while and every minute we have is a blessing. When you move forward in your life, you'll carry me with you."

Scott couldn't deny the truth of those words. No matter what, he'd think of his dad and this period of time with fondness. "It's not enough."

"Maybe not right now, but in time it will be." Dad closed his eyes. "Bad memories have a way of fading away. It's human nature to heal. You'll feel pain, at first, but memories of these past few months will be what sticks, and someday..." his voice cracked, and he paused before speaking again. When he did, the words came out through a strangled voice. "Someday, when you have kids, you'll be the kind of father to them I was able to be now. Hopefully, you'll tell them the good stories we created together, and let me live on through them."

Scott shook his head. "You're talking about things that may never happen."

Dad leveled Scott with a gravely serious expression. "Oh, they'll happen. I'm positive." He reclined against the pillows, a new sheen of sweat emerging along his clammy skin. "You and Derek will live a long, happy life together."

Derek. Earlier he'd wanted to wring his boyfriend's neck for keeping all of this from him, but sitting by his dying father's bed, he wanted nothing more than to have the safe, loving embrace of strong arms holding him close.

Like magic, Derek appeared in the doorframe. Without saying anything, he rushed to Scott and pulled him into a tight hug.

"Ask the nurse to come in, would you, Derek?" Dad tried to sit up, shaking arms forcing him to give up the effort.

Derek darted out of the room.

Alone with his father again, Scott did the only thing he could think of to do. He helped Dad sit up. He'd make himself helpful even if he didn't know what to say.

"I'd like you to spend the night. The nurse can bring in a cot. I'd like you to be here if I need you." Dad reached his hand toward Scott. "Would you?"

"Sure, Dad." What else could he say? What more could he do?

The nurse put in a perfunctory objection at his father's request, but caved in far too easily to convince Scott he had any real objection.

"Derek. You'll be staying too." Dad hadn't asked a question.

"Yes, sir." Derek stood to the side as an orderly wheeled a cot into the room, then climbed onto it after Scott has taken his spot nearest his father.

Sometime, in the middle of the night, Scott stirred, then opened his eyes. His father watched him, light from the hallway sparking in his eyes. "You okay, Dad?"

"It's nice being able to see you here whenever I open my eyes. You look so peaceful when you sleep. Always did."

"Mmm." Scott closed his eyes, drifting back to the blackness.

"Scott. How did you do today?"

In all the confusion, Scott had never told his father about the second day of the tournament. "I made it to the finals. Second place is fine. I need to be here."

"No." Dad's voice rose just above a whisper. Derek stirred next to Scott drawing both of their attention. "No," he said more quietly. "You have to finish this. For both of us."

Too tired to argue, Scott nodded, then closed his eyes.

Scott pretended to be asleep. Dad stood in the doorway. He could tell by the scent of coffee perfuming the air. He was in his childhood bedroom, the one before his family started moving all the time. "Good night," Dad whispered, his voice now right next to Scott's ear, followed by an equally tender kiss to his forehead.

The floor boards creaked as his father tiptoed toward Scott's bedroom door. "I love you, little man, always will."

The door closed with a soft clicking sound.
And then, a steady buzz…

Scott woke up, glanced around the unfamiliar room until he remembered where he was, then reached out to take his father's hand.

He recoiled at the touch of icy skin. Bolting upright, he swiveled in the cot. His father lay in bed, his skin a pale shade of blue, eyes closed, and arms folded peacefully across his very still chest.

Dim morning light filled the room, the beginning of a new day. A day without Ronald Thayer.

Derek wrapped his arms around Scott, hot drops of wetness falling on Scott's shoulder.

"He's gone." Scott turned in Derek's arms and sank into the loving embrace.

TWENTY-SIX

THE NEXT HOUR PASSED BY IN A BLUR, SCOTT SIMPLY MOVING from place to place, directed by either Derek or Mom as nurses and other medical staff buzzed in and out of the room.

The doctor announced the time of death and completed all paperwork. Scott found himself stranded, although surrounded by loved ones, in the middle of the hospital hallway.

Mom took action. "Honey, I have to arrange a few things, and I know you came with Derek, and…" Tears welled in her eyes as she pulled Scott into a tight embrace. "I'm so sorry, baby."

Scott wrapped his arms around his mother, engulfed in the familiar scent of lavender, but he'd cried all the tears he had in him. At least for the morning. "Okay, Mom. I love you."

His mother stepped out of the hug and cupped Scott's cheek. "You've grown into a man. When did *that* happen?"

"I dunno. I guess while you weren't looking." He hadn't meant the words to hurt, but he could see the pain flicker in his mother's eyes. "Sorry."

"I'll see you back at the house." She glanced at Derek and nodded.

Scott caught the tail end of Derek's return head nod. Scott felt his body clench and then heard the words spill from him, "Hell, no. No more secrets. No behind-the-scenes plotting about what's best for me. Talk. Now."

Several nurses glanced in his direction, but Scott didn't care. The whole floor could watch and it wouldn't change a thing he'd say if they didn't spill the beans right then and there.

Derek placed a tentative hand on Scott's shoulder. "We think you need to finish the tournament." To his credit, he didn't flinch as he spoke.

"You thi…you exp…you wan…are you fucking *crazy*?"

This time, Derek shrunk back, but only slightly. "No. well, yes to the tournament part, but only because of Ronald."

"What in the *hell* does my father have to do with this? He's dead, Derek, he has no opinion about this."

"Actually, he does." Derek reached into his pocket and pulled out an envelope, the manila kind with a clasp. "Ronald wanted me to give you this."

"What? When did he…*that's* why he wanted you to stop by?" Scott struggled to find the words to express his anger, but his tongue apparently decided to take a vacation. Wordlessly he yanked the envelope from Derek's hand.

Scott recognized his father's handwriting. Funny how a few months ago he wouldn't have had a clue what his dad's handwriting looked like. Slowly, as if each moment of revealing the letter's contents prolonged the loss ripping his heart out, Scott tilted the package until something fell into his hand.

He ambled over to a couch and sat, placing the envelope on his lap. He held up a hemp necklace with an amulet attached. When he recognized the object, his chest constricted, solitary tears forming in each eye and running lonely paths down his cheeks.

The four-leaf clover, encased in glass or plastic, pressed flat and surrounded by sterling silver. The actual necklace part was dark brown, about three millimeters in width.

An image of his dad's face, smiling with the excitement of a toddler, flashed in Scott's head. He'd been so happy when he found the clover. To think, he'd taken the time to make it into something Scott could actually wear.

Clasping the gift around his neck, Scott returned his attention to the envelope. Reaching inside, he felt what he knew would be there. Slowly, desperate to know what his father wanted to say, yet fully aware this would be the last communication from the man, Scott withdrew the letter.

Words only covered one side of one page. Scott smoothed the paper on his lap, drawing in a shuddering breath. His father was still with him, still had something to say, as long as he didn't read the letter.

Seconds ticked by, Scott covering the final words of Ronald Thayer.

Then, he read the letter.

Dear Scott,

If you're reading this, it means I'm gone. I know we both wanted a different outcome, but life gives us what we get and it's up to us to make the most of it.

Which is why I want you to finish the tournament. Do your best, as I tried to do mine, and see this thing through to the end. I won't be there the way you want me to, but I'll be there just the same.

Victory or not, you win when you seize every moment.

In the times when you're feeling down and doubt seems to pile, remember you have that four-leaf clover to keep me close by, looking out for you.

There's always hope for happiness, Scott. So be happy. It's the best thing you could ever do for me.

I love you, my son.

Dad

. . .

Scott folded the letter and closed his eyes. Hot tears streamed down his cheeks, yet the ripping torment of the past few hours seemed to ease a bit. He tried to feel his father's presence, breathing in, focusing on signals inside to indicate Dad's presence.

Nothing.

Reaching toward his face to rub the sting from his eyes, his fingers brushing against the pendant. He gripped it between thumb and forefinger, the smooth surface pressing comfortably against his skin, and he could see his father, smiling, on top of the mountain. He snapped his eyes open. The shift from a vision of his dad to the blaring lights of the hospital made him a bit dizzy.

Derek came into focus first, standing a few feet away, his face radiating love and concern. "Derek." Scott stood and closed the distance between them. So many questions to ask, yet he simply wrapped his arms around the man he loved and squeezed him tight. No matter what else happened, he had love and safety and everything good that came from having Derek in his life.

"You okay?" Derek whispered in his ear.

"I am." He didn't have to think about his response. "We need to get to the athletic complex."

Derek held Scott at arm's length. "You sure?"

Scott's response flew out of him without hesitation. "Yes."

He took Derek's hand and led him toward the elevators. "But I'll need to completely lose it later on."

Derek nodded, a mixture of humor and sadness keeping his smile from spreading too far. "Good." He took Scott's hand and together they walked to the parking lot.

They drove in silence, a peaceful relaxation filling the space they shared. Scott rolled the pendant in his fingers, picturing various times he's spent with his dad over the past few months, all of them happy.

As they arrived at the athletic complex, an electric buzz

blasted through the serenity inside the car, yanking Scott from his reverie. People milled about the parking lot, every school color waving in all directions.

He stepped out of the car. "Jesus. I forgot how intense the final day can be. Let's get to the locker room. I want quiet before I wrestle."

Derek tugged at Scott, dragging him past hordes of people, and yanking with special force whenever they approached someone they knew.

"Hey, there's Marcus. Shouldn't we tell him?" Scott said, barely slowing his pace as Derek dragged him along.

"I already called him. You had enough to worry about." The slight squeeze to Scott's hand let him know Derek only had good intentions, even if the news wasn't really his to share. At least it explained the odd looks he received from the guys on the team.

Safely inside, Scott relaxed and air filled his lungs. "Stay with me?" Scott almost laughed at how innocent he sounded, like when he'd been young and clung to his father's hand at bedtime, not wanting him to leave. Like his dad had made him feel back then, Scott knew he needed Derek by his side if he were going to make it through the next few hours.

Derek sealed their lips together in a brief, yet intense, kiss. The kind that told Scott how powerfully Derek loved him. "You never have to ask."

Most of the guys on the team gave him space, glancing in his direction, giving him a head nod. Scott would break the ice and talk to them later, once he'd gotten himself in the right head-space for his finals match.

Derek remained by his side, playing bodyguard whenever someone approached who didn't have enough sense to read the scene. Still, in his own talented way, he diverted people tactfully. God bless him, he tried his best to keep Marcus away, failing, to no one's surprise.

Marcus plunked down next to Scott on the bench where he sat, slinging an arm over Scott's shoulder. "I'm so sorry about your dad. You know I'm here for you. You're my brother."

Scott leaned into Marcus. "Thanks. I'm gonna need you. Right now I want to get ready for my match. Then I'm takin' off."

Marcus nodded. "I hear you, but when I'm done, I'm swinging by, even if it's just to sit around staring at your ceiling."

"Okay, you got it," Scott said on a sad chuckle.

"Good luck." Marcus clapped Scott on the back, and left him in far more capable hands.

Derek took the spot Marcus left. "You okay?"

"Yeah. He's a good guy. One of the best." His mouth curved up a fraction of an inch. "But he's not the *best.*"

Derek pressed his forehead against Scott's. "I love you."

"I love you too."

Scott savored Derek's warmth, inhaling his slightly musky scent. *Poor guy's been through nearly as much as I have today.* "I think it's time for me to grace the gymnasium. One last match, then we can deal with the rest."

Grasping Derek's hand, Scott led him out of the locker room.

The din of hundreds of voices filled the air when Scott entered the gym, soft and blurry, but filled with excitement. The room seemed much larger, only one mat lying in the center of the room. The sole focus on this last short day of the tournament was the final matches.

"Nothing like a stage." Scott swallowed back the lump in his throat. Whether from nerves, sadness, or maybe even some fear, he wasn't sure, but he'd be on display during one of the most private moments of his life.

"You don't have to do this, Scott." Derek squeezed his hand. "If it's too much, you can say so. No one would think any less of you."

"Dad wants me to." Scott, gazed about the room, soaking in the ambiance. People-filled bleachers surrounded an open floor with laughing groups of wrestlers intermingling with players from other schools. Finalists stretched and jumped rope.

Scott normally loved championship matches. The final battle to claim the title of champion. Not today. Dad should've been there to share in the excitement.

Scott pressed his eyes closed, willing the tears to retreat. He swallowed hard, forcing the lump back down to his stomach. "I can do this. I *have* to."

Derek simply nodded and followed Scott to the BU finalists' warm up area.

Marcus spotted them and rushed over. "C'mon. Let's do some spins."

Scott followed his friend to an open space along one wall. The three other wrestlers from his team nodded at Scott as he passed them, one mouthing "Sorry" before looking away.

"Forget them. They don't know what to say." Marcus got down on all fours. "You go first. Thirty seconds."

Scott lowered himself onto Marcus's back. He spun as fast as he could, switching direction every time Marcus called "Switch!"

When he finished, he fell back onto his haunches, blood pounding through his veins. "Awesome. You go now."

Marcus lowered his weight onto Scott's back. "Be harsh, man. Make me work."

Scott laughed and braced himself to support Marcus's weight. The friction from the spinning, Marcus's chest in constant contact with Scott's back, helped nudge Scott into the mood and tone of the room.

After two more rounds, both wrestlers rolled into sitting

positions and grabbed for their water bottles. Scott took a long drink, savoring the coolness of air brushing against his dampened neck. Derek plopped down next to him, not saying anything, not having to.

Several beads of liquid ran down Marcus's neck and arms, so he'd likely had a good warm-up too. "I'm ready to crush it today." He held up his hand for a high-five, which Scott gave him immediately. "It's been one hell of a year, huh?"

Scott wasn't sure whether Marcus meant the season, or everything going on in Scott's life since Christmas. Probably a bit of both. "Yeah. It has."

Marcus nodded, his silence creating a bubble surrounding the three of them. "I don't know how you're doing it, man. I know I should probably shut up right now, but I couldn't be here if I'd gone through what you did."

Derek angled forward, only a bit, imperceptible to anyone who didn't know how to read his body language.

Down boy! Scott squeezed Derek's knee, but directed his words to Marcus. "I know and I don't want to talk about it. We'll talk later. Promise."

Marcus placed his hands on the floor and pushed himself up. "I'll hold you to that." He nodded toward Derek and ambled back to the other BU finalists.

Alone with Derek, Scott stretched out his legs into a V shape and stretched forward, grabbing his right toe with both hands. No sense in talking since Derek would surely have something to say.

Not disappointing, Derek tucked his legs to his chest, hugging them and resting his chin on his knees. "You okay?"

He hadn't meant to laugh, but predicting Derek's actions was as natural to Scott as breathing. "I'm in the right place for wrestling my match." He gazed directly into Derek's eyes, wanting Derek to see as well as hear Scott's reassurance. "I can do this and later, I can handle that too. With you."

Scott stretched, oblivious to his surroundings, until Derek nudged Scott's leg. "I think someone wants to talk to you."

Scott followed Derek's line of vision. Zane stood, sort of awkwardly, a few feet away. Under normal circumstances, he wouldn't want to talk to the person he'd have to wrestle for first place, but nothing fit into the category of "normal" anymore. "Hey."

Zane sat on the floor so the three men formed a triangle. "I heard about your dad. I'm sorry."

Scott fought back the urge to question him how he knew.

Zane had an answer for him anyway. "I saw you when you entered the gym and wanted to come talk to you some more about transferring to BU, but you seemed so…distracted, I guess, so I kept my distance. Then I saw your captain. Marcus, is it?"

Scott nodded. "Yep. Good old Marcus." He'd have to remember to give the guy a speech about discretion.

"Anyways, he told me what happened." Zane stared at the empty portion of mat between them. "Actually, he looked at me like I had two heads, asked me why I wanted to talk to you." He lifted his head, making direct eye contact with Scott. "He told me what happened when I mentioned my interest in joining your team."

That sounded like the Marcus to Scott. Probably thought Zane wanted more than just wrestling and got all defensive. "I wonder if he's smart enough to put two and two together. If you come to the team, I have an excuse to bump up a weight class, which means he'll have to as well. You may have saved me a tough conversation."

Derek punched Scott's arm. "Be nice. Marcus is very smart."

"I know." Scott kissed Derek's cheek.

He glanced up to Zane's dreamy-eyed expression. "You two are so perfect together."

And did he detect a hint of sadness lurking under the surface of his tone? Scott remembered feeling the way Zane looked. "Man, you come over to BU and guys will trip over each other to get to you."

Derek shook his head. "You talk about him like he's a piece of meat." He disregarded Scott and turned his full attention to Zane. "We have a very strong alliance on campus and we're quite active. I actually hold an office, so if you decide to transfer here, I'd be happy to let you know about our meetings and activities."

"You don't even know me and you're already inviting me to be a part of your group?" Zane's eyes shimmered.

Scott clapped him on the shoulder. "My man is the absolute best possible sort of person. He'd help a skunk find a tree to spray if he thought it would make the skunk happy."

Both Derek and Zane stared at him, mouths slightly ajar. "Uh, thanks?" Derek finally chimed in.

"You know what I mean." Scott stretched toward his other foot until his chest touched his knee.

Zane chuckled. "Well, I wanted to say I'm sorry and good luck in the match later."

Is this guy for real? "Thanks, man. You too."

Zane nodded and hopped up. "I guess I'll talk to you later." He strode across the room.

Scott followed his retreat for several seconds, only drawn back to Derek at the sound of a breathy huff. *Uh oh.* "Something on your mind?"

Derek remained silent for a moment and shook his head. "No. I really wanted to *not* like him. But he's awesome."

A smile tugged at Scott's cheeks. "Is my little Derek jealous again?"

Derek shot Scott a glower. "I'm not so little anymore if you haven't noticed."

Holding up his hands in surrender, Scott felt a piece of

heaviness fall away for the first time all day. "Believe me. I've noticed."

"Besides, this time, I wanted to dislike him because he stands between you and the championship." Derek's cheeks pinked, but he also scooted a little closer to Scott. Close enough so Scott could kiss the man of his dreams on the lips. "And maybe I got a little jealous."

The two BU wrestlers preceding Scott won their matches, giving the team an energized buzz and drawing a great deal of attention from other teams. The crowd congealed around the mat in time for Scott's match.

Derek and the team held a prime spot at the edge of the circle, but the electricity in the air outweighed any comfort Scott could draw from their presence. Zane stood opposite him at center mat. A talented wrestler, and, it turned out, a really nice guy. Someone Scott could see calling *friend*. On top of everything else, when the match ended, Scott would have to deal with the loss of his father.

Weird day.

Zane extended his hand and Scott shook firmly. The two wrestlers locked eyes, a silent *good luck* passing between them, and then the ref blew the whistle.

Scott found himself locked in an equal match right from the start, Zane gripping his arms, circling in time with Scott, and Scott focusing on Zane's legs, looking for a takedown.

Each time Scott saw an opening to swoop down and claim Zane's leg, a sharp tug pulled him off balance and he'd have to start all over. They continued like this for the remainder of the first period, each of them missing the first strike move by split seconds.

By second period, Scott dripped with sweat. Zane chose to start in bottom position, giving Scott a chance to observe him.

He seemed no better off, his skin reflecting the overhead lights. He'd be hard to hold onto because of the slickness.

As expected, Scott's hand slid along Zane's sweaty arm as he took the top position. When the ref started the period, Zane shot out of Scott's grasp, earning one point for escaping. They spent another two minutes circling each other from neutral position.

Scott earned the one point back at the beginning of the third period when he started from bottom position.

His muscles wobbled as he stood in neutral position again with his worthy opponent. They crashed together in two exhausted heaps of muscle. He couldn't remember the last time he'd felt so spent from wrestling. Even his thoughts blurred as he tried to process his next move.

He only lost focus for a split second, thinking of his dad, sadness crowding out thoughts of championship titles.

All the time Zane needed.

With a firm tug, he pulled Scott's arm, forcing him to brace the movement with a stabilizing leg. A leg which ended up in Zane's grasp. Scott crashed to the mat, Zane coming down with him.

For the remainder of the match, Scott struggled to crawl back to his base and escape.

There was still time.

Until there wasn't.

The buzzer sounded.

He'd lost.

Defeated in more ways than one, Scott rolled onto his back, his chest heaving as he sucked in air. Sounds blurred, colors swirled together, and a wave of nausea washed through him. He closed his eyes, the darkness easing the disequilibrium. He'd lost. He'd let his dad down. In the end, nothing worked out the way it should have.

All of this in a split second, then he opened his eyes and forced himself to stand.

Zane also struggled to get to his feet, his arms trembling as he supported his weight.

When they both finally returned to center mat, they shook hands and the ref lifted Zane's into the air. Scott kept his eyes on Zane, who stared back at him, something like an apology in his eyes.

Sorry for beating him? Sorry about his dad? Scott didn't have time to contemplate the answer, finding himself pulled forward into a hug.

"Great match." Zane squeezed once, patted Scott's back, and broke away from him.

Together, they trudged off the mat. Derek and the team silently parted for them as they passed.

A million thoughts crashed together in Scott's head. *Is this what crazy feels like?*

Zane stopped walking and tilted his head to the side. "You're laughing?"

Am I? The ridiculousness of his behavior crashed into Scott and he felt his lips tug further upwards and then, against his will, into heartier laughter. "I don't know why." As he spoke, he couldn't tell whether he talked or cried.

Derek appeared at his side, sliding his arm around Scott's back. "C'mon. Let's go to the locker room."

The world came back into focus. People watched as Derek led him out of the gymnasium, some with disapproval, others with genuine concern. He glanced over his shoulder before exiting the gym, his team standing as a group, all eyes on him.

Derek steered him through the doors, and the craziness vanished.

Scott inhaled deeply. "I need to get outside."

"No, let's—"

Scott was already halfway down the hallway. He burst through the front doors of the athletic complex, earning the shock to his system he so dearly craved. The wind bit at his wet skin like tiny ice-pics. Fresh, chilled air filled his lungs, pouring energy back into him. Better than water.

Derek stepped beside him. "Scott, look at me."

Scott whirled, shivering a bit, having adjusted slightly to the cold. Greeted by Derek's wide-eyed gaze boring into him, he finally let go. His muscles relaxed. His mind unclenched, and he collapsed against Derek, sobbing onto his shoulder.

He didn't know how he ended up in Derek's car, dressed in his regular clothes. The heat from the dash blasted on full, bouncing off Scott's impenetrable ice shield.

He touched his face, his fingers and cheeks numb. His feet too.

"Scott!" Derek's shouting cut through his random attention to his limbs.

"What?" Scott lolled his head to the side so he could see Derek. Pale cheeks. Tight lips. Knuckles pressing through the skin of hands gripping the steering wheel tightly. All of these registered in a flash, snapping him to attention. "What's wrong?"

Derek visibly relaxed, his entire body sinking into the driver's seat. "I called your name three times before I had to shout to get your attention. Are you okay?"

Scott reached over the console, placing his hand on Derek's thigh. Heat radiated against his palm. "I lost. Dad's gone and I'm really *not* okay."

Reaching down to grip Scott's hand, Derek drew in a sharp inhale. "You're freezing. I'm taking you home and you're getting right into the shower."

Scott nodded. "Will you shower with me?"

"Seriously, Scott, talk to me." Derek snapped a quick glimpse at Scott, then returned his gaze to the road.

"I'm not joking around. Please shower with me. I want to be with you for a while. To hold you, with the water sealing us together." Scott dropped his head back, closing his eyes and sighing. "I'll talk later. Right now I need to think."

Derek responded with a soothing gentleness. “I can live with that.”

Mom was busy on the phone when they arrived at Scott’s house. She glanced in their direction, but turned her attention back to the person on the other end of the line. “No, we won’t be needing the large room…yes, cremation.”

Scott glanced at his watch. Only two o’clock. Dad had only been gone for about six hours. He took Derek’s hand and dragged him toward his room, not wanting to listen to the logistics of the plans for his father’s remains.

Under the spray of hot water, Scott simply hugged Derek, replaying the past few months through his head. The letter at Christmas. The museum. Meets where his father’d cheered him on. Camping. Visits to Dr. T. Time spent at Dad’s hotel. All ending with their final moments together in the hospital.

Scott pulled Derek closer, a shield against the final thought Scott didn’t want to face. The one where he’d have to admit total failure. Both he and his father lost their battles. *Don’t hope for the best.* The apparent lesson from his dad coming back into his life, then exiting it again in such a final way?

Scott broke the silence, spitting his words out bitterly. “It wasn’t worth it.”

Derek remained silent.

“I feel like my heart’s been ripped out of my chest and thrown away. I was angry before, but now I’m devastated, which is worse. I never expected to have Dad as part of my life. Then he comes back, and now…” The words caught in Scott’s throat.

“It *was* worth it.” Derek rested his head against Scott’s shoulder, running his hands in a soothing path up and down Scott’s back. “Now you know your father loved you. He *always* loved you and didn’t know how to show it.”

“What does it matter? He’s gone. I couldn’t even do the one thing he asked of me. I lost my match.” Scott closed his eyes. Maybe blocking everything out would make his pain go away. “I couldn’t even honor my father’s last wish.”

"Are you sure?"

The question hung in the air, Scott struggling to sort through a multitude of possible responses. Dad wanted him to wrestle. To win. Well, he hadn't actually said he wanted Scott to win. He wanted him to see the tournament through, but what difference did it make if he lost in the end?

"You honored your father by doing one of the bravest things I've ever seen anyone do." Derek's voice echoed softly in the closed room. "There's no way I could have pulled it together the way you did."

"Yeah, right," Scott huffed, his tone dripping with sarcasm.

"Seriously. The way you finished what you started. It's what Ronald wanted for you. I don't think he really cared whether you won or lost. I think he wanted you to complete the journey you and he started together."

"For what? He's not around to comfort me. He won't be here next season. Or the season after that. Or ever." Scott released Derek, resting heavily against the tiled wall. "He won't be here when you and I get married and have kids. He's gone."

"Is he?" Derek stared at Scott.

"What do you mean?" Anger licked its way up Scott's throat like a flame crawling along a piece of dry wood.

Derek forged on before Scott could say anything. "I mean, is he really gone? You opened your heart to him. You bonded."

He had to admit Derek's words made sense. "Not in the way I want. He's not here, physically. It's not good enough." At least he could hold onto his stubbornness for a while.

"I know." Derek hugged Scott again. "But you got the dad you always wanted. You got the answer to the question you'd always been asking yourself."

Scott wanted to lash out: *Oh yeah, what answer is that?* But he already knew the answer. His father loved him. Scott knew, although the realization offered no comfort, Dad's love would help the empty place inside him to heal. In time, he'd be able to live his life with a whole heart.

Too much. He wasn't ready to accept anything good could come from losing his father. He refused to admit the time they'd spent together over the past few months was anything but a huge reopening of an old wound. One that wouldn't heal this time.

TWENTY-SEVEN

SCOTT PROGRESSED IN A HAZE THROUGH THE NEXT FEW DAYS. The hospital released Dad's body to Mom. The only people attending the small wake were friends of Scott's. No one his father had even known. Then the cremation.

Back home, a crowd of about twenty filled the living room and kitchen. Some of the guys from the team spilled out into the back yard, milling about, probably waiting for an excuse to leave.

Scott sat on a couch, Derek on one side, Mom on the other. Derek's parents arranged for the food and busied themselves with details Scott couldn't have focused on if he tried.

"I sure am sorry about your dad, Scott." Coach sat in a chair facing Scott, his forearms resting on his knees. "And I'm sorry about your final match, too. You sure put your whole heart into it."

"Thanks, Coach." No matter how much time passed, Scott would always remember how Coach tried to intimidate him into prioritizing wrestling over time with his father.

Derek and Mom maintained small talk with Coach while Scott reached to his neck, cradling the clover pendant in his closed fist. *Yeah, Dad. I made you the priority. Right up until the end.* A fraction of heaviness lifted, providing a minuscule amount of peace to settle in, only to be wiped away by grim reality.

Coach stood and Scott stood with him. "Well. The boys and I carpooled here, so I guess we'll get out of your hair. We wanted to stop by and express our sympathies."

Scott shook Coach's hand. "I really appreciate it."

Mom led him away and Scott sat back down.

Derek rubbed Scott's leg, warmth seeping through the fabric of his pants. "What were you just thinking about? You had that look you get."

"It's a good thing we have the no secrets rule because I can't hide anything from you." Scott chuckled, although the act didn't bring him much happiness. "I was thinking about how Coach tried to strong-arm me into putting wrestling first."

Derek's jaw clenched, causing Scott to laugh. The look meant Derek worked overtime to bite his tongue before saying something he'd later regret. Once the muscle relaxed, Derek spoke. "You made the right decision."

Scott slipped his arm around Derek's shoulders, pulling him close. "I sure did."

The guys from the team streamed through the living room, each stopping by to say goodbye, then hustled out the front door, leaving the room quiet for the first time all day.

Scott was about to excuse himself to lie down for a while when the doorbell rang. He started for the door, but Claire whisked by him, stopping only to peck him on the cheek and utter a quick, "I'll get it, sweetheart. Go sit down."

Obediently, he trudged back to the couch.

"Scott." Marcus's unmistakable baritone voice rang out.

Scott turned to face his friend. "Marcus." Sherry, Marcus's girlfriend, stood next to him. Scott hopped up from the couch and strode to them. "You came too." He embraced her, trying to remember how much time had passed since they'd hung out.

Too much, he decided. He'd have to make amends when life settled down.

Mid-reach to pull Marcus into a hug, he noticed a third person with them. Zane.

Marcus must've been nervous because he started babbling like he always did when he got nervous. "Zane and I got to talking after your match and he's staying in town for a few days. He decided he'd stop by the admissions office and set up an interview at BU, so he asked if he could hitch a ride to express his condolences." Marcus rocked back and forth on his feet, glancing between Scott and Zane as he rambled. "I figured, hell, if he's gonna be on the team next year, may as well bring him by." The tense laughter, which came out more as a breathy *heh-heh-heh,* let Scott know Marcus wasn't so sure he'd made the right decision.

Strange as it seemed, Zane coming by felt right. In all his years of wrestling, Scott had never met an opponent quite as sportsmanlike. "It's fine."

Marcus heaved an audible sigh. "Whew!"

"C'mon. Take a seat before Derek's parents sweep you into the kitchen to eat." Scott pointed to several chairs and took his spot on the couch again.

"How're you doin'?" Marcus, always good for filling awkward silences.

"As well as can be expected, I guess." Scott shrugged, earning a sympathetic head tilt from Sherry.

"Well, you know I'm here for you. Anything you need." Marcus clapped Scott on his leg, giving it a squeeze.

"I know. Thanks, man." Scott smiled at his friend, then turned his attention to Zane. "Not to be rude or anything, but what are you doing here?"

Zane's eyes popped open and he darted his gaze around the circle of people. "I don't know. I feel like we connected. Your team, your school, it feels like the place where I need to be. I hope," his cheeks flushed, "maybe we could be friends." He nodded at Derek and Marcus as well. "I mean all of you."

Marcus fist bumped him. "If you're a part of the team, you're family."

Zane nodded. "I can tell, but talking to Scott is what really convinced me to pursue a transfer." He shifted attention from Marcus to Scott. "What you have. This amazing family surrounding you. A great friend who's also the captain of the team. A boyfriend who stands by you. You're so lucky." He studied his hands. "Which is such a horrible thing to say at a time like this. I'm so sorry."

Scott couldn't suppress his chuckle. Funny how Zane brought the inappropriate, yet cleansing reaction to the surface. "It's not horrible. Everything you said is true. We're a family and we stick together."

"Thanks for understanding. I felt like a stalker asking Marcus to bring me along." Zane reclined in his chair, seeming a bit more relaxed than he had a few minutes earlier.

"So, Thayer. When were you planning on telling me you want my spot?" Good old Marcus, always keeping it light.

"Well. You see. I wanted to tell you, but then I remembered, you obsess about shit. I didn't want to get you all worried before your big match." Easy banter. Normal. Maybe things would be okay. In time. "You know how sloppy you get when you're distracted."

Marcus opened his mouth, his finger raised in the air, then cut himself off. Regaining some composure, he made a show of settling back into calmness. He even crossed his legs in a grand motion, although the effect made him look like he had to pee. "In light of your current situation, and because I won my match, I refuse to sink to your level, my dear friend."

All eyes fixed on Marcus, followed by laughter. First Scott, and then everyone else. Hearty, body-shaking laughter, releasing pent up tension. Scott wiped the tears from his eyes, trying to manage his breathing. "I so wish I'd recorded that. The guys would eat you alive."

Marcus dropped the funny-guy act, unfolding his legs and straightening in his chair, his commanding presence drawing everyone's attention. "Seriously, though. If Zane comes to BU, and you," he glanced at Derek, a heavy silence hanging in the air for about three seconds, "join the team, then we'll be unstoppable next year."

Scott nodded. "Yup. I agree."

From his vantage point, Scott could observe the people he cared about most in the world, interacting in various ways. Making memories. Sharing in the good and the bad.

Henry and Claire stepped out of the kitchen, probably to see why everyone had become so noisy, and ended up joining the crowd.

Mom eased next to Scott on the couch, rubbing his back in a rhythmic circle. "I love you, honey." She whispered into his ear. "You did a good thing, Scott." A secret exchange, just between the two of them. She kissed the top of his head.

Scott could have fallen asleep right there in his mother's arms, but he caught a glimpse of Derek, watching the two of them, his eyes shimmering. No, he'd fall asleep in those arms, and he'd do it again and again, for the rest of his life.

Around eight, everyone helped clean up and put things away. One by one, they hugged and kissed Scott and finally, Scott found himself in his room, alone with Derek.

Derek climbed into bed, pushing the sheets aside for Scott.

Scott ambled to Derek and kissed him on the lips. "I'll join you in a minute. I want to write something down first."

A slight crinkle of brows, then a happy sigh, and Derek lay back, sinking his head into the pillow.

Scott turned from the beautiful sight and crossed the room to his desk, switching on the desk lamp.

Opening a side drawer, he pulled out a clean piece of white paper. He unclasped the clover necklace from around his neck and set it on the table next to the paper, then picked up his favorite pen, one with a Taz logo on it.

And then he wrote.

Dad,

I don't know where to begin, and that's what my life feels like right now. A beginning.

He eyed the pendant, remembering his father's broad smile.

I thought it would be easier to hate you. To believe my life had been rotten luck up until I moved to Boston. I was wrong. At first, when you sent me the letter at Christmas, each meeting felt like work, but seeing you, spending time with you, became easier.

Scott pictured Coach, looming in his chair, all but threatening him. Scott had chosen his dad over wrestling.

Letting you in became the most natural and easy thing in the world to do. Because I opened my heart to you, I got the one thing I'd always wanted.

His eyes burned and unshed tears pooled at his lids. He grabbed a tissue to dab the moisture away.

I don't know how our journey will continue, but I do know you'll always be with me. I know you loved me and that's all I ever wanted.

. . .

Scott turned in the direction of the bed, studying Derek's resting frame. His heart fluttered and he drew in a ragged breath. A wave of love flooded through him.

Now I can love Derek with a healed heart. I have you to thank for that.

Until the next time, I love you.

Scott

He read the letter once and placed it back on the desk surface. He turned off the light, then hustled to bed, sliding into place next to Derek.

Derek kissed Scott's cheek, then lay his head on Scott's chest. "Night."

Scott closed his eyes, resting in the one place he knew he'd always be safe. "Night."

EPILOGUE

SUMMER

THE BACK YARD WAS LIKE A JUNGLE OF WILD ANIMALS. THE entire team pushed and shoved, vying for chips and burgers faster than Claire could put food on the picnic table. Henry, Mom and Greg stood by the grill, his mother having recently decided to introduce her new companion to the family. Derek sat in the shade with Zane, who'd been accepted to BU and would be moving to Boston in the fall. Scott watched the two of them, pleased with how easily Zane seemed to fit in with the rest of the group.

Marcus, on the other hand, hung sheepishly on the outskirts of the crowd.

Scott took pity, strolling to where he sat under a tree. "Dude, you're sucking the life out of the party."

Marcus shrugged. "Just thinking."

Scott channeled Derek's inner psychotherapist. "About?"

"You." Marcus locked eyes with Scott, his expression unreadable. "If you move up to my weight class, I might not make the varsity team next year."

Scott shook his head, his laughter automatic and, based on the way Marcus hunched into himself, entirely inappropriate.

"Dude, no one, and I mean no one, can beat you. We'll work out all summer and make sure the extra weight we need to put on is all muscle. Derek can join us too. Hell, he's been a beast working out this year. Have you seen how big he is now?"

Marcus glanced to where Derek and Zane sat chatting. "Yeah. What's that all about anyways?"

"He said some stupid shit about wanting to keep up with me since he's not doing sports like I am." Scott pushed aside the hint of guilt at how much he'd had to lean on Derek for the past six months.

"Really? I can't picture him as insecure at all." Marcus waved his arm dismissively.

"I know." Scott observed Marcus, pleased to see life fill his friend again. "You said it before. Next year's gonna rock."

"Yeah. I did, didn't I?" Marcus punched Scott playfully in the arm. "Man, I didn't realize how hungry I am. Wanna grab some grub with me?"

Scott chuckled. "Nah. I'm good for now."

Marcus stood and headed toward the picnic table. After a few steps, he turned. "Thanks, man, I feel a lot better."

Scott gave him a thumbs up then watched him cross the yard to join the rest of the crew.

Finally ready to join everyone, Scott stood and ambled towards his friends. He stopped mid-stride when a brash voice sliced through the air. "All right, ladies, the party can begin now."

Scott ran his hand over his face, preparing for the onslaught.

Beck.

Hopping to his feet, Scott strode to the brazen girl who'd crawled into his heart years ago. "It's about time you showed up."

Beck crossed the yard in two strides and yanked Scott into a hug. "I'm so sorry about your dad. I know I called, but nothing says I love you like a hug. Damn my choice to take a semester abroad."

Scott stared at her. She stared back. Finally, Scott felt his lips twitch and then the laughter spilled out of them both. Beck remained undefeated in their little game of who-can-keep-a-straight-face-the-longest. "It's good to see you."

She scanned the lawn, gasping with a sharp intake of breath about halfway through her inspection. "Scott, you fart-sniffing, butt-licker. You didn't tell me the new guy was so *hot*."

"Didn't I?" Scott smirked, enjoying this planned victory. "I sent you photos."

"You most certainly did *not*!" Beck placed her fists firmly on her hips.

Scott could barely maintain a serious expression. "I swore I did."

"Well, you didn't. It's about time the team got an available hottie." Beck ran her hands over her dress, smoothing out the wrinkles.

The entertainment of watching Beck hit on a gay guy would provide him with years of ammo to use against her, but he wasn't feeling particularly sadistic. "Uh, Beck–

"Scott Thayer. You look more squeamish than a cat in a room full of rockers. Tell me what I need to know right now or I'll—"

"Tie my balls up with twine and sheer them off with gardening clippers. I know. I've heard it a million times." He made an exaggerated show of protecting his junk.

Beck raised her brows and gripped Scott's shoulder, giving him a slight squeeze. "Well, at least one of you has the good sense to know the way of things."

"Self-preservation." Scott slipped an arm around Beck's shoulder. "He doesn't play for your team."

Her cheerful expression melted away. "Why are all the best guys gay?"

"You'll find someone and when you do," he paused, waiting until he had her full attention. "When you do…I'm gonna pay you back for all the shit you've laid on me and Derek for the past two years."

Beck's eyes widened, then a grin lit up her face. "Don't tell Derek, but I think you're my favorite person to vamp with."

Great. Another secret. "Well, you and I are bitches. What do you expect?"

She cackled, drawing the attention of everyone on the lawn. "Well, I'm off to wreak havoc on the people. The new meat needs to learn his place if he's gonna be a part of our lives." She marched to Zane and grabbed him by the hand without hesitation. Scott had to fight back his laughter as she dragged him toward the food.

A minute later, Derek stood by Scott's side, gazing worriedly toward the disaster-about-to-happen unfolding. "What on earth is she doing?"

A conversation for another time. "Just being Beck." He slid his arms around Derek's waist, drawing him close and stealing a kiss. "So, you gonna join the team next year?"

Derek rested his head against Scott's shoulder. "Yeah." He glanced toward Beck and Zane again. "Maybe I should save Zane before Beck does anything crazy."

Scott held Derek tight. "You know better than to interrupt Beck when she's on one of her missions." Besides, Scott had something far more important to discuss. "Listen, before we shift gears into summer mode, there's something I need to do, and I'd really like you to do it with me."

"Anything."

"Good. Tomorrow, I want to drive up to Mount Washington to release Dad's ashes. I think it's what he would have wanted."

Derek hummed, a contented, relaxed sound. "Sounds like a great idea."

Scott kissed the side of Derek's head, then took him by the hand and led him towards the largest group of his friends. "I'm being a terrible host right now."

Before he joined his teammates in a rough game of something between wrestling and touch-tackle football, but without an actual football, Scott paused, staring up at the cloudless sky. "I'll see you tomorrow, Dad."

Derek hugged him. "I love you."

Simple words, reliable and stable, filling Scott with overwhelming happiness. Eventually he'd get used to loving Derek with a healed heart. "Love you too, forever."

ABOUT THE AUTHOR

D.H. Starr is an educator by day and an author at heart.

Writing erotic romance in any genre and young adult stories as well, he likes to explore the emotions of discovering oneself while also allowing someone else into your heart. His style has been called angsty at times, and he takes pride in torturing his poor protagonists, making them work for their happily ever after.

www.dhstarr.com
dhstarr@dhstarr.com

ALSO BY D.H. STARR

Meant for Each Other

Meant for Him

Perfect For Me

The Spirit of Kilapea (YA)

The Wrestling Series:

Wrestling With Desire

Wrestling with Love

Wrestling With Passion

Join the Rocky Ridge newsletter for the latest on Doug, the Wrestling series, and more.

ALSO FROM ROCKY RIDGE BOOKS

Spokes by P.D. Singer

The Angel of 13th Street by Eden Winters

Fallen Angel by Eden Winters